CW01676528

A London Apprentice

by

JUDY GRAHAM

First published in 2019

Thames Press

IBSN: 978-1-9160865-0-0

For Don

'WHEN A GIRL IS TIRED OF

LONDON, SHE IS TIRED OF LIFE.'

With thanks to Samuel Johnson

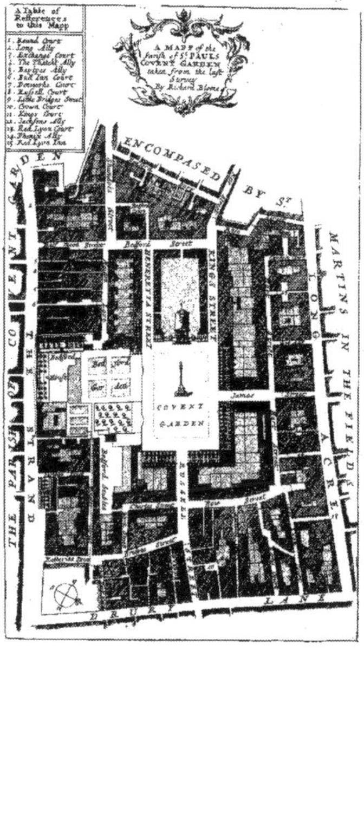

Drink thirstily from the spring of experience

CHAPTER ONE

Tyburn 1726

The moment had come, and horror engulfed the eighteen-year-old. She'd chosen the longest straw from the choice of three, scattered over the filthy floor of Newgate's condemned cell, while the men jested about their fate with pitiful bravado.

The Ordinary recited the funeral prayer. 'He that believeth in me.'

Her fellow prisoners took their turns before her, and now they dangled from Tyburn Triple Tree. The hangman bit on the silver bribes, as he pulled the twitching legs to hasten death and removed the nightcaps rolled down over their eyes. This incited the crowd, drunk on gin and hanging day lust, to roar again as the corpses stopped dancing and hung motionless, with their tongues lolling, eyes bulging and bowels voiding.

The horse snorted, impatient to pull the wagon from under the feet of the prisoner, causing the slip knot to throttle her. As the executioner grasped the long end of the rope and threw it over the gibbet, she felt a gentle tug from the hemp halter around her slender neck. The girl faltered as she stood up next to her coffin on the death cart, whilst the crowd jeered and pelted her with mouldy fruit and night soil.

The rope tautened, her chest tightened. Panic seized her breath. She looked down at the clergyman and pleaded for succour. 'Please, mercy.' Ignoring her, he continued to read from the Book of Common Prayer.

'Though he were dead.'

Stealing a purse holding eighteen guineas had demanded a death sentence. She'd got away with many crimes of thieving, all necessary acts to augment her earnings as a London whore. Steal or starve. Die either way. She screamed. 'Please God, help me.'

'Yet he shall live.'

Shuddering, she whispered, 'Lord, have mercy on me.' Lifting her eyes to the horizon, she prayed to see something good in the last minute of her life. In the far distance, across the fields, she recognised the shape of a covered country wagon making its way towards London from the west.

On the scaffold, the Ordinary of Newgate prison looked into her face with little compassion. He spoke the final words.

'And whosoever liveth and believeth in me.'

The signal was given. The horse jerked forward.

'Shall never die.'

The Wiltshire wagon rolled along Orchard Road, passing the gardens of Kensington Palace to the south. On the driving-box sat a young girl named Fanny Tomlinson, who examined her dirty hands. They were not the fingers of a needle-woman and she feared her aunt Marie, the milliner, would not want her as an apprentice. Fanny's mother, Anise, always made sure her daughter was clean and tidy, saying she must be ready for fine things to come into her life. That dream had faded the day her mother died, now she was alone. To keep her mind occupied, she imagined what her aunt would look like and wondered if she would be happy living in the city. The rhythm of the cart's wheels began to dull her senses and she fell asleep, unaware of the dangers that lay ahead in London.

A cold, east wind whipped up and a cheer disturbed her peace. Shaking herself awake, her muscles contracted as a fear rose in her. She looked towards the horizon where the swarm of unruly, hanging day addicts chanted for death. A sense of premonition engulfed her. She turned to Finch the wagon driver; a sullen lump of a creature with a strangulated glottal stop. 'What is that noise I can hear?'

'Tis a hanging day at Tyburn, a good holiday for Londoners. What a welcome for you all, they'll be merrymaking in the streets tonight.'

Fanny bit her lip. 'Do we have to ride past it?'

'I knows you all wants to see the gibbet, but I have to take the path across the fields to the north, I don't want to get slowed down in them lot. They'll be cutting the corpses down for the surgeon's knife. It always excites the crowd and they'll be after a piece of old rope from the hangman.'

The nervous perspiration from Fanny's palms mixed with the grime as she wiped them on her apron, the blackness matching the smoke hanging over the city before her.

Finch cleared his throat in preparation of his welcoming speech. 'Welcome to London, peasants. The city of thieves, robbers and killers, good ale and even better thrupenny uprights.' He paused for a laugh, which didn't materialize. 'Pity you had to miss the hanging, next time it might be Jack Mann at the end of the rope. Tyburn Triple Tree has got his name carved on its gibbet, three times he's slipped the noose has Gentl'man Jack. The thief-takers are out looking for him, a ruthless villain with a bloody knife and a hot temper.' His theatrical delivery became more colourful as he chewed the words around his slack, near-toothless mouth, putting the fear of God into his listeners. 'There's many a bludgeoned head and a slit throat that Jack leaves his mark upon. Ladies and gents, better ye be very afraid of the long shadows of the alleys and courts and hold on tight to your valuables, be they coins or quim.'

The old gentleman from inside the wagon pushed forward from under the canvas and retorted, 'Mr Finch, please desist with your coarse language, we carry with us innocent, impressionable children and young ladies. Such talk will disturb both their waking and sleeping dreams.'

'I'd like to disturb them sleeping dreams,' Finch muttered under his breath. The wagoner sighed and raised his eyebrows. He hawked and spewed up a stream of black speckled, grey phlegm that flew passed Fanny as she sat next to him on the exposed driving box. Never, had Fanny so wanted time to pass quicker.

Without warning, a man jumped in front of the wagon. 'Whoa!' Finch shouted, as he tightened the reins trying to control the horses. The wagon lurched and pulled up sharply, nearly toppling over.

Fanny was thrown back into the dark, canvas abyss, joining the tangled passengers who cried out in alarm.

Finch swore. 'You flat, swift, dull-headed lobcock!' The cart horses reared in fright, both from their master's commands and the dirt-encrusted vagrant who barred their path. Drinking from a bottle, he danced and sang, begging for food or coins.

Fanny managed to scramble back onto the driving-box and said, 'Pray, is he a fool or a mad man?'

Finch looked at her and answered with a snarl. He had no mercy. He raised his whip and with his full strength, brought it down upon the filthy wretch, slashing the beggar's cheek. The blood slowly seeped and spread until it dripped into the man's hands as he tried to hold his face together. The bundle of rags screamed then fell to the ground and crawled away into the gutter where, Fanny predicted, he would spend the rest of his sorry life.

'Making me late, may he burn in hellfire! I need my full wages not docked for slowness!' said Finch as he whipped the tired and foaming horses into a gallop.

The uneven road and Finch's irritated driving made the wagon dangerously unstable, but Fanny managed to keep her balance by grasping the cold iron handrail with both hands. She was exhausted and disorientated by grief and travelling for days, with little sleep and not much food. She felt tears of unhappiness running down her cheeks but wiped them away, determined to be brave.

She asked Finch, 'When shall we reach the coaching inn at Holborn Bridge?'

Lifting a small bottle from his pocket, he raised it to his lips and took a swig. 'We'll be slowed down by the bustle of the city, but I have to get the horses in by nightfall. Another hour if all goes well.' He leaned into her, smiled and belched in her face. 'Where's your Ma, then?'

'She's dead.'

'Any family?'

'My grandfather, but he's in the workhouse now.'

'Ah.' He sniffed and considered. 'If you want a lady to look after you in London, I know a kind one who will let you live with her. She likes young, pretty girls.'

'No, thank you, my aunt is meeting me.'

'Oh.' Finch lost interest and turned away.

Reaching Holborn Bridge, Finch turned the wagon sharply into the cobbled yard of the Swan Inn. He yelled, 'Hungerford coach coming in,' as they entered into the noisy hubbub of porters and stable lads, all shouting different directions as they steered the clattering horses to a standstill.

'Make way for his lordship's wagon,' laughed a stable lad as he caught and led the horses in. 'Alrighty boys, easy, you're home now. Nice bag of oats for you.'

'And for Finch?' the other boy joked.

'Respect boys, respect if you don't mind,' said Finch.

'Where you been, Finch, on a merry-go-round?'

'Two hours late again, old man,'

'Awl, leave the old bugger alone.'

The teams snorted, their tack rattling, and they

shook the sweat off their coats adding to the smells of wet leather, wood smoke and spilt ale: a masculine odour unfamiliar to Fanny. It both revolted and attracted her. She sat patiently on the country wagon as it lined up with other larger and grander carriages and coaches, and watched the passengers spill out dressed in all types of warm traveling clothes, greeting friends and family with warm embraces. Fanny felt colder and very alone.

Dusk was falling and the ghostly full moon could be glimpsed between the gathering clouds. Fanny shivered and looked longingly towards the yellow flames of the fire, illuminating the leaded windows of the Inn. The sound of chatter and laughter of the patrons drinking was seductive.

Finch dismounted the dray and for the benefit of prospective clients, he displayed a new, more genteel character. 'May I help you step down, Mistress Tomlinson? Please be notifying of the foot iron, my good lady.'

Fanny looked at Finch, opened-mouth. She was so shocked at the change in him she couldn't speak. Finch came close to her ear. 'Give me the shilling you owe me, you little waif. For that's what you are now.'

Fanny scrambled to find the coins in her apron pocket but stopped. In a voice that carried, she said, 'Lift my box down first, if you please, sir.' Now it was the turn of Finch to look at her in surprise.

'Well, well, I didn't know you had it in you. Young lady.'

He went to the rear of the wagon, shuffled the luggage around and lifted Fanny's travelling box down.

'There you are, your Majesty.'

'Thank you, Finch,' Fanny replied and passed the

money to him.

'You'll do all right,' he said and immediately turned away to collect his other fares.

Fanny scanned the yard looking for her aunt Marie or the old gentleman who was paid to make sure she was handed over safely, but he'd disappeared. The receiving yard was crowded and noisy, but she noticed the stillness of a thin, ethereal young woman wearing second-hand clothes over many petticoats, no cap but a plaid shawl covering her head. The girl nodded at Fanny, amused at the scene she had just witnessed. Fanny smiled back. She turned to pick up her box containing all she had in the world. Despite its weight, with two hands she managed to drag it to a bench near the tavern's door where she had seen the girl, but she had vanished like a phantom.

Fanny sat down and waited as per instructions. Her aunt would come and greet her and take Fanny to her dwelling place. There was a faint rumble in the air and a strike of lightning tore through the sky followed by a huge crash of thunder. Three seconds later the heavens opened, soaking Fanny to the skin. As she took off her cap and was wringing it out, the Innkeeper's wife came outside to watch the storm, framed by the light of the fire from inside the Inn.

She saw Fanny and said, 'Come inside sweeting, there's already too many drowned rats in this city, best you not be another one. Whoever is greeting you will find you. London is a dangerous place for an innocent girl, you'll have to find your feet and stand your ground if you want to enjoy it. Bring your box.' Fanny heaved the small trunk over the slippery cobblestones.

'Here I'll help you, take one of the handles and we'll

carry it in together. You're only a mite, how old are you?'

'I'm fourteen, I know I'm small for my age, but tomorrow I shall be fifteen. Will I look old?'

Chuckling, the woman replied, 'No, my dear, you are petite and pretty. Remember, you will never be as old as me and that good things always come in little parcels. What's your name, lovely?'

'I'm called Fanny,'

'And I'm, Annie. Pleased to make your acquaintance and I wish you a very happy birthday for tomorrow. Come on in now, it's cold and wet out here and I'll be wanting a dram of ladies delight to keep me old soul case warm. Mind the steps.'

Crossing the threshold of the tavern Fanny stepped into an unacquainted world, alerting her senses to the new colours, sounds and smells of this vivacious group of characters whose main purpose was to enjoy themselves. Here, in the embrace of liquor, they forgot their troubles for a while and celebrated without restraint, both great or small successes. The room was veiled in smoke and bathed in the glow of the fire, softening furrows in faces and turning rags into amber cloth.

Amongst this false golden illusion, Fanny noticed some of the men looked dangerous and others, wary of them, kept their distance. The warm room drew out fine steam from the wet clothing, which permeated the air with a mixture of rank body odour and mouldy dampness. The patrons, whether drunk or not quite drunk, chose to be either extrovert or introvert, some pronouncing strong views on their captive audience and others immobile, whispering their troubles to themselves.

Annie pointed to a space at a long trestle table, next to a man wearing an oiled coat with the collar turned up and a tricorn hat pulled low over his eyes. 'Sit yourself down by the fire.' The man inclined his head, listening to what Annie was saying. 'You'll be safe there. Your aunt will find you. I must get to work.'

'Thank you, Mistress, for your kindness.'

Fanny pulled her box in front of the bench at the refectory table, it faced the tavern's entrance and was close to the roaring fire. Although crowded with several groups, she was small enough to wiggle in beside the tall man who kept his head down, mesmerised with his pot of ale. Fanny placed her feet on the box and looked around the drinking parlour. She felt her fear begin to subside until a loud, painful groan startled her. She turned and recognised the girl who'd been watching her in the yard, the phantom.

Sitting on a table, the girl clamped back the head of a portly man, holding it tightly between her thighs as he squirmed on the bench below her. She examined the inside of his mouth.

Standing above him was a woman, whose hair hadn't been brushed since birth. She held a brandy bottle tightly in her fist while she commanded, 'Now, Abe, you listen to your good wife and stop your fidgeting and let the lady draw the tooth.'

A youth bent close to Abe's ear. 'Yes, Pa, and enjoy her legs around your ears.' The mother slapped her son's head.

Abe windmilled his arm around trying to catch the bottle of liquor, but his wife held it out of reach and said, 'You've had half a bottle of brandy, if you want the rest you have to behave yourself.'

The tooth drawer fixed Abe's mouth open with a bone prop then looked down at the instruments next to her on the table top. She lifted up the bloody rags to reveal the previous broken extraction, a dental pelican and a tooth key. Abe screamed in agony.

The pain and frustration were too much for him as he continued to flap his hand. His wife took another swallow of the warming liquid. 'It does help the nerves, Abe.'

He stamped his feet and tried to speak. 'You bitch, give me the bottle.'

Fanny winced at Abe's suffering and the blood oozing from his mouth as the gory show continued. The girl took a braced position and hooked the key over the remaining lower molar and rocked it back and forth to loosen the root.

'Aarrgh, aaaww.'

'All right, Abe, I'm nearly done. It won't hurt much, not to a strong and brave man like yourself.' While Abe was off his guard, unhesitatingly and with great strength, she yanked the tool down and with it came the rotten tooth. Abe swore, although Fanny found it difficult to hear the precise phrase, as his mouth had been stuffed with almost clean rags to stem the bleeding.

The spectators cheered as the tooth was held up high in victory. The operator for the teeth turned around, bowed and said, 'Thank you ladies, and gentleman. Apart from drawing ale for you, I shall be here next week to draw your teeth, stopping the misery of mouth pain. It'll cost you only sixpence a tooth. And you can have a nice smile, like what I got.'

The good hearted-laughter was unexpectedly halted by the sound of the Inn's door opening and slamming against the wall. A group of rough men burst in. 'Stand firm, Jack Mann, we have you now. Back to Newgate gaol for you,' yelled a pocked-faced man who headed a viciously armed posse that barred the way to the yard and freedom.

At the speed of light, Fanny felt a strong arm grab her around the waist and she was lifted to near standing height. The fugitive brought a knife to her throat and she felt the soft touch of its well-honed silky edge. Fanny smelt oil on the coat sleeve and she knew this was the man who had been sitting next to her. She was breathing fast but trying to not breathe at all. Her mouth fell open, her throat so dry she couldn't swallow, she hoped this would be enough to keep the blade a hairs breath away from cutting her throat. 'Stay back, Cribbage, with your scurvy crew, Jack Mann ain't going to be caught and dragged back to Newgate so easily. Stand off you traitorous villain.'

'I am no villain now, I am a thief catcher and your head has a fortune on it. Don't make me take it off, Jack.'

My god, thought Fanny, I'm in the hands of Jack Mann. He will kill me, he will slash my throat without a moments thought. He lifted her free of the bench and dangled her directly in front of him.

'Be off, or I shall cut her,' Jack said. 'My fipenny will slice through her neck like cutting butter. Stand off the lot of you.'

The crowd rose up in defence of Jack. Three villainous men advanced towards the thief-takers accompanied by a cacophony of chants, 'Out, out, out.' One of them spoke quietly but menacingly to Cribbage. 'Give Jack another day. He is one of us. Or by God, we shall hunt you down.' Jack took this opportunity to run and he let his grip loosen.

Before Fanny could take a breath, a hand grasped her left wrist and she was yanked away from Jack, her feet slipping on the sawdust as she struggled to find purchase. She was dragged backwards through the mass of drinkers who parted to make a narrow pathway for both she and her abductor. She turned her head and saw the Innkeeper's wife pulling back a curtain and opening a small door at the back of the tavern. Fanny was hauled towards the doorway and almost flew through it, to find herself in a back yard full of wet mud and driving rain, which made it impossible to focus on who was pulling her. She slithered along, shackled by the vicelike grip. Temporarily blinded by sludge in her eyes, Fanny had no idea where she was or what was happening to her. Terror overwhelmed her.

Just when she thought she could no longer go on with her lungs aching from the exertion, they slowed down and came to a halt. Fanny pushed back the rat-tails of wet sticky hair from her face whilst panting. Trying to catch her breath above the wind, a young woman's voice said, 'Wipe your eyes, we have to cross the Fleet ditch. There's a long narrow plank spanning the stink. We have to go separately, it won't take the weight of both of us together.' Fanny was shaking violently from head to foot, bent over trying to catch her breath. 'I'm sorry, but we have to keep moving. 'Tis dangerous what I've done. If they catch me, one of them lot will kill me, whichever side. It's not far now. I'm taking you to a place where you will be safe. You have to trust me.'

Fanny lifted her head up so the rain could wash away the muck from her face allowing her to see again. She looked at the girl. It was the phantom, the tooth-drawer at the Inn. Although slight, the girl had immense strength in her arms and hands, enabling her to run fast and far with the dead weight of another fighting against her all of the way. 'It's you, you saved me. Thank you.'

'Not yet, we still have to save the both of us. Are you ready to balance the plank?'

'Yes, I can do it, I'm light and nimble.'

'Good girl. What's your name?'

'Fanny. What's yours?'

'Betsy.'

Fanny took a deep breath to gather her confidence and said, 'I'm ready, Betsy.'

'There's the plank.' Betsy pointed her finger through the driving rain towards a perilous makeshift bridge on stilts, made from a system of narrow boards nailed roughly together spanning the bubbling grey waters of the Fleet. 'You first,' said Betsy. Still shaking, Fanny placed her right foot onto the wood. It rocked, unsteady and unsafe and the flimsy handrail promised no assurance. Her weight caused the precarious structure to bow and lurch from side to side. The slick of wet moss and slime covering it would make it treacherous to keep sure-footed. She could easily slip off into the reeking deep ditch, where the human effluence and animal remains would hold her feet firm and where she would be trapped in the muck, while the storm rain and wind raised the rapid waters high enough to drown her. How to rid herself of fear?

She closed her eyes and imagined warm summer sun and clear blue sky above her, and the feeling of surety she had when she climbed onto the narrow willow branch bridging the fast running River Kennet outside her home in Chilton Foliat. She remembered how she would stretch her arms out for balance and how determination would see her safely across. She had done it a hundred times, she could do it, she was sure of success. Fanny opened her eyes and stepped out.

They were over.

'Where are you taking me?' Fanny asked, still shivering.

'To the little people. Come on.'

Betsy took Fanny's hand and together, leaving the rushing waters of the ditch they headed towards a cats cradle of flimsy wooden tenements, held together by ladders and ropes that rose out of the shore of the Fleet.

It didn't look possible the structures could hold the weight of even one person, but Fanny would learn there were hundreds of people living here in dire poverty. The dwellings had grown room by room on all levels with bridges made of boards, stitching them together into a matchbox warren of slums. The phantom opened what only just passed as a front door, hanging at an angle from one remaining hinge. Once inside, Fanny saw a twisted staircase winding up four stories with leaning landings and warped doors, all with bolts or chains.

'Up you go, top floor and watch out for missing floorboards, 'tis a long way down to fall,' Betsy warned.

Fanny could hardly put one foot in front of another, she was so exhausted and cold. Through the open holes in the side of the building, Fanny saw where they had crossed the Fleet. Anyone not knowing there were open areas on the stairs, would certainly fall down the huge gaps. Various lengths of frayed and knotted ropes dangled from the rafters, which she used to pull herself up. At the very top, in the eaves where she could hear the rain pounding down was a small door, even she would have to bend down to get through it. It looked like a cupboard.

Wet and muddy, Fanny's rescuer knocked three times on the door. A woman's high voice asked, 'Who is there?'

'It's Betsy.'

There was a dragging of something heavy and the sound of a bolt being drawn across. The door opened to reveal a room in pitch darkness, except for the low light from the pitiful fireplace. As Fanny looked in, she felt herself spiralling up high and just before she fainted she saw, staring at her, a room full of talking dolls.

CHAPTER TWO

Friends

THE NEXT MORNING, Fanny, delirious with fever, lay on a simple cot. Standing over her, fretted a twenty-seven inch high, perfectly proportioned woman. She had the kindest of faces framed by curls of sable tresses, neatly dressed up and secured by ribbon and velvet flowers. Mrs Big was foster mother to all her husband's sideshow performers, who were known as 'Mr Big's Little Troupe'.

With great tenderness, she mopped Fanny's brow and fussed over her. She spoke to Fanny in her high tinkling voice, a little more refined than the common dialect of a Londoner born within the sound of Bow Bells. She turned to her husband sitting next to her.

'Poor little darling, her temperature is high and I'm worried Mr Big, she has no strength after her travels and her escape from Jack. Just wait till I see him. I know he escaped Newgate, but he's done it before so it ain't no excuse for bad behaviour towards a little one. Betsy's gone to fetch Theo, he must be able to help. I do hope so.' She placed her cool hand on Fanny's forehead. 'Come on my dear, break the fever. I'm here so no need to be fearful and my Mr Big will protect you, my lamb.' Mr Big, a little taller than his wife at thirty-two inches, held Fanny's hand safe between his. There were three knocks at the door and Mrs Big called, 'Who is there?'

'Betsy.'

'I am coming.' She patted the entwined hands of Fanny and her husband and hurried over to the little door. She slid back the large bolt and the phantom entered.

Following her was a tall, lithe young man who carried himself with grace and self-assurance and in his hand was a well-worn leather bag. He removed his hat to bend low through the doorway. He greeted Mrs Big, 'Good day, my dear friend.'

'Theo is here now, so stop your worrying, Mrs B,' said Betsy.

'Yes, of course. Theo will know how to make her well again, he is so knowledgeable and dependable. Welcome back from France, Theo. How good to see you again.'

Theo approached the cot where Fanny lay on straw and opened his bag.

Mrs Big held Betsy's hand as they joined Theo, asking, 'Betsy, what do you know about this girl?'

'Her name is Fanny, and Annie at the Swan Inn said she's going to apprentice with her aunt, as a milliner.' At that word, Mrs Big raised an eyebrow. 'And she's got good teeth. I could make a nice pile of money out of those.'

'Those teeth are staying right where they are,' said Mrs Big.

Theo shook his head at Betsy's comment and turned to more important matters. He knelt by the cot and gently lifted Fanny's wrist to take her pulse and felt her forehead. With a kind smile, he said, 'Hello,

Fanny, my name is Theo and I am an apothecary, I'm here to make you feel better. May I examine you?'

From the depths of tangled, muffled consciousness, Fanny nodded.

'Her pulse is fast,' he moved his ear close to her chest to listen for congestion, 'the lungs seem clear.' He checked her all over and apart from some bruises and swelling, he reassured Fanny all she needed was warmth, nourishment and sleep. He turned to Mrs Big and gave her instructions on how to care for Fanny. 'I shall prepare a bark potion, it will help reduce the fever and some chamomile for a tisane.' He reached into his medical bag. 'In the meantime here is some vinegar and clean rags. You know what to do: heat the liquid and soak the bandages in it. Wrap them around her hands and feet: it should break the fever. Once the sweat subsides, remove them.' Betsy distracted Mrs Big by tapping her foot throughout Theo's recital of directions, her natural impatience rising to the fore. Mrs Big gave her a stern look and Betsy ceased her fidgeting. Theo closed his bag and said, 'Keep her body at an even temperature. I shall return later. Do not fret, Mrs B, all will be well.' Theo stroked Mrs Big's arm and looked straight into her eyes. 'I shall keep a close eye on her.'

Theo turned to Betsy. 'You have a quick and intelligent mind, Betsy, but sometimes it is better to take time to listen and consider. To seize Fanny from Jack was rash. You did it without thinking of the consequences. When Jack finds out you took his hostage, he is not going to be happy, for all your calf-eyed looks. Do not test him'.

'Yes, Theo, I know,' said Betsy.

From his inside coat pocket, he brought forth a package the size of a book, wrapped in brown paper, sealed with wax and stamped with the letter M, which he handed to Betsy.

'Give this to Jack. He is expecting it. And Betsy, it is sealed.' Theo lifted his bag and said, 'Mr and Mrs Big I wish you farewell, I must return to the apothecary before my father finds me missing. I shall see you soon, bless you both.' As Mrs Big opened the door for him, he took from his pocket a small bottle with the word PORT on the label. He bent low and said in a quiet voice, 'Here is your tea, Mrs Big. The usual herbs, pennyroyal, more of the opium, rue and tansy. I hope it helps the ladies.'

Theodore bowed and left the attic and Mrs Big bolted the door behind him.

'What a gentleman he is, so good to those of us who have no money for medicines. Betsy, he is a fine young man, you should look upon him with a sweet eye and forget about that rogue Jack who will hang, be in no doubt, my girl.'

Betsy frowned and countered, 'They will never hold Jack. He is too clever for them and Theo may be confident, but he is too young for me. Just a boy.'

'My poor girl, you will suffer great sadness whether Jack lives or dies. He fights within himself and has a dark side to him.'

'I have to go. Are you practising tonight?'

'No, the boys did it this morning. I want Fanny to rest, they can rehearse again tomorrow. Off you go, Betsy, thank you for your help. Do not worry, Mr Big and I will look after Fanny throughout the night.'

'I shall take my leave of you, Mrs B, and see you tomorrow.'

It must have been late morning when Fanny rejoined the world. The sound of soft thuds and squeaking of loose floorboards nudged Fanny's dreams to evaporate as she opened her eyes to a room she barely recognised. Pushed against the wall to make an open central space was a highly polished round table with chairs set around it, each one with its own short ladder rising to the cane seat. In the centre of the room were a troupe of very small men leap-frogging, tumbling and balancing on each other's shoulders. The men may have been short, but they were strong. The performers lifted up each other to make a tower of four people and when the man at the top cried, 'Hoopla,' one at a time they somersaulted to a lower tower of two and then again, down to the ground. In an immaculate straight line, they turned to face Fanny and took a bow. Fanny clapped her hands and said, 'Oh, how wonderful, you are so clever.'

The troupe ran over to her, all talking at the same time. Over the rainfall of excited chatter, soared the high, crystal voice of Mrs Big's authoritative voice, 'Please boys, let Mr Big through.' A moment of respected silence was held, then the group parted to reveal their director as he regally approached the cot. He looked at Fanny, felt her forehead and nodded his head as a huge smile broke out on his face. He kissed his wife and a relieved Mrs Big asked Fanny, 'Are you feeling better, my dear?'

'I think so. I don't remember much. I know my aunt Marie was meant to meet me and I remember running from the Inn, but there is confusion in my mind. Are you a friend of my aunt?' Fanny asked.

'No, my dear. Do not worry yourself at the moment. All will be well, trust me.'

'I am worried though, my aunt will have gone to the Swan Inn to find me and she won't know where I am. She will be very concerned. Where are my clothes?

I think she lives somewhere called the Inner Temple. I must go and look for her.' She tried to stand up, but her full strength had not returned.

'No, my dear, you must rest today.' Mrs Big eased Fanny back down. 'Annie, the Innkeeper's wife, will find out where your aunt lives, and she will send word to us. Now, settle yourself,' she said as she tucked the blanket around Fanny. 'I shall care for you until you are fully recovered and reunited with your family. You're safe here, Fanny.'

She studied Mrs Big's face. 'You are very pretty. I have never seen such a small person before. Where are you from?'

Mrs Big chuckled. 'The same place as you came from, my dear. But my mother was a little person too.'

'What is your name?'

'Mrs Big.'

'Mrs Big?'

'Yes, because I am so small.'

Fanny took a moment to think about this, Mrs Big tilted her head and waited. The penny dropped, 'Oh, I see,' said Fanny and laughed.

'My friends call me Mrs B. Are you my friend?'

'Yes, of course I am, Mrs B.' Fanny smiled at her new friend.

'Well, now you must be formally introduced to Mr B. Husband, please come over here. Mr B is a mute, my dear, however, his conversation is as educated as the best in the land. People assume he is deaf, but he is not. He hears a lot of secrets, 'tis useful is it not, Mr B? He directs the troupe by sign language and can converse without others knowing what he is saying. Maybe you will learn some words, Fanny. He likes being spoken to from the heart, through the hands. What is your full name, my dear?' asked Mrs Big.

'I am Frances Tomlinson from Chilton Foliat, Wiltshire.'

'Well, Frances Tomlinson, welcome to our home. Now,' said Mrs B, 'Let me introduce the boys to you. Come forward, gentlemen, please. This is Livewell and Noble, they are twins. Useful for magic tricks, eh, boys?' The two small men were perfectly in proportion as Mr and Mrs Big were. They flourished a bow. 'And here we have our anchors, the strongest little men to be found in any fairground booth: Matthew, Mark, Luke who is the main support man and John, all originally from Ireland. If they're missing you will find them in the nearest tavern. We send Samuel the Strongman to round them up, if we need to.' Mrs Big clapped her hands twice and said, 'That's enough excitement for one day, Fanny is to rest. Noble, as it's Sunday and the baker's oven is free of bread, please go and get three large pies. Luke and John can escort you.' She took some coins from her pocket and placed them in Noble's palm. 'Theo left some money for food, God bless his soul. Bring back some mild ale from Annie, off you go. I've counted the pennies, so don't think you can get away with extra beers.'

Luke picked up a woven hemp bag and pulled it over his shoulder. 'Now, Mrs B, don't send Samuel to find us, we shall be back within the hour. Goodbye, Fanny.'

She was enveloped by the kind-heartedness of these little people. She would always be grateful to them, but once recovered she must discover her own way to be free of danger and threat. To stand alone, sure and confident. She had no choice, she couldn't go back to her old life. London was her home now.

Mrs Big unbolted the door and gave her parting

words to the three men, 'Tell Annie and Betsy, I will see them presently.' She lowered her voice, but Fanny could still hear her. 'Not a word about the girl being here, we don't want no trouble from Jack.'

The Swan was in full flow when Noble, Luke and John strode into the yard. The simple act of opening the tavern's door immediately welcomed the customer with a blanket of warmth, fun and good cheer. Taverns were like theatres, both promised a dream world of heightened reality, a more colourful and pleasing life than the patron's own dreary existence. The Inn had its own principle actor: the Innkeeper. At the Swan, Annie took the place of her late husband. Competent and respected, she always introduced herself as the Innkeeper's wife, it being safer for the public to think there was a man about the house. As her spouse had been rather weak in physique, she now reinvented him as a strong, thick set ex-wrestler who was always, "Just in the next room".

Annie greeted them. 'Mr Noble, once again the Swan welcomes you and your companions. May I offer you a small pot of ale, sirs?' Noble looked and Luke, Luke looked at John and John looked back at Noble. 'On the house, gentlemen, be it my pleasure'.

'We thank ye, Mistress Anne. Beer is very welcome and in gratitude, may we tumble for the patrons?'

'That is kind of you. Find room on the floor and I shall draw the ale ready to refresh you.' She leant close to Noble's ear and asked, 'What news of Fanny?'

'All is good, Mistress, the fever is broken. Mrs B says she will visit you presently.'

'Good. What swag is in the bag, Luke?'

'Best meat pies for the boys, Mistress Anne, and we'll take a flagon of small beer to wash it down.'

'Leave the bag with me and I shall fill the jug whilst you do your tricks.'

'Is Betsy here?' asked Luke.

'She left but a moment ago, to help a friend.'

The room was full and noisy, but it didn't take long for the three acrobats to be noticed as they cartwheeled across the trestle tables causing the drinkers to lift their pots out of the way. After jumping high in the air they somersaulted off the tables to people's applause. As they took their bows, a very well dressed young man, who was in liquor, brazenly came forward and shouted, 'Monsters, freaks, get out of here or damn it, I shall step on you. Vermin.' He spat on the floor and continued to demean the acrobats against the calls from the crowd. Annie called for her two largest draymen.

Noble and John held Luke back. 'No, Luke, we cannot fight. We must get back to Mrs B.' Luke struggled to be released. Noble insisted, 'Leave it, Luke, wait until another time.'

The two draymen picked up the troublemaker, each taking an arm whilst his feet threshed about never touching the ground. Annie opened the tavern door and they threw him unceremoniously into the yard, an efficient and well-tried manoeuvre.

'Better to leave by the back door, gentlemen.'Annie handed the troupe their belongings and the full flagon and they left by the taverns rear door leading out to the Fleet.

'You should have let me at him,' Luke said, shaking off John's hand from his shoulder.

'We would have done if it had not been for our errand today,' answered John.

'I shall remember his face. His time will come,' said Noble. 'At this moment, it's more important to get out of this mud. Annie should have thrown him out this way, he would sink in it. At least we can skip across the top 'cos were as light, fast and as smart as rats. Ha.'

Outside the front of the Inn, Annie's henchmen entertained the drunk young man. Having laughed at him scrabbling on the ground, they lifted him up and twisted his arms painfully behind his back. He shouted, 'I am of the Woodford family. Take your filthy hands off me, let me go.'

'Ah, that we would sir, if only ye could stand steady on your feet. We cannot let you fall, you may injure yourself, sir. Ain't that right, George?'

'Indeed, Little John, let me be coming to the front of the young man, so as I can support him. Oh, dearie me, the gentleman does indeed seem unstable on his legs, don't he?'

George pushed the youth forward and he fell into the chest of Little John, who turned him around and without care, threw him back. They repeated this action, again and again, faster and faster until the young man became disorientated and unbalanced.

Little John held firm to his left shoulder and said, 'Take care now, sir, or you may slip and do yourself harm.' He threw a right hook, knocked Woodford down and bloodied his nose. 'Up-a-daisy sir, watch your step now,' said John, who helped him up only for him to fall again as George tripped him up. The young man spreadeagled himself at the feet of a beggar sitting on the bench next to the tavern's door.

'What entertainment boys. Two strapping lads against a streak of piss.'

'All right, Tinker, keep out of this one. You've enjoyed the show, now scuttle off back to your hole.'

George kicked Woodford as he writhed on the ground. 'You, piss off.'

'I'll send you to Newgate, I am a gentleman of the law at the Inner Temple.' Woodford's eyes rolled up and he collapsed, out cold.

Betsy lived her life between one slum and another. Around noon, she headed to the river and crossed London Bridge with its shops and houses packed as close as a pack of cards. She weaved her way through the throng of citizens and crossed over the drawbridge.

'A few pennies for my baby, dear?' begged a woman too old to bear children.

'Not for you to rent another child,' said Betsy and moved on.

The smell from the river reeked with no wind to disperse the stench. Betsy hurried towards Southwark and the Mint, a haunt of criminals, fugitives and debtors. Sited below the water level of the Thames, maladies from sewage or the foul stagnant water were rife. She held the corner of her shawl over her nose and mouth in the vain hope it would protect her. Nobody lived here unless they had nowhere left to go or they were hiding from the law. And now Jack Mann was one of those.

Something darted out of the darkness and startled Betsy, it wasn't a rat, it was a hand. Desperately, it locked on to Betsy's ankle and she nearly fell into the filthy open sewer. The human vermin threatened, 'Give me some money, you whore.'

'Get off me.' Betsy shook her leg hard enough for the vagrant to release his grip. She regained her balance and kicked out blindly with the other foot, managing to smash the man's nose as he lay amongst the filth.

'You bitch.' He spat and slunk back into the shadows. Betsy escaped down into dark warrens of the courts where underfoot was wet and slick. She stopped only for a moment to check her whereabouts and looked up at the warehouse looming above her, then dodged into the entrance before anyone could see her. Nothing or no one would get Betsy to come to this hell on earth, except Jack. She knew she was foolish, but she couldn't say no to him.

The stink was appalling as she climbed up the rotten staircase. Keeping her back to the sweating brick wall, she slid up the stairs hoping the edges of the steps would be more stable and hold her weight.

Two floors up, she found a door with a torn piece of rag attached to it. She knocked. 'Jack, Jack it's me, Betsy.' She waited. A grimy eye looked out at her from a crack. The door was forcibly opened and Jack caught her by the neck, roughly pulling her inside.

'I should squeeze the last breath out of you, Betsy. You've crossed me one last time.' Desperately, Betsy fumbled with his fingers trying to release his hands to stop him from choking her, but he held her firm. Just as she had no air left in her lungs, he slapped her face hard and threw her across the floor. 'Next time, you're dead. Remember that, girl.' Betsy crawled to the corner of the room. Jack demanded, 'Where's the food?'

'I have it, Jack, I have it,' she whispered, her throat sore and her voice nearly gone. In silence, Jack waited. 'She's just a child Jack, she ain't no value to you.'

'She was my hostage, not yours, hag. Give me the food and gin.'

Betsy opened her bundle and pushed it along the floor with her feet. 'Here's the packet Theo gave me.'

Jack snatched the neat box and hid it deep in his waistcoat pocket. He pulled out the bread and tore off a chunk, before ripping into the meat and cheese Betsy had taken from the store at the Swan. After filling his mouth, Jack took the top out of the bottle, swigged back several slugs of gin and sat down.

'Nobody saw you come?'

'No, Jack, I was very careful.'

'Didn't tell no one where I was?'

'No, Jack.'

He hooked some meat gristle out of his mouth. 'Where's the girl now?'

'No need to know, Jack.'

He slowly stood up tall, changed tack and swooped, his face an inch away from hers. 'But I do need to know, Betsy.'

'She's no worth to you or to no one, she's a waif.'

Jack sighed and shook his head. 'Where is she, Betsy?'

'She's on the road with a travelling group. I sold her. To get money for the food and clothes what's in me bundle. If you had her, people would notice, with me she could pass as my girl. That's why I took her. Safer for you, Jack. She was just worth money to me. I did it to help you.' Betsy looked straight into his eyes without blinking, praying he would believe her. 'Neither of us wants an urchin hanging around us. Leave that to the bawds and pickpockets.'

Jack took his penknife out of his inside pocket and turned it around in his hand. In the still silence, Jack studied her. With her most innocent gaze, Betsy offered, 'We've got better crimes to do, Jack, ain't we?'

He cupped her chin ready to kiss her, holding her head steady. Then he cut off the tip of her earlobe.

Jack knew he'd hurt Betsy. This time, more than before. But he couldn't stop the blind fury he felt at the thought of her, not needing him. She'd acted on her own, taking his hostage. That was breaking their rules. By controlling Betsy, it helped him to check his unpredictable emotions. To test her by challenging her love, to be sure she would not desert him, to know she would always forgive him and come back. That was the certainty he needed. He craved unconditional love.

Careering out of the door and down the stairs, he tried to call her back. But she was gone. The fear of abandonment overtook him, and he thrashed out at the walls until his knuckles bleed. Back in the cold, dark prison he'd created for himself, he wrapped himself into a ball and squeezed into the corner of the room, trying to contain the burning rage that consumed him.

'Betsy, come back. I need you,' he pleaded to no-one. Jack Mann, vicious villain and master thief, wept pitifully and hit his head, over and over again, with his fists. There was only one thing that would stop this mania, the only solution he had found. Total absorption in beauty. He took from his pocket the package Theo had given to Betsy. Breaking the wax seal, he wiped his eyes with his oily sleeve, smearing his tears over his unwashed face.

'Come on, I must see you,' he said, as he panicked to untie the knotted thongs.

Released from the leather wrappings, was revealed a heavily embroidered handkerchief which encompassed the treasure within. As he gently unfolded the French silk, his heart rate slowed.

'Concentrate, you madman. Give me back who I really am.'

He lifted the monogrammed corner to uncover a

diamond encrusted, enamel box. The little light that entered into this squalid attic, was enough to set the faceted stones sparkling. Jack breathed out slowly, while meticulously examining the exquisite workmanship. His demons began to flee. Once more, he became a connoisseur of fine craft and style. He turned the box over in his hands, feasting on the intricate design. When sated with the outside, he clicked the fastening to open the lid and read the inscription written in French, etched into the gold. It was genuine. His heart jumped, as he held it close to his chest. The treasure was back where it belonged.

CHAPTER THREE

The Tiny Pearl

MR BIG LIT a fire in the small grate making the garret cosy. To make sure Fanny was out of any draughts, he pulled up a chair, close to the flames and hung a blanket over the window shutters. 'Thank you, Mr B, you look after me so well, I feel like a princess.' Mr Big blushed.

His wife stopped stirring the vegetables which she was heating up. 'A princess. Yes, of course,' She moved the pot to the side of the fire and ran over to a mound of skips and theatrical props waiting to be stacked and opened the lid of a long wooden box. Turning her back on Fanny in order to conceal what she was rifling through, Mrs Big found what she was looking for and said, 'This is the one.' She closed the lid, placed smaller boxes on top and turned to reveal the treasure she carried in her outstretched arms. She approached Fanny with the highest respect, knelt down before her and said, 'Your Highness.'

Fanny had never seen anything so beautiful, a young woman's gown made out of a patchwork of rich velvets and silks, sewn together with gold thread. Attached to it, like twinkling diamonds were hundreds of mirrored spangles and around the hem and sleeves were bands of tiny bells that tinkled as the garment moved.

'Oh, Mrs B, what a magical gown. What is it?' asked Fanny.

'It is the dancing gown of a Maharaja's daughter. The young princess fell in love with a poor young carpenter who saw her dancing in the lotus garden, but their love was forbidden. He was banished and sent away across the seas to England. The Princess Jahanara cried a river that she swam along until it reached the sparkling ocean. The captain of a silver hulled galleon ship saw her floundering in the deep, turquoise waters and saved her. The Princess sailed to London where she searched for her love, dancing at all the fairs, hoping one day to see him again.'

'And did she?' asked Fanny.

'Oh, yes, she told me the tale.'

'You met her?'

'How do you think I have the gown? When I was your age and showing at Bartholomew Fair she came to view me. She and her carpenter ran away deep into the forest, where the young man cut trees down to make a glade and where he built a wooden house to her design, her own Taj Mahal where they lived happily ever after. She gave me the gown to me to pass on to another Princess.'

'I don't suppose you get to meet many Princesses, do you, Mrs B?'

'Well, I have one in front of me now.'

'Mrs B, thank you. I shall never take it off.'

Although the attic space doubled as lodgings and a rehearsal room, Mrs Big had made it homely with the barest of things. Her big personality of love and laughter made it a happy, family home. She cleaned regularly, washing the floors and the small amount of linen they owned. Buckets of water were hauled up from the well in the tenement's small yard by an iron hoist fixed to the last surviving wall of the original warehouse. The whole rookery was latched on to it. Each time she went downstairs, she would fill the pail with water ready to be winched up and lifted through the shuttered window on the top landing. By cleaning relentlessly, she managed to stop her neighbour's lice and fleas from taking residence in the garret and Mr Big often picked up the heavy shovel to flatten a rat or mouse if they dare slink in. It was a never-ending job.

Mrs Big didn't perform with the troupe any more, her acrobatic routines being in the past. She did practise sometimes, to keep her bones and muscles strong and supple. These days, her main task was to care for all the fair acts and they loved her for it. Together they made a large, eccentric family, not at any time boring and never normal. Physically, big or small, with extra or missing limbs, they all had warm hearts and enjoyed extraordinary lives.

Mrs Big was the tiniest of small women this century, so people paid a premium to view her privately in their houses. She dressed up and painted her face as a Bartholomew Fair baby doll, and Samuel the Strongman carried her in a box. Placing her on a table, the viewers gathered around as Samuel ceremoniously untied the red ribbon and carefully opened the lid. Mrs Big kept her eyes closed.

'Wake up dear, you need to come to life for these good people,' Samuel would say. The circle of faces drew nearer. 'Give the lady some air, if you please.' Samuel propped up the top of the box and Mrs Big flickered her eyes and rolled them open. Some of the people were fooled and they exclaimed, 'This is not a woman, this is a poppet. We are cheated.' Mrs Big knew this was her cue to move her head in a circle as though the doll was waking up. When she had the spectators full attention, she sat up, turned around and curtsied, smiling at the stunned faces.

Not being one to show off, unlike the rest of her found family, Mrs Big rarely spoke about her expensive appearances, as she knew that to talk of money was abhorrent and common and that was one thing Mrs Big wasn't. If pressed, she was proud to announce, 'I am known as The Tiny Pearl and I have been to Kensington Palace and presented to the late Queen Anne who gave me gave me a little pearl necklace.' This could not be trumped.

There were three loud knocks at the door of the garret. Mrs Big explained to her husband, 'That will be Sam the Strongman. We have a special private show today, he will present me to a little ladybird who is too fearful to have a baby.' Mrs Big opened the door. 'Good day, Samuel. Come in, please pick up the doll box. It is ready with clean rags, bucket and apron. I shall bring my instruments. Now, where is my PORT tea?'

Mr Big passed her the blue glass bottle Theo had delivered to the garret. 'Thank you, Mr Big. I shall return later today.' She reminded him with a kiss, 'Pray for the mother whilst I help the poor little child to pass. When all is well, Samuel will carry the box down to the river. I shall leave the holy launch to him whilst I go to the Swan.'

Samuel confirmed to Mrs Big, 'I'll wait for the tide to turn, allowing the current to carry the precious innocent soul to heaven. Amen.'

'You are a good man, Samuel.'

Fanny's heart went cold. This small, kind woman showed boundless empathy, love and enduring concern for others. Why would she speak so?

'Samuel, meet Fanny. She is the latest member of our happy family.'

'Hello, Fanny, welcome to our small band of performers.'

Three more knocks fell upon the wooden door, and Mr Big drew the bolt. Noble, Luke and John stumbled into the room, teasing each other and laughing. 'Ah gentlemen, I thought the expedition would take longer.'

'Cut short by a rude fellow at the Swan,' said John.

'I'd have wrung his neck if you'd given me the chance,' said Luke, still angry.

'Don't worry Luke, if you don't do it, someone else will,' Noble said.

'It'll be me that does it, make no mistake,' insisted Luke.

Mrs Big decided to put a stop to all this bickering. 'Well, you are here now, Luke. So make yourself useful and get everyone a spoon and a bowl. John, please cut the pies. Come on everybody, I must hurry to my job and then on to the Swan.'

With a high and fast running tide, Samuel finished God's work quickly whilst Mrs Big left her ladybird to recover. Carrying her roll of instruments, she hurried to the Inn to meet Annie where they sat in her private room, away from the drinkers.

'Please, sit down, Mrs B,' said Annie, 'May I get you anything?'

'No, thank you, my dear, but it's very kind of you to offer. Is Betsy joining us? I pray Jack has not found out what happened?'

'Not as yet, he has been keeping low. She took him some food and gin, sweetening him up in case he hears the truth. She'll join us soon.'

'Annie, what do you know about Fanny and her aunt, the milliner?'

'Finch the wagoner, says she is a destitute orphan from Wiltshire and her aunt is French. I have made some inquiries, and I believe there is a milliner of that country residing at the gate of the Inner Temple. She is a respectable woman and married to a God-fearing, strict gentleman merchant. He is a freeman of the blacksmith company who had an accident, which took off the fingers and thumb of his left hand. From what I know, Fanny will be safe and cared for there.'

'We must be sure they will not treat her badly or she may go the way of other milliner's apprentices, the streets are full of game pullets.'

'Betsy has the same worries, she decided to make enquiries about the lady earlier today.'

The door was thrown open, and Betsy staggered in, holding herself up by the doorframe. Blood had dried on her elbows and mouth and fresh blood still leaked from her left earlobe, covering her badly bruised cheek. To complete the suite, she had a vicious black eye.

'Oh, Betsy, come and sit down and I'll get something to help clean you up,' said Annie.

'Not learned yet, Betsy?' said Mrs Big.

'I love him.'

'And I can see just how much he loves you'.

After Annie had cleansed the wounds, she left the tavern to fetch some calendula and arnica ointment from Theo's apothecary. Once again, Mrs Big had helped to patch up Betsy and she wanted to repeat her warnings of Jack's irrational behaviour, but she held her tongue as she knew it would make no difference. Instead, the two women discussed how to go about ensuring Fanny's immediate future. 'What did you find out about Fanny's aunt, Betsy? Are there other children in the family?'

'There are no children, Fanny is the only relative, except for one other. Are you ready to hear this?'

'Yes, get on with it, Betsy.'

'Theo is the nephew of the milliner's husband, Humphrey Busby.'

Mrs Big took a big intake of breath. 'Are you sure?'

'Certain.'

'Fanny and Theo, are cousins?'

'Yes.'

'Oh, Betsy, it means he will keep an eye on her. That's a relief.'

'Indeed, fortune shines on her, so far,' said Betsy.

'Well, her aunt must be worried sick, thinking God knows what. Now Fanny is fit and well, we must return her to her family as soon as possible. We cannot risk Jack finding out she is with us, he is in a bad state.'

'I told him I had sold her to a travelling group. We have to talk to her explaining she cannot speak of us, for all our safety.'

'Indeed. No mention of you, poor Betsy.'

The two women held each other's eyes until Betsy asked the question, 'Can we trust her? '

CHAPTER FOUR

The Inner Temple

BETSY VISITED THE rag market late the next morning, ready to haggle for garments to replace Fanny's ruined clothes. Her travelling box was nowhere to be found at the Inn, the contents no doubt, sold on. Betsy headed to the stall of one of her customers.

'Blimey, Lizzy, it ain't ermine, it's a bit of rabbit trim. Come on ducks, it's me you're selling to. Look, I'll be fair as we're all in the same game, I'll give you sixpence for the coat, cape 'n petticoat. The boots are worth fourpence at the most and you make sure you throw the laces in for nothing. What you got in lace trim?'

'Here is a stretch of nice Belgian lace, my dear,' said the second-hand garment seller.

'Belgian? That's never crossed the Thames, less the Channel, I give you a farthing for it.'

'Betsy, have pity, I'm a poor woman, do not cheat me, dear. I have to take what's given to me.'

'And it was me what gave you all this nicked stuff, and if I remember correct you only give me sixpence for the whole bloody lot. Take it or leave it.'

'Nice to do business with you, my dear'.

Betsy tucked the purchases under her arm and made her way back down Field Lane ducking under the strings of stolen garments and silk handkerchiefs, still warm from the previous owner's pockets.

Betsy entered into the match built castle where the Big's lived and climbed the stairs to the top.

Stepping into the attic she saw Theo had already arrived and was talking seriously to Fanny. 'So you see, it is vital you do not mention Betsy by name or tell of what has happened to you in the last week since you arrived at Holborn Bridge. You have experienced the anger of Jack Mann, Betsy would be at the receiving end of this rage and then he would find the little people and punish them. Do you understand?'

'Yes, Theo, I owe my life to these good people, I would never put any of you in danger.'

'There is something else I must tell you, Fanny. The people you are going to know me. I am Mr Busby's nephew. You will see me in the shop at times,'

'Oh, Theo, I am so pleased.'

'You must never mention we have met before, I help a lot of people whom your aunt and uncle would disapprove of and I've become friends with many of them. If your uncle found out, he could make my life very difficult. Will you keep our friendship a secret?'

'For you to be my friend, I would do anything.'

'Good. Now, do you remember what we agreed to say, about what happened to you after you arrived at the Swan Inn?'

'Yes, Theo. I will do as you wish.'

Betsy passed the bundle of clothes to Fanny and said, 'Dress yourself in these, dear.' Fanny took them behind the dressing screen, which was draped with tasselled and embroidered shawls.

'Do you think her aunt will accept her explanation?' asked Betsy.

'Theo has such charm she'll not question him,' said Mrs Big.

Fanny came from behind the screen all dressed up but not quite as if she had travelled from Wiltshire. There was more of an air of London about the style. It would have to do. Fanny handed back the Indian dancers gown. 'For another Princess.'

'It's yours, Fanny, it will always be here.'

'Ready?' asked Theo as he took Fanny's hand.

'Yes, I'm ready. I hate to leave you. Please will you say goodbye to Noble and Luke and John and…'

'Yes, my dear, I shall give them your farewells, fear not,' said Mrs Big and she wiped her eyes with her handkerchief.

'Don't cry, Mrs B. I shall see you again, I promise.'

'Well, take this handkerchief until the time comes around.'

Fanny turned to the shadowed corner of the room and saw Mr Big sitting in the dark. She knelt in front of him and signed a message. She kissed his damp cheek. He signed back.

'What is he saying, Mrs Big?' asked Theo.

'He says, she is his daughter now, and he loves her.'

Theo and Fanny walked down to the end of Field Lane where they turned right into Holborn. This was a new world to Fanny, her eyes and ears filled with images and deafening sounds, wagons, carriages and carts fighting for space along this muddy, major route west out of London and the hawkers calling, each shouting louder than the other. Along the sides of the street, under the overhanging floors and keeping close to the houses were throngs of people rushing by in both directions, hurrying to do business. Although they should all bump into one another and cause chaos, somehow they flowed like a river around stepping stones. Fanny was dragging her feet, looking sullen.

'Don't be so downhearted, Fanny, you are beginning an adventure.'

'My whole life is now an adventure, not a nice one. I'm at other people's mercy.'

Theo stopped Fanny and crouched down to speak to her. 'Your aunt will love you, she will be kind and look after you. Very soon you will feel in harmony with the pulse of the city and you will make friends and find your strengths, I know you will. Promise me you will.'

Fanny hated this childish angst of the unknown and chastised herself, she must learn to conquer this weakness.

'I promise.'

Theo kissed her hand, making Fanny smile. 'Shall we pass your shop, Theo?'

'Yes, I have to pick up a package delivered from France. We're nearly there, just a little further down Chancery Lane, opposite the gatehouse of Lincoln's Inn.'

'Is it an inn like the Swan?'

'No, Fanny, it is one of the Inns of Court. Where lawyers do their work. You will be lodging at the Inner Temple.'

'Is it like a Roman temple?'

Theo laughed. 'In a way. The Inns do have their own little gods. We're here. Will you wait outside, Fanny? Stay right here, I shall not be long.'

After Theo entered the apothecary, Fanny wandered further down the street looking at the delights in the shop windows. Without realising it, she had strayed quite far. A woman spoke to her.

'What pretty things they have. Which ribbons do you desire, my dear?'

How friendly people were in the city. 'I love the pink rosebuds woven into the silk, they would look beautiful as a tie for a bonnet.'

'How clever you are, what is your name?'

'Fanny.'

'Are you new to London?'

'Yes. This is my first day looking around the city.'

'Are you waiting for your mother?'

'No, my mother is dead, I am an orphan.'

'Oh, how sad. My dear, please allow me to be your friend. Come, let me buy you some ribbon, it will look enchanting with your fine features. My name is Betty, and I care for some lovely girls. I give them pretty things to wear and they pay me back by entertaining my friends. We are a loving little family. Let us go to a haberdasher that I know well, it's not far, just down here.' The woman looked over her shoulder to see if anyone was looking. 'Hold my hand and don't let go.'

'Fanny. Fanny, stop.' Theo ran towards her.

'That is my friend, I must go to him.'

'Oh no, my dear. You are coming with me.' The woman dragged her into the alley.

'Please, let go. You're hurting me.'

'Shut up, or I'll slap you.' The woman clamped her hand over Fanny's mouth and pulled her down into a small cubby hole, which hid them from Chancery Lane.

Fanny's heart raced, once again she was being manhandled against her will. How stupid she was, why had she trusted this woman? It all happened so quickly. She must get away. Fanny bit down hard on the side of the woman's hand, Betty screamed and let her go. Fanny rushed out into the daylight where Theo opened his arms and grabbed her.

'Fanny, what happened?'

The woman screeched out of the shadows, 'You little bitch, you'll end up whoring be it with me or another bawd. I'll look for you in the murky lanes of St Giles, filthy and starving, riddled with pox and I won't give you a farthing. No one crosses Betty.'

'Be off with you, before I call the constable,' shouted Theo.

The woman spat at Theo and slunk away into the maze of back lanes.

'Fanny, are you alright?'

'Yes, Theo. It was my own fault, I should have stayed outside the apothecary and waited for you. It will never happen again. I have learnt my lesson.'

Fanny calmed herself as they walked down Fleet Street. Opposite the gate of the Inner Temple, Fanny's attention was diverted and she tripped over somebody's leg and stumbled.

Theo laughed loudly and said, 'I'm sorry Fanny, I forgot to warn you of Mrs Salmon's House of Wax. This match seller is to entice people in, it's carved out of wax and dressed as a real person. You were kicked by the clockwork figure. See her crutches? They support the weight of the waxwork, while the clockwork kicks the foot out.' He laughed again.

Fanny didn't find it funny, as her shin hurt.

'We go through here. Are you ready to play your part, Fanny?'

'Yes, Theo.' Despite her best intentions, Fanny couldn't help but ask, 'May I hold onto your hand as we go in?'

'Of course,' Theo said. She held it fast for protection,

never wanting to let go. But one day soon, she would.

CHAPTER FIVE

Aunt Marie

THROUGH THE INNER Temple archway was a small row of shops. The first one, a bookseller, was busy with gowned lawyers studying the shelves and talking to an old gentleman with pince-nez spectacles, wearing a yellow and purple checked waistcoat and of all things, a Fez. The second bow window displayed printed ephemera in every pane, samples of the printers art; business cards, examples of the Inn's notices and some fine etchings. At the lower, left-hand corner of the window was a print of attractive ladies, semi-naked at their toilette with their maids helping them dress. The script at the bottom of the paper was in French so Fanny could read it. She stopped and peered closer, but Theo pulled her away and said, 'Fanny, stand up, we're here. Do you see your aunt in the shop?'

This window was full of hats, braids and ribbons and gold embellished robes for the legal profession of the Inn. It looked bright and welcoming inside and Fanny could see a small woman, bustling about busying herself with boxes of stock.

'Ready?' Theo whispered.

'I think so,' replied Fanny and she touched the sky-blue, frayed ribbon her mother had given her for luck. The bow was always pinned to her corset. It made her smile.

The coiled sprung bell rang out their arrival and as Fanny entered the shop her first impression was of cleanliness. There was an aroma of newly pressed linen and something else Fanny hadn't smelt before, she thought it very delicious: a green, waxy, floral perfume. At the back of the shop, the milliner used a wooden step to reach the highest shelf. She balanced a box with her fingertips. Her aunt was very petite with similar features as Fanny, a very tidy and pretty lady wearing a small lace cap over slightly greying hair and enveloped in a beautiful scent.

'Forgive me, forgive me, I'm rather engaged at the summit of French lace.' She laughed at her own joke and said, 'Pray, one moment.'

Madame Marie pushed the box of lace back safely onto its shelf, stepped down and managed, by much experience to turn, curtsy and speak all at the same time. 'Bonjour, Monsieur et Mademoiselle, welcome to my humble establishment. How may I be of service to you today?' Once she had come to a standstill, she peered over her brass-framed spectacles and focused her eyes on Fanny's cobbled together apparel. The milliner's smile dropped. Passing over Fanny's sweet smile she turned away to discover Theo. 'Ah, 'tis you my dear boy, how happy I am to see you. Your visits should more often, Theodore.' Madame Marie looked from Theo to Fanny several times, as if trying to work out the relationship between them.

'Dear Aunt,' said Theo, 'This is Frances, your late sister's child. She was lost but now she is found.' There was a moment of hesitation from all. Fanny could see her aunt turning over these details in her mind and piecing together the many questions raised from this revelation. She started to open her mouth to speak when Theo said, 'Frances, give your aunt a kiss, for she must be relieved to see you are safe and not in danger of the city.'

Fanny stepped forward, put her arms around Madame Marie and tenderly kissed her. As if Fanny had opened a sluice gate, her aunt broke out into violent weeping. So much so, that Fanny kept her arms tightly around her, looking back to Theo, wondering what to do.

'Oh, my dearest, dear child, I feared you were lost, disappeared into the sinful ways of London. Oh, my dear, will you ever forgive me for not being there to greet you? Mr Busby had a prayer meeting and as the wagon was late arriving, I had to attend or he would have been so disappointed. I hoped the old gentleman who was travelling with you would have brought you to me the following morning but no. Oh, my dear. Oh, my dear.'

'Aunt,' Theo said. 'Pray, do not upset yourself so. This is a happy greeting, your niece is with you now.'

'Yes, yes, of course, how foolish of me. Mr Busby will be so relieved, he has been praying for your salvation, every day.' Madame Marie had a thought come into her brain, which wasn't a frequent occurrence and asked, 'How did you meet upon each other?'

'Dear Aunt, it was a happy and fortunate occasion, providence was kind to us all. What matters now, is not the past but the future.'

'But—' her aunt started another question. Theo interrupted her.

'Dearest Aunt, may I ask you for some refreshment,

please?'

'Of course, how silly of me. Please, please come and take a seat. I'm afraid we shall have to stay in the shop as my dear husband, Humphrey, is absent this morning and I have to be sure I do not miss a customer. He would be very disappointed if it were to be the case.' She turned and decided, 'I shall make some tea.' Madame Marie passed through a lace-edged linen curtain leaving Fanny and Theo alone.

'I think we have put her at ease, Fanny. My aunt has a sweet nature, but her thoughts are inclined to fall through the bobbin lace so she may not put all the facts together. It is what I hope, anyway'

'Theo, can I come back with you to Mrs Big's home?'

'No, Fanny, that's impossible.' Her face dropped. 'You will be happy and safe here.'

Madame Marie returned, carrying a china teapot and cups on a small tray. Of course, Fanny had heard of tea, people spoke of it in awe in the village and Fanny used to put her face to the windows of The Bear coaching Inn in Hungerford, where the gentry took tea. Now, here was the tea ceremony, right in front of her. Fanny had no idea how to drink it correctly, so she observed her aunt pour the steaming liquid and watched Theo bring the cup to his mouth and drink it. Fanny copied him, but the liquid was too hot and she burnt the roof of her mouth. However, she persevered and soon its bright taste refreshed her. 'I like tea,' said Fanny and her aunt smiled and patted her on the knee.

When the conversation stilled, it signalled the time for Theo's departure. Fanny wanted to rush up to him and give him a warm embrace, but she knew she couldn't. She must keep the secret, as promised. She felt tears stinging her eyes as once again she was thrown into an unknown world. Theo took his aunt's hand and kissed it. He turned to Fanny and said, 'Goodbye Fanny, I know we shall meet again soon.' It couldn't be soon enough.

As Fanny had lost her box, she had nothing that belonged to her. She would never forget this time when she felt so vulnerable; one day she would want for nothing.

Her aunt pulled out some clothes a previous apprentice had worn and started to alter them. Madame Marie set Fanny to work immediately and gave her a piece of linen to embroider and was delighted to find she was adept at the fine needlework. While she stitched, Fanny considered how her life would be at the milliners. Her aunt was warm-hearted and she was sure Theo's uncle would have the same attributes as his nephew: intelligence and affection. But something in her aunt's demeanour made Fanny uneasy, she sensed nervousness disguised another emotion.

Once her aunt had performed her magic on the shop's clothes, she handed them to her niece to try on. Fanny drew the lace curtain aside and skipped down the two steps into the workroom. At speed, something flew towards her and landed on her head. She screamed out. It was too heavy to be a bird, what was it? Her aunt came running to her and when she parted the curtain said, 'C'est mon petit monkey, Frances, he will not harm you. Come to Mama, Sous-sous.'

The monkey jumped high off Fanny's head onto her aunt's shoulder. Fanny looked at him in complete fascination. He was a very small creature, wearing a velvet waistcoat the colour of a summer sky. Attached to the top button hung a small, light silver bell to alert

Madame Marie to his whereabouts, and on his head sat a turban decorated with silver metal thread.

'This is my partner in cards, Frances. When I am alone I play patience, and Sous-sous places the cards for me. Sometimes I think he knows the cards too well and will cheat me. Have you heard of the game of chance, Pharo? Do you know the rules of Quadrille?'

'No, Aunt.'

'Well, you will learn, if you are to be in society, which I hope you will rise to, you must play these games. We need four players for Quadrille, but I shall think of something. Now let us sew and sing, do you know "Lavenders Blue", Frances?'

'Yes, I do, Aunt.'

'Good, then we shall start. Here is some lace to sew onto this cap.'

'That is exactly what I wanted to do,' said Fanny.

They both settled down to their work, sang songs and spoke in French. 'Oh, c'est formidable, I am so happy you are here, Frances.' The monkey swung around the shelves and peered into the boxes until Madame Marie chastised him and he jumped back on to the countertop and preened himself.

The afternoon passed comfortably and happily. The light lowered as the sun began to set and Madame Marie said, 'It is time to stop working. I never stitch in candlelight, Frances, many a seamstress has gone blind from straining her eyes.' As Fanny placed her work in a linen bag, she noticed a shadow creeping across the window, consuming the last rays of the days sunshine. The door opened, the bell attracting the attention of Madame Marie who had her back to it and causing Sous-sous to dart into the workshop. A tall, cadaverous man entered. He was stooped and dressed in a black wool coat and wearing a full bottomed wig under a tricorne hat. He bought with him a cold, oppressive atmosphere.

'Husband, you quite surprised me. I hope your business has been fortunate today?'

'Who is this?' said Humphrey Busby, indicating Fanny with his right hand.

'Husband, such joy this day has bought. This is Frances, my niece.'

'Your niece? Make sense woman.'

'Why, she is my late sister, Anise's child. From Chilton Foliat.'

Busby removed his hat and thrust it to his wife's hands without looking at her. He moved over to Fanny, who curtsied and looked at the floor, thinking it more friendly than her uncle's face. He bent down, looked closely at her and asked, 'Where have you been?'

'Husband, she was found.'

'Quiet woman. Where were you found, girl?'

'By a young man who helped me when I was exhausted from fear and walking the streets of London looking for you, Uncle.' Fanny bit her lip and waited for his next question.

'What young man?'

'By good fortune, sir, it was my cousin, Theodore Busby.'

'By good fortune, I see. Not by chance, girl?'

Humphrey never blinked during this interrogation. She continued, 'I found myself before an apothecary in Chancery Lane. My cousin took me in and was kind to me.'

'How did you get there?' Humphrey asked.

'Please sir, I have done no wrong. The wagon was late from Hungerford, and I waited an hour for my aunt. When she didn't arrive, I went to look for her and became disorientated by the maze of courts and alleys around Holborn. Soaking wet from the heavy rainstorm, I took shelter in a church. I knew not what to do. The rector took pity on me, fed me and let me sleep in a pew.'

'Why are you not still there?'

'Uncle, I overheard the rector tell a parishioner to get the constable, I was frightened I would be sent to the workhouse like my grandfather. I couldn't bear to be taken, I so wanted to find my dear aunt and uncle. I ran away from the church until I could go no further and I fainted outside a shop full of bottles with herbs, and a skull hanging in the window.' She waited silently, in anticipation.

Humphrey rubbed his chin, judging if her explanation was believable. Fanny noticed his left hand had no fingers or thumb. Instead, she saw a heavy boned club of a fist. She didn't react.

'On your knees, girl, thank the Lord and pray for your salvation.'

Fanny dropped down and said the Lord's prayer. When she opened her eyes, her uncle had disappeared into the back workroom and her aunt said, 'Come, my dear, stand up. All is well. Your uncle is pleased to see you.' There was a beat of silence, followed by a thunderbolt of profanity from Humphrey Busby, as the monkey flew passed them and smashed into the shop door, the bell ringing in alarm.

CHAPTER SIX

Settling In

MADAME MARIE RAN to pick up Sous-Sous to assess his injuries, but the little monkey was resilient, and Fanny was sure her aunt's petting would soon revive his lively character. 'He will be alright, dear Aunt.'

'Of course, he will. He is like me.' It seemed a strange thing to say, but before Fanny could inquire further, she was distracted by her aunt placing her beloved pet on the velvet cushion of her chair. Madame Marie put on a brave face, as though nothing upsetting had happened and said, 'Well, Frances my dear, the day ends and we shall cover the items on the counter with this muslin.'

Fanny took one end of the long length of fabric, and her aunt held the other. Madame Marie counted, 'Un, deux, trois,' and the two of them threw the cloud of gossamer linen up in the air and watched it settle, like early morning mist over the company of bonnets, lace and feathers. 'Come, my dear, it is time I showed you to your room.'

Fanny looked back at the monkey to check if he was recovering. He seemed very happy, sleeping peacefully on his mistress's chair.

Madame Marie showed Fanny the back workroom. Here, were stored bolts of fabric, boxes of trim, a wooden and iron mannequin and in the middle of the room stood a large cutting table. Fanny felt the warmth radiating from a small stove, heating the slug irons of various sizes resting on trivets. The whole room felt safe and welcoming. Madame Marie explained, 'This is where our making is done, it must be kept clean and tidy with everything in its place, so as no time is wasted in the cutting and sewing of the garments. Through here are the living quarters.'

Madame Marie led Fanny through a door, to a building attached to the bow fronted shop. The parlour, though small was beautifully decorated, and the first thing Fanny noticed was a stone fireplace with a basket grate made up with coals, ready to light. 'Come in, my dear, this is your home now.' Fanny remained in the doorway as she was too apprehensive to get any closer to such delicate items, fearing she may cause damage. 'Oh, Aunt Marie, what fine furniture and ornaments. In our cottage we had so little, simple country carpentry except for my mother's rocking chair.'

'Ah, yes, that was a gift from me.' She coaxed Fanny to enter. 'Please, my dear.'

'Shall I take my boots off, Aunt?'

'You do not have to do that, Frances. Please, come in.' Fanny stepped further into the room. She touched the abundant variety of surfaces: the smoothness of polished wood, the wild silk that gently caught her skin and the rough nap of woven course linen. She swept her fingers along the over-mantle, where a pair of blue and white ginger jars were placed either side of a ticking, white marble and ormolu clock. The walls were panelled and painted in pale, grey-blue and under Fanny's feet was an oilcloth.

Fanny studied the floor covering, the design being extremely intricate. 'Oh, how beautiful. What does it all mean?'

'That is for a future time, Frances. It will all become clear to you.'

Fanny thought it depicted a sundial, but on closer inspection, she realised it was the astrological heavens. The constellations of the zodiac were overlaid with a six-pointed star and at its centre was a monogram with the initials M and R entwined. This was partly obscured by a wooden gate-legged table, its top so highly polished, Fanny could see her reflection in it. Four high-backed walnut chairs completed the small dining set and there were two comfortable upholstered chairs placed either side of a folding card table, where a pair of brass candlesticks waited for a spark from the tinderbox. The two sash windows were hung with blue, toile de jouey silk. The room delighted Fanny.

'Aunt Marie, what a lovely parlour,' said Fanny. 'I see you have beeswax candles, my mother made them from the honeycomb, but only rarely. We normally had tallow, it smelt awful.'

'No, no, beeswax has a lovely light and a delicious smell. I cannot abide bad odours or bad taste. We should surround ourselves with the best we can and always choose beauty, if possible. Come, I wish to show you something.'

Madame Marie ushered Fanny towards a glass-topped display table that held a group of painted miniatures. 'This is my mother, Celeste.' Madame Marie pointed to a small oval pendant with a portrait of a vivacious young girl, with dark velvet hair and eyes the colour of honey. The face looked out provocatively at the transfixed viewer.

'She is very beautiful and mesmerising, Aunt. Who is the gentleman in the picture next to her?'

'She was very attractive to all gentlemen, but this one was very special.'

Fanny looked closer at the image of a handsome man wearing exquisite clothes and a sash of blue, the colour of the walls. 'Come, Frances, let me show you to your room.'

As they left the parlour, Madame Marie trilled out a girls name. 'Martha?' Through a small door leading to a scullery, came a worn out young girl, who was obviously the maid of all work. She wore a dirty apron from cleaning the range and a cap with her brown hair poking out. 'Martha, tidy yourself and make some tea, please. This way, Frances. You will be sleeping upstairs.' As they approached the narrow staircase, Fanny noticed a door ajar. Glancing into the room she saw her uncle sitting at his writing table, reading a leather-bound ledger. Through the narrow crack, she caught sight of Humphrey's hand moving back and forth, piling up gold coins. 'Frances, follow me,' her aunt said.

This disturbed Humphrey in his counting house. He kicked the door shut, ordering, 'Quiet.' Fanny and Madame Marie crept up the stairs, making sure they didn't disturb him.

On the first floor was her aunt and uncle's bedchamber, and on the higher landing was a little room in the eaves. It contained simple furnishings: two narrow beds, a jug and bowl for washing and a small table with a candlestick and a bible resting on it. A plain hemp curtain hung at a small window, looking east over the Temple church. 'It's lovely, Aunt. Thank you for welcoming me into your home. I shall work hard for you,' said Fanny, and Madame Marie wept a little once again.

'I know you will, my dear. You have no idea how pleased I am to have you with me. I shall leave you to settle yourself.'

Fanny sat on the bed and for the first time in months, she felt secure. Her uncle's stern manner troubled her, but she tried to put it out of her mind. Maybe it was something he'd eaten. Her mother always put bad behaviour down to indigestion. She loved the milliner's house and all the wondrous treasures in it, and she loved her aunt. But it wasn't enough. 'What is it that's missing?' Fanny talked to herself to find the answer. Despite her Aunt's kindness, she didn't want to be dependent on them. 'I need to be free to make my own life. I must find a way to make this city work for me.' She stood up and turned around, ready to air the bed. 'But at the moment I'm safe, and I shall be as long as I am here with my aunt and uncle.' She turned down the linen sheet. Concealed under it, lay a small piece of crumpled paper. On it, in scratchy pencil was written, "Beware Mr Busby."

The dawn light, tinted with rose, filled the window panes and stretched its fingers along the unpolished floorboards, touching Fanny's eyelids open. Her initial thought was the written warning, but she dismissed it as mischief. For the first time since her mother's death, she was happy.

There came a knock at the door. It opened and Martha was revealed on the threshold, holding a bowl of chocolate. After two flights of stairs, half the contents had slopped into the saucer. Never taking her eyes off the stormy waves of warm liquid, she announced, 'The mistress says it's only for this morning, as it's your first day. Sorry about the –'

Fanny yawned. 'Thank you, Martha, don't worry. How very kind of you to bring it to me.'

Martha looked at her askance. 'It's me job, miss.'

'Yes, I know, Martha, but I'd like to thank you for your trouble and hope we may be friends?'

'Oh, I dunno, miss. I mean, you being the mistress's family and all that.'

'Well, we can keep it our secret if you prefer?'

Martha gave Fanny a queer look. 'Er, all right, miss.' Confused, she started for the door.

'Martha, where do you sleep?'

'In the scullery, miss. It's warm from the range.'

'Do you not have a family, Martha?'

'No, miss. I'm a foundling of the Temple, my name being Martha Temple.'

'I see. Well, Martha, thank you again and I shall look forward to seeing you presently.'

Martha shook her head as she closed the door behind her.

Fanny dressed and ran down the stairs with a light step, looking forward to joining her aunt in her lovely parlour.

After a breakfast of oatmeal and a small beer, Fanny and her aunt opened the shop and went into the workroom to look at patterns. Madame Marie showed her how to work the scissors and press the fabrics. There was a lot to learn, so the morning passed swiftly, the instruction occasionally being interrupted by a tenor voice in a foreign language.

'Who's singing?' asked Fanny.

'It's Signor Boldini, such a charming man. He wishes he were an opera singer, but he is the printer next door. My dear, there are some trade cards to pick up from him. Would you go and see if they are ready?'

'Of course, Aunt.'

Fanny listened to the shop bell as she left the milliners. She had mixed feelings about the sound. The tinkling was associated with her aunt Marie and it heralded Fanny's homecoming, both happy occasions. But the feeling of wellbeing was bruised, by the memory of her uncle's cruelty to her aunt Marie's pet monkey.

She opened the door of the printers and waited, whilst a rotund gentleman sang loudly in front of his printing press. He didn't hear her come in, as he was lost in the upper tenor notes of his voice. His arms gesticulated freely, narrowly avoiding the drying prints hanging above the press. Despite his large size, Signor Boldini moved elegantly within his working space in a rhythmic dance. Fanny was fascinated by the printing process and the magic of seeing images appear on the plain paper; the Inn's news illustrated with woodcuts of Middle Temple Hall, broadsheets of folk and popular ballads and playbills of Lincoln's Inn Field Playhouse and The Theatre Royal, Drury Lane. Signor Boldini approached the crescendo of the last verse and graciously and theatrically, took his bows to every part of the invisible auditorium, to pay homage to his adoring audience whilst twirling his brightly coloured, voluminous handkerchief. He was surprised to see Fanny standing there.

'You sing very well, Signor Boldini.'

'Scusami, signorina. I did not know you were there.'

'Pray, do not apologise, I enjoyed your singing,' said Fanny, smiling.

'Um, do you speak Italian, Signorina?'

'I am sorry, no.'

'Well, that's fortunate,' murmured Mr Boldini. 'How may I help you?'

'My aunt, Madame Marie, has asked me to collect her order.'

'Ah, you must be her niece, yes? She has been so looking forward to your arrival. But you were delayed, no? She was very worried. What happened to you?'

Fanny hesitated and said, 'I have put it from my mind, Mr Boldini. May I take the order?'

'Si, si, of course.' Mr Boldini turned, wiped his hands, dipped them in chalk again and lifted down from a shelf, a small neatly wrapped packet of printed cards. 'Here you are my dear. May I ask your name?'

'Frances, but I'm known as Fanny.'

'How do you do, my dear. It is a great pleasure to meet you. I am sure our acquaintance will grow into friendship. I am always here, should you need me.' He opened the shop door for her. 'One more thing, Fanny.' He drew his breath. 'Do not upset your uncle.'

'I shall try not to. Why?'

The printer looked intently at Fanny. 'Your aunt is like one of her fragile china ornaments. Donna bellissma. Handled without care, she could break.'

A ripple of dread passed over Fanny. 'I shall remember your warning. Goodbye, sir.'

Before she could leave, Mr Boldini called out to her as he started to work some more ink. 'Fanny my dear, visit Mr Jordan the bookseller next door. He is a fine man, despite his waistcoats.'

'I have just a little time now to introduce myself. Thank you Mr Boldini. Goodbye.'

In farewell, he sang a rising scale.

Mr Jordan had no customers and Fanny could see him

sitting in a comfortable chair reading a book, his head to one side. A blanket was draped over his knees and he was wearing his Fez. Today, he was sporting a fine waistcoat in yellow silk, embroidered with turquoise blue peacocks.

The shop bell jingled and he looked up above his pince-nez spectacles.

'Good afternoon, Mr Jordan, I am the niece of Madame Marie, the milliner. My name is Frances and I have come to introduce myself.'

'Come in, my dear. Welcome to my library of knowledge. Our little row of shops is honoured to have such a pretty young lady amongst our midst.'

The aria Mr Boldini was singing next door increased in volume and Mr Jordan called out, 'Not again, Mario, please. Do expand your repertoire.'

'It is the first time I have heard opera,' said Fanny.

'Opera?' Mr Jordan broke into laughter. 'It is not opera, my dear. He may have a natural tenor voice and love music, but it certainly is not opera. That, my dear,' he said, as he jabbed towards the wall between the two shops, 'is a broadside ballad. Just one of the many he prints. He has learnt the tune by listening to a ballad singer on a street corner or in a tavern. Opera. It is a bawdy song, my dear, not for your delicate ears. Thank goodness he sings it in Italian.'

Fanny laughed with the bookseller and said, 'Well, I must take my leave of you, Mr Jordan, as I have my work to do. I look forward to speaking to you again soon.'

'Indeed, is my wish too, my dear. Please feel free to borrow my books should you wish. I am happy to advise you, should you need it.'

'Thank you, Mr Jordan. Do you have any of Shakespeare's works? I have never read him, but I have seen scenes acted out at the Marlborough Mop Fair.'

'I shall be honoured to introduce you to the Bard, Frances. We shall have many interesting hours discussing his work. There are other playwrights we can study too, if it would be pleasing to you.'

'Indeed it would, sir. Thank you,' said Fanny.

'Not at all my dear child, it is my pleasure. Here, please take this small book of sonnets.'

'Thank you, Mr Jordan, I shall take great care of it and return it to you very soon,' said Fanny.

'Do not worry, Frances, I am happy to open your mind to the best use of the English language. I am pleased your aunt Marie has you to look after her. Take care, Fanny.'

'I will, Mr Jordan. Farewell, for now.'

He held the door open for her. 'God bless you, Fanny.'

As Fanny left the bookseller to walk a few steps to her aunt's shop, standing in front of her with the sun behind him was Jack Mann, his long shadow casting its gloom over Fanny's body. She was startled for a moment, but as he extended his hand, she turned and raced in the opposite direction onto Fleet Street. She ran for her life, as fast and as far as she could to take the danger away from herself and her aunt. She collided with several people who shouted at her in anger.

'Watch it, love, where's the fire?'

Another, chastised the man. 'Don't speak of such things, you will start a panic. Don't run, you foolish girl.'

'Oi, look where you're going, knocking me down. You owe me a shilling, all my muffins are in the dirt.

Just wait till I get hold of you.' The young man rushed after her in a fury.

Her pace didn't slow until she darted into the churchyard of St Dunstan's and hid behind a grave. After her heaving chest eventually relaxed, she peeped above the headstone to see if Jack Mann was about to catch her. There was no sign of him or the muffin man. Fanny slumped down, relieved but annoyed with herself not to have been more vigilant. This was London, where bad things happened. Jack Mann was dangerous and he was looking for her. She would have to be more careful. Waiting a few more minutes to make sure of her safety, she crossed the street and took a more inconspicuous route back to the milliners, through Serjeants' Inn.

Her aunt was not in the shop, so Fanny walked through to the workroom. There was no sign of her. Fanny called out, 'Aunt Marie, I have the order,' and she moved towards the connecting parlour door. 'I met Mr Boldini and Mr –' when she entered the room she saw her aunt lying on the floor with Sous-Sous sitting beside her, whimpering quietly and shaking. 'Aunt Marie? What happened? I'm here. Aunt Marie?'

Fanny put the package on the table and knelt down to help her aunt, who was stretched out on her side. When she turned her aunt's face towards her, she saw there was blood on her lip and eyebrow, and a bruise was swelling up around her eye. 'Aunt, please wake up, it's me your niece, Fanny. Please, Aunt, open your eyes.' Fanny lifted Madame Marie's head up and cradled her body close to her, rocking her like a baby. 'Please, Aunt, speak to me.' Madame Marie opened her eyes and although at first they were rolling back, they gradually focused on Fanny's face. 'Oh, Aunt, thank the Lord. What happened? I shall go to our neighbours for help.'

'No,' said Marie as she clutched on to Fanny's sleeve. 'No, do not involve them.'

'But Aunt, you are hurt, they will come to your aid. Please.'

'No, Frances. Hear me, they are not to know about this.'

'I don't understand…'

'There is nothing for you to understand. I fell, entirely my fault. I'm all right, help me up and place me in the chair.'

Fanny helped Madame Marie into the special, comfortable chair with the bleached cotton cover. It protected the upholstery made from woven French silk. 'My dear Frances, not this chair, I may bleed over it. Please, place me on one of the high backed chairs.'

Her aunt did have blood on her bodice and sleeves, but it was dry and she couldn't see any deep wounds still bleeding. She settled her aunt and collected clean linen from the workshop and dampened it with water from the jug in the scullery.

'Where is Martha?' asked Fanny as she cleaned the wounds.

'She has gone to get milk. I am all right, Frances, so do not worry. It is only a scratch, I bumped into the table and I fell, very silly of me. I am always doing it.'

If Fanny had been at the Swan the day Betsy returned from The Mint, she would have recognised the wounds her aunt had suffered. This first time, she believed her aunt's explanation.

Fanny cleaned off the blood from Madame Marie's face and insisted she move her aunt to the armchair, where she bought up the small foot stall for Madame Marie to rest her legs.

'Thank you, Frances, you have been very kind. Now, promise me, you will not tell anyone of this?'

'If it is your wish, Aunt,' promised Fanny.

The shop bell rang and Fanny rose to greet the customer, but it was Martha who came into the parlour. Fanny was standing in front of Madame Marie and said, 'My aunt is sleeping. Please do not disturb her, Martha.'

'All right, miss.' Head down, she hurried towards the scullery.

'Martha. Bring me tea, now.' Fanny, surprised, spun around towards the counting-house next to the scullery. The door was slightly open and through it, she saw her uncle, Humphrey Busby looking straight at her.

Fanny didn't know what to do. She didn't understand. Her uncle had been there all the time, he must have listened to the conversation. In that case, he must have heard her aunt fall. Why didn't he do anything to help her?

'Fanny,' her aunt whispered, 'Remember your promise, do not say anything about this, especially to your uncle. He would be very disappointed.'

The next few days, Madame Marie stayed out of the shop. When not busy and her husband was out, she asked Fanny to bring the sewing into the parlour to join her to play cards. They sat either side of the card table, and Madame Marie dealt the pack. The teaching began.

'The first and most important play you must learn, Frances, is how to take tricks. To do this you must remember which cards have been played, so when you trump or play your highest suit card, you know there are no higher cards in your partner's hand.'

Fanny was excited to tell her aunt that she could remember the cards. 'I have done so for many years. As a little girl my mother would test me, she had a memory system that she taught me. I know what order the fifty-two cards are in a pack, and I can count the cards that have been dealt.'

Madame Marie clapped her hands. 'Dear Anise, she did not forget our little game. I am so pleased to hear of your ability, Frances. We can move forward very quickly. Now, did she show you how to palm the cards?'

'Yes, she did. We made it our entertainment in the country.'

'Well, well. All we have to do is polish your skills and teach you the rules of card games. C'est formidable. It is time I passed on my secrets.'

Fanny became familiar with the complicated rules of Quadrille. The game required four players, making it difficult to play with just two and a monkey, although Sous-Sous was extremely adroit. They used a dummy hand whilst Fanny learnt the game.

One day, Madame Marie placed on the table a plain wooden box and explained, 'In this box are several packs of playing cards. I bought them over from France with me. They are specially prepared for use in games such as Pharo, Quadrille and Vingt-Et-Un. Ladies love these games, I played them many times before I married. All the cousins were clever with the cards, I think the hereditary skill passed down to them from their great-uncle, who believed in divination and other truths or tricks.' Fanny's eyes widened. 'My cousins still use their powers to attract and captivate. But, enough of such stories.' Fanny wanted to hear more of these mysterious cousins of her aunt Marie, but further conversation was diverted. 'This is most important Fanny. My husband disagrees with gambling, so he cannot know about this box and certainly not be reminded of his wife playing such games. You must hide the cards and box in your room. For now, we shall play. We can use buttons for money.'

And so, Fanny laid down not only cards but also the foundations of becoming an excellent gambler. She was nimble with her shuffling and would win by counting the cards. Her aunt was serious with her teaching, 'No, Frances. I can see you place the card at the bottom of the pack. You will be found out and dismissed from the gambling circle. Be more precise and clever.'

'Like you, Aunt.'

'But, of course. I was the best, the most daring of all the beautiful, young girls in Paris. I had an exhilarating life.'

'Maybe I shall have such a life?'

'Be careful what you wish for, ma petite. With excitement comes danger.'

CHAPTER SEVEN

Mr Big

THEO HELD FANNY'S arm as they crossed Chancery Lane and passed through the large gate into Lincoln's Inn.

'I'm pleased you have settled so quickly into the ways of London, Fanny. It is only a month since you arrived.'

'I think it will take a long time for me, not to be called an outsider, Theo.'

'Maybe it's because you speak well and have no country accent. Why is that, Fanny?'

'My mother was strict about my speech. I wanted to talk like my friends in the village, but she reprimanded me and said I was above others, therefore, I should behave like a gentlewoman. It was complete foolishness. Why should I speak good English when she spoke with an accent when not talking in French? She spent money we could not afford, on lessons with the schoolmistress.' Fanny laughed. 'We were poor, it made no sense and I was teased. But here in London, nobody takes any notice. As there are many different people living here, I can be who I want. I don't know why she insisted I speak this way.'

'Your Aunt is refined, your mother would have been brought up in the same way. Maybe something happened to them in the past, which changed their intended future.'

'Perhaps. It doesn't matter, though. Now, I can make my own destiny.'

'Indeed, Fanny.' Theo smiled at those wise words.

'Maybe I should start adding some London slang to my conversation. Betsy can teach me. But don't tell my aunt, she wouldn't like it.'

'Your secret is safe with me, Fanny.' Theo turned to more important matters. 'You haven't mentioned my friendship with Mr and Mrs Big, have you?'

'No, Theo, you asked me not to.'

'Good. They are fun, aren't they?'

'Yes, they are.' She loved the showmen's exuberant life, it was far removed from the sometimes oppressive atmosphere at the milliners. Fanny's behaviour became tentative around Marie and Humphrey, as she observed them closely. Her aunt was a very clever and creative woman, something her husband did not value, and this caused him to make sarcastic and derogatory remarks. Marie's response was to shy away and become more invisible. She was a different person when in the company of Fanny or her monkey, Sous-Sous, or indeed alone. She could often be heard singing and talking to herself, laughing at the little jokes she made. Her disposition was completely benign. Humphrey Busby tried to stifle both this kindness to others and her natural love of life. It came very easily to her, whereas he had to try to be charming but, of course, never to his wife. He was jealous of her.

Humphrey Busby's disappointed episodes became

more frequent and each time, her aunt withdrew a little more from her outgoing character. Her nervousness had increased and Madame Marie didn't speak to her husband, unless in reply. It still didn't appease her uncle's displeasure, in fact, it seemed to make it worse. Fanny wondered if his behaviour could be tainted by what had happened to his left hand. When Theo and Fanny rested on a bench in Lincoln's Inn, surrounded by crisp dry leaves, Fanny asked Theo, 'Would you tell me what happened to your uncle's hand?'

'Of course. It's a terrible story. My uncle was a talented and hardworking blacksmith. He was working with an apprentice named Thomas Steer on a large commission for iron railings and Humphrey had worked out a method of speeding up the production.'

Fanny asked, 'How was it done? I have seen a blacksmith at his forge and it seems a slow action to heat up the iron to malleability.'

'Humphrey has an analytical mind, and he worked out it would be faster to create all the parts first. Once made, he and his apprentice would fuse them together. First, they cut all the posts, spears and collars. Thomas, at the forge, heated up each of the iron rods for the posts, on the red hot coals, and Humphrey, who was at the anvil, hammered them into shape.'

'Very clever,' Fanny said.

'Yes. The two of them fell into a rhythm and they were able to produce the ironwork quickly. By the third day, both were tired, and Thomas made a dreadful mistake.'

'What happened?'

'The anvil was at a right angle to the forge, so Humphrey had his back to Thomas. Humphrey held out his left hand, ready to receive the next post in order to draw it out with his cross-plied hammer. Thomas heated the tip of the posts until they were yellow-orange, but his time, instead of using his tongs to hold the hot end of the iron, he mistakenly held the cold end and passed the melting metal into Humphrey's unprotected left hand.'

Fanny put her hands over her mouth. 'Oh, how awful. The poor man.'

'The pain must have been excruciating. The searing iron burnt through his fingers and thumb and blistered the skin off of his palm. He plunged his hand into the water trough, but nothing could stop the smell of burning flesh and his screams were heard all around the blacksmiths forge. Humphrey was never the same man after this disaster. A year earlier he had married an exceedingly pretty, but frivolous French milliner and he was very happy. After the accident, he changed.'

Fanny began to understand. Marie as was her nature, was kind and loving towards Humphrey and she must have looked after him well, but over time he began to resent her and turned cold and remote. Theo explained more.

'He directed his passion towards the church and money. He is a clever man and never misses an opportunity to better himself. He set up his wife and himself as milliners at the gate of the Inner Temple and became the main maker of legal apparel and paraphernalia including robes.'

Fanny was in awe of her aunt's needlework. She made exquisite mantuas and accoutrements for the ladies and perfect jabots for the gentlemen of the Inn.

Theo continued. 'Humphrey kept his ear to the ground and was not shy about offering to be part of property acquisitions. He owns the freehold or demise of several tenements, dwellings and land. The most valuable part of his property portfolio is fourteen acres in Kensington, close to his Majesty's Palace. He has become well known amongst the legal profession and is held in high regard.'

Respect was what Humphrey Busby needed above all. It was like oxygen to him. Without admiration, he became a dangerous man. Fanny decided to keep out of his way. In his presence, she would do her best to disappear, as her aunt did.

Every Sunday morning wearing their best clothes, a small line of worshippers crossed Fleet Street to St Dunstan-in-the-West. Humphrey Busby led the train with a wide stride and a slight stoop. Following three steps behind, his short wife trotted along, supported by freshly starched lace. Madame Marie concentrated on walking to heel behind this man who kept her wound up as tight as a watch spring. If she lagged behind he would whistle, as though training a dog. Fanny completed the trio, wondering why people needed religion to be judged good. By ancient habit, the three crossed themselves as they passed through the porch. At the back of the church was the high-boxed pew, in which the fragmented family sang hymns, chanted psalms and listened to the long, dry sermon, promising terrible things sinners would have to endure. Fanny wondered, where was the radiant and caring man depicted in the stained glass windows of this cold church? The bible tells of him bringing love and charity to his flock, but Fanny never saw it in the people of London, who lived in poverty and hardship.

At last, the service was over and Fanny bid farewell

to her aunt and uncle. The rest of the day was hers to do as she wanted, and she craved the joyful company of Mr and Mrs Big. Halfway to Holborn, she met up with Theo at his apothecary where she gave her salutations to his father, Charles Busby.

'Hello, sir. I trust you are well today.'

'I am, Frances. How are you settling in at my brother's house?'

'Very well, sir. I am most grateful to Mr Busby.'

They took their leave and continued towards Field Lane. Theo asked Fanny her news and was as charming and amusing, as ever. Sometimes, Fanny would catch him gazing intently at her for no reason she could make out.

Entering the crooked tenement, they climbed the rickety staircase, knocked on the door and expected the usual happy welcome, but today something was different. Betsy opened the little door silently and said, 'Mr Big has the smallpox.'

'Do not allow them in, Betsy,' said Mrs Big. 'It is too contagious.'

Theo pushed the door open and said, 'It's all right, Betsy, I shall take my chances. I have seen smallpox before, let me see if I can help. Go home, Fanny, this is not for you.'

'Yes it is.' Fanny was insistent. 'Mr B is like a father to me. I shall do anything to help him. Let me in, Theo.'

'It's too dangerous, Fanny. You must go home.'

'No, Theo, I shall not. Stand aside.'

Fanny pushed Theo out of her way and headed straight to Mr Big. His face and lower limbs were red.

Theo approached the sick man and asked Mrs Big, 'How long has he had this rash?'

'It appeared during the night. He seemed fine and was sleeping well: a sudden recovery from the headache, sickness and high fever he had been suffering. He complained about his back aching, I thought he'd just overdone one of the tricks with the boys. How foolish I am. 'Tis the pox, isn't it Theo? Oh, he will die.' Mrs Big wept.

Fanny asked, 'Is it smallpox, Theo?'

'Yes, Fanny, I have seen this stage before.'

'Will he die?' Fanny's eyes started to fill with tears.

'Left as he is, yes. There is a chance, but a very small one that he may live. I know of an eminent physician who is experimenting with a treatment called inoculation. It is a very new discovery, and there is evidence that some people have survived the virus and others, who have been exposed to a patient with smallpox, can be protected if administered early enough.'

'Bring the doctor here, Theo, at once. We must do everything to save Mr B.'

'I am sorry, Fanny, the treatment and the doctor attending is very costly, far more than any of us have saved.'

'We must get the doctor to treat him. We must,' said Fanny as she looked around at her friends.

'Fanny, even if we did have the money, Mr B would have to receive the vaccination by tomorrow night before the blisters appear or it will be too late. I'm sorry, Fanny.'

'Stop saying you're sorry, Theo. We shall find the money, somehow. Let me think.'

Betsy said to Fanny, as kindly as she could, 'There's nothing we can do, Fanny, we cannot change nature.'

'No. There must be a way,' said Fanny.

Theo turned to Mrs Big who, wearing a deep frown,

was wringing her hands. He put his arms around her and said, 'If there was anything I could do, I would, Mrs B.'

'I know.' She leant against Theo and wept.

'I can help,' said Fanny.

'What?' said Theo.

'I can help. There is a way to get the money. I can get the money,'

'What are you suggesting, Fanny?'

Fanny turned to Besty and asked, 'At the Swan, is there a room that can be seen from the drinking parlour?'

'Yes, there is. 'Tis not used much and it may have storage in it. Why?'

'I shall win the money.'

'Just a minute,' said Theo. 'What do you mean, Fanny?'

'I shall gamble.'

Mrs Big, Betsy and Theo were astounded and stared at Fanny. 'Gamble? You do not even know what gambling is, you are little more than a child, Fanny. You cannot gamble. Anyway, it is a sin,' said Theo.

'It's not a sin to save someone's life,' said Fanny.

Theo took a moment. 'Fanny, are you saying you know how to play such games?'

'Dear cousin, our aunt is not what she seems.'

'Marie? What can you mean?' Theo asked Fanny.

'Aunt Marie was a courtesan gambler before she married your uncle.'

'What?'

'I don't have to repeat myself, Theo, you heard me. She worked the salons in Paris and when she came to England she continued to be very successful as a sharper, if you know what I mean.'

'Sharper? What do you mean by sharper, Fanny?'

Theo was looking for confirmation of his worst conclusion.

'Aunt Marie had dexterous fingers from stitching. She could manipulate the cards to her advantage.'

'Aunt Marie was a cheat?'

'A very coarse description, Theo. She was a highly skilled risk taker. Also, exceedingly beautiful.'

'Are you saying Aunt Marie has taught you to cheat at cards, Fanny?'

'Yes.'

Theo fell back into a chair. 'Somebody else say something.'

'What do you want us to do, Fanny?' asked Betsy.

'Go to the Inn and tell Annie to prepare the room ready to play cards. Make sure the patrons have sight of the table and what is going on inside, we shall lure them in. Annie will agree as she is a good woman, I shall meet you at the Swan, Betsy.' Turning to Mrs Big, she continued, 'I intend to hold the bank throughout the evening. I need a fair amount of money to do that, do you have any, Mrs B?'

'I don't believe this, I must be dreaming,' said Theo.

'I have some savings, Fanny. It is all yours.'

'Thank you, Mrs B. I shall win, I promise. Now tell me, do Luke and John know the game of Vingt-Et-Un?'

'There're Irish, they know all the games and every deception. They are good showmen, Fanny, the best supporting actors you could wish for. And if there's any trouble, they will see you safe and away.'

'Tell them to be here within the hour, and I shall instruct them as to what our plan will be around the table.'

Fanny demanded of Theo, 'Are you with us or not?'

'I know when I am outnumbered, and who knows

where we shall all be next week. How can I assist?'

'You are to go and find the physician, make sure he has the vaccine for us all. If he knows you, he will trust you to pay him. And you will do so, by the end of this night. Collect your medicine for Mr B on your way back and I will meet you all here. We must go, now.'

As they all left the room Fanny moved close to Mr Big and signed to him, 'Trust your daughter. I love you.'

Fanny was out of breath by the time she reached the gate at the Inner Temple. There were no candles burning in the two shops or at the milliners. Her uncle was building a house on his land in Kensington, and this afternoon they had been checking the progress. Now, most likely they were visiting friends and ironically, they were probably playing cards.

As Martha did not work on Sunday afternoons, Fanny was alone. By the time the maid returned later tonight, the household would all be fast asleep.

Fanny ran upstairs to her room and took from a chest some of the clothes Betsy had bought for her. Once they were rubbed in the streets filth, she would blend in with the hundreds of other poverty-stricken girls of London. When dressed, she removed the small wooden card box hidden under the floorboards and placed the little money she had saved, into her pocket. Tucking the box under her arm, she went downstairs to the kitchen where she collected an old bowl and added some water. She picked up a floor rag and took it into the parlour. From the fireplace, she scraped off some soot and mixed it with the water. She began to paint her hair with the mixture and when done, she tied it back with a red ribbon. Fanny closed the shop door, dirtied her coat and made her way out of the Inner Temple to Fleet Street, dropping the rag and bowl, but holding on tightly to the box.

Fanny knocked three times on the small garret door and Mrs Big questioned as usual, 'Who is there?'

'It's Fanny.'

Mrs Big opened the door to a black-haired girl. 'It's me, Mrs B, Fanny.'

'Oh, my dove, your beautiful hair.'

'Tis just soot, Mrs B. May I come in? I promise not to make anything blackened.'

'Of course, my dear.'

Fanny moved over to the dressing screen and asked, 'May I borrow this black and gold silk shaw?' It had a long, heavy knotted fringe and Fanny always wanted to wear it, never imagining it would be for such an adventure. 'Do you have some hoop earrings, Mrs B?'

'Yes, here.' Mrs Big opened up a treasure box filled to the brim with gold and silver metal and glass gems of every size and description. She pulled out a pair of huge gold hoops. 'Will these do?'

'Perfect,' said Fanny, as she put them on.

Mrs Big opened another box and pulled out a black oil stick. 'Let me add some black to your eyes and brows.' She guided Fanny to a broken looking glass. 'Is this how you want to look, Fanny?'

Her reflection was of a gipsy girl. No one would recognise her, it was a perfect disguise.

Fanny held Mrs Big's eyes.

'Yes, dear. Is there something on your mind?'

'Why do you destroy life?'

Mrs Big knew what Fanny was referring to. 'To return it to the mother. All I do is correct a mistake.'

The door flew open and Luke and John came in followed by Theo. The gipsy girl standing in front of them startled all three.

John said, 'Very good, Fanny, and clever. Let us get started.' He rubbed his hands in delight.

Fanny looked at Theo and she could see he was wondering what had happened to the fragile girl he knew this morning. He opened his medical bag and began to place items on the table. 'I have bought the medicine and the doctor will come at midnight. Will it be enough time, Fanny?'

'It will have to be.' She turned to Luke and John and said, 'We shall have to fleece them fast, boys.'

CHAPTER EIGHT

The Game

FANNY PREPARED THE cards for Vignt-Et-Un. She had several packs to choose from, plain or marked. She chose the biseauté deck, with the long sides of the cards being slightly tapered off. If all laid the same way, the four edges were smooth. She primed the pack before play by turning the tens and aces upside down, allowing her to feel the projecting corners. She could easily lift them from the pack, during a shuffle. As dealer, she handled all the cards, so was able to expertly manoeuvre her chosen ones to the base of the pack, where she could bottom deal them. Also, by sleight of hand, she would hold the required top cards and second deal the card beneath.

Two accomplices, John and another man, would join the table. Luke was to stand behind the players, watching for cheating.

Fanny would make sure some of the gamblers won money, so as to tempt others to join. Once the table was full, the winning cards would be dealt to John and the plant.

'Who have you have to play with us, John? Is he trustworthy?' Fanny asked.

'No one will consider him to be anything but. No one will doubt him,' answered John.

'What's his name and how shall I know him?'

'You will know him when he sits, Fanny, have no fear.'

Fanny practised her sleight of hand and the two men were very impressed. Her expertise in shuffling and dealing the cards was perfect, but she would act as though she was not proficient. To be able to palm the cards slowly, was far more difficult.

'Ask Betsy to join us and we four will sit down. Luke, open the door halfway, please. I shall start by reading the cards, revealing your good fortune, indicating success and luck. The people know you as performers and 'tis very acceptable you should enjoy a fellow showman's talent. Make noise to attract attention. Once there are a few punters, suggest we play another game to wager on, Vingt-Et-Un. That is our moment. We shall begin.'

All went to plan and as the gambling started, it drew in more players and bets were raised as the excitement grew. Fanny conducted the game with the sensitivity of the finest maestro. She hoped the accomplice would appear as she sensed the betting progressing to a crescendo.

A tall man ambled towards the table and took hold of the neckerchief of the player who was sitting immediately opposite Fanny. He pulled him up from his chair and sat down himself. Fanny smelt the distinctive odour before she saw the man. She looked up as she dealt the cards. Facing her was Jack Mann in his oiled coat. She froze, remembering the fear she felt when he drew a knife to her throat, in this very inn. She scowled at him, he was going to expose her and the night watchman would be called. Her hands began to sweat, soon the cards would slip. She wiped them on her shawl and looked straight into his eyes, defying him to betray her. Instead, the corner of his mouth turned up slightly and he winked at her. Fanny stalled, realising Jack Mann was part of the deception.

She must stick to the plan. Jack's generous betting raised all the other punter's stakes. The first three deals, Jack lost, the next four he won, on the eighth he bid a great deal of money. Fanny wondered where such a sum had come from. She knew he would lose the hand, and they both knew he would win it back. He lost. The punters now gambled serious money. Fanny gave the secret signal that this deal, would be the one that lost the banker a fortune and put her in the clear. Out of the corner of her eye, she saw Luke lick his lips. She dealt Jack the first card and his hand darted out to trap it. He challenged her stare, looking deep into her eyes, daring her to lose control. She took a long intake of breath and refusing to break the eye-line, she pulled her hand away and dealt the cards. Fanny knew the value of every card on the table. One by one, the players lost, their last card taking them over twenty-one. As Jack looked at the last card Fanny dealt him, she saw a twinkle in his eye as though he was proud of her. It was an Ace. He held, King, Jack, Ace: Twenty-one. Fanny's two cards were fives. She turned over another card. A Queen: Twenty. Not enough to beat him.

'Luck is with you tonight, sir.' Fanny said.

'I'm a lucky man,' said Jack, as he scooped up his winnings.

Was that the last she would see of the money to save Mr Big?

Luke took Jack's place at the table and John took his turn at spying on the group of excited gamblers. The gaming continued, Fanny must make as much money as she could in case Jack vanished. They carried on for a few hours with Fanny raking in the coins. The players enjoyed their evening and were content with both their gains and losses. Without knowing it, they had made a generous donation to saving one small man's life.

When the last punters finished playing at the gambling table, Fanny got up and thanked them as they all disappeared back to the drinking parlour. She spun around to face John, slamming the door behind her.

'Jack Mann? The criminal, Jack Mann? Are you touched in the head? He is the last person in London to trust.'

'He is one of us, Fanny. Have you never heard the saying, honour amongst thieves?'

'But, Jack Mann?' She stamped her foot and turned on the spot, looking up to the ceiling.

'Fanny, your time to repay Jack will come, be in no doubt. Him being there made the game look genuine. It worked, Fanny, it worked and you were quite something. The best I have seen.'

'Thank you.' Fanny felt a little foolish. Of course these men knew what they were doing.

Luke explained further. 'What you don't know, Fanny, and no one should, is Jack is a friend of Mr and Mrs B. They do some business together. I don't know what it is, but they will always look out for one another. He was happy to help.'

Although Fanny's head spun with these new revelations, something inside told her to welcome them, they were markers to guide her towards a fate she would control. She'd proved herself today, she was no longer a weak child and she would not be frightened or cowed. She would do everything in her power to become a strong and independent woman.

Betsy popped her head around the doorway. 'You lot better go home. You can't hang about in a tavern all night. Well, not tonight. Off you go, I pray all goes well. Oh, you better take this, Fanny.'

Betsy handed her a leather bag. Fanny looked inside, it was the money Jack had won and it included his huge stake. He was honest. At least, for tonight.

Fanny rinsed the soot from her hair, in the water-filled trough, before the three tricksters left the Inn. It was only Fanny who saw, slinking out of the shadows, Jack Mann watching her.

The shop bell gave a loud jangle, objecting to the interruption of its slumbers. Fanny silenced the protest by clamping her hand around the cold metal.

During her walk home, the excitement and nerves that buoyed her confidence trickled out of her. She looked at her hands to find them shaking. She grasped her wrist to still the tremors, but the energy flowed through the physical connection and flooded her entire body. Her brain began to project vivid images of various scenarios, which could have happened at the Inn. She knew she was too unstable to climb the stairs to her room, so she made her way to the parlour, steadying herself by sliding her hand along the walls. The fire embers were still glowing and the room's warmth began to comfort her. She fed the fire with sea coal and it soon caught. Surrounded by darkness, she focused on the flames turning from yellow to orange. She let her mind float freely, as she read the ribbons, dancing in the grate. They took her back to a world fast fading from her, seeming further away with every step she took in her curious new life in London. As she moved deeper into her memories, she caught a familiar smell of food cooking in a cauldron, set above the burning logs of the inglenook fireplace, at her home in Chilton Foliat.

Her mother hung the iron pot early in the day, to simmer the fatty pork and potatoes during the working hours. The heat from the fire allowed the bread dough to rise until it was ready to bake in the bread oven. Every day was the same: repetitive with similar activities, creating a perceived safety. This world was small; the cosy thatched cottage, Sunday church and the close village community, where newcomers weren't accepted until fifteen years of residence. Fanny was protected. Today, she hadn't been. She'd put herself at risk. Nibbling at her nails, she considered her feelings: did she like the excitement or hate it? She stared into the flames and thought about who she was and how she'd been nurtured. Certainly, love had been all-encompassing. But had it stifled her? Her upbringing was all about keeping safe. But why? The world wasn't safe. She should have been prepared for danger. Her mother kept her from harm, by isolating the small family. She was wary of strangers, whereas Fanny longed for new company. Until now, she'd not thought about her childhood, it all seemed so natural. But it wasn't. Her mother insisted on teaching Fanny good diction, urged her to read well, to have correct manners, be a fine needlewoman and to handle cards. This was incongruous with her social place in life. She was a poor peasant girl. She wasn't going to be a lady. Fanny never questioned any of this before, but being exposed to the perils of living in a great city, she now realised how unequipped she was to confront such a mercurial world. She made up her mind. No longer confused, Fanny relaxed and sat back in the chair. She closed her eyes and called for sleep, having decided to take on London, and win.

CHAPTER NINE

Backstage

TWO MONTHS LATER at Christmastide, there was a lot to be thankful for. Mr Big had survived smallpox with just a few battle scars on his face, Mrs Big never contracted the disease and the others were also immune to it. Theo was elated and excited about inoculation as a new advancement in medicine, and he wanted to become involved with the practitioners who prescribed it. He was welcomed into the medical circle for his respected, extensive knowledge of plants and herbs, as it completed the synergy between the physician, surgeon and apothecary. His life became full of lectures and study and he had less time to spend with Fanny.

Her life at the milliners was more settled. She enjoyed working, whilst she and her aunt sang and talked together about Paris, and in the afternoons they sometimes played cards together. Between them, they had taught Sous-Sous to recognise the difference between the playing cards, and he would make small gestures enabling them to know their face value. It was fun teaching him these tricks, but difficult when they wanted to play a serious game without cheating.

In the evenings Fanny visited Mr Jordan the bookseller, who was well-versed in Shakespeare.

'Learn your favourite passages, Fanny. Recite them to hear the Bard's rhythmic music of the English language. Never, was there a greater master.'

Soon, she had a small repertoire of ingénue speeches and she acted them out, to entertain Mr Jordan and Signor Boldini.

Mario, of course, insisted he read in the part of Romeo to her Juliet. 'Ah, Fanny, my dear, allow me to play your Romeo.' What he lacked in talent he made up with enthusiasm. Fanny did have reservations about a stage balcony not being able to take his weight, and when he embraced her, he nearly crushed her. All this vigour added to the fun and enjoyment of the evenings. Signor Boldini insisted she learn some of the ballads he knew, and Mr Jordan insisted he chose only the ones suitable.

'You have a lovely, crystal clear voice, Fanny. I think you have a talent for the stage.' Mr Jordan was delighted with his protégée. Fanny dropped a curtsy in appreciation.

'I have a small gift for both of you, to thank you for the sunshine you have brought into my life here, at the Inner Temple,' said Fanny.

'My dear, it is not necessary. It is your company that brings us much pleasure, we should thank you,' replied Mr Jordan.

Fanny gave them both their presents, wrapped in silk and tied with ribbons. For Mr Jordan, she had stitched a waistcoat in patchwork, made from the silk scraps left over from cutting patterns. She remembered the Indian princess's gown she wore at Mrs Big's, oversewn with metal thread. Although she couldn't use the silver wrapped twine, she picked apart strings of fringing and attached it to the fabric using tiny overstitches. The waistcoat had buttons of different sizes and colours to match the crazy design.

'My dear girl, it is truly a piece of wonder. It will be greatly admired by my customers. Thank you.' Mr Jordan immediately tried it on.

For Mario, she had made two large silk handkerchiefs made to the same design as the waistcoat. The silk was so fine he could scrunch it up in his hand, and when released it would explode into the world, as did Signor Boldini's personality.

'Beautiful, Fanny. Thank you, my dear.' He smacked her with a big kiss on her cheek. 'You are a fine seamstress and you have a talent for the stage. Tell me, have you ever been to the theatre?'

Fanny laughed and said, 'No, sir, I have no idea what it is like'.

The two gentlemen spoke in whispers together. Mario turned back to Fanny and said, 'Come to my shop tomorrow, about ten o'clock. I have someone I wish you to meet. It will be our gift, to you.'

Fanny was intrigued, she would be there on time.

At ten precisely, the printers shop bell rang and Fanny entered. Standing at the serving counter was a young man dressed in flamboyant clothes, with a fine powdered wig and an immaculate manicure. Fanny had never seen such clean hands before. She quickly hid hers behind her back when the gentleman espied them, raising his left eyebrow.

'Such excellent timekeeping. So necessary in the theatre. May I introduce myself, Mr Thomas Mercutio,

at your service, assistant theatre manager of His Majesty's Theatre Royal, Drury Lane.' He flourished a deep bow.

'Thank you, sir, the honour is all mine. Your name is familiar to me, Mercutio?'

'Indeed, fair lady, the great tragic hero from the world's finest love story, Romeo and Juliet. I hope I carry some of the perfect features of such a brilliant character,' he said as he put his hand to his heart and lowered his head in respect.

'Yes, sir, indeed. I see before me a man of such graciousness, humour and taste.'

'I like you, Fanny Tomlinson. Now, Mario and Charles tells me you have a liking for the theatre, and they wish to give you a present. I cannot imagine a better gift than an evening embraced by the exquisite sights and sounds of excellent performance, in the gilded temple of art. Tomorrow, come to the theatre's stage door and ask for me. They will be expecting you. You need not arrive an hour before curtain up as you, my dear, will be watching from the wings.'

'The wings?' Fanny asked.

'The side of the stage, Fanny, you will be as close to the action as possible,' explained Mario.

'How wonderful, I don't know how to thank you, I am overwhelmed.'

'Well, you can thank me, by delivering my order of playbills later today. Bring them to the box-office at the front of the theatre, you may access it from Brydges Street. Just mention my name and doors will open for you. I wish you all, arrivederci. I must away.' He waved his hand and left the printers in a waft of citrus fruit, bergamot and rose.

'How exciting. Thank you, gentlemen, for this exceptionally kind gift, I shall remember it, always.' She stretched up and kissed each of them on their cheeks.

The afternoon was wet, and Fanny wanted to keep the mud off her shoes and gown. If she walked along the Strand, she would not be able to avoid the splashes from the busy street, so she cut through Middle Temple, passing the 12th-century Crusaders church and made her way along the narrow lanes, leading from one court to another. She emerged onto Milford Lane that led up to St Clement's and crossed the churchyard onto Wych Street. This was still lined with medieval shambles from before the great fire. All along Drury Lane, she passed groups of girls who were fashionably dressed with the side of their petticoats raised a little. They were conversing with various gentlemen and occasionally, would lightly brush their hands along the gentlemen's sleeve. Sometimes they would link arms and stroll along the street together. Fanny supposed they all seemed very friendly.

Russell Street was upon her, so she turned left until she met with Brydges Street, where Tom had told her to go. She came to the narrow passage leading through to the theatre, and once inside she approached a small opening in a wall. Filling the ticket window was a stern looking woman.

'Please, madam, I have these for Mr Tom Mercutio from the printer, Mario Boldini,' said Fanny.

'Give them to me and leave,' said the woman.

'May I see him, please?'

'Why?' asked the gorgon.

Fanny considered this and answered, 'He asked to see me.' She waited.

'About what?'

What could she say? She looked down at her feet, hoping an idea would spring into her mind. 'He has some work for me to do.'

'Really? What would that be? To play the leading

lady?'

'No, madam, to be given some needlework to do,'

'Ah, you are a milliner's apprentice? Be off with you, we do not have your sort hanging around outside this theatre.'

'No, we have plenty of them inside,' a voice jested and laughed. 'Let's have look at her.' A head came into view, which was Tom without his wig. 'Oh, it's only Fanny, she's a friend of mine,' he said, winking at her. 'Do not be nasty, Barbara. Just because she is prettier, it does not mean I shall not adore the bella Barbara forever.'

Barbara blushed, smiled and giggled.

'Come through, Fanny, the door is to the right,' said Tom.

And so, Fanny entered the outer portals of a theatre for the first time. The narrow box office was a mess, with paperwork strewn over every surface. Barbara sat in a high chair, against a shelf, sorting theatre tokens ready to be delivered to the gentry, for the coming season. Tom swept up some of the piles of paper and offered Fanny a seat. The chair was well worn, the cracked leather seat deeply moulded, having caressed many a clerks bottom. All around the room were shelves holding rows of dusty ledgers. As Fanny would find out, dust seemed to be the prevalent smell of backstage.

'Fanny, may I introduce you to Barbara who is hard to take at first, like the first sip of gin, but with the second sip you fall in love. Ain't that right, Barbara?'

'Stop your teasing, Tom,' Barbara said.

'Well, I shall tickle you instead.' And he did, much to Fanny's amazement and Barbara's obvious delight. 'Goodie, it's the playbills. Do you want one, Fanny? It's what you're going to be watching tomorrow: The

Miser. A grotesque entertainment, it says. The only grotesque thing about it, is Mrs Wetherilt. She can be a bitch, that one.'

Fanny listened intently to his manner of speaking, unsure if she should be appalled, or amused. She decided to offer no comment, allowing her to enjoy the moment.

'Now, Fanny, as you can see, Cibber Jibber is top of the bill and he will be passing you sitting in the wings, as he goes on and off stage. Do not get in her way, and do not upset her whatever you do, she is god around here. She's a good comedy fop, but excruciating as a tragic actor. Fortunately, she will not be speaking much in this extravaganza.' He looked at Fanny, who was totally confused by the switched gender. 'I'm talking about Colley Cibber, actor-manager of this company of spoilt, infantile troubadours. He gets final say in casting, so I suppose he is a god, at least in this theatre. Actors. Who'd love them, darling?'

Fanny counted the hours before her return to Drury Lane Theatre. They seemed to pass so slowly. When she did arrive at the stage door, her heart began to beat a little faster. The doorkeeper called a boy to run and tell Mr Mercutio, his guest had arrived. After only a minute or two, Tom appeared and took her through a double door where backstage began. Running up and down a flight of steps were an army of people: some carrying costumes and props and actors and actresses wafting about in silk damask banyans. Some had only lengths of fabric wrapped around their near naked bodies. Whether they be cupids with arrows or fairies with wings, all these people were totally blasé about their state of undress. There were sounds of shoes clattering on the stone steps and everyone was chattering. High above her she could hear scales being sung, voices trilling and strange phrases being repeated over and over again. Above all this noise was the wonderful sound of laughter.

Coming down the stairs were two girls, one of whom was rather cross. 'I've told you, Dolly, if you take my stockings one more time, I'll clout you.'

'Briddy, I didn't have no time to go up to wardrobe to get mine darned.'

'Well, take them off before scene three 'cos that's when I have to wear them. If you don't, I'll flatten you,' warned the girl who wore a wide-brimmed hat, low cut stays and carried a basket full of oranges.

An older woman pushed Fanny aside as she complained, 'Excuse me my lovely, I have to get by and sew Mr Cibber into his Quaker collar before the five, he's ripped the button off again. Tom, a word, if you please. I know it's not up to you, but I'm one girl short in wardrobe and I got twelve low comedians to keep under control, which is nigh impossible I might say, and a troupe of flighty girls always wanting more lace to be stitched on everything. I can't be expected to do all this work myself. I warned this would happen, I knew Polly let out her front room and lay backwards, if you'll excuse the term, young lady. I know she'd get one in the basket quick. She should have called for the little woman, but she left it too late. I don't know how she'll care for the poor little mite, but she ain't coming back 'ere, all right? I'm an over busy woman. I know I'm at the King's draughty stables and we all should be grateful for the honour, but Mr Mercutio, I can't be expected to run up and down, up and down these stairs at my age, I really can't. I'm not young anymore. It's not that I'm complaining 'cos I need the work and I'm deserved of it as I am the best costume mistress in

London. But give a poor woman some help, love. I can't be exp—'

'Mr Cibber awaits, Mrs Bovel. Have a word,' interrupted Tom.

'Oh, me Lord,' and she shouted as loud as she could up the stairs, 'I'm coming, Mr Cibber, I'm coming.'

'That will be the first time in years, dearie.'

As Fanny and Tom rounded the corner, a little man appeared holding a large coil of rope, almost as big as him. It was one of the boys of Mr Big's troupe.

'Matthew, what are you doing here?' asked Fanny in surprise.

'Fanny? Oh, Fanny, how good to see you. I've gone legit, at least over Christmas and the New Year. This should see me through to the May Fair. I'm the rope dancer in this one, and Livewell is playing the Toy Woman. Can't miss him, he's the one with the ginger wig and oh, he's short.' Matthew nudged Fanny and touched his nose as he laughed. 'Let us talk after the show, yes?'

'Yes, I look forward to it, Matthew.'

'What you doing here, anyway?'

'Mr Mercutio is kindly letting me watch the show, from the wings tonight.'

'Oh, right. Well, I'll see you later. 'Tis the quarter, I must set up me props, excuse me.' He ran up in front of Fanny and disappeared through a heavy door with the words, STAGE QUIET, stencilled on it.

'Tom, he's my friend, what a surprise to see him here.'

'Not really, love, this type of show is full of turns,' said Tom as he flicked his head up and to the side, as though he had noticed a bad smell. But strangely, it wasn't a rude gesture at all, it was endearing.

Mesmerised from the moment the overture started, Fanny watched, enthralled at the first scene with the colourful Harlequin. She didn't notice Mr Cibber enter the stage area until he came up beside her in the wings. She knew at once who he was, as he was wearing the Quaker collar. She was so still, he could have taken her as a dressmakers dummy. But no, he turned his head slowly around to face her and said in a measured way, 'And who are you?'

'Fanny, Frances Tomlinson, sir.'

Emphasising every word, Mr Cibber continued, 'What are you doing here?'

'Mr Mercutio allowed me to watch the performance from the wings, sir.'

'Did he now?'

'Yes, sir.'

He moved his head around in a deep circle and chanted, 'Ber ber ber, der der der, ter ter ter,' and trilled from high note to low. Fanny swallowed hard as Harlequin came off, and Mr Cibber swept on stage.

He was magnificent, and she applauded as he exited stage left, towards her. He stood close to her and whispered, 'Difficult house tonight. Need a lot of work to get them going. Good that I ate pie earlier, I shall need a lot of stamina.'

'Yes, indeed sir,' said Fanny, although she had no idea what she should say.

'Next scene, tricky with Mr Clark playing Harlequin. I hate to say it but he's not a jot on Mr Rich. Now, you keep a watch out and see if Harlequin does any sudden movements to distract the audience, right?'

'Yes, sir. Certainly sir.'

'I shall have him, if he does.'

As the pantomime continued, Fanny was easily drawn into the magic: spirits, fire eaters, clowns, a flying cupid, toys dancing, caskets of jewels, Pierrot, and lovers sitting on the silver moon, rising. She fell in love with everything; the transformations, the sound of dancer's feet pounding the stage as they leapt and pirouetted, the smell of the wax from the hundreds of candles that lit the make-up of ceruse powder and rouged cheeks and lips, and even the whiff of sweat from well-worn costumes. She would never forget the dust catching the back of her throat as it flew off the stage cloths and flats when changing scenes. Fanny became intoxicated by the colours, aroma and the intangible enchantment that was the essence of theatre, and she wanted to stay there forever.

The actors took their bows to great applause. Fanny was surprised how noisy the performance was, the audience shouting to the actors and the repartee and flirty conversation from the rakes in the stage boxes, engaging with the young dancers who coyly flirted with them. As the curtain fell, these gods of the theatre became mere mortals again, talking of things going wrong, assignations settled and discussing which tavern they would retire to.

'Did you enjoy it, Fanny?' asked Matthew.

'Yes, it was wonderful. You were so good, Matthew.'

'Just doing my job, Fanny,' he beamed. 'I liked the new bit I put in, when I spun the rope around me in a circle on the floor and jumped over it. It went down well, I think I'll keep it in. Are you joining us at the Rose?'

'I better ask Tom what he wants to do, but I would love to. It's on the corner, is it not?'

'It is. Us lot go there, the leads go to Tom's coffee

house and talk about literature and politics. We stick with gossip and, well, more gossip. See you there, Fanny.'

Tom arrived through the pass door connecting backstage to the auditorium. 'Well, Mistress Tomlinson, did you like our little entertainment?'

'Yes, yes it was beautiful, funny and magical.'

'You did not see the rags, dirt and perspiration?'

'I could see the hard work, making it look easy. Thank you, Tom, I had the most exciting evening of my life.'

'Ah, we have captured another poor girl, have we?'

'I have my trade as a milliner and mantua maker. I would love to go on the stage, but I can't see it in my future.'

Tom had an idea. 'Well, to be a part of it, you could help out in wardrobe after your work during the day? Mrs Bovel is desperate for a needle-woman. You would be paid, Fanny, and I would be grateful to you. Mrs Bovel knows all the stories never told to the punters, you may enjoy spending time with her.'

'Thank you, Tom, I accept with no apprehension and much appreciation. When do I start?'

CHAPTER TEN

Foes

TOM ESCORTED FANNY to the Rose. 'I'll not be joining you tonight as I have been invited to a wedding at Molly's.'

'A wedding, Tom? At this hour?' asked Fanny.

'Well, yes. A sort of wedding.' Tom hesitated. 'It's like a droll, a funny play on a wedding.'

'Oh,' said Fanny. 'I don't understand.'

'Neither should you. Don't worry about it.'

'Why isn't it in a church? Why at Molly's?'

'Oh, good grief, Fanny. Stop interrogating me on a simple sentence.'

'I just want to understand what — '

'In you go, Fanny, I'll see you tomorrow.' Tom kissed her on the hand, turned and rushed off to avoid any more questions.

The Rose was full of people. Fanny looked around and noticed Briddy being ushered upstairs by a stout gentleman, whose hands squeezed her ample rear. She wondered where she was going. Briddy waved to Fanny, stuck her tongue out and put two fingers in her mouth. She laughed as she rubbed her fingertips together to indicate money.

'Over here, Fanny, I've got a seat for you,' called Matthew, who stood on a stool, beckoning her to the table. Fanny sat next to him.

'How are Mr and Mrs B, Matthew?' she asked.

'Very well, Fanny. Mrs B is busy sorting out next year's calendar of the Fairs. We've added some tricks to our routine, which requires new costumes, so things are very busy at the garret. We shall play our new show in the Spring, at May Fair and come the summer we all caravan to Cambridge Midsummer Fair. This year we have decided to stay several weeks to make a holiday out of it. We can work as fruit pickers during the day, and in the evenings we shall perform at the local taverns. You should come with us, Fanny.'

'I would love to, Mathew, but I have work to do. I'm really enjoying myself, and I'm very happy.'

At Fanny's moment of unblemished contentment, she was unaware that her life and those of two others were destined to meet. With every hour, the angle of collision became more acute, predicting catastrophe.

She'd only seen the innocent side of the Rose Tavern. Upstairs, the bedchambers were rented out for the communion of the flesh, Covent Garden offering the widest choice of sexual entertainment. The London clouds darkened over Fanny, as in the room directly above her, were the two people whose actions would bring ruin and despair.

The dark haired girl lay on her back with her hands above her head, loosely tied to the post of the bed, by the man's stock. Her breasts spilt out from her stays, enticing the young man to ravish her. He was stripped to his shirt, wearing no breeches, erect and ready. Climbing onto the bed he pushed up her petticoat and opened her legs.

'Kitty, my dear, I see you are waiting in anticipation for my desire of you, all rosy and glistening.' He slowly slid into her. 'Is it like the first time, Kitty?'

The girl panted through her teeth. 'Yes, Gideon. When I did not know you, as you took me against the porch wall of Temple church.'

'You were a bad girl, Kitty, caterwauling on holy ground.' He slowly withdrew, waited a moment, then thrust into her. Kitty winced.

'I am a bad girl, sir, when I'm with you. What will do to me to correct my behaviour?'

'Turn over and I shall show you.'

Gideon twisted her round and raised her rump until she was kneeling. Holding her fast by the waist, he took her from behind. Gideon's sexual desire was insatiable and the rutting continued with Kitty calling out repetitively, in either desire or pain, until he was finished with her.

'That was nice, Kitty, was it not? Did I hurt you enough? Do you want more next time, my dear?'

'I shall do as you want, Gideon, you know you are the only gentleman for me.'

'You could find no better.' He slapped her buttocks so hard, it left a red mark. Untying her, he asked, 'Wine, my dear?'

'That would be very pleasant.'

Gideon went to the door and shouted down the stairs. 'Bring me wine and cold cuts, Filth. And be quick.'

Kitty sat on the side of the bed, still with her breasts uncovered but her petticoat down. She rubbed her red wrists to ease the marks. 'Gideon, as you are my master and want me all to yourself, will you pay for lodgings for me? I am about to be thrown out of my residence and I have nowhere to go.'

'What residence? It's a slum, I have no doubt. A whore's usual habitation.'

'Gideon, you are my protector, I see no other gentlemen, but you. If you refuse me, I shall have to go back to my colonel and offer myself solely to him.'

'No, not the fat pig with the gout, I'll not have it. I shall ask about in the Temple to find someone who will take you in, but you must say nothing of our arrangement, do you understand?'

'Of course, Gideon. Do you have someone in mind?'

'Yes, an obsequious man who craves my position in life. He comes from a poor family, but he has been clever and has a good clutch of properties. He is married to a silly French milliner. He will agree to take you in, in order that he may be attached to my influence, within the Inner Temple.'

There was a knock at the door and a boy opened it, carrying a tray laden with wine, meat and two glasses. 'Ere you are, Mr Woodford.' He offered the platter to Gideon.

'Put it on the table, idiot.' The boy placed it on the serving table and left the room. Gideon stared at Kitty, his lust rising again. He approached the bed, came close to Kitty's face and pressed his stiff prick against her mouth. 'You must sing for your supper, Kitty.'

A few days later in the milliner's workroom, Fanny and Madame Marie were busy pressing yards of silk, ready to cut on the pattern table, when Humphrey called them into the parlour. He told them his news. 'I have a gentleman visiting us today. He has a young niece called Katherine, who is looking for lodgings. We are honoured to take her. Gideon Woodford is from a great legal family, well-educated and charming. I look forward to our friendship growing more intimate. I know you will treat him with the utmost courtesy, which must extend to his young niece.'

'Of course, husband. We shall welcome Katherine as one of our own. Fanny, she will be sharing your room, please be sure she has all she needs before her arrival,' said Madame Marie.

'Of course, Aunt, it will be pleasant to have a new friend, who is close to my age.'

'I believe her to be seventeen years of age. She will be a good example of a well brought up young lady. One you can aspire to, Frances.'

'Indeed, Uncle. I shall learn many things from her.'

Fanny went out to the Strand to buy a nosegay for Katherine, and on her return she placed it in a small vase on the bedside table. Next to the flowers, she left her book of Shakespeare sonnets, hoping Katherine would enjoy reading them. As a welcome gift, Fanny had embroidered a lawn handkerchief. She'd stitched it for Mrs Big, but it would be a nice gesture to give it to a young girl, arriving at a strange house. Fanny would do all she could to make Katherine welcome.

The shop bell jingled, and Fanny ran down the stairs to the workshop so she could peer through the lace curtain to view the visitors. She'd been instructed to wait until called by her uncle.

Sous-Sous jumped on her shoulder and followed her gaze. 'Shush, be very quiet and don't move around,' said Fanny to the little monkey.

A very pretty, young girl entered, wearing a dark blue mantua and a stylish lace cap. She was slim with long, luxuriant brunette hair, pinned up with combs made from tortoiseshell and paste diamonds. However, it was the man behind her who Fanny was unable to wrest her eyes from. A gentleman in every way, elegantly dressed in a coat of finest wool the colour of dove grey and a long waistcoat of midnight blue silk. His face was as though carved from alabaster, his perfect complexion creamy with highlights of rose, and his blond hair caressed his head in crests of waves. His eyes were of such azure blue, that they were mesmerising.

Gideon introduced himself to Madame Marie. 'My dearest Mrs Busby, how charmed I am to make your acquaintance. Your talents are known throughout Middle Temple for such fine stitching and design. Maybe you would be so kind as to create something exquisite for my niece, Katherine?'

'I would be delighted, Mr Woodford.' Madame Marie dropped a curtsy. She was as giddy as a filly and melting under Gideon's lagoon eyes. After a long pause filled with anticipation of whether Madame Marie would faint or ever speak again, she took in a deep breath, found her composure and although in a voice higher than normal said, 'Please allow me to introduce my niece, Frances. She is an expert needlewoman herself.' The milliner called for Fanny, 'My dear, our guests have arrived.'

As Fanny drew back the lace curtain, Sous-Sous jumped off her shoulder, flew close to Kitty's face and landed on the counter. Kitty screamed. Humphrey Busby shouted at his wife, 'Take that disgusting animal out of here, and lock him in his cage, now.' He calmed Kitty with apologies. 'My humble apologies, Katherine, please take a seat to recover. Frances, give our young guest some water.' He gave his wife a look that should have turned her to stone. Madame Marie, in a fluster, said, 'Please accept my sincere apologies, I am mortified to have shocked you so, Katherine.

Please do forgive me, it is entirely my fault.'

Through clenched teeth, Humphrey said, 'Take him out, woman.' When Madame Marie and her beloved Sous-Sous had left the room, Humphrey resumed his social tone and introduced Fanny to Gideon and Kitty. 'Frances, come here and greet our guests properly,' said Humphrey.

Fanny felt her legs fail her. She held onto the door frame for support as she stepped into the shop. She couldn't look directly at Gideon or speak, because of the overpowering beauty of the young man. She was in love.

Gideon bowed to Fanny. 'What a delightful, young lady you are, Frances.' He looked so deeply into Fanny's eyes, she had to turn away. Fortunately, the reappearance of her aunt into the parlour distracted the company from Fanny's blushes.

Quickly, Kitty interrupted, 'Thank you, Mr Busby, for your kindness of inviting me to live with you. Please do call me Kitty, it is a pet name my family call me by, and you are now my family.'

Humphrey looked at Gideon and said, 'What a charming young lady.'

Gideon explained, 'Sadly, Kitty is without family, her parents being prematurely deceased. Alas, she has no one but myself. I shall continue to take the greatest care of her and visit her often, offering my guidance and friendship.'

'It is true, Gideon and I give to each other, all our desires…' said Kitty, looking knowingly at Gideon.

'Kitty, I shall leave you in the gracious care of Mr and Mrs Busby and return this evening, to take you for a late supper. My best wishes to you and your dear wife, Mr Busby, and, of course, to dearest Frances.' Gideon bowed to Madame Marie and Fanny, looking deep into her eyes. This time, for a second too long.

Fanny showed Kitty the way upstairs to her bedchamber on the top floor. As they passed through the workshop, Kitty saw the cage Sous-Sous was locked in. He was running around grasping the bars with his tiny paws, demonstrating his dislike of the confinement. When he saw Kitty he started to scream. She ran past the cage and up the stairs. Once Kitty had closed the door, she turned on Fanny and said, 'Don't let that rat anywhere near me.'

Fanny tried to calm Kitty. 'He is very sweet, he's just shocked by the shouting, I'm sure you will become fond of him and enjoy his company.'

'No, I shall not. Keep him away from me.' She stuck her chin in the air and looked around the room. 'Not bad. Is this my bed?'

'Yes, I hope you will be comfortable, here is another blanket should you be cold at night.'

Fanny handed her a woollen coverlet. Kitty snatched it and asked, 'Are you the servant?'

'No. Why would you say such a thing? You know I am Madame Marie's niece, I'm apprenticed here.'

'A milliners apprentice. Butter wouldn't melt, eh?' Kitty dropped her accent back into the gutter.

'Forgive me, I do not understand?'

'Come on, you need not keep up the pretence with me, dearie. When do you do your walking?'

'Walking? I run errands during the day and in the evening, I go to Drury Lane,' explained Fanny.

'A Vestal, are we?'

'I do not know of what you speak.'

'Wait a minute, are you telling me you don't do a bit of business on the side?'

'I just assist my aunt, in her work.'

'Blimey, you must be the only milliner's apprentice in London who's not a prostitute.'

'Katherine, I am a girl of virtue. How could you think such a thing?'

'Keep your hair on. Let's start again, shall we? I'm sorry, I got you wrong. I can see now, you're an innocent and just an apprentice. I want to be your friend. Please call me Kitty.'

'I won't be an apprentice all my life, I am going to work hard and make a good life for myself.'

'Yea, yea, yea. It's what all London girls say. A lot of them end up in the swirling waters beneath London Bridge. First, you have to get money. And you know how you do that, don't you?'

'I will work for it.'

'You certainly will, dear.'

Fanny couldn't follow this strange conversation. She changed the subject. She wasn't sure of this girl. 'Are you really Mr Woodford's niece?' inquired Fanny.

'Yes. I'm the poor relation he has taken under his wing, and very good to me he is too.' Kitty sat on her bed and bounced up and down to see if it is was comfortable, 'Um, nice. What's the old man like, Fanny?'

'He is a God-fearing gentleman with strict moral values. He has a temper, do not cross him,' warned Fanny.

'Strict, eh? I shall remember that peccadillo, Fanny. Thank you.'

Whilst Fanny was gathering her sewing notions to put in her bag, ready to take to the theatre, she heard Kitty talking to Madame Marie and Humphrey, as they took tea in the parlour. Her uncle offered sympathy to Kitty, over the loss of her parents. She recounted the tale of horror in vivid detail.

'My parents were missionaries who left me in the safe hands of the preacher of our parish. Over the next two months, they sailed far away across the seas to the Americas, following the journey of the first pilgrims. They wrote to me, telling of the hard life they suffered, of crops failing and illness. But most of all, they were afraid of the threat of violence. They were scared the native Indians could attack their settlement, at any time. One hot night, it happened. The compound was lightly defended and the raiding party easily outnumbered the missionaries.'

Kitty had repeated this story many times and she knew she told it well. It never ceased to lose its immediacy.

'The Christians knelt in prayer as their pastor tried to ease their fear by saying, they must put their trust in God.'

Kitty knew it would have been wiser, to put their trust in firearms.

But Humphrey agreed with the innocent preacher. 'Indeed, our salvation is in our Saviour.'

Madame Marie felt she should acknowledge her husband's belief, 'Amen.'

Now that Kitty had their full attention, she continued the story. She brought to life, the horrendous events of that fateful night.

As the believers recited words from the Bible, their attackers shot flaming arrows over the wooden defence enclosure. They ignited the tinder-dry roofs of the homesteads and the fire spread quickly and ferociously.

Kitty's father turned to his wife and said, 'We can't stay here, we shall be burnt to death. We must take our chances and run towards the woods. Hold my hand.' They ran for their lives.

Outside the blazing settlement, emerging between clouds of choking black smoke, furious young men rode bareback. Both the warriors and horses were painted with red ochre and burnt black pigment, in patterns only the tribe understood.

In the glow of the angry flames, the man and woman saw scalp trophies of long hair, hanging around the warrior's necks. Some of these were braided with beads which were, paradoxically, traded by the British. Kitty's mother recognised the gruesome pendants. She prayed, 'Oh, dear God, save us,' as her husband pulled her towards the trees. A horse was reigned in close to them and the animal pawed the ground, impatient for action. As they trembled in terror, a young man, no more than a boy, with shaved head and teeth bared, sat up high on his horse and pulled back the taut string of his bow to let the arrow fly. It passed straight through Kitty's father's eye until its point lodged deep in the soft tissue of his brain. Her mother screamed, 'Edward. No, please God, no.' She fell on her husband, embracing her lover for the last time. As she dropped, a hand grabbed the neck of her nightgown, wrenching her head, up and back. The tomahawk cleaved open her neck and barely conscious, she heard the rushing sound of pulsating blood escaping. Finally, a blade sliced across her skull.

'They died, as true followers of Christ.' Kitty lowered her head and crossed herself.

Madame Marie put her hands to her ears, closed her eyes and wept, Humphrey Busby bowed his head and recited a prayer and Kitty, raised the corner of her pretty rosebud mouth into a sly smile.

A noise alerted Kitty to Fanny crossing the doorway behind her. Piously, she rose and said, 'Please excuse me, I need some peace.' She gently closed the parlour door behind her, turned and whispered, 'Where are you going, Fanny?'

'I have to go to work at the theatre'

'The theatre? I love theatres,' said Kitty.

'I overheard you speaking, I'm very sorry your parents died so far away and in such terrible circumstances.'

'Oh, yes. Can I come with you?' asked Kitty. Fanny was taken aback by this question, so soon after giving her condolences. 'I can act, I am very good at it. I shall accompany you, Fanny, I'll get my cloak.'

'No,' said Fanny and held onto her arm. 'It's not possible.'

'What do you mean? The theatre is open to everybody.'

'No,' insisted Fanny, 'I'm not going to watch the theatre, I'm working backstage.'

'Backstage? Fanny, how very exciting, come on let's go.'

'Kitty, I cannot take you with me, I am working in a sewing room high up in the roof. I have nothing to do with the performance. I repair the costumes, that is all.'

'I knew you would not be involved with the art. Of course, you are just a seamstress. Off you go.'

CHAPTER ELEVEN

Led Astray

THE DAY ARRIVED when Fanny started work at The Theatre Royal, fondly known as The Lane. She announced herself to the stage doorkeeper, who sent a boy to get Mrs Bovel. Fanny waited for her to come down but instead, the boy reappeared out of breath. 'She says, she ain't gonna come down these blessed dancers no more today, and tells you to send the girl up.'

Fred the doorman moved his clay pipe to the side of his mouth to make room to speak. 'What's your name? I have to put you in the book. Sign in and out every time, do you understand?'

'Yes, sir. I know how to sign my name, it is Fanny Tomlinson.'

Fred turned the large book around showing the pages marked in columns. The first one contained a list of names and to its right, were more columns labelled, date, in, and out. Under these headings were the marks of those who worked in the theatre. Fanny picked up the stub of pencil, hanging from a string securely nailed to the wall, and wrote her name neatly at the bottom of the list.

'An educated one? Well, Mistress Tomlinson, welcome to Bedlam.'

Fanny climbed the stairs finding each floor quiet now, as the company was not in the theatre this early. The silence was eerie. The last time she visited, the building was full of bustling people and commotion. Now, the theatre was sleeping, awaiting actors and actresses to breathe life into it once again, to make it sparkle.

Climbing the stairs to the top floor, Fanny passed the different landings where the tiring-rooms were all empty. She saw the rows of hooks with costumes hanging, waiting patiently for the warm bodies to turn them into living characters. She pushed a door open to see inside. There were tables jumbled with make-up, hairpins and wigs. And, either side of the mirrors were candlesticks, to illuminate the actor's faces. All of these accoutrements were covered with a gossamer of white powder.

Fanny jumped when she heard Mrs Bovel call to her from the next landing. 'Is that you, Fanny?'

'Yes, Mrs Bovel, I'm coming.' Fanny pulled the door to behind her, and ran up to the highest floor, where she was called into the theatre's wardrobe.

'In here, dear.' The costume mistress opened her arms in homage to the room. 'This is where the insanity starts. Well, I says that. Mr Cibber would say it's where the magic begins. It's where the bloody hard work is done, that I do know.'

The large room had racks filled with every garment imaginable. From Britannia to butterflies, garments of all sorts resided here: costumes for angels, devils, Kings and Queens, beggars, gentlemen, soldiers and jesters. All waiting patiently for their turn to shine on stage. Fanny thought of how Mrs Big would be overwhelmed and excited by such an eclectic choice. On Sunday, Fanny would tell her all about this treasure trove.

'Follow me, Fanny. Over here, and get to work taking up the hem of these breeches an inch and tighten the band, Mr Cibber wants to show off the turn of his calves. When you've done that, you can run down to the girl's tiring-room and get Dolly's stockings, they need darning again. Sit here, Fanny.'

Fanny sat at a huge table, supposing it must be used for cutting the long lengths of fabric into pattern pieces. The table at Aunt Marie's was sometimes too small, and they would have to bring in the gate-legged table from the parlour, to extend the surface. It made the work awkward, whereas here, there was enough room for the fabric and trimmings as well as pins and scissors, all at arms reach. Fanny itched to make something.

'You had better learn a bit about the company, my girl, before you put your foot in it.' Mrs Bovel came close. 'Not to be spoken about outside these four walls mind you. Understood?'

'Yes, of course,' agreed Fanny, wide-eyed.

'Now. Mr Cibber is a gentleman and one of England's finest actors and managers. He runs the place. Keep him happy, always be adoring and tell him how good he is, after each and every performance. Nice and simple, and he won't give you no trouble. Next in billing, comes the leading ladies and gentlemen. Nance Oldfield is known as Queen Anne in this theatre. She is truly, a wonderful actress and she's all right that one. Nance started reciting plays at her aunt's tavern when she was just a girl. Now a lovely lady, she's one of me favourites. There are others, who you will get to know.' She pointed to a playbill on the wall.

'Most of them have done the rounds of the theatres before coming here, to the Lane. Some of them know each other very well, very well indeed. But what goes on in the theatre, stays in the theatre.' She gave Fanny a knowing wink. 'The young girls will flirt with anyone who they think can further their career, whatever profession it may turn out to be. Some of them only last a season. Later, you'll see them in the taverns or in the Piazza, looking for a gentlemen's company for the hour or, if lucky, the night. A few of the Drury Lane vestals do well and find protectors and if they are very good at their trade, these may be members of the aristocracy. I have to admit, many a Lady or Countess has started her rise in life, either walking the boards or walking the streets. Men will be men, they can be very stupid when it comes to sex.' Here, Mrs Bovel moved close to Fanny and spoke a little more softly.

'Finally, I must warn you about the sexual activity bubbling up in the cauldron of these hallowed halls.' As if a title of a book she said, 'The Young Men.' Mrs Bovel crossed her arms and sucked in her cheeks. 'Most of them are back door ushers, not interested in ladies, so they will look elsewhere. But I warn you, Fanny, the rest are continuously on the hunt for new, tender young meat.' She nodded at Fanny. 'They will make all sorts of promises to virgins, in order ravish them. And not a by your leave, the next day. Remember, your maidenhead is worth a lot more than a quick upright in the wings. Watch yourself, Fanny, do not be seduced by their smooth, fine words and flattery. Keep your ears open, your mouth shut, your legs together and your nose out of other peoples business, and you will survive this madhouse.'

Fanny learnt more about the world in that short speech than during her entire life. Sex? She had heard the word before but had no idea what it meant. It was obviously something very powerful and she decided to learn more about it. She would ask Kitty if she had any understanding of it.

As Fanny was about to leave the theatre, Tom arrived at the stage door and asked her, 'Did everything go well tonight, Fanny?' He looked her up and down and said, 'Well, it must have done, as I see no wounds have been inflicted by the bossy Bovel. Good house tonight Fanny, the play should run its length, so we, the spirits behind the great temple's proscenium, have the money to eat, drink and be very merry. Come, wise Athena, do join the happy jesters in a glass or two at the Rose.'

'Thank you, Tom, it's very kind of you, but I shall retire early tonight as I am rather tired. May I join you another evening?'

'Yes, of course, my dear. Off you go, watch out for those naughty gentlemen in Drury Lane. Straight home now.'

Skipping down the backstage stairs, came a slim young dancer still wearing makeup, who draped himself over Tom's shoulder and said, 'Come on, Miss Molly, let me guide you to Hades.' And he kissed Tom fully on the mouth.

By the time Fanny reached the milliners, all was dark and quiet within Mr Jordan's and Mario's shops and her aunt and uncle were in bed, asleep. Just as she turned the key in the door, a man stepped out of the shadows making Fanny start, until she recognised the exquisite face of Gideon.

'I have one moment ago said goodnight to Kitty. She told me you were working at the theatre. I decided to wait for you to make sure you reached home, safely.'

'How kind of you, Mr Woodford. Thank you.'

'Are you tired, Fanny?' asked Gideon. 'Or, would you take a little wine with me at the tavern before retiring?'

'Thank you, but after my first evening working at the theatre and I am a little weary, and I do not drink wine.' Fanny blinked with embarrassment. 'Is that very unsophisticated of me?'

'My mother never drank wine, she didn't need to, her vivaciousness filled my heart with joy. You do not require any stimulant, Fanny, your beauty glows naturally.'

'Thank you, Mr Woodford. I am honoured that you see a little of your mother in me. I hope to meet her one day.'

Fanny watched in astonishment as the colour drained rapidly from Gideon's face, and he stood transfixed. His eyes wide open, he stared vacantly into the distance and stood as still as a marble statue. Seconds passed and Fanny became concerned.

'Mr Woodford.' No response. She touched his arm and that tiny human contact caused a powerful reawakening. His face flushed red, as blood pulsated around his body, his respiration raced and his pupils dilated.

He began to quiver and as his eyes focused on Fanny he said, 'She left me.'

Fanny asked as carefully and kindly as she could, 'Did she die?' She understood this extreme response to fearful quietus. Gradually, came a calming of his soul. His anxiety faded and when his heart slowed, he was able to say,

'Yes.'

'I'm very sorry. I lost my mother not long ago. I understand.'

Gideon shouted at her. 'No, you don't. I loved her so much.' He blinked twice, took a deep breath and once again his demeanour changed abruptly. He continued as though nothing upsetting had happened. Fanny was confused. 'Well, my dear, we shall have to leave our happy liaison until another time. I wish you goodnight. Ah, it may be wise not to mention our meeting to Kitty. Let it be our little secret, yes?'

'Of course, Mr Woodford.'

'Please, my dear, do call me Gideon, now we are friends. Au revoire, ma belle,' and as quick as a moth he brushed her cheek with a kiss and disappeared into the dark night. The kiss shattered her disquiet. Her stomach filled with fluttering as she walked back to the milliners. All was silent except for Fanny's heart beating loudly.

When Fanny opened the attic door, she found Kitty sitting up in bed, full of excitement with words tumbling out of her, as she described the wonderful evening spent with her young uncle.

'I met Gideon after he'd been playing at the Cocoa. He was rather upset at losing a great deal of money at the gambling tables again, he so loves Hazzard, but sadly it does not like him, I hope he will be lucky at cards this evening as he will be playing Pharo. Silly me, what would you know of gambling, Fanny, you know so little of the world.'

'I know about Vingt-Et-Un,' said Fanny.

Kitty quipped, 'Such a common game, Frances.'

Put in her place by the giddy, sharp-witted Kitty,

Fanny wondered what happened to her own confidence and feistiness. Where was the self-assurance that fired up her energy, enabling her to turn card sharp to save Mr Big? She was no longer a simple country girl, the time had come to be noticed. Fanny looked at Kitty, who was comfortable with her surety and beauty. Fanny decided to study her closely. She would become her friend.

Undressing, she said to Kitty, 'I have no work tomorrow, shall we pass the day in each others company? We could play cards,' said Fanny.

Kitty gave Fanny her annoying, kittenish smile. 'And I shall win, and you will lose.'

'We'll see about that,' thought Fanny.

The next afternoon, the girls put together new outfits using each other's clothes and dressed their hair in different ways. They talked and laughed, finding they liked each other. Kitty insisted Fanny rub a little rouge on her cheeks and lips, and she gave her a straw hat bedecked with ribbons to wear for the day. Fanny wore it tilted on the front of her head with a dormeuse cap. As they both shared the same foot size, Kitty lent Fanny a pair of beautiful green silk shoes with a higher heel than she usually wore.

'Fanny, do you have some money? I am afraid I gave all I had to Gideon last night. I'll pay you back.'

'Yes, of course. I'm saving up to make my own way in life but what I have, I shall share with you, until you can repay me.'

'That is kind of you, Fanny. Thank you.'

When ready, the two girls left the milliners and gossiped their way to the tea room, close by in the Strand. Fanny felt uncomfortable, as her normal position was as server, not customer, but Kitty's intrinsic self-assurance secured them a steaming pot of Bohea tea, at the best window table.

'Kitty, I feel so special, what a luxurious room. Look at the ladies wearing the newest fashion.'

'We could wear the same style. I could ask Gideon to buy me the silk, and you could make it up?'

'I would be happy to. Do you think there would be enough length, to also make a mantua for me?

'You tell me how many yards we require, and I shall ask him to order it.'

'My aunt has a cousin who is a silk weaver in Spitalfields. If we find a pattern we like, he could weave the design. It would be expensive though, I cannot afford it myself.'

'Do not distress yourself, Fanny, Gideon is from a wealthy family. The cost is nothing to him.'

Fanny took a sip of the hot tea and inquired with innocence, 'Is the gentleman betrothed to a young lady yet?'

Kitty laughed and replied, 'No, he enjoys his bachelor life too much. But he told me, he has lost his heart completely to a beautiful young girl. Sadly, his family would not approve of her lower status. He is quite besotted with her.'

Fanny's heart missed a beat. 'Does he see her often?'

'He creates instances of meetings, as to spend time in her presence. It has to be kept secret for now.'

'A secret, yes, of course.' Fanny remembered what Gideon had asked of her, "Let it be our little secret." Her breath was caught for a moment, and a blush blossomed in her cheeks. She would not confide in Kitty, she would keep the secret. She would do anything for Gideon.

Towards late afternoon Kitty suggested, 'Let us go to

Covent Garden and take a glass of wine in a tavern.' Fanny hesitated.

'I am not sure about that, Kitty.'

'Why?'

'I do not drink liquor.'

'Why not?'

'I have been brought up, not to do so.'

'Fanny, you are in London now, and you are a young woman. Do not be silly, 'tis time you grew up. Let us go to the Fleece.' Kitty grasped her hand and led her to the tavern.

The Fleece was located opposite the theatre, its reputation as rough as the Rose. The moment Kitty opened the door, Fanny smelt the mutton roasting on the spit in the fireplace, and it made her feel very hungry. Little daylight entered the tavern through its few dirty windows and the condensation obscured the outside view. The only illumination came from the cooking fire, and a few candles, throwing dancing reflections on to the black glass beer bottles. As they entered, the Innkeeper gave Kitty a deep bow. 'Well, well, what has this humble tavern done to deserve your presence? It's been a while, Kitten. You are looking very la-de-da. Found yourself a rich protector, have you?'

'Take no notice of him, Fanny. We would like a separate table and two glasses of Canary, if you would be so kind.' She gave him a beady-eye, daring him to question her further.

'Certainly, madam, and if you want anything in the back room, you just let me know.' He gave her a wink.

'What does he mean by, you have a protector?' Fanny recalled Mrs Bovel speaking of such.

'I have no idea. Such a common man, I hardly know him.'

They stayed at the Inn for a long time and Kitty plied Fanny with wine until she could neither walk nor think straight. Fanny had something on her mind that she needed to ask Kitty about, and the liquor had given her the courage to speak.

'Kitty, what is sex?'

Kitty spluttered her wine all over the table. 'I beg your pardon?'

'You heard me, what is it?'

Kitty set down her glass and looked straight at Fanny, reading her expression. She took her time to think and leaned back in her chair. 'My, my. A little virgin. You are of great value, girl.' Kitty moved in on Fanny and spoke rather severely to her. 'Listen to me. You must retain your maidenhead, do not be stupid to give it away for free.' Kitty smiled. 'Let your friend Kitty advise you in such matters, I shall see you right. We shall come to some arrangement.' Fanny had no idea what she was talking about. Kitty drained her glass and caught Fanny's hand, 'Come, let us go. I know a place where you can observe all matters of vice. It will be easier to understand than to be told.'

CHAPTER TWELVE

A Narrow Escape

KITTY TOOK FANNY to a bawdy house just off the Piazza. Commonly known as a bagnio, this house of vice had no steam room or masseur, except for Miss Gratify. The only container for water was a tin bath, which remained unused in the cellar.

The entrance was presumptuously grand with flaming torches either side of a portico. The door was painted scarlet. Visitors made known their desire to enter via a large, iron door knocker in the design of a naked woman arching her back, with her hands above her head. To the side of this, was a small wicket with a sliding panel. Kitty knocked and the wooden board slid open. A woman's voice said, 'Hello, dear, what is your business?'

'Tell Mother Stroker Kitty is here, and I have someone I wish her to meet. She is an innocent who has run goods.' Kitty looked at Fanny, checking she didn't understand the slang for maidenhead.

'I shall, dear. Wait there.'

Kitty looked at Fanny and saw the wine was having a strong effect on her. 'Stand up straight, Fanny. You're a bit pale. Here, I'll soon sort that out.' Kitty pinched

Fanny's cheeks, hard. It hurt enough to rouse Fanny from her fuzziness.

Whilst they lingered, three gentlemen approached the door. One of them removed his hat and asked Kitty, 'May I escort you two young ladies inside? Are you working together this evening? Maybe you would both like to join me in a dram?'

'Thank you, sir, but I am on different business this night. I must sadly refuse your kind offer, however, please do remember my name. It is, Kitty. Pray enjoy your night with good or bad company, whichever is your preference, sir.' One of the men gave Kitty a crooked smile as he rubbed his thumb over the iron door knocker's breasts.

Fanny whispered to Kitty, 'Do you know these gentlemen?'

'Not yet,' answered Kitty.

'I want to go home.'

The door opened to admit the three male visitors and was swiftly slammed shut again. Kitty knocked louder then turned on Fanny and said, 'You ain't going nowhere. We got business to do.' The panel slid open. 'Tis bleeding perishing out here, I can't wait. Tell Mother Stroker I shall take my proposition elsewhere.' She turned to go. Immediately, the door was opened.

Confronting them, filling the doorway, appeared a woman with a full mane of curly, fiery red hair pinned up haphazardly, by a pair of enamelled chopsticks. She was dressed in a vibrant Chinese silk embroidered robe of red, orange and green and wore a quantity of large gold and silver jewellery. She smoked a long clay pipe. 'Kitty, my dear, to what do I owe this pleasure? Please do enter. And pray, who is this beauty?'

'We shall get to that at a later time. Let us in, and I shall have a glass of brandy. Your best stuff, mind you.'

'All my pleasure, my dear.'

Kitty took Fanny's hand and they stepped into the hall. The air was filled with heady, cloying scent coming from smoke trails, emitting from the smouldering joss sticks. The walls were hung with red damask silk and the many looking glasses reflected candlelight from baroque candelabras and crystal chandeliers. On a pier table was a large bible opened at Revelations and a prayerbook with a notice above, reminding the girls to read their scriptures twice daily. Hanging from silk braids and ropes was an array of paintings of biblical and allegorical scenes, with naked women in various positions, and French engravings of the type printers kept under their counter.

Kitty could see the drink had gone to Fanny's head and was making her sleepy. She guided her to a stuffed, gilded begère. 'Sit there and don't move. I'll come back for you.' Kitty and the eccentric woman retired to an adjoining room, to talk business.

'Well, Kitty, what do you have to tell me?' The Madam relit her opium pipe.

'This girl is new to London and brings with her the most valuable asset: her virginity. She is fair looking and manageable, because of her virtue. As I bring unsullied goods to your door without any procuring on your part, I am willing to accept a fifty-fifty split with you, less her fee for the tap.'

'Kitty, my dear, you may have considerable knowledge of the horizontal in this business, but please leave the acquisition of goods to me. It is very kind of you to offer me this young lady, but I could not offer you more than ten per cent of the transaction and certainly no payment of the tearing of the hymen.'

'Out of the question, you old bawd. I know the worth of a virgin. No negotiation, I want fifty.'

'Now, my dear, let us not be hasty. May I ask you, what experience does the girl have?'

'None. That should tempt the old buggers. She is a true innocent. However, I agree she does need to know what is required of her. May I take her to the voyeur room ?'

'Yes, my dear, I can see no reason not to. We shall speak of this potential agreement later when we have both had time to consider. Visit me tomorrow at four o'clock. The house is yours, please enjoy.'

Fanny was nodding off to sleep in the comfortable chair when Kitty shook her. 'Wake up, we have work to do. Follow me.' As Kitty led the way along the hall, Fanny noticed the rooms had small, framed engravings secured to their doors. They depicted different Roman goddesses, in a variety of energetic poses and all were naked. From behind the doors came the noise of laughing and moaning, which disturbed her.

'Kitty, I want to go home. I'm tired and I need to sleep.'

'We shall not be long. Come, climb the stairs.' Kitty looked at her sternly. 'And put a smile on your face.'

Reaching the landing on the first floor, a serving girl walked towards Fanny carrying a tray laden with a decanter and two glasses. She was dressed theatrically, on her head she wore a peruke, powered with a dusting of violet, pink and blue that was sprinkled with silver spangles and swansdown feathers. Her stays were low and with no handkerchief to hide her breasts she displayed her rouged nipples. Below, she wore nothing but a short tasselled shawl tied around her hips, with black lace-up boots and silk stockings, gartered with pink ribbons. As she passed, the perfume of civet, ambergris and lilies was overpowering.

Fanny felt her palms sweating and her heartbeat racing. 'I really want to leave now, Kitty.' She tried to turn, but was too giddy from the alcohol. Fanny held on to Kitty's arm for support as a servant girl passed them and opened a pair of double doors to a large drawing room. This was furnished with an abundance of sumptuous chairs and day beds. Fanny tried to focus as the room floated around her like a whirlpool.

Liveried footman served an array of roasted meats and filling the air was a sweet aroma from the burning incense, mixed with the tobacco from the men's pipes. The room looked dreamlike, softened behind a mist of blue smoke. Opulent as the hall, light reflected and sparkled off crystal and gilding. Classical music played. Three girls, naked but for one swathe of cream silk between them, played homage to the vestal virgins. Lounging around on every surface, were men in various states of undress, with nude girls writhing over them.

Fanny's attention turned to one tall man leaning against the over-mantle. He wore only his shirt, which was lazily open to show off his fine physic. He poured wine into a glass while a woman kissed his neck and slowly made her way down his body, gathering up the hem of his linen shirt as she got lower. He turned towards the door and saw Fanny. Immediately and roughly, he pushed the girl's head away, and she fell to the floor. Fanny recognised him as their eyes met. Jack Mann.

Both were paralysed until Kitty grabbed Fanny and dragged her upstairs to the second floor of bedchambers. Some doors were shut, a few ajar. As Fanny peered in, she realised an ornate bed was the main attraction in all the rooms.

'Let me see what's going on,' said Kitty as she disappeared through a narrow door, leaving Fanny outside.

Silently, Jack Mann came up behind Fanny and through his teeth, seethed furiously, 'Come with me, you stupid girl. Keep quiet. Not a word and we may get you out of here, without the bawd stopping us.'

Kitty called, 'Come in, all is ready.' But Fanny was halfway down the staircase with Jack. By the time Kitty came out to see where she was, the front door closed and Fanny was once again, being dragged along by someone.

'Let me go, you brute. Leave me alone.' She struggled with all her might and anchored on her back weight to try and stop him pulling her forward. Jack looked at her and to her surprise, let go, causing her to topple backwards onto the mucky street, dirtying her dress and breaking the heel of one of Kitty's shoes. She was furious. Fanny sat up in the gutter, pushed back the hat covering her face and stared at her muddy and grazed hands. She looked ridiculous, and it broke his anger.

'That will teach you a lesson not to struggle with Jack Mann.' He laughed at her, a lot.

'How dare you. Go away,' she said, kicking him in the shin.

'That's not nice, Fanny.' He held out his hand to help her up. Fanny brushed it away in temper.

'I can get up myself.' She struggled to her feet and tried to keep from crying.

'Fanny, what were you doing in that place?'

She retorted, 'What were you doing there?'

'I was doing what men do.'

'I mean, oh, I don't know what I mean.'

Jack looked around and invited Fanny to sit on a doorstep with him. She nodded and gave him wry smile. She gazed at Jack as though for the first time. She noticed he wasn't wearing his usual oiled coat and dirty clothing. He wore an elegant wool coat and breeches. His shirt was still untied. It was obvious he'd dressed in haste. Fanny realised Jack was a very good looking man, but one who had an unexpected and violent temper.

'What are you dressed like that for?' she asked.

'Well, I don't always dress like the villain I am. I've had a bit of good luck and I've come into some gold.'

'You mean you stole it.'

'It just dropped into my hands.' He held his hands up to the sky. 'A gift from a wealthy gent.'

'Enough of this nonsense, leave me alone. I want to go to bed.'

'You were about to do that at the bagnio.'

'No, I was not.'

'Yes, my dear, indeed you were.'

'No, I wasn't, I was just going to watch something. I heard them talk about me as run goods. What is that?'

Jack leaned back and looked at Fanny anew. 'Ah, now I understand. My girl, you are worth a lot of money to some people. Who took you to that place?'

'Nobody.' Fanny said.

'You just walked in all by yourself, did you?'

'A girl befriended me and took me.'

'What was her name?'

'I do not know. We had a few glasses of wine.'

'Were you born yesterday?'

'Well, many years after you were.'

'Fiery little thing, aren't you?'

'I'm all right, nothing happened. Forget about it. I'm going home.'

She tossed her head as she turned from Jack and limped proudly away, carrying her broken shoe in her left hand, her head held high. After a few steps, she stopped abruptly, realising how comical she must look. She became very cross again when she heard Jack laughing at her.

'Wake up, Fanny. I want a word with you.' Fanny roused herself to see Kitty staggering around the attic. More Canary had been drunk.

'Shush, Kitty, you will wake the household.'

'Shut up. I don't care. Who do you think you are? Making me look stupid, I was trying to help you, but you made a fool of me. I shall not forget it.'

Fanny propped herself up on her elbows. 'I am sorry, Kitty, I had too much to drink and knew I was going to be sick, so I ran out into the street. I came home and went straight to bed.'

'I don't know why I bother. I've tried to be friends with you. You just treat me badly.' Kitty dropped down onto her bed.

'Kitty, forgive me. I do want to be your friend.'

'I don't believe you.'

'Please, Kitty.'

Kitty looked at Fanny for a long time, judging her sincerity. Fanny could see how much she wanted a friend.

Kitty tossed her head. 'Well, you must listen to what I say in future. Do you understand?'

'Yes, Kitty. I am sure you have my wellbeing at heart.'

Mrs Big went through the usual security routine

before she opened the little door. 'Who is there?'

'Jack.'

She unbolted the door and pulled away the heavy chest that was set against it, allowing it to be opened.

'Jack, how are you? It's good to see you. We have missed you. Come in.'

'I've had a bit of luck and have something to add to my stuff, Mrs B.' He handed over a pouch that was heavy. Mrs Big knew it was gold.

'Don't you be worrying, Jack, I shall add this to your stash and keep it safe until you need it. I shall guard it with my life and tell no-one.'

'Thank you, Mrs B. I do have another matter I need to involve you with. It concerns, Fanny.'

'Fanny? Is she all right? Is she in trouble?' Panic passed over Mrs Big's face.

'Do not worry yourself, Mrs B. She is safe, but I found her in a place she should not have been, and I pass the information on to you because, as you know, I cannot take on responsibilities, my business as it is.'

'Of course, I thoroughly understand Jack. Unburden yourself, please.'

Jack told Mrs Big the whole story and she was shocked. 'Leave it to me, Jack. You get on and forget all about this. Thank you for what you did, it was kind.'

'That is the first time I have been called, kind.'

'It is in you, Jack. Mrs B can see deep inside of you.'

CHAPTER THIRTEEN

Complications

THE FOLLOWING EVENING Fanny was busy in the theatre wardrobe with Mrs Bovel. While they worked, they sang some of the bawdy ballads that Mario printed for the broadside sellers. They sang lustily and giggled, enjoying each other's company.

Mrs Bovel complimented Fanny. 'You have a fine voice, my dear. As good as some of those song thrushes what tread the boards. They had better watch out.'

The message boy appeared at the door. 'Old man Cibber wants you, Fanny.'

'Less of the old man, Benjamin. It's Mr Cibber to you, or you will be out on your arse if he hears you being disrespectful,' Mrs Bovel said.

'Well, Mistress Tomlinson better get her arse down there, quick.' And he disappeared faster than he came.

'Cheeky bugger. Take your sewing kit, dear.'

Fanny knocked on number one tiring-room. She preened her frock and chewed her nails while she waited for an answer.

'Enter,' Mr Cibber roared. 'Ah, my child, how may I be of service?'

'You asked for me, sir.'

'Did I? What for? Oh, I did. Indeed. Come in.' Fanny closed the door behind her. The room was small but full of all the necessary items required for a legend of the stage: a day bed, dressing screen, a side table with a water jug and basin and a chair to relax in. On the actor's high altar, which is his toilette table, a handsome walnut looking glass waited to reflect the great man's image and close at hand, was a selection of make-up and a small box of patches. On the wall opposite the single sash window, was a shelf with a selection of wigs on stands and a powder shaker with a cone close by, and under the shelf were about six pegs to hang the costumes. On the floor was a row of shoes, ready to trip their way across the Drury Lane's famous stage. Central to all this, sitting right in front of Fanny, was the leading man himself.

'Now, my dear, can you read?'

'Yes, sir.'

'What can you read?'

'I can read English, French and some Italian.'

A pause in the conversation. 'Do you jest?'

'No, sir, my mother was French, and I have a friend who has taught me Italian.'

Colley Cibber settled back into his chair. 'Tell me more about yourself, Fanny.'

'There is little to tell, sir. I am an orphan and an apprentice milliner. I live at the gate of the Inner Temple.'

'You tell me you read. What do you read?'

'There is a gentleman whose trade is bookselling. He is very learned and is kindly instructing me in the reading of Shakespeare, which I find beautiful to recite. My other friend is a printer who supplies broadside ballads for the sellers, and he teaches me the rhymes.' Cibber lowered his head, frowned and looked up at her under hooded eyes. Fanny took this as disapproval. She quickly added, 'I hope I have not offended you, sir, they are only for singing whilst working. Mrs Bovel and I enjoy the tunes and the silly words.'

'I'm certain Mrs Bovel does.' He reached for his clay pipe and in silence, ritually filled it with tobacco and lit it. Fanny waited in apprehension, picking at a hangnail. Cibber stretched to the side of his dressing table and leant down to a pile of books on the floor. He picked up the largest one, opened it on his knees, and flicked through the pages until he found what he was looking for. 'Ah, yes,' he said, passing the book to her and pointing to some dialogue. 'Read this.' Fanny recognised the piece as one of her favourites.

'Come, gentle night, come, loving, black-brow'd night,
Give me my Romeo; and when he shall die,
Take him and cut him out in little stars,
And he will make the face of heaven so fine
That all the world will be in love with night
And pay no worship to the garish sun.'

'Enough,' instructed Cibber. Fanny stopped. 'I am reworking an unfinished play by Vanbrugh. I need someone to read in for me so I can hear the music of the words. I do not want an actress as they will irritate me to cast them. You, my dear, can read the words correctly and do not hanker after the profession of acting. Or, do you?'

'No, sir, I am very happy working with Mrs Bovel and as a milliner.'

'Good, then let us begin. Here are the first pages. You can read it seated, you do not need to use your diaphragm for this.' He passed Fanny a sheaf of handwritten pages, unbound. The writing was difficult to decipher, but Fanny could just about read it. 'The play is called, "The Provoked Husband" or "A Journey to London". It is a comedy: well, one hopes. I shall play Lord Townly, and you will read in Lady Townly. Are you ready?'

'Yes, sir, I shall do my best'

'Giving your best is not good enough, Fanny, you must be the best. Now, Act I, Scene I.' Fanny watched Colley Cibber's stomach extend as he took in a deep breath and with such enormous vocal power, he began to speak. 'Why did I marry? Was it not evident, my plain rational scheme of life was impracticable, with a woman of so different a way of thinking…' and on and on this great actor read. Fanny was overcome by his majestic performance, given only to her, in this private space. She read quietly but accurately, carefully pinching herself, not believing this was really happening.

By the time Fanny returned, the wardrobe mistress was beside herself. 'Where the hell have you been, my girl? It's nearly the half and we have to set the quick change costumes in the wings. Come on, Fanny. What you been doing?'

'Mr Cibber needed me to read in for him, he is writing a new play, and as I was free at the time, he asked me.'

'Well, he can't use you this late to curtain. I'll have a word. Hurry now, bring those breeches and hats.'

Fanny followed Mrs Bovel and the work began. It was a busy evening. The house was full and rowdy, and Fanny was rushed off her feet with the many costume changes. 'Fanny, where are my shoes?' 'The seams split, me arse is hanging out.' 'Fanny? No, not you, I want Fanny to do my change.' The hectic pace continued throughout the show. She mended, pinned, dressed, undressed and redressed the performers, always remembering the hierarchy of the actors, as to help the most important first. Friendly as actors were, their billing was very important to them, if you got it wrong, they could easily be offended.

After the curtain fell and before she could relax, Fanny collected all the soiled garments from the tiring-rooms and took them down to the stage door for the washerwoman to pick up. The laundry girl would return the items, clean and ironed, the following afternoon. Fanny was pushing the dirty clothes into large linen bags when she saw Theo.

'What a lovely surprise, I am glad to see you. How did you know I was here?'

'I visited your aunt, and she explained you were working at the theatre in the evenings.'

'I'm nearly finished. We could go to the tavern if you wait for me?'

'I am here on a serious matter. I must speak with you privately.'

'Is all well in Field Lane?' Fanny asked with concern.

'Yes. Let us go somewhere quiet.'

'I have to tidy things in the wardrobe and collect my sewing bag. I shall be as quick as I can. Wait here, Theo.' She hurried toward the stairs, turned around and said, 'It is good to see you again.' Theo's heart jumped a beat.

The theatre emptied as fast as chucking a pail full of water into the gutter, the gullies finding the fastest route to the nearest taverns. As Fanny turned the corner of the second-floor landing, she faced a ball of petticoats and boots tumbling down the stone steps. The action and the sound didn't match, the girl fell in silence when she should be screaming. It frightened Fanny, but her reaction was fast, she bent down and held her arms out to scoop up the confusion of arms and legs, halting the fall.

'Oh, my god. Are you alright?' Fanny lifted the yards of cotton covering the girl's face. It was Dolly the dancer, Briddy's friend. 'What happened?'

The girl glared at Fanny. 'Why did you stop me? I have to get rid of it.'

'Get rid of what?' asked Fanny.

'Oh, you stupid, innocent girl. You have no idea.' Dolly spoke in panic, the words exploding out of her. 'I'm ruined. I've got a jack in the box. I dunno whose it is. What am I going to do? I live in a room with three others, and they won't share it with a squealing brat. I ain't got no money, and I can't work if I have a baby. I'll have to beg. What will happen to me? I'll starve.' She tried to stand up. 'I have to kill the baby or myself. Let me go.' Dolly struggled and pushed Fanny down to the floor in order to lever herself up. In total distress, she ran up the next flight and threw herself high into the air, plunging herself down the staircase.

'No, Dolly, no,' cried Fanny and she clambered up after Dolly, trying to stop the girl's descent. Dolly knocked Fanny over, and they both spilt down to the lower landing in a heap. This time Dolly was not silent, but hysterical. Fanny untangled herself from this desperate woman and jerked her into a sitting position, grabbing her shoulders. Dolly wailed and flayed about trying to free herself from Fanny's clutches. Still holding her fast, she released her right hand and with all her force, slapped Dolly across the cheek. The surprise shocked the girl into submission and her screams turned into uncontrollable tears. 'There must be a way out of this, Dolly. Do you have family?' Dolly wasn't listening. Fanny struck her again. 'Look at me, Dolly. Listen. Is there anyone you can visit, to bear the child and who will look after you both?'

Dolly raised her head and looked at Fanny in desolation. 'No, nobody cares for Dolly.'

Fanny calmed her mind and considered what could be done. Her mother had helped with birthing and Fanny had accompanied her, so she had some experience of pregnancy.

'How far are you?'

'I dunno.'

'Yes, you do. Have you felt the baby quicken?'

'What you mean?'

'Butterflies in your tummy?'

'No.'

'When did you last bleed, Dolly?'

'A couple of months.'

Fanny shook her head. 'All right. I'll help you. You mustn't tell anyone, do you understand?'

'Yes, Fanny. I'll do anything you say, but get rid of it. Please.'

'I know a woman.'

'I know of one too, but I a'int got no money. And she's filthy. But there is talk of a little woman who does not charge. Do you know who that is, Fanny?'

Fanny paused for several seconds. 'Yes, Dolly, I do.'

A wave of excited and joyful sounds flowed down the backstage stairs as the very last of the company left the theatre. Briddy, stocking guardian and dancer, signed out with Tom's young friend, Oliver. She looked up at Fred the doorman, blew him a kiss and wished him,

'Goodnight, sweet prince.'

The painted young man added, 'Wretched queen, adieu.' Laughing good-naturedly as they stepped out into Little Bridges St, they didn't notice Dolly creep out of the theatre behind them.

Briddy approached Theo, who was standing against the wall. She promptly dropped her hand from Oliver's elbow and said sweetly, 'Well, hello, pretty one. Would you like to buy a girl a dram?'

'No, thank you, I'm waiting for Fanny.'

'Fanny? I didn't know she had an admirer.' She looked Theo up and down approvingly. 'Lucky girl.'

'She does not have an admirer, I am her cousin,' said Theo stiffly.

'Yes, dear, of course.'

'Briddy, come on, I'm parched. Let us withdraw.' Oliver slipped his arm back through hers, and off they tripped, gossiping all the way to the Rose.

Fanny came down from wardrobe, signed out and said, 'Goodnight Fred. Would you check that the washing is picked up? My friend is here, waiting for me.'

'Yes, Fanny. Have a good evening.'

'Thank you, Fred.'

Dolly's predicament was preying on her mind, but she didn't want Theo to know something was distracting her. She tried to appear normal. 'Here I am, Theo, where do you want to go?'

'Nowhere around here, this area is a den of iniquity at this hour.'

Tired and worried, Fanny snapped at Theo. 'Why are you so dismissive of the people who live and work around here? Most of them are good and kind. Please do not condemn them all.' She had begun to understand this multifaceted quarter and working amongst its inhabitants, her respect for them had grown. They worked hard for a meagre living from selling or begging. Their lives may be bleak, but they had astonishing energy, making light of their difficult circumstances by using humour and generosity. In this underworld of London, good and bad, right and wrong, were not independent of each other, and it was unfair to denounce these people's behaviour. They did what they had to do, for survival, and it was pointless to deny them. She would help Dolly.

'Well, we could sit in the porch of St. Clement's in the Strand. That is half way home for both of us.' Fanny suggested.

'Yes, let us go.'

Theo was silent and tight-lipped as they passed the girls on Drury Lane who let him be, with just the odd remark by habit. Word spread fast in the area around the theatre, and they knew Fanny was not competition. As she passed them by, Fanny smiled and said hello in recognition.

It didn't take them long to reach St Clement Danes. They sat in the church porch, sheltered from the January weather and although the stone was cold, it was reasonably comfortable and private.

'Fanny,' Theo started, 'it came to my ears you were seen inside a disreputable house in Covent Garden.'

'How did you find out about that? Oh, I know, Jack Mann. I wish he would mind his own business. Look Theo, I was there and now I'm not, and I won't be there again. All right?'

'Fanny, you are innocent of the ways of London,' Theo said, embarrassed and not looking at her. 'A young girl like you can easily be led astray.'

Fanny interrupted him. 'Theo, my innocence

diminishes with every hour I live in this great city, and the more experience I get from the straight and crooked paths, the more I understand and learn how to judge wisely and make correct decisions.'

'You are too young to make those decisions, Fanny.'

'You are wrong, Theo. I am an orphan, I travelled here alone, I had a knife put to my throat, I cheated at cards, I work all day and nearly every evening, and I walk unaccompanied through the streets of the city. Now I find I have to explain all this to a man who is older than myself. I think I'm rather grown up. Please leave me alone. If I should need your help, I hope you will allow me to ask for it, but I am quite content and happy now.'

'Fanny, I want to look after you.'

'I don't want anyone to look after me. I want to be able to look after myself.'

Whilst Fanny talked to her protector, Theo, Kitty conspired with hers. In a room above the Fleece tavern, they ate cut meats and argued, naked.

Gideon, gesticulating with a leg of capon, paced about the chamber shouting at Kitty. 'You are a stupid, ignorant wench. A maidenhead is not to be sold to the lowest bidder but to the highest. To tell a bawd, nay, to take the girl into a tawdry bagnio was stupidity of the highest order. Mother Stroker could have kicked you out and kept Fanny for herself.'

'I expected you to be glad I had such a plan to gain money. I only want to please you, Gideon. As I do, in every way.'

'Well, Katherine, you do not please me. All we can be thankful for is that she escaped and is now back in our control.' He threw the gnawed leg into the flaming fire and jumped on to the bed where Kitty was lounging against a bolster. He sat astride her and with his right hand he clasped her cheeks together, distorting her mouth into an ugly pout. 'Listen to me, you simple whore. You are not to take that girl to any brothel. You are to keep her clean and pure, become her closest confidant and when the time is right, I shall find a group of wealthy satyrs and sell her to the highest bidder.' She felt him hardening. 'You, I shall have for nothing.'

CHAPTER FOURTEEN

Chief Lightning Thundercloud

FANNY LED THE way to Dolly's lodgings. She had given the dancer nearly all her money, some to use as a bribe to keep her fellow lodgers absent for a few hours and the rest to keep Dolly in food and lodgings until she was fit enough to dance again. Once more, Fanny had to rely on the goodness of others to keep her from penury. Fanny knew she was now part of this underworld, her dreams of being independent and making something of herself being thwarted at every turn. But she refused to give up her dreams, something would change.

Mrs Big walked alongside, her instruments in a linen bag, whilst Fanny carried the bucket filled with the other necessities. Fanny had explained Dolly's position and suggested to Mrs Big that Sam the Strongman's assistance was not required. The two women could make their way along the back streets of Covent Garden, not looking out of place. The charade of the Bartholomew doll presentation was unnecessary. Dolly was not a well-to-do ladybird, more of a London sparrow. Fanny and the little woman were safe from any fear of revelation.

Although uneasy, Fanny would assist Mrs Big.

When they arrived, Dolly was quaking from fear. Fanny introduced Mrs Big as Mrs Gabriel.

'Is this your first time, my dear,' asked Mrs Big.

'Yes. Sorry.'

'No need to be sorry, dear. We can all make mistakes. This one can be set right. As long as you do exactly what I tell you. Do you understand?'

'Yes.'

'Right. Fanny, get the water boiling over the fire.' She took out the small blue bottle of PORT from her pocket and asked, 'Do you have a cup, dear?'

'Yes.' The girl picked up a once elegant china cup, now cracked and handleless. She spat in it, wiped it with her finger and said, 'Here, it's clean now.'

Mrs Big sucked in her cheek and raised her eyebrows. She poured the potion into the cup and said, 'Well, my dear, drink this. And let me know when your tummy starts to ache.' Mrs Big took out of her bag a large bottle of gin. She opened the top and passed it to Dolly. 'Drink as much of this as you like. When the water has boiled, I will cut up some onions and mix them with the steaming water in your piss pot. I want to take off your lower garments and sit on the pot.'

'Why?' Dolly asked.

'We agreed you will do what I say, didn't we, dear?'

'Yes, Mrs Gabriel.'

'Good girl, not to worry. All will be well. Now drink the tea first and then the gin. Fanny, scrub the table and cover it with the paper I brought.'

'What happens now?' asked Dolly.

'We wait, my dear.'

Dolly became very happy once the gin took hold of her, and the opium floated her above the real world.

They had to quieten her down as she started to sing with great volume. Occasionally, Mrs Big suggested she dance around and to jump up and down energetically.

Then it started.

'Awww, ohhh.'

'All right my dear, off the pot,' said Mrs Big. 'Hop on the table now. Mrs Gabriel is going to rub your tummy. It will help the pains. Fanny, pour boiling water over my instruments.'

Fanny unrolled the linen to reveal Mrs Big's tools including a long glass rod, two types of extended forceps, a curette and a sharp knife. Fanny tasted bile rising.

Mrs Big said to Dolly, 'I want you to relax dear. I'm going to put my tiny hand inside you, to make the passage wider. Pass me the rod, Fanny.'

In many ways, Dolly recovered quicker than Fanny, who found the whole experience distressing. She repeatedly looked back on that day and gradually came to understand the hardships poor people had to experience in the reality of survival. She never wanted to be in Dolly's situation.

Fanny's life relaxed back into a routine, and she hoped any other excitement would be of the enjoyable type.

As Kitty got to know Fanny, she softened her arrogance and the girls became close. Although keeping their lives separate, they made time to enjoy the special, isolated world they'd created together. Kitty was the gatekeeper to Gideon, the man who Fanny longed to see and who they both idolised. Kitty was obsessed with him and Fanny captivated. Neither told the other of their feelings. As an addicted gambler, he showed particular interest in Fanny's talent with playing cards. Gideon knew she could be valuable. He took the girls with him to the tables and while Kitty looked pretty on his arm, Fanny would play. At the beginning, he provided Fanny with money. When she won he gave her a small cut, which he always borrowed from her the next time they met. Round and round it went, with Fanny not earning anything.

When at home at the gate of the Inner Temple, Madame Marie, Humphrey, Kitty and Fanny tried to be a normal family. The atmosphere was lighter and more amenable. Kitty accepted Sous-Sous the monkey, but only at a distance and the feeling was mutual. Madame Marie complemented Fanny on her proficient sewing and allowed her to make up some of the orders for their best customers. For pocket money, Fanny altered secondhand clothes to make them more fashionable and sold them on to the girls in Drury Lane. They gave her what they could afford, which wasn't much. Fanny didn't mind, she was happy to help. The word spread, and soon the actresses at the Lane wanted Fanny's skills. She was able to put a little money aside, keeping it in her card box, but it would never be enough to make her self-sufficient to live on her own.

The one person who threw a shadow over the milliner's house was Humphrey Busby. Fanny felt a menacing undertone to him. However, recently he seemed more relaxed and much happier. He became very fond of Kitty. He was polite to Madame Marie, and kept out of Fanny's way, which she welcomed.

The Sunday before the May Fair, Fanny visited Field Lane to enjoy the fun and laughter of Mr and Mrs Big and their friends. Theo hadn't joined them at the garret, since the evening when he and Fanny spoke in the church porch. Fanny wasn't sure if he was avoiding her, or if he was immersed in his medical studies. Either way, her life was too busy to worry about it.

Fanny helped Mrs Big prepare the dinner for the assembly of theatricals, who came in all shapes and sizes. To make a large table, they placed a row of boxes on the floor and created a top from the knife thrower's target board. Eagerly, they awaited William Bull's arrival. Not only was he the famous showman known as Chief Lightning Thundercloud but more importantly, he was the best butcher in Leadenhall market. William was a gentle giant of a man with a gruff voice, and today he was bringing a large roasted rib of beef. Fanny had never tasted this expensive cut of meat, and the company were full of excitement as they explained its lusciousness to her. The description made her salivate and when footsteps on the stairs were heard, all voices hushed to see the imagined turned into reality. William carried the hot spit roast into the room. Licking their lips as the sight and smell of the sumptuous, roasted beef, they found themselves ravenous.

'A toast to the best roast meat of Old England.' John lifted his pot of ale and all the diners toasted the platter.

'Do you have a sharp knife, Mrs B?' joked William, the butcher. A gale of laughter rose from the company. 'Fear not, I happen to have one upon my person. I shall carve.' The knife thrower began to cut through the oozing flesh.

Fanny had never seen people eat so much, so quickly, and she had to push forward to get her share.

The meat was truly delicious.

'Where is your good wife today, William?' asked Mrs Big

'Alas, she had to go to her sister in Kent, who is poorly. That is why I cannot show at the May Fair next week.'

'What a shame, William. Do you not have another assistant, who you may bring in to replace Lizzie for this short while?'

'Alas, no. As you know, Lizzie is very small and I am confident of the knife positions around her.'

Mr Big started to sign. Mrs Big answered. 'What a good idea husband, I shall ask her.' Mrs Big turned to Fanny, who was savouring the sweet meat she had scraped off a bone with her teeth. When she saw Mrs Big was about to speak directly to her, she froze. After a few seconds, still with the bone at her mouth, she looked around the table to see faces smiling and nodding at her.

'Mrs B, I'm not sure of this, I have never done anything like it before. No, I do not think so, thank you very much.' She waited. There was silence. To fill the quietness, she added, 'I would if I could but I can't. I am most sorry.' All her friend's eyes were upon her in absolute stillness. She looked at the butcher. 'Mr Bull, I am sure you are very practised in your art, but I cannot imagine having knives thrown at me.'

Mrs Big climbed on her chair and bending over with her hands on the table top said, 'Well, Fanny, you do not have to imagine it, as you may try it. Here and now, on this board.' She knocked on the wood. 'Up you get, all of you. Place the board in its usual position, resting against the end wall.'

Fanny realised she still had the bone in her hand, worried she may not be alive to savour rib of beef, ever again.

The troupe of little people cleared the table and Samuel the strong man lifted it into position.

Chief Lightning Thundercloud assured Fanny, 'Do not worry, I shall not hurt you. Keep still and trust me.' Fanny could hardly breathe, let alone speak, as she was led towards the old door that his usual assistant stood against.

Livewell offered his hand up to her. 'Perhaps, Fanny, you may like to give me your chewed bone.'

Fanny nodded and gave him the rib.

William said, 'Fanny, if you would be so kind as to stand like this.' He placed both her hands on her hips to create a triangle each side of her waist, this was where two of the knives would land. 'Would you like to have a blindfold, dear? At least until you get used to the sound of the knives. Very soon, you won't be aware of me throwing them.' Fanny didn't believe him. He put his hand in his pocket and bought forth a long strip of black silk. Just for a moment, Fanny queried why he should have a blindfold on him, to eat dinner. Just before he tied it around her head, she saw Mrs Big open the roll containing the set of knives and noticed a knowing look pass between her and William. With her eyes staring into the cloth's blackness, she listened to William's heavy footsteps walk back five or six times.

'Keep quite still, my dear. Are you ready?'

'Yes,' Fanny said in a quavering voice.

'Good, I shall begin.'

Fanny heard a sound like a sword cutting quickly through the air, swiftly followed by a firm thud. She felt a tiny amount of air pressure as the first knife landed close by her right ear. Fanny was sure he had aimed at the most vulnerable and noticeable position first. She was correct, the second knife stabbed the wood next to her left ear, the sound matched the first throw exactly, the positioning being the perfect mirror image. With each thud of the knife, she worried less, proving William was correct. There were so many knives being thrown, so fast, that in the end, she didn't notice them at all.

'All finished, Fanny. Well done, my dear. Would you like to try again, this time with the blindfold off?'

'No. Not really,' said Fanny. And they all laughed.

A week later, Fanny felt at ease having nineteen knives thrown at her. Her costume was a leather shift, calf length, with beaded fringing all along the hem and around the neck. From a headband stood an eagle feather. This attire kept clear the outline of her body so William could be sure of her silhouette.

William dressed as Chief Lightning Thundercloud. His costume was of soft leather: a tunic and wide breeches with a breastplate of glass beads. On his head, he wore a full-length ceremonial feather warbonnet. Fanny hoped its magnificence would direct the crowd's gaze towards William and away from her, who would be shaking with fear. Fanny was very nervous. This was the first time she had ever performed and as she was working with her dearest friends, she didn't want to let them down.

As William had a business to run, he only performed on certain days. This suited Fanny, as she could take only a little time away from her work at the milliners. As for Mrs Bovel, she understood, as it was the world of performance. Chief Lightning Thundercloud was a very popular showman, and a huge crowd jostled for a better view. Part of this attraction was the fact he performed sporadically, so when dates were announced, word of mouth sped across London like wildfire.

The first day of the May Fair arrived and the show people were at their peak of energy. Matthew, Mark, Luke and John with Noble and Livewell, had been practising a new routine with rehearsed mishaps. It was exciting and also funny. The Troupe had a good pitch, facing north: the sun never being in their eyes, to blind them.

Mr Big also ran the booth next along the line. Here, showed the posture-masters, with their marvellous body manipulations. Before a show, the performers teased the mob by posing on the narrow outside gallery. The punters couldn't wait to climb up the wooden steps, to get a closer look. Before they realised it, Ned Boyle with his white painted face and black eyes would take their entrance fee off them.

Sam the Strongman, was working this act for the first time with a slim, young and pretty contortionist, billed as Letitia from Lithuania.

'Lithuania, where the hell's that?' asked Noble. 'Letitia? That's Letty from Limehouse, I'd know her anywhere. Blimey, you don't forget a girl who can bend her leg around the back of her neck.'

Luke tutted. 'Samuel looks enchanted with her.'

'Yes, he looked very happy when she bent over backwards and put her face between her feet.' Luke slapped Noble around the head and told him to behave. 'Then she winked at him.' Luke slapped him harder this time.

'She looks nice,' said Luke.

Noble gave Luke a sideways look and said, 'Wait until she gets a couple of gins inside her. She can swear worse than a Jack Tar drunk as a wheelbarrow. Sam better watch out.'

Mr Big came from behind the curtain and rang a handbell to attract the crowd.

William Bull wearing his normal clothes, announced the next show would begin in ten minutes and tickets were on sale now. 'Hurry, hurry, ladies and gents, first come get the best seats. Hurry, hurry to sit close to the actors. See the sweat of the acrobats and the glint of the knives. See the little people tumble and stumble. Shake with fear for a brave young woman who will have many knives thrown at her by Chief Lighting Thundercloud. Will she survive? Or will she die of a hundred cuts? Do not miss this exciting moment. Hurry, hurry. Book both shows for a discount. Marvel at the dangerous feats of Mr Big's entertainers.' Mr Big took a bow and rang the bell again.

During this three o'clock show Fanny saw Jack Mann in the crowd, he watched the knife throwing and when Fanny and William took their bows he lifted his hands in the air and applauded above his head, his eyes on Fanny. She smiled, for all she despised him, there was something attractive about Jack, and he always seemed to be just on the edge of her existence.

During the last show of the day Fanny heard Kitty shout, 'Fanny, it's me. Meet me after.'

As the girls walked away from the May Fair, Kitty asked Fanny, with an air of disdain, 'What are you doing here? Why are you doing this common entertainment?'

'These people are friends of mine, and I am helping them out. 'Tis just for the two weeks of the Fair.'

'Well, it's a sideshow. Look at the freaks you are working with.'

'Don't call them that.'

Kitty ignored her. 'Don't think it's the real theatre. You're not that good. It's easy if you ask me, you just have to stand there, doing nothing. Come on.' Fanny raised her eyes up to the sky, Kitty had no idea. They held each other's hands and made their way back to the Fleece Tavern in Covent Garden.

'A gin, Fanny?'

'No, Kitty, I don't like the taste.'

'Have two and you'll get used to it.'

'Kitty, I do not like it, I shall have a small beer.'

'Fanny, really, what am I to do with you?'

When the Innkeeper bought the drinks over, Kitty raised her pint tumbler and clinked it against Fanny's pot.

'Will you drink all that, Kitty?'

Kitty paid no attention to her remark. 'Good health and wealth,' Kitty toasted. 'I saw Gideon last eve and he gave me money for the silk, to sew our new gown. I tried to get more out of him, but he insisted this would have to do. So we can only make one mantua. As we are the same size, we can share the wearing of it. When shall we go to Spitalfields to see your aunt's cousin?'

'Once the May Fair is over.'

'What a waste of time helping others who are poorer than you. You will have to learn how to have conversation with those of a higher class than yourself. There are ways.'

'Kitty, I am as poor as my friends, and it is my pleasure to help them. I do not speak about them as I know it makes you angry. I shall not stop seeing them, do you understand?'

'I suppose so. It makes no sense. Do as you wish. Soon, I shall be above all that.'

'What do you mean, Kitty?'

'I shall, no doubt, marry into a family of substance quite soon.'

'Really? Have you fallen in love with a suitor?'

'Yes, and I am sure it is only a matter of time before it is announced,' said Kitty, in what Fanny took to be a rather smug manner.

'How exciting for you, Kitty. Who is the fortunate gentleman?'

'You will find out, soon enough.' Kitty was not going to tell her anything more. Fanny wondered where she found the time for courting, Kitty was always with her or out with Gideon.

'Let us take a stroll and see the ladies and gents in their finery and carriages.' Kitty got up expecting Fanny to follow her every desire.

They cut through Maiden Lane and headed west across the Hay Market into St. James's Square. Fanny noticed Kitty's eyes dilating when she espied gentlemen emerging from sedan chairs and ladies in beautiful gowns, stepping down from carriages.

'Come, Fanny, let us go to Kings Place and watch the girls arrive with their clients.'

'Kitty, I must go home to bed, I am very tired. Do let's go.'

'You can go, but the night is just beginning for me. It's my birthday today and I want some fun.'

'Oh, Kitty I didn't know. I would have made you a gift. I'm sorry.'

'Don't be sorry for Kitty. What's a birthday anyway, nobody's never given me nothing. I don't care.' Kitty grabbed her shoulder. 'Don't tell anyone I'm eighteen. That's getting on a bit, in my trade.'

'You don't have a trade, Kitty. Do you?'

Kitty ignored the question and told Fanny, 'You trot home if you want to. I want to see the horses. I'm off to the stables. Don't leave the candle burning, it will be dawn before I retire.'

'My aunt and uncle will be displeased if they discover you have been out all night, on the streets of London.'

'Who's gonna tell them, Fanny? I don't think so. I'm fed up being the good girl and having you always around my neck. I'm going to have some fun.' Fanny knew this was the Madame Geneva talking. 'Off you go, don't you worry about me, Even if Humphrey does find out, I can talk him round. Gideon tells me he owns property in Kensington, is that right?'

Fanny, bored with the liquor talking, said, 'Yes, I believe so, but I know little about it, it is not my business.'

'Not your business, what is your business, Fanny? Stepping in the footsteps of Holy Mary, Mother of God? You ain't Mary Magdalene, that's for certain.' She laughed coarsely.

'Kitty, please do not blaspheme.'

'Why, shall I go to hell?'

'Indeed, you may.'

'Leave me alone, you little saint. I cannot stand to look at you tonight.' Kitty turned and tottered off unsteadily, towards the stable yard, off St. James's Street.

There was nothing Fanny could say or do. She had seen Kitty like this before, and it took a night's sleep for her to forget what she had said and behave normally once again. All Fanny could do, was to head back to the Inner Temple to enjoy a quiet night alone in her attic bedchamber.

CHAPTER FIFTEEN

The Whip

KITTY SMELT THE horses before she saw them. The sweat from the stallions raised her blood, and when she saw the liveried drivers and footmen looking splendid in their uniforms she knew she was in for a good night. She approached a stall where a groom was sponging down a horse. The carriage driver was leaning against the open stall gate.

'Hello, my name is Kitty. May I stroke your beautiful horse?'

'Indeed you may, Kitty,' replied the good looking young man.

The other men watched what was happening and made lewd comments under their breath.

'What's your name?' asked Kitty.

'Thomas.'

Kitty stroked the hindquarters of the animal and asked, 'Well Thomas, do you like to ride?'

'I ride every day.'

'What do you ride every day, Thomas? What is your preference, a stallion or a filly?' She smartly slapped the buttock of the horse.

The animal reared a little but was held firmly by the

groom. 'Don't do that,' he said.

'Why not, I think he liked it.' She turned to Thomas. 'Being held down, he was safe and in no danger, do you not think, Thomas? I would never hurt him, just correct him lovingly should he need it, guide him and bring him to his full potential.' She put her cheek against the horse's thigh and slowly slipped lower, as her hand moved towards the animal's scrotum. The horse was very still and as an erection grew, Kitty moved her hand over his penis. She read Thomas's reaction. 'What a big boy you are, Thomas. Would you like to come over here to Kitty?'

The groom just stared at what was happening. The coachman said, 'How much?'

'Just you, Thomas?'

Thomas looked behind him at the other young men and one answered, 'After you, Tom,' as he rubbed his crotch.

'One after another, with the others looking,' Thomas said.

'Three guineas and I'll take one of your whips with me.'

'Not a chance, I don't have that sort of money.' Kitty knelt down closer to the horse's underside. 'One guinea, that's all I have.'

'Don't believe you. Two quid,' said Kitty.

'All right.' He grasped her hand and took her to the next stall strewn with new hay. She lay down, raised her petticoat and opened her legs. Thomas fiddled with his breeches while the other man rushed in and knelt down close to see what would happen. Pulling out his prick, he started to masturbate. Thomas was over excited and entered her immediately, he was all too quickly spent.

The other man pushed him aside, and he rode her to

his own finishing line. Kitty, pleased this bit of business was done quickly, pulled down her petticoat and pointed to one of the leather whips hanging with the rest of the tack.

'That one will do.'

As the men fumbled to find the money, Thomas said, 'That's an expensive whip.'

'As you know, Thomas, I am an expensive girl.' She pointed once again. 'That one, Thomas. Now, please.'

He took it from its hook and gave it to her.

She approached a tall footman, her face close to his. 'Would you like to buy a good girl a dram, sir?'

'Indeed I would Kitty.' He offered her his arm and they began to leave the stable. Kitty paused, looked over her shoulder at her small audience and turned to give them a farewell curtsy. 'I hope you enjoyed the show, gentlemen. I may visit again should I be passing. I wish you all a good night.'

The dawn was just breaking when Kitty stumbled into the parlour, placing the whip on the table. She looked at it with a conniving smile and went into the scullery to get some water to drink. She dipped a pewter ale pot into the bucket of fresh spring water, drawn from St. Clements Well, and carried the cold liquid up the stairs to her bedroom, being careful not to make a noise. She collapsed onto her bed fully dressed and was asleep immediately.

Humphrey must have been disturbed enough by Kitty's homecoming, to stir himself into wakefulness. He saw the sky was still heavy with darkness and not bright enough for him to rise for his early morning prayer. He turned over to sleep again but only for a while, as he had reached a state of consciousness that required sustenance on waking. He slid out the chamber pot from under the tester bed and relieved himself. Standing up, he reached for his woollen banyan draped over the bedside chair and put on his slippers. Once robed, he opened the door and crept downstairs to the parlour. Martha was up, the fire was lit, and the kettle hot.

Humphrey was hungry. 'Martha, hot chocolate. Now.'

'Yes, sir, coming sir,' Martha quickly showed herself in the scullery doorway and gave her master a small curtsy. 'Good morning, sir.'

Humphrey found his spectacles on the side table, by his reading chair. He picked up yesterday's newspaper, ready to settle at the dining table. Reading as he sat down, it was only when his hand nudged something laying on the table, did he see the black leather riding whip. 'Martha, what is this instrument doing here, pray?'

Martha put her head around the door. 'I do not know, sir. It was here when I come in this morning.' She curtsied again and disappeared as fast as she could.

Humphrey moved the whip away from him and stared at it for quite some time, thinking of how it could have possibly appeared in his house.

Madame Marie was the first to join Humphrey in the parlour. 'Good morning, husband, I hope you slept well?'

'Yes. Annoyingly, I was disturbed early and awoke before dawn.' He pointed at the whip. 'What do you know of this?'

'It's a whip.'

'Very observant of you, wife. But how is it here?'

'I have no idea, husband. I did not see it last

evening, I am certain.'

Fanny came down from her room, and when she saw the riding crop, she stopped and asked, 'Are you riding out today, Aunt Marie?'

'Your aunt does not ride. Do you know anything about this?'

'No, Uncle. It was not there when I retired to bed.' Fanny's mind turned back to last night and remembered Kitty saying she was going to the stables. This must be something to do with what happened after she left her in St James's. Fanny was frightened of what her uncle's reaction may be to Kitty's late return. Her aunt and uncle were speaking of the possibility of an intruder.

'…but what would he need a whip for, Humphrey? And why would he leave it here?' asked Marie.

While they were talking, Fanny ran upstairs to warn Kitty of what was being discussed downstairs. 'Kitty, wake up.'

'Go away. Let me sleep.' Fanny shook her again,

'Kitty, my uncle has found a whip on the table and he wants to know how it got there.'

'Oh, that. Tell him it's mine.'

'I shall not do that Kitty, please come down and explain yourself. Be quick.'

Kitty sat up and smoothed her hair down. She stood, still half asleep, and Fanny tried to smooth her frock and tidy her up. She didn't want her uncle to think Kitty had slept in her clothes.

'Kitty, why did you bring it home? He will know you returned after we had all retired for the night.'

'Stop your fussing, Fanny. It will be fine, trust me.'

'I hope so.'

Kitty led Fanny down the stairs with not a worry in

her pretty head. Fanny, on the other hand, was very concerned. Her uncle demanded total obedience and good social appearance was paramount. He had a sharp temper, and Fanny knew if Kitty disrespected his hospitality, he would tell Gideon that new lodgings would have to be found. Fanny feared for Kitty, having come to a conclusion that she must have a secret life. The closer she became to her friend, the more she worried for her welfare.

Humphrey was talking loudly at Madame Marie. 'Woman, stop your prattling, I am going to get my pistol and keep it at hand until I have found an answer. There may be a thief close by, and I intend to protect my property.'

Kitty entered the room just as Humphrey opened the wooden corner cupboard and took out a small flintlock pistol. He heard her come in and turned, the weapon pointed directly at her.

'Husband, what are you doing? Put the pistol down.'

'For goodness sake, wife, it's not loaded, I am only looking down the barrel, checking the weapon. I shall, however, prime it later today.'

Kitty did not flinch an inch. Calmly, she said, 'Oh, I see you have found my crop. Gideon gave it to me at supper last night, he wishes me to learn to ride. My regrets for leaving it on the table. I quite understand it would suggest an intruder, how foolish of me. Please forgive me, Mr Busby.'

Madame Marie and Fanny waited for the torrent of anger. It didn't materialise. Instead, he said, 'My dear Kitty, what an excellent idea. Of course, a lady of your standing must be taught to ride. Would you like me to keep the whip safe for you?'

'How very kind of you, Mr Busby, but it is so new, I

wish to hold it and feel the soft leather in my hands and become comfortable switching it. It must be a powerful feeling to ride a wilful beast and to be able to control him with a light but well-positioned lash, don't you think?'

Humphrey unconsciously licked his lips and said. 'I do indeed, my dear.'

'Well, if you will excuse me, I shall return to my toilette and prepare myself for the day ahead.' She looked at the pistol in his hands and moved towards him. 'What a fine weapon, Mr Busby,' she said, as she stroked the barrel up and down. 'Take great care of it and keep it in good working order.' Coyly, she added, 'Let me put it where it should be.' She took the pistol and placed it back in the cupboard, never once taking her eyes off Humphrey. She turned back and raised up close to his face. In a honeyed voice, she said, 'Dear Mr Busby, do prime your weapon, in readiness to be fired in a moment of passion. It may be soon.'

Kitty left the room like a leading lady exiting the stage, leaving her fellow players in stunned silence, all for different reasons. Humphrey Busby watched with glazed eyes every movement Kitty made, and Fanny could see all he wanted was to follow her upstairs. She looked at her aunt's reaction to this and saw she was standing completely still and staring obsessively at the floor.

There was nothing for her to do except follow Kitty to the attic. Kitty was undressing as Fanny closed the door and said, 'I don't know what you are up to, Kitty, but I know you have some plan in mind. Do not upset Humphrey Busby, you don't know what he's capable of.'

'Fanny, I don't need you to tell me what to do. Old

men like a young pretty girl. Well, it's simple: he is an old man with property and I'm a pretty girl. I would like to get to know him better.'

'I beg you, Kitty, do not raise the devil within him.'

'I'm going to sleep a little longer.' She lay on the bed and closed her eyes to end the conversation.

From downstairs, Fanny heard weeping, shouting, a short scream and someone falling to the floor. Her uncle was disappointed, once again.

Fanny collected her cape, ran downstairs avoiding the parlour and passed through the shop, out into the Inner Temple passage. The tinkling of the shop bell no longer rang out in welcome but in warning. As she hurried past the printers and the bookseller. Both custodians raised their hands in greeting, but Fanny disregarded them. She had to get away to somewhere not oppressive, a place of light and laughter. She headed for the theatre.

'Good day, Barbara, is Tom here?' asked Fanny through the ticket window.

Barbara looked up from the pile of admission tickets and tokens she was counting. 'Try keeping him away, Fanny.' Like the movement of the sun and moon on a clocks dial, across the small window, Tom Mercutio's face began the eclipse of the waning Barbara's.

'Greetings, fair Ophelia. Do I not send you into delirium with my charm, wit and intelligence? What is your desire, sweet girl?'

In one sentence Tom had broken through the dark clouds enshrouding Fanny, and she saw a shaft of sparkling daylight to be guided by.

'Is there any work for me to do today, I feel in need of company.'

Tom looked closely at Fanny. 'Yes, I can see. Wait

there.' He turned to Barbara and waggled his finger. 'Keep a firm hand on the tiller Barbara, as I hear you do every night, you naughty girl. I shall return soon.'

Barbara giggled and shooed him away. 'Be off with you, you exceedingly incorrigible man.'

Tom came through the connecting door and seized Fanny's hand. 'Come with me,' he said as he led her outside. From Little Brydges Street, they turned into Vinegar Yard that led to the stage door. Tom could hear Fanny crying, he stooped down to look her straight in the eye and asked, 'What's wrong, Fanny? This is not like you.'

'I'm all right, really, Tom. I'm just a bit upset.'

'About what, Fanny?'

'I can't say,' she said, bursting into tears.

'Get it out dear, tell your Uncle Tom.'

'I'm being foolish, I'm sorry. Please forgive me.'

'All right, Fanny, I shall not pester you for what is ailing you so.' Tom came closer to her. 'You know I am always here with a listening ear.'

'You are very kind, Tom. Thank you.'

'Don't tell too many people, or my fragile shell of aloofness will shatter.' Tom gave her a flamboyant bow making Fanny smile and laugh. She threw her arms around him and gave him a huge embrace. 'Careful now, Fanny, people may begin to gossip. Follow me, I have an idea.'

They entered the theatre where Fanny could hear voices reciting lines. Tom led Fanny through the pass door from backstage, into the large auditorium where Fanny had never been before. She was bewitched by it. Tom opened the door of one of the stage boxes. 'Sit here, Fanny, and keep quiet.' Fanny sat snugly in the corner, out of the sight of Mr Cibber, whose voice was filling the theatre from the table set up down stage left.

The auditorium was not brightly lit as it was during a performance, so the darkness of this cavernous space, against the candlelight on stage from the few chandeliers necessary for reading, gave the theatre an intimate atmosphere. There was something special about being in an empty theatre with only the people that really belonged within. The actors settled on their chairs, in a semicircle, whilst a stagehand hung about in the wings waiting, should he be required. Sitting next to Mr Cibber, was the stage manager who followed the lines in a book.

Fanny recognised most of the actors, they were the very best of Drury Lane and here she was, so close to them.

Mr Cibber spoke, 'I have brought you all together for a read through of "The Provoked Husband". A play, that you all know was started by Vanbrugh. This is an early draft and there may be, or indeed, will be changes. I know there has been much conversation of this strange collaboration between the living and the deceased, so let us begin.' He looked at the one empty chair. 'Where is Miss Cibber'

From the wings came Tom. 'My pardon, Mr Cibber, but I have news that Miss Cibber has hurt her ankle and cannot attend.'

Colley Cibber lifted his eyes upwards and slowly followed the curve of the proscenium arch. As they lowered he said, 'Apologies, my good friends, it seems young Charlotte is indisposed. Who do we have to read in, Mr Mercutio?'

'Fanny.' He pointed his finger at her.

Colley Cibber turned and saw Fanny pressing her back against the side of the box.

He was considering the possibility when Ann Oldfield said, 'What an excellent idea Mr Mercutio.

Come on, Fanny, join us on stage.'

Fanny, convinced she had misheard, sat stock-still.

'Come, Frances. Tom, go and bring her to the stage.'

The box door opened and Tom with a broad grin, said, 'This should cheer you. Quick.'

Fanny joined the actors on the stage.

Colley Cibber put his hand on her shoulder and smiled. 'Now, Frances, you know us all. There is no need for nerves.' He then turned and spoke directly to the actors. 'I would like to tell the company that Frances has been kind enough to read in the parts as I have been writing this comedy, therefore, she is familiar with the plot.' He picked up a copy of the play and handed it to Fanny. 'You will be reading in for the part of Jenny. Act II Scene I: Jenny's entrance. Do you see your first line?' Fanny flipped through the script and nodded. 'Good. Now, Frances, I want you to walk on from the wings, and say this first line. Off you go.' As he ushered her to the wings, he whispered, 'I know you can do this, Fanny, it is only an exercise. Walk on stage with your head high, back straight, speak from your diaphragm and make the audience see and hear only you, no one else is of importance. Off you go, and wait for me to speak your cue, then come on.'

Mr Cibber returned to his table and all the other actors turned in their chairs to watch Fanny's entrance.

Cibber spoke his line. 'Come forward, Jenny.'

Fanny felt her legs wobbling, but she took a deep breath, stepped out and said, 'Sure, Papa, do you think I don't know how to behave myself?'

A moment of silence. Had she done it badly? A murmur of appreciation. She hadn't done it badly. Light applause. She had done it well.

And that, was how Fanny Tomlinson from Chilton

Foliat, Wiltshire, spoke her first lines on the great stage of the Theatre Royal, Drury Lane.

CHAPTER SIXTEEN

Celebrations

SUNDAY WAS A perfect English spring day with fresh, clean air and a sky clear and bright, the colour of a bluebird. Theo waited for Fanny outside the apothecary, and the two of them walked together towards Field Lane, passing through the medieval Staples Inn. Theo was full of excitement and tales of the advances of medicine and his decision to study in Edinburgh, for a short time this summer.

'Not for too long, I hope, Theo? I shall miss you.'

'Will you, Fanny? I do hope so.' He stopped and faced her, held both her hands and looked into her eyes.

Fanny lowered hers, blushed and said, 'Of course I shall, Theo. You are my truest friend.' Theo sighed, released her hands and they continued their journey.

What Theodore could not know was Fanny had given her unexperienced, and therefore vulnerable, heart to the dashing Gideon and until this infatuation passed, he had no chance of winning Fanny's love in the way he wished.

Arriving at Mr and Mrs Big's, Fanny gave the little door the usual three knocks and called, 'Tis Fanny.'

Opening the door, Mrs Big wore a smile that would light up the whole world. 'Come in, my dove, we are all here and what news we have to tell.'

The usual warm welcome from the troupe was followed by Samuel the Strongman, in great solemnity, walking up to them with Letitia on his arm, her head slightly bowed.

'May I introduce my beloved, who had kindly agreed to be my wife.'

Fanny threw her arms around Letitia and Theo shook Samuel's hand rigorously.

'Blessings be upon you both and may I have the honour of sewing the bride's gown?' asked Fanny whilst Theo embraced Samuel and clapped his back in congratulations.

'Oh, Fanny, that I'd be loving you to do. I ain't no bleedin' idea about all that stuff,' Letitia said, with her strong zest of Limehouse.

'Oh, I shall help you in any way you wish, Letitia,' offered Fanny.

'Call me, Letty, do. What colour do you think, Fanny?'

'China blue is very becoming and would suit you well.'

Arrangements for the wedding continued with Mrs Big adding inspirational touches, such as little silver stars and waxed flowers in Letty's hair. The ladies moved into a corner and discussed a plan, oblivious to the men who were at a loss of what all the excitement was about.

Theo asked the future bridegroom, 'When is the wedding to be, Samuel?'

'Letty has decided on Christmas week. I am happy to oblige, as I care for her so. Oh, what a fortunate man I am, to have found such a gentle angel.'

From the huddle of ladies, came a squawk. 'Aaaooww. You don't half make me laugh, Fanny. I can't wear such fine garments. I ain't at court. Something plain is all I deserve.'

Both Mrs Big and Fanny were aghast. 'Certainly not,' said Fanny. 'You are going to be the best dressed bride in this parish.'

Letty's eyes glistened. 'My dear friends. Thank you'.

Samuel gazed at his chosen one, with adoration, 'So happy, ain't she. My dearest love.' And he shed a small, devoted tear.

After a hearty meal and much ale, Mrs Big climbed up on her chair and tapped one of the drinking glasses, saved for special occasions.

'May I have your attention, dear friends? Mr Big has asked me to invite you all to a party at the Swan, two weeks on.' A cheer went up and toasts were made. 'All our acts will be present to enjoy wine, ale and food and most of all, good company. It is Mr Big's and my way of saying thank you for a successful May Fair.' Another cheer from all present. Mrs Big paused and gestured her hand towards Samuel and Letty. 'It is also, to celebrate the betrothal of our dearest Samuel and his Christmas bride. Will you all be coming?' The biggest cheer of all was raised and, of course, more ale was drunk.

Fanny knew how fortunate she was to have such joyful friends. She prayed nothing would change.

Gideon held Kitty by the throat. 'What don't you understand, you stupid whore? Listen to me and maybe, the words will penetrate the fog of your brain.' He shook her neck on every word, 'I don't have any money to buy you stupid gifts.' Gideon let go of her, and she fell back holding her throat, gasping for air.

Gideon paced the room. 'My creditors will not lend me any more money, and my father will not raise my allowance, I am in debt to the gambling houses. I have to find gold.' He took a gulp of claret and spun around, kneeling in front of Kitty, their faces almost touching. 'I need Fanny to play cards again. Arrange it.'

Tense and troubled, Gideon picked up the wine glass and threw it in the fire. Opening the chamber door he shouted down, 'Boy, bring brandy.'

He threw himself into the winged chair, resting one leg over the arm and ruminated about his diminishing prestige.

For the first time, Kitty was nervous of Gideon's mood. With caution, she crept around him and settled on the bed. 'Gideon,' she started.

'Quiet, woman, or I shall shut you up with a blow.'

Kitty remained motionless whilst Gideon searched for a way to save himself from ruin. The silence was broken by a knock on the door. 'Enter,' Gideon shouted.

'Your brandy, sir.' The boy poured two glasses of the burnt wine and withdrew, not bothered about the argument as he'd seen it all before.

Gideon sprang to his feet. 'I have it.' As he strode up and down the room, he explained his plan to Kitty. 'Humphrey Busby will have a counting house in his lodgings. This is where he must keep his money. We shall do this slowly, coin by coin. For every ten crowns, guineas or sovereigns he has, you are to take one of them. He will not notice such a small loss. Over time, you will steal a large amount of the gold. Flatter him and watch him. Find out where he keeps the strongbox keys and take them to copy. Make sure you put everything back in exactly the same place, so he does not see it has been disturbed. See what other treasures are in there. Do you understand?'

'Yes, Gideon.'

Kitty was used to pilfering; however, if she was caught for this kind of theft she would hang. 'Are you sure this is the only way, Gideon?'

He carried the bottle of liquor to Kitty and topped up her glass. Sitting on the bed, he moved in on her, nuzzling her neck and whispering into her ear, 'Yes, my pretty girl. With Fanny winning at cards, together with Humphrey's gold, it should be enough for me to recoup my losses at the tables. At least, for a while.'

He slid his hands up her petticoats and touched her where she could not resist him. 'Let me rub some French brandy onto your rosebud, my dear.'

Kitty arched her neck back as she breathed deeply, and pleaded, 'Gideon, please be it your pleasure.'

The morning of the party, Fanny and the troupe collected the garlands of May blossom and pine sprigs, ordered from the market at Covent Garden. As cotton or silk was too expensive, Fanny planned to wind swags of thin paper through the garlands, from the rolls Mario the printer had given her. These ropes of evergreen and hawthorn would decorate the interior gallery balustrade and the stairs at the Swan Inn.

The sky was overcast and just as she reached the Inn, it turned dark grey and rain broke through in torrents.

'Always trying to be a drowned rat, Fanny Tomlinson?' welcomed Annie.

''Tis true. Do you think the rain clouds follow me about and when I visit the famous Inn on Holborn Bridge, they can no longer hold the water for excitement?'

'A bit like me these days.' Fanny didn't understand what Annie found so amusing but laughed along with her.

The rain was constant and the streets turned to rivers, churning up the mud but washing away some of the stagnant filth down the kennels.

'I've never seen it rain like this before,' said Annie, as she looked out onto the courtyard from the shelter of the threshold. 'See the yard? The water is two or three inches deep in some parts. 'Tis good we are two steps higher. At least the horses shall have clean water today, the rain has refilled the troughs.'

Annie returned inside, shut the door against the weather and said to Fanny, 'Well, my dear, the room is all yours. I shall leave you to it.'

Fanny worked hard and Betsy helped her to wire the garlands to the stair spindles. The two of them were sitting down admiring their labours and enjoying some cold meats and bread when Annie came to see the decorations. 'Fanny, you are a wonder, the garlands are beautiful and I can't tell the paper ain't silk.'

'Thank you, Annie. Shall I put the foliage cuttings and scrap paper, in the back yard?'

'No, my dear, it is too wet out there. They will not burn when I want to use them as faggots for the fire. Place them in the old barrel under the stairs. There is some sawdust in the bottom but plenty of room on top.'

Fanny collected up all the mess and wrapped it in a large piece of printers paper. She pushed it down into the barrel and asked, 'How may I help you now, Annie?'

'We should move the tables and make room for the

musicians and dancers. The heat of the fire is such now, the cook will put the meats upon the spit soon, and Betsy will mix the punch and spice it well. Come, let us check all the candlesticks and sconces have candles. You must change, did you bring your party clothes?'

'Yes, Annie. I'm very excited. It will be an evening to remember.'

The rain stopped during the late afternoon and Fanny watched the water gradually subside and drain away, down to the Fleet river. When evening fell, Fanny changed in Annie's bedchamber at the top of the stairs, over the bar area. Fanny looked around the room and was surprised at its luxuriousness. Annie had a four poster bed with red damask hangings trimmed with fringe and a counterpane stuffed with swansdown, it was the softest bed covering Fanny had ever seen. Annie explained, 'Me old bones need a bit of comfort when I put them to bed at night. I work hard and deserve the best to sleep in.'

'Indeed you do, Annie. You are the kindest of people, and you should have a bed fit for a Queen.'

Annie laughed. 'Thank you, Fanny. I must be away and check all is in order downstairs.'

Fanny put on the gown she shared with Kitty. It had been a joy sewing it. The silk was shot with two colours of gold and green, and it was embroidered with delicate flowers. Fanny checked herself in Annie's looking glass. She took a sharp intake of breath when she saw her reflection. It was of a woman, not a girl, and a very beautiful woman at that. She saw herself in the blink of an eye and dismissed it immediately, as pure vanity. Fanny opened the door and stepped down the staircase, brushing the May blossom and needle-shaped leaves with her hand as she descended, causing the pine oil to disperse in the air.

Annie greeted her at the bottom of the stairs. 'My, my, sweeting, you are a lovely looking girl. Better watch the gentleman tonight, Fanny.'

'Annie, stop your teasing.'

'No, my love. You are on the cusp of womanhood, a girl never looks lovelier.'

The tavern door opened and the rest of the troupe all fell in, laughing and joking. Mark saw Fanny and stopped mid-step, causing all the other dwarves to fall over each other, and Livewell and Noble had to jump over the pile of tangled showmen. They all tried to disengage themselves whilst staring at Fanny.

'Yes, well gentlemen, what have you got to say?' asked Annie.

Their words were as jumbled as their bodies. 'Fanny, you look beautiful', 'May I have a dance tonight, Fanny?' and 'Will you marry me, fair maid?'

'I shall dance with all of you, in celebration of our betrothed couple. Where are they?'

'Just behind us, hand in hand and looking soppy at the moon,' said Mark.

'Where is your romance, Mark?' Fanny asked.

'In the alley behind the Fleece Tavern.' Luke slapped him around the head. 'Would you stop doing that Luke, it's becoming a habit.'

'Behave yourself then,' and he slapped him again.

Theo appeared at the door, removed his hat and greeted everyone. He took one look at Fanny and anyone could see the love radiating from his eyes. 'You look wonderful, Fanny.'

'Thank you, Theo. Come and drink some punch. Betsy's best.'

The guests arrived, excited and happy to celebrate

together and soon the room was crammed with fellow entertainers, friends and customers. Fanny laughed as she joined in the gossiping between the different vibrant groups. They came in all shapes and sizes. Showman of all kinds coming together to celebrate the future Mr and Mrs Samuel Bennett. The party had started.

Jack Mann never left Betsy's side, and she sat on his lap when she wasn't serving or singing. Fanny realised their relationship was complicated and passionate, a heated cauldron of love and jealousy.

The fire glowed, the candles flickered, the food was abundant, as was the gin, wine and beer. As the evening wore on, the enjoyment became more vocal and there was much loud singing and country jigs to the music of the fiddlers, pipes and drums. Betsy was filling glasses behind the bar when Annie said to her, 'The party is a great success. I'm going upstairs to get a short rest as I feel a little tired. No one will miss me, and you can wake me later, to help you get this lot off home to their beds.'

'You're not ill, are you, Annie? It's most unusual for you to rest during the evening.'

'I'm quite well, Betsy, do not fret. I shall take my candle up to bed and I shall see you again, soon.'

'Sleep well, Annie,' said Betsy.

CHAPTER SEVENTEEN

The Party

AS ANNIE CLIMBED the wooden steps, she watched Samuel lifting Mrs Big onto his shoulders. Once comfortable, the little woman announced, 'Quiet, please. May I have your attention, ladies and gentlemen. I have a new artiste to introduce. Tonight, you will be the first to view this Eastern dance, and I don't mean it's from Hackney village.' The crowd laughed uproariously. 'All the way from the Ottoman Empire comes an exciting lady who has never been seen before in England. She uses two musical instruments unknown to us, the calpara, which is a wooden clapper stick, and a tambourine. The Midsummer Fair punters will love this act. Let us show her our warmest appreciation, and welcome her into our special family. May I introduce to you, for the very first time, having travelled over the seas from the far off land of Turkey, the delectable, the desirable, dancing, Fatima.' Applause filled the room as the performance began.

Annie, in the doorway of her bedchamber, looked over the balustrade, smiling at her friends enjoying the spectacle of the exotic dancer. Feeling a wave of tiredness spread over her, she entered her bedchamber and closed the door behind her. She started towards the bed to place her lighted candle on the side table, but before she could put it down, she felt a pain so vicious and unbearable she clutched her hands to her breast, letting the candlestick fall onto the bed dressings. She fell forward, grasped the bed hangings and slowly collapsed into a heap, on the floor. The flame from the candle caught the silk and a stream of shining gold, snaked upwards towards the canopy pelmet. The revellers downstairs were unaware of the danger above them: the beginning of a silent vortex of fire trapped in a room, which would devour everything it touched.

The dancing girl, dressed in a highly decorated costume with jingling filigree jewellery, wore a large diaphanous scarf over her head that floated as she spun around in circles, whilst shaking and beating her tambourine. The crowd around her shouted and clapped along with the rhythmic music that stirred up frenzied excitement in them.

The bed was alight with licks of jumping flames and smoke began to build up.

Fatima bent over backwards, shaking her hips and every time a man placed a coin on her forehead, a cheer went up.

The smoke curled seductively out from under the bedchamber door.

The dancer shook her shoulders and moved her hips in a suggestive way, causing the men to go wild while the women copied the dancer's movements. She started to spin around again but abruptly stopped, looking up to the gallery. The crowd were noisily wondering what was she going to do next. What she did, was to scream.

Fanny followed Fatima's eyes and saw the smoke and a narrow band of flame, shining from under the bedchamber door. Fanny shouted, 'Betsy, look,' and pointed upstairs. Betsy pushed people out of her way and rushed towards the staircase. 'Annie is up there. She's in that room.' She ran up the stairs.

Fanny pushed through the crowd shouting for Jack Mann. 'Jack, Jack, help!'

His attention was caught and when he realised what was happening, he forced his way through to join Fanny at the bottom of the stairs and shouted up, 'Betsy, stop.' Betsy had reached the door and as she put her hand on the latch, Jack bellowed out, 'No, Betsy. No.' Opening the door caused the fire to breathe in oxygen. The flames reinvigorated, grew larger and leapt out onto the gallery. 'Come back down, Betsy,' Jack yelled. When she didn't, he took the stairs two at a time but too late. Betsy had walked into the fire.

Fanny shouted, 'Betsy, I'm coming to help you.' She dashed up the stairs behind Jack. Fanny reached the bedchamber door as Jack disappeared into the void of dark smoke. She couldn't see anything inside the room. Water was needed. She looked around the gallery and noticed a piss pot outside another chamber. Picking up the hem of her gown, she ripped the seam and tore off a long rag of silk. She dipped it in the urine and wrapped the fabric around her face, then disappeared into the fire.

Down below, the guests were startled and stared up at the landing, not moving. Theo, now aware of what was happening, knew the shock would soon change to panic when the fire spread. And it would, fast. He raced through the wall of people, shouting, 'Fanny, wait.' When he looked up towards the gallery, what he saw frightened him. The fire had ignited the thin paper swags and they bloomed into flames with the pine oil acting as an accelerant, setting alight the garlands in a chain reaction. 'Fanny, come out!'

The onlookers around him saw the fire spreading and realising the situation, they started to scream as pandemonium broke out, memories of the Great Fire filling them with terror and fear. In the panic, tables were turned over and candlesticks fell, setting fire to the sawdust on the floor. Drinking vessels flew through the air and bottles of brandy and rum smashed and spilt their alcohol. Men rushed about shouting, 'Get water,' and women cried, 'Get out, save yourselves.' Some of the men ran into the yard to fill buckets with water, fortunately, most were full already from the torrential rain. Those that did not flee, made a chain to carry the water into the Inn to try and douse the flames, but the fire spread faster than they could control it.

Inside the smoke-filled room, the bed was fully alight, illuminating Betsy who was unconscious on the floor, with her chemise and stays alight. Standing by her was Jack, coughing whilst he tried to beat out the flames and attempting to drag her from the room at the same time. Fanny touched him on the shoulder and grabbed Betsy's other leg and the two of them pulled her away from the flames onto the landing. The smoke had found its way into Jack's throat and he couldn't speak. Fanny screamed for Theo. He bounded up the stairs and she told him, 'Theo, carry Betsy down and care for her. She's badly burnt.'

'You go first, Fanny, quickly,' said Theo, fearing she

would refuse.

'I'll follow. Do as I say, Theo. Carry Betsy down. Now. Jack will help you as much as he can, he will be fine with some fresh air in his lungs.'

The two men picked up Betsy and made their way down the stairs where the garlands were now fully flaming. Whilst the men were looking down and not at Fanny, she dipped the silk back in the urine and re-entered the inferno.

Theo turned in time to see her go back into the bedchamber. 'Fanny, come back. Stop. Please, come back.'

Jack coughed, found his voice and looked at Theo directly. 'Theo, take the weight of Betsy and do what you can, I'll get Fanny.'

'No, I have to go to her. Help me, Jack.'

'Take Betsy outside, Theo, I shall go to Fanny.'

Theo looked at his patient and knew he had a duty to her, he needed to reduce the heat and burning on her arms. He remembered the rainstorm that refilled the horse's troughs, cold and reasonably clean water. He would lay her in the stone trough to cool the skin of her burning body. It may help. He carried Betsy outside and put her in the bath of cold water. He watched steam rise from her. He was not sure she would survive.

As Jack leapt up the stairs, he saw it happen. The paper swags on the staircase and the burning pine leaves fell through the gaps of the treads and into the barrel full of the leftover sprigs of the garlands. The thin paper eagerly joined the dance of the flames that set fire to the sawdust in the bottom of the barrel.

The heat built up quickly and soon it became

searing. The flames started to burn the staircase treads above.

'Fanny, I'm coming in,' shouted Jack.

He looked into the room, now fully alight. The wooden bed was burnt black with red hot embers. Jack saw Fanny trying to pull Annie away, but he knew it was too late. He turned Fanny around by the shoulders and looked at her, shaking his head and grabbing her hand. Both of them stumbled out of the room. Fanny's gown was alight and he rolled her over on the floor, smothering the flames.

'Quickly, Fanny, down the stairs.'

'I can't see them, Jack, I'm blinded by the smoke. You will have to lead me.'

'All right. Keep hold of my hand.'

Maybe it was good that Fanny's eyes were watering and smarting, as she could not see the flames jumping all along the gallery and down the staircase.

The room below was now empty except for the troupe, Mr and Mrs Big, Samuel and Letty. They would not leave without Fanny, even if it meant dying with her, she was part of their family.

'Ready, Fanny? We are going to walk down the stairs now. Don't reach out for the bannister,' said Jack. 'I'll go first, a couple of steps in front of you. I know you can't see. You have to trust me to be your eyes.'

Fanny nodded. He started to step down. He was only on the third step when there was a loud, cracking sound and the staircase began to collapse in front of him. He tried to go back up, but it was too late. He was carried forward and down with the falling staircase. He had to let go of Fanny's hand, or she would fall straight to the floor. He jumped away from the burning stairs that broke into pieces around him. He managed to get clear, landing safely on the ground.

When he looked up, as all the friends did, they saw Fanny standing alone at the top of the stairs with her arms outstretched, blinded for the moment with the fire raging around her.

Jack looked towards the roof and saw a beam. He shouted at Samuel, 'Get a rope.' He looked across to the landing. 'Don't move, Fanny. Not an inch. Stay just as you are.'

He beckoned to Mr Big and the troupe, pointed to the beam and mimed swinging on a rope. They all nodded, understanding what they had to do. Samuel ran in with the rope and Jack tied a double knot in at one end. He gathered it up and with great force, threw it over the beam. Now, he had to get the end of the rope to Fanny. Mr Big signed what the boys were to do, and Mrs Big acknowledged what her part would be.

Samuel and Jack were the anchors of one end of the rope, and the four dwarves created a tower as they had done many times before. They moved slowly to grab the knot of the rope hanging over the beam and carefully moved closer to Fanny.

'Can you see now, Fanny?' shouted Jack.

'Yes, Jack, I can. What do you want me to do?

'The boys will pass the rope to you and I want you to wind it around your arm several times and stand on the big knot. Once secured by the rope, you will step off the platform and swing down. We'll catch you. Do you understand?'

'Yes, Jack, I think so.' Mrs Big looked at Jack in doubt.

The tower of little men moved closer to Fanny, only to realise they were too short to reach her, she wouldn't be able to take the rope from them. They all looked down at Jack. Mrs Big stepped forward and said, 'I shall climb up and swing down with Fanny. I can tell her what to do.'

'Are you sure, Mrs B?' asked Jack.

'Of course. I am saving my child.'

Samuel dropped his end of the rope, picked up Mrs Big and held her until she got her balance to stand on his shoulders. Once next to the tower, she reached out and climbed on the third man, John. She scrambled up into Mark's cupped hands and onto his shoulders. Miraculously, the tower didn't topple over: so good were the men at shifting their balance. Mark took the rope from between his teeth and passed it to Mrs Big. She held on to it and nimbly jumped from the tower onto the landing and joined Fanny. The boys broke the tower, and John ran outside to the yard returning with a tarpaulin that they stretched out and held at waist height, to make a blanket to break the fall of the two beloved women.

Mrs Big was calm and spoke quietly to Fanny, in order to make her concentrate. 'My dearest, do exactly as I say and we shall be down on the ground in seconds. It's easy to do. Here, let me twist the rope securely around your left arm and waist. I want you to carry me down with you. We shall be together all the time. All right, my dear?'

'Yes, Mrs B.' She could see Fanny shaking. She handed the rope to Fanny and told her where to hold it tightly.

'Now, my dear, we are going to push this burning balustrade away, so we have a clear platform to swing from. Place your left foot to the side of the knot to feel it against your leg, and push us off the landing with your right foot. You will have to take the weight of both of us as we step into the air.' Mrs Big smiled at

Fanny. 'Only for a moment, my dear. Quickly place your right foot on the other side of the knot. This will take our weight, and the counterweight of Samuel and Jack, who will guide our swing down to the blanket. Are you ready? Hold me tightly on your hip with your right arm. And if you do it well, you can join the troupe.'

Fanny managed a small laugh and said, 'Wait a moment, I have to take my stockings off. I must be able to feel the grip with my skin.'

'Quickly, time is short,' said Mrs Big, and she signalled to the troupe to be ready for the escape.

Fanny did exactly what Mrs Big had told her, and they both flew away from the burning gallery, swinging across the room and back again. Samuel anchored the rope around his waist whilst Jack pulled it in, bit by bit. This controlled the descent, and very soon the women found themselves on the tarpaulin and safe. The boys gently lowered the blanket and ran to embrace Fanny and Mrs Big.

Jack broke up this reunion by shouting, 'Get out now. Run.' Just in time, the band of showmen escaped the Inn before the burning rafters began to fall and break.

'Help me.' It was Theo. Jack and Samuel joined him and gently lifted Betsy out of the horse trough, she was moaning and in great pain. 'Where can we take her? She needs clean linen to bind her burns and rest, lots of rest.'

Letty voiced her Limehouse instructions, 'Take her to my lodgings, 'tis opposite in Plumtree Court. It may be small, but it's as clean as laundresses copper.'

The men followed Letty, carefully carrying Betsy, who was unconscious again. Before leaving the yard,

Fanny turned towards the burning building and said, 'God bless you, Annie, we shall meet again when the time comes. I shall carry your kindness with me for the rest of my life.' And she blew a kiss.

CHAPTER EIGHTEEN

Recovery

TRUE TO HER words, Letty's room shone as bright as a new pin, and the bed was made up with newly washed linen. She never stopped surprising people.

'Lay her down, I'll care for her. Me and my Samuel will see her right, I promise. How long will Theo be? She'll be needing something to stop the pain. Samuel, go to the box under the window, where you will find a bottle of rum. Bring it to me, and we shall wipe her lips with it. Mrs B, please take a sheet of clean linen from the same box and Samuel will tear it into strips for dressings.'

The adrenaline that kept them all going started to drain and these brave performers felt tiredness settling over them. They found places to sit on the floor and talked in hush tones, about the events of the night.

Mrs Big came over and sat next to Fanny. 'You were very brave and did all you could to save Annie. Sometimes things are beyond our control. It wasn't your fault, something set the room alight, it didn't go up all by itself. What exactly happened, we shall never know.'

'But I was the one who put the garlands together

with that stupid paper. The fire would never have happened if I hadn't made them.'

'No, the fire started in Annie's bedchamber and it spread. No one was hurt outside that room. It was a terrible accident, Annie would want you to know that.'

'What about Betsy?' She began to weep.

'Jack told me you helped him save her, and he couldn't have done it without you. You saved her life, Fanny. And knowing how strong Betsy is, she will survive. We just have to look after her.' The little woman put her arms around Fanny and stroked her hair.

After Theo had administered various medications and treated Betsy's burns, he squatted down in front of Fanny and said to Mrs Big, 'May I speak to Fanny alone?'

'Indeed, dear Theo.' She moved across the room to put her arm around her husband.

'Fanny, I was so scared I would lose you. I have to tell you that I love you, and I always shall. It doesn't matter if you don't feel the same way, I just want you to know I shall always be here for you. I may not be as brave as you, but I shall keep you from harm and love you for the rest of my life.'

Fanny didn't know what to say, she cared for Theo, but Gideon's image came to her. 'I do not know a truer man than you, apart from Jack Mann, although he has a dark side to him.' She smiled. 'I could not do better than to have you as a husband but not now. I would have to be certain of my feelings and at the moment I am not. Please forgive me, Theo, I do not wish to hurt you. I cannot promise you anything.' Theo's heart was heavy, but he admired her honesty.

'I understand, Fanny, I shall wait.'

Theo took Fanny home and explained to his aunt how they had been caught up in a fire, whilst celebrating a fellow apothecary's betrothal. He gave Madame Marie some herbal tisanes and powders to help Fanny relax and sleep. When certain that both women were calm and without worry, he bid them farewell and returned home, for a good nights rest.

Madame Marie helped Fanny up to bed. She slipped a clean nightgown over her head and tucked her in ready for sleep, like a small child.

'Where's Kitty, Aunt?'

'She's out with Gideon. Martha will bring you some hot milk and once you have drunk it, you must sleep. I shall leave a note telling Kitty what has passed, asking her to be as quiet as a mouse when she gets ready for bed.' Madame Marie looked at the tatters of the beautiful gown Fanny had made for herself and Kitty. She tutted and said, 'Nothing can be done with this. We shall sew another, even more beautiful. Now, Fanny, you are not to do anything tomorrow. I shall come up to see if you are awake, and we shall talk and play cards. The day will be ours alone, and Sous-Sous of course. Your uncle is going to Kensington to speak to the men who are building the house, as they don't seem to be doing the work quickly enough. This is nothing new. I have the perfect excuse not to travel with him.' Madame Marie smoothed the blankets around Fanny, as her mother used to do. 'Now, I wish you goodnight, my dear. You will feel better tomorrow.'

Martha came up with the milk. 'You been caught up in that Swan Tavern to-do? News spreads as fast as fire, miss. Weren't there freaks there?'

'Don't call them that,' shouted Fanny. 'Forgive me, Martha, I am not myself. Theodore and I were celebrating in a private room at the Inn. I do not know what was happening elsewhere in the Tavern. Thank you for my milk, Martha. Please don't mention the fire again, I find it very upsetting.'

'Yes, miss, whatever you say, miss. I'm sorry for the upset, I'm sure I do. I wish you a good night.'

Fanny drank her milk, took her powders and fell into a deep sleep.

As promised, Madame Marie gently stroked Fanny awake to spend a peaceful day together. Kitty had gone with Humphrey to Kensington, taking her aunt's place. Madame Marie brought Fanny downstairs and made her comfy in the stuffed chair and put her feet up on the little beaded stool, whilst she searched the workroom for a book of designs and silk swatches. The two women picked out several patterns.

'It will be the best mantua I shall ever make.' Madame Marie was excited. Not only about stitching the garment, but to have Fanny to herself, all day. 'I have a box of very best trimmings saved over the years, hoping one day I would use them to make your wedding gown. I think, now is the time to bring you some cheer. What better way, than a new gown? There will be time to make another before you wed.'

'Thank you, Aunt, you are very generous.'

'Now, you will need new petticoats, so we shall start with them. I'll go to the workshop and cut the pieces out. Would you like to start the flat pleating?' Fanny nodded. 'Good. I will find your sewing bag, and we shall begin.'

They sang as they worked until the light faded. Madame Marie reminded Fanny, 'Remember what I told you. Stop sewing with the lowering of the light.

You need to keep your eyes strong to be a seamstress. I shall light the candles and we shall play cards. Who will be the cleverest and win today? How is your counting?'

Whilst they were playing cards with Sous-Sous, who changed allegiance frequently, they heard the shop bell ring.

'It will be your uncle. Quick, Fanny, hide the cards.'

Fanny collected the packs and the buttons, which they were using as chips and put them in her sewing bag, placing it down by the side of her chair.

Humphrey Busby was in a good mood, they listened to him laugh and talk with Kitty.

'I must return tomorrow afternoon to discuss further plans for the building, are you free to accompany me, Kitty?'

'Alas, no, sir. I have a dancing lesson. Maybe the next time you visit?'

'I shall look forward to it. Mrs Busby will join me tomorrow.'

Fanny and her aunt sat still and in silence in the parlour, waiting for them to enter. Kitty walked in, with her head turned back towards Humphrey. 'Excuse me, Mr Busby, I must take off my travelling clothes, I wonder if you would help me—' As she turned her head forward, she was greeted by the two women, who anticipated her next move. 'Oh, I didn't realise you were sitting in here.'

'No, indeed,' said her aunt.

'Ah, Marie,' Humphrey said, without welcome. 'Would you organise tea for our dear Katherine? Fanny, do you not think it would be wise to take a rest up in your room for a while? Kitty may have your chair.'

'My pleasure, uncle. Aunt, please excuse me.' She

picked up her sewing bag and retired upstairs.

Fanny fell asleep but was soon awakened by Kitty.

'Are you feeling better? What happened to you? Tell Kitty the truth now.'

'I don't want to talk about it. I'm tired.'

'Fanny, I have a message from Gideon for you.'

Fanny sat up immediately.

'He is in a bit of trouble, his finances are sort of stuck at the moment. He was hoping you would accompany him to the tables and use your skill to, hopefully, win some money that you could then lend him. What about tomorrow afternoon?'

'I shall make sure I'm free.'

'Good. I had better get back to Humphrey, now his wife has retired to bed.'

'Kitty… no, it doesn't matter.' Nothing she said would change this strong-willed girl's intent. 'Do you have a dress I could wear? I'm afraid the one I made for us to share was destroyed during the fire, last evening.'

'My beautiful gown? How could you, Fanny. There must have been a way not to get involved. Really, Fanny, you think only of yourself.'

'I couldn't help it, Kitty, everywhere was covered with a coating of black soot from the fire. There was nothing I could do to keep the gown clean.'

'Oh, all right. I'll lay one out for you tomorrow.'

The next evening, Kitty and Fanny meet Gideon outside the Temple Chapel.

'Fanny, how delightful you look. It is an honour to be in your company,' flattered Gideon. 'We have been invited to a private gathering to play cards and dice. As there will be ladies playing, you will feel quite comfortable. Are you happy with that scenario?'

'Yes, Gideon. But I do not have any money to wager. I've gambled away all my savings and given you the winnings.'

'Do not worry, I shall provide for you to play. Kitty tells me you will be so kind, as to lend me what ever profit we should make?'

Fanny didn't want to, but she couldn't refuse his wishes. 'Indeed, Gideon, I shall help you in any way I can.'

'My dear, how exceedingly gracious you are.' He glanced at Kitty and said, 'I have to speak to Katherine, would you excuse me?'

'Of course.'

Kitty smiled at Fanny as Gideon led her away for a private conversation. 'How are things proceeding with Busby?'

'He is falling under my spell and soon he will trust me implicitly, and I have seen where he keeps the keys.'

'Where?'

'On a chain around his neck.'

'How will you get them?'

'I shall have to exhaust him.'

'How?'

'How do you think, Gideon?'

'I don't like to share you, Kitty.' He kissed her. 'I shall have to, this one time.' Gideon squeezed Kitty's forearm, hard.

'You're hurting me.'

'I know. When will you do this?'

'Sunday, after church. His wife is visiting her cousin in Spitalfields to order some silk, and she will worship with them at the new church there. She will be away all day'

'What about Fanny?'

'Stop worrying about Fanny. She never returns home with us after Matins. She won't tell me where she goes. It really irritates me. I shall be alone with him all day.'

'Good. Start to take the coins as I told you and bring them to me tomorrow. Don't have ideas about keeping any of the money for yourself. See what else is in the box.' He delved into his waistcoat pocket and bought out a small pad of wax in a metal box. 'Take an impression of both sides of the key and I shall have a copy made. With it, you will have free access to siphon off the money each time he adds to it.'

'Yes, Gideon. Now, please release me.'

He let go of her and said, 'To other matters. There will be men playing the tables this evening who will be interested in our young lady's innocence. I shall present her and subtly indicate what may be for sale. This will require a delicate negotiation, not to be rushed. Keep that girl innocent and unsullied'

'She is. So much so, she could be canonised.' She spat on the ground.

Walking to church on Trinity Sunday, the usual cast of three had changed. Madame Marie did not to join them, feigning a headache. Taking her place on Humphrey Busby's arm, Kitty showed-off in her Sunday best. Fanny trailed behind: an unwilling chaperone.

Inside this place of worship, the temperature rose one degree higher than out on the street, but the welcome seemed a lot colder. The service droned on. Fanny wondered if there was anything that could be done to make Matins a bit more interesting. Maybe the dour preacher could speak with some rise and fall in his voice, that would help. The flat delivery made it impossible not to be bored. Fanny found she couldn't keep her concentration on God or the preacher, so her mind wandered. During the long sermon, she watched the dust motes floating without rest until her eyes finally focused on the congregation. Fanny could only see the back of the heads of the parishioners. This view was enough, as her interest was in the hats. She knew who everybody was by their Sunday best millinery. Margaret Much was good to her name with her over laced cap and Widow Stone was wearing grey again, matching her complexion, set off with no smile. Fanny sighed and resigned herself to sit patiently in her seat, counting the minutes until she could be free for the rest of the day.

The box pews were high sided, each with its own carved door making them very private. The Busby pew was the furthest away from the altar. The occupants were not overlooked by anyone and could sleep, if so inclined. Today, Fanny was sitting by the aisle, Kitty in the middle and to her right, Humphrey, close to the corner. The sermon droned on as usual and many of the men had their heads down either in prayer, or sleep. Occasionally, there were strange sounds as people made involuntary noises. Sometimes, they snored and jerked awake, had coughing fits or even talked to themselves. But now, she heard something closer to her. Out of the quietness, she listened to her uncle take a short intake of breath, and she turned to see if he was unwell. Her view was blocked by Kitty leaning forward and slightly to her right. Kitty was quivering slightly and looking down at Humphrey's lap. Fanny concentrated on his controlled breathing that seemed to get deeper and faster. As she leant forward, Kitty caught her looking and snapped her head round and whispered, 'Be still.' Fanny looked to her front and tried to focus her attention on the bewigged preacher in the pulpit. But again, she heard her uncle quietly groan. She turned round once more and saw Kitty's right arm shaking up and down in small movements. When she looked at her uncle, his mouth was slightly open, his eyes closed, his breath short and trembling. Kitty whispered something into her uncle's ear and he took a deep breath and held it for a few seconds then exhaled in an exhausted manner.

Kitty reached into her bag, took out a lace handkerchief, wiped her right hand then passed it to Humphrey.

CHAPTER NINETEEN

Involvement

THE MOMENT THE service ended, Fanny lifted the latch of the pew door and fled from the church. She had agreed to meet Theo at the apothecary shop but instead, she ran up Fleet Street and into Shoe Lane. Her head was spinning as she tried to make order of her jumbled emotions. She may not be experienced in sex but instinctively, she knew she had seen something private, and it made her feel uncomfortable.

Fanny was relieved when she reached The Bull Head Tavern, which was just around the corner from Letty's lodgings in Plumtree Court. In this corner of Holborn, the buildings were packed close together, creating a perpetual dusk in the narrow alleyways. On the front door of Letty's tenement, was a freshly carved heart, a love token. Fanny traced the design with her finger. It made Fanny smile, and she knocked three times. Whilst waiting, she noticed a pot of rather sparse honeysuckle, desperate to weave its way up the brick wall, out of the shadows and into the light: a fitting metaphor for the people living here. Samuel answered. 'Fanny, come in.' He called into the room, 'Another one to see you, Betsy.'

'What is that delicious smell?' Fanny asked.

Letty looked towards the fire. 'It's William Bull's new receipt for his sausages, he adds fennel seeds. We're trying them out on you lot, before he cooks them at Cambridge Midsummer Fair. Help yourself.'

'I shall. Thank you, Letty. How is Betsy?'

The patient was sitting up and Fanny could see the red skin and blisters on the side of her face. Her left arm and leg were wrapped with dressings under which were various salves. Fanny held back her tears. 'Hello, Betsy. I do hope you are feeling more at ease. I'm so sorry about the fire.'

'Don't be distressed, Fanny. It was you and Jack what pulled me out of the burning room. If it weren't for you both, I'd be as crisp as them there sausages.'

'Betsy, I do love you.'

Theo arrived next and asked Fanny where had she been, he had waited for her.

'I'm sorry, Theo, I had to run an errand for my aunt after church.' He nodded and smiled. 'How are you treating Betsy?'

'She has first and secondary burns, so I am using several mixtures of ointments such as aloe vera with tincture of myrrh, oil of rose and linseed oil. My idea of the cold water seems to have helped, I shall discuss it further with my tutor in Edinburgh.'

'When are you going to Scotland?'

'In two weeks. I am hoping Betsy's skin will show good signs of recovery by then. I shall ask a colleague to keep an eye on her.'

Mrs Big approached Theo, and he sat on his haunches. Their eyes were level. She took both his hands in hers and said, 'Theo my dear, we cannot thank you enough. Your tender heart is of such importance to us.' She touched his cheek. 'What we should do without you, I do not know. God bless and keep you.'

'Mrs B, you are good people, and I am honoured to help you.' He turned back to the convalescent. 'Forgive us, Betsy, we are not paying attention to you. How are you feeling?'

'Shall I be badly scarred?'

The group of friends looked at each other and waited for Theo to speak.

'I know you are a brave young woman, and I cannot lie to you. The truth is no one knows how you will heal. There will be some scaring. I shall do all I can to reduce it. You must understand that all those who care for you, love you for who you are and not what you look like.'

'But Jack…'

Mrs Big moved close to the bed. 'Jack has been to see you every day, usually when you're asleep. He doesn't want you to know he cares so much, but it seems he does, and maybe this event will change his ways. I pray it does. To all of us, you will always have a beauty that is deep and radiant.'

'I must farewell,' said Theo. As Mrs Big escorted him to the door, he took from his pocket another wrapped item, sealed with the usual letter, M. 'Please give this to Jack, Mrs B'. The little woman nodded.

'I shall accompany you,' said Fanny. 'I wish to spend the best of my time in your company.'

'Don't forget your sausages,' called Letty, as she wrapped up two in scraps of paper, for Fanny and Theo to take.

They talked all the way to the Old Square Gate, where Theo took his leave of Fanny, and she felt very alone knowing her friend was leaving her. He had always been just a head turn away.

After saying farewell to Theo, she drifted reluctantly back to the gate of the Inner Temple, hoping she had imagined what had happened in the pew. But she knew what she had seen.

Usually, Fanny arrived home much later on a Sunday. As she was early, she hoped her uncle was still in his counting house. Not to disturb him, she reached up to silence the shop bell as she carefully opened the door. She noted the quietness and felt relief flowing through her, as she tiptoed up the stairs to the attic. When she was half way up the first flight, she heard noises coming from her aunt and uncle's bedchamber. Madame Marie must have returned early from Spitalfields. But it was not her aunt's voice she overheard. It was Kitty's.

Fanny gripped the bannister rail until her knuckles turned white. She lowered her breathing as she looked through the open bedchamber door. There was clothing shed in haste, tossed all around the room and in the middle of the bed, Kitty was on all fours with Humphrey kneeling behind her, in a manner Fanny had seen dogs do. The rump of this particular cur was crisscrossed with red welts.

She raced up the bare boarded stairs, the clatter interrupting the couples sexual pleasure. Both turned their heads and Humphrey whispered the name with malice, 'Fanny.'

She closed the attic bedchamber door and put the chair against it to try and secure herself a safe place. Her heart pounded as she waited for her uncle to break down the door and storm in. Nothing happened. This scared her more. What was she to do? Should she tell her aunt? How should she behave towards her uncle? What would she say to Kitty? All these questions both scared and revolted her.

To calm herself she lay on the bed, closed her eyes and remembered the bedtime stories her grandfather would tell her. Grandpère Pierre had been a domestic servant to the French mistress of King Charles II, who held extravagant and splendid salons at her home, the Little Palace, which was next to St James's Palace. The best of London society attended, celebrated people in literature, politics and philosophy, dressed in the newest fashion as their diamonds sparkled in the flickering candle light. Fanny concentrated on this dream world of grandeur to stop her thinking about what she had just seen. She imagined herself moving amongst the guests, admiring the gowns. But she knew in her waking life as a seamstress, she would only touch the silk through the needles used to stitch them. Eventually, Fanny fell asleep.

So did Humphrey Busby. But not Kitty. Whilst Busby was sleeping, she slipped the key to the strongbox from around his neck and went down into the counting house. She lifted the heavy box from the shelf above the chimneypiece and placed it on Busby's writing table. Firstly, she took a wax impression of the key as Gideon had instructed. When done, she replaced the lid and placed the tin box it in her pocket. She listened intently for any sounds of movement, and when she was certain no one was around, she turned the key and opened the lid. The box was full of deeds to property and many sovereigns, guineas and crowns. She counted them and took a share of the coins, dropping them in her other pocket. Kitty was careful to move the papers with little disturbance. Underneath them were several gold snuff boxes and a leather case. She flipped the catch. Nestling on fitted emerald green velvet was a beautiful diamond and ruby demi-parure. The drops of the earrings were fashioned as waxing and waning crescent moons, and at the centre of the necklace hung a large cabochon ruby, set in a gold mount of the sun's rays, reaching out towards six round diamonds. Kitty's hand automatically reached for the glittering jewel. She stopped herself, she would leave them for now. Maybe Gideon would let her keep it, as a thank you for her help.

'Some chance,' she said, snapping it shut. She locked the strong box and went back to the bedchamber, where she stealthily put the key back around Humphrey's neck. Everything was back in its place. Except the gold.

Gideon was waiting in the porch of the Temple Church, to receive the stolen money. She dressed, held the shop bell to silence it and left the shop.

'Well done, my clever girl,' he said. 'I must rush to meet friends at the Cocoa. Tonight, I feel lucky.' He kissed her, biting her lip. Kitty returned to the milliners, very pleased with herself.

Fanny needn't have worried about a scene, as nothing was said. Her aunt returned late from visiting her cousin, and Kitty came up to the attic, to ask Fanny if she would like to join Mr and Mrs Busby for evening tea. Her uncle behaved in his usual severe manner, and the butter Kitty held in her mouth didn't melt.

The next afternoon, Gideon was waiting at the Temple church, this time for Fanny. They were to visit the gaming tables again. He chose different venues to keep Fanny relatively unknown and to not raise suspicion. Fanny was clever, in that she didn't win noticeably large amounts but gained a steady, moderate profit. Gideon now recognised she was a cheat and a good one, but he didn't say anything to her as he secretly commended her skill. This admiration grew in a different way too: her beauty and innocence was becoming beguiling to him. By choice, he would see her every night, but she worked at the theatre wardrobe.

He didn't hear Fanny approach. She was standing in front of him. 'Good evening, Gideon.'

'Fanny, how delightful you look this evening.' He kissed her hand. As he bowed he noticed her forlorn look and asked her, 'Is something troubling you, my dear?'

'No, Gideon, I'm all right.'

'No, Fanny, you are not. We shall go to the Crown and Anchor in the Strand, it is a reputable house and we can talk privately. Let us walk.' He took Fanny's arm in his and they meandered through Fountain Court, to the small streets that led to the tavern's side entrance, on Arundel Street'.

'Would you like some wine, Fanny?'

'A small glass, if you please,'

'Certainly. Shall we have some cold roast meats and cheese?'

'How very pleasing. Thank you.'

'Oh, I seem to have forgotten my coins. My dear, would you be so kind as to lend me a little?'

'It would be my pleasure, Gideon.'

He ushered her to a small table in the corner shadow of the room, where they would not be noticed nor overheard.

When he returned, he held Fanny's hand in his and said, 'Tell me your troubles, Fanny, I'm here to listen and help you.'

Fanny sighed as if weary of carrying her burden of

worry. She looked into Gideon's blue eyes and started to cry. 'Gideon, I don't know how to tell you, something shocking has happened at the milliners.'

'Unburden yourself, Fanny.'

The wine and food arrived at the table. 'Take a sup, it will give you courage to tell me your concerns, although I am certain they are not as bad as you fear.'

Fanny took a deep breath, lowered her eyes and said, 'It concerns your niece.'

Gideon had to think for a moment who Fanny meant. 'Ah, Kitty. What about Kitty?'

'How can I tell you this? You will be so angry, I fear for what you may do.'

'For goodness sake, Fanny, it can't be that bad. Just tell me what has happened.'

'I believe my uncle has taken advantage of her.'

'Oh,' Gideon said noncommittally. He didn't know what to do for the moment, he considered how he was going to play this hand. 'In what way, my dear?'

'He has drawn her into his wicked ways of the flesh.' Fanny drew on biblical text to help her.

'Oh,' repeated Gideon and decided it must have been a very quick seduction.

'When did this happen, Fanny?'

'Last Sunday'

'And how do you know this?'

'I saw them.'

'Did they see you?'

'Yes.'

'Ah,' said Gideon, thinking Kitty had conveniently omitted to tell him of this piece of information.

'What are you going to do, Gideon?'

'I am shocked. He is a beast. I shall confront him and tell his wife he is a lecherous man.'

'No. Please, Gideon. My aunt does not deserve such

humiliation, and I fear what he may do to me if he finds out I told you. He can be violent. I want him to suffer but no one else. There must be another way.'

'What is most dear to him?'

'Money.'

'Yes, I believe that to be so. Allow me a moment to ponder over this situation.' Gideon's refined face showed its future ageing, as wrinkles appeared due to his concentration and concern. 'I have nowhere for Kitty to lodge at the moment, so we shall have to continue to appear unconcerned and hope she will avoid him.'

'I don't think that will happen. I'm sure she likes him.'

'Ridiculous, she is being led astray. She doesn't know what she is doing, unlike you, Fanny. I shall remove Kitty from that dwelling as soon as I can, in the meantime let us plan what we can take from this monster that will give him pain. I wonder, has he small items of silver around his home?'

'There are pieces, but he would notice if any were removed. Fanny thought for a moment. 'I have seen him hide gold coins. I don't think he has any idea of how many he's collected.'

'Is that so? Do you know these hiding places?'

'Some of them.'

'Search around Fanny and find these hoards. Take a couple of pieces now and again, that way he won't notice they reduce in number. Will you do that, Fanny? You can bring them to me when we meet to gamble.'

'Yes, I shall do that.'

'Good. Now, you are looking very beautiful this evening, my dearest. Allow me to get nearer to you, I want to take in your essence.'

Gideon moved closer to Fanny, his cheek touching

hers and his breath warm on her neck. She shivered and let her head fall backwards. Gideon recognised the young woman's yearning, as he placed his hand over her breast.

'Oh, my,' she whispered, as he kissed her neck just below her ear. Her head rolled down in a circle and as she lifted it, Gideon kissed her on the mouth.

'Gideon.'

'Fanny, my dear, you are too tempting. I should stop.'

'Yes. But no, please don't.'

He knew she couldn't resist him. He kissed her again and slid his hand under her petticoat and slowly brushed it higher, up to her thigh.

Fanny was spellbound by his actions and was fully accepting of them. Gideon remembered his plan for her. He checked himself and said, 'No. I must not.' He removed his hand and cradled his head in it.

'Fanny, I'm sorry. You bewitch me, I cannot help myself. Please forgive me.'

'There is nothing to forgive, Gideon. For you I would give myself to.'

Tempting as it was, Gideon desired money more. 'We must go. Remember Fanny, this is our secret.'

CHAPTER TWENTY

The Molly House

FANNY HAD BEEN thinking. London was full of citizens doing a myriad of business, trying to make a living. The one thing that seemed constant and paramount in this kaleidoscope of a city, was sex. She didn't know much about it, but she was sure that money was to be made from it. She needed to learn more. She couldn't ask Kitty, their friendship was sullied, so she decided to enlist Tom Mercutio's help.

That evening, after Fanny finished working in the theatre wardrobe, she met Tom at the stage door, expecting to accompany him to the Rose. 'I can't tonight, I'm going to the Molly house to meet some friends and have some fal-al-deral.'

'Can I come with you?' asked Fanny.

'No. It's not a place for girls.'

'What do you mean, Tom?'

He stopped and looked at her. 'It's a place where boys like me go for a good time. If you know what I mean.' Fanny continued to look straight at him, saying nothing. 'Fanny, you really don't want to come with me.'

'Yes, I do. Stop treating me like some girl just up

from the country.'

Tom lifted an eyebrow, sucked in his cheeks and said, 'So sorry, Frances. How silly of me, I should know you was a mistress of experimental sexual experience.'

'Stop it. Tom. Look, you're my friend, aren't you? I need to get some of that experimental sexual experience.'

Tom laughed and spun around with his knuckle between his teeth. 'What did you say? Fanny, you are so amusing, you should get on stage, quick.'

'Tom, I'm serious. I am beginning to realise I'm some milk-sop, virgin of a girl and yes, I am not long up from the country, but I want to know as much as I can about this city. And…'

'And what?'

Very quietly she said, 'And what sex is all about.' Tom gasped theatrically. 'Will you help me? Or shall I go and ask Briddy.'

'Now, listen to your uncle Tom. Firstly, a virgin in this city is a rare asset. Hold onto it as long as you can, it's all downhill from then on ducks, and secondly, Briddy ain't going to get her dirty little mitts on you. If anyone is going to show you the divine and unimaginable things going on in the backstreets of London's maze of vice, it's going to me. I can keep an eye on you.'

'Thank you, Tom.'

'If you really mean it?'

'Yes, Tom, I want to learn all about sex. Once I have the knowledge, I will be able to understand and deal with it.'

'Well, if we are going to the late Mother Clap's understudy's abode, you will have to act as a drawer and fill the liquor glasses, I'm a good friend of Mother

George, so she will let you in. Keep quiet and try not to be too shocked at what you see. Run up to wardrobe and get an apron and cap, you can serve the drinks and observe. They don't let women in just to look around and get ideas about decoration and fashion. Hurry up, I need a gin. A big one.'

Tom and Fanny crossed the Piazza towards a coffee stall, where the gamut of society met for liaisons of dubious nocturnal activity. The shed, always busy and rowdy at this late hour was hosting a drunken brawl between two young men of nobility. Stepping nimbly around the fight, Tom led Fanny towards the portico of St Paul's church. 'Here's someone you know, Fanny.' Stepping out from behind one of the pillars was a very elegant lady with a powered auburn wig and a gown of scarlet. Hiding her eyes behind an open fan, she lowered it at the sight of Tom. Her face was lit with desire. As she extended her hand to Tom, he interrupted the gesture by saying, 'You remember Fanny?'

'I do. I saw you just three days ago, my dear.'

'Forgive me, madam, your memory serves you better than mine,' said Fanny.

Tom whispered in her ear, 'It's Oliver.'

'Oliver?' Fanny was lost for a moment.

The lady bent close to Fanny and said in a normal man's voice, 'It's me, Oliver, the lead dancer at the Lane.'

'Oh, Oliver.' Fanny was very surprised. 'You look so beautiful. I can't believe it's you.'

'I don't know how to take that. What are you doing here, Fanny?' asked Oliver.

Tom answered for her. 'Fanny has decided she wants instruction in the full spectrum of naughty goings on, in this degenerate area around the Piazza.'

'Not physically I hope. She'll be worn out, dear. Anyway, she won't get any of that tonight, going Mollying.'

'Exactly. She's not to be touched, she is like my own child.'

'Stop it, Tom,' said Fanny.

'Yes, stop it, Madame Madge,' said Oliver.

'You know what I mean. I shall not allow her to go the way of the rest of tiring-room five.'

Oliver pursed his lips. 'I see, and will you be escorting her to the bagnios too? After all, she has to see how the boring people, do boring things, down there.' He pointed to his crotch. 'A girl like you can't take her, Tom.' He stopped, thought clearly for a moment and continued, 'What am I saying? This idea is ridiculous. Tell her to go home, Tom.'

'Go home, Fanny,' Tom said.

'No. I want to come with you.'

'Go home, Fanny,' said Oliver.

'If you don't help me, I'll ask Briddy.' Silence for a second or two.

'No. You can't fall into her clutches,' said Oliver.

The two men folded their arms, looked at each other, shrugged their shoulders and Tom said, 'All right Miss Molly, have it your own way. Don't come crying to us if you don't like it. Sex, I mean, Well, watching it. Oh, Cibber Dibber, what have I got myself into?'

They walked back to Drury Lane to the Three Tobacco Rolls Tavern. These premises also advertised as a tallow and wax chandler. At first floor level hung a sign with the arms of the guild: three doves holding olive branches in their beaks. Tom knocked at the door and told Fanny, 'Put on your apron and cap.' The door opened, the noise flooding onto the street. A long shadow was thrown from the young boy who stood blocking the entrance. He wore a coat, two sizes too big with the sleeves turned back, but it still limped over his hands. Identifying the callers, he gave a short bow. 'Welcome, gents. Please enter.' He gave Fanny a shifty look, draining her bravado in apprehension of entering this underworld.

'Get Mother George for me, Valentine,' said Tom. 'Go in Lady Olive, I won't be long, I have to present Fanny to his Majesty, King George.' Oliver tutted and lifted the fan to his face. He threw back his head whilst quickly and impetuously, shutting the fan before he swept inside.

Fanny was confused. Here they were, in a tallow chandlers house that was a Tavern, with a closed door. Oliver was now a lady, in both senses of the word and she was going to be presented to the King of England.

'He says, come to the back parlour. Follow me,' instructed Valentine.

As they moved down the hallway, they passed a large room where fiddlers played, and the men dressed in women's clothing. They spoke to each other in an affected and effeminate manner. Fanny dawdled for too long and Tom took her hand and said, 'Quickly, Fanny, his Majesty doesn't like to be kept waiting.'

'In here, Mistress Madge,' said Valentine, as he opened the door to the receiving chamber. He proffered a bow and backed away out of the room. Tom went in first, and Fanny stuck her head forward to see round the doorway before she reached it. It was a throne room. The floor had a narrow red carpet leading up to a dais set between the two sash windows. These were hung with rich, shot silk and were edged with heavy rope fringing. Fanny noticed they had a lot of dust on them. On every surface were candelabras and the walls were covered with Venetian looking-glasses. These reflected the light from hundreds of candles and the effect was dazzling. Fanny now understood how the tallow-chandler trade fitted in with the Molly House: all the candles were in the shape of penises.

On the step up to the dais were two tasselled cushions and towering above, sitting on a severely gilded throne, was a tall woman in a full bottomed wig, dressed as a king and wearing a golden crown. Fanny looked twice at His Majesty and was certain the crown was from Richard III and was used at the theatre. Mrs Bovel had spent three days searching for that diadem and it would be her, rather than the false monarch, who would have the head of the thief. She looked at Tom and pointed to the king's head. Tom took no notice of her. He knelt down and gestured to Fanny that she should kneel next to him.

'Your Majesty, may I present, Frances. I hope you will allow her to serve the ladies tonight. She is discreet and hard working. I shall take full responsibility for her.'

In a bad German accent, the king replied in a woman's voice, 'Vy is she here?'

'She has nowhere to go, and she is my sister. I must look after her. She will serve well,' said Tom.

'Ummm,' considered the king. The monarch stood up, told Fanny to rise and threatened her with the words, 'Or it will be off with zer head. Zu may retire now.'

The new brother and sister walked backwards, bent at the waist, until they were outside the room and Valentine had closed the door. Fanny stared at Tom with her mouth wide open.

'What was that all that about?' Fanny asked.

'It's what we do, boys are girls and girls are boys,' explained Tom.

'I see.' But she didn't.

Valentine came up to them and haughtily asked Fanny, 'What's your name, girl?'

She looked back at him deciding he was playing at superiority, although younger than she. 'Frances,' she replied stiffly. Tom picked up the animosity and decided to take a great interest in the ceiling.

Valentine looked Fanny up and down, and he obviously wasn't a bit impressed. 'You'd better come with me, I'll jolly you up a bit, and I tells you what's what. Don't touch anything, don't nick nothing, and do as I say. Follow me.'

Fanny took a deep breath and looked at Tom, who turned a blind eye to the whole conversation. She said, reluctantly, to Valentine, 'I am at your service.' She added pointedly, 'Just for tonight.'

Valentine led Fanny to a back room where the alcohol was kept, not accessible to the punters. The liquor served here was carefully accounted for and sold at inflated prices. Each customer ordered what they wanted and a record was kept, the bill being paid at the start of the next visit, or the gentleman was not allowed admittance and banned. There were several servers including Valentine and Fanny, who would replenish the guest's glasses that were never to be less than half full. Each refill was charged at a full glass rate. The profit was high, but as the service of this particular Molly House was very good, the men were happy to pay. The room next door was where the food was cooked and prepared, and it was of excellent quality. Tonight, there were capons roasting over the fire and large cuts of cold meats ready to carve. A variety of cheeses and expensive fruit, some sugared, were portioned out on plates in a row, ready to take upstairs.

'We have the best grub in Drury Lane,' Valentine boasted. 'Here, carry two plates of sweetmeats, and I'll lead you up to The Chapel. Better put a couple of these strings around your neck.' He handed Fanny some long ropes of fake pearls and spangled necklaces. Picking up a small pot containing rouge, he dipped his finger in, then rubbed it on Fanny's cheeks. 'That's better, you look happier now. I'll show you around the house, so you know where all the ladies are.'

He led Fanny in and out of the rooms that were full of men dressed as women, from milkmaids to duchesses. They called each other by their maidens names, which were given to them on the first visit to the Molly House.

'Miss Betty, you are such a tease,' said a highly made-up older gentleman, sitting in a chair wearing only a shirt. Sitting on him was a slim young man, dressed in women's stays and a wig that was seriously askew, who was feeding the older man grapes with one hand and rubbing himself with the other.

On a bed next to a marble-topped table laid with a feast of meats, was a boy sitting back against the wall whilst a corpulent man with his breeches open, sucked the boy's toes and groaned.

'Come on, girl. We got to get the service ready,' said Valentine as he climbed the stairs. On the first floor landing, Valentine opened the double doors to the front room. It was The Chapel. They entered under a bridal arch of flowers and taking the most prominent place in the centre of the room was a large bed. There were various types of costume laid out on it. In the middle of the eiderdown was a bridal gown of pink and gold and a posy of beaded flowers. Next to it, lay wedding attire for the bridegroom. Various bridesmaids gowns and a bishop's regalia of cope, mitre and crozier were placed around the edge. Valentine spoke, 'Put the plates on the marble and pour out the Canary in the glasses for the toast before the betrothal.' As Fanny was pouring the wine, behind her, she heard a familiar woman's voice speaking to her. The king had dropped the awful German accent.

'Frances, you're a sweetie and you'll look good as an angel for the happy couple. Val, go and get the Christmas wings and a white nightgown from Rosa. Pull the chair to the altar and get Frances up there with the thurible. Light the incense soon and show her how to swing it to keep it alight. The wedding takes place in half an hour. I'll get the happy couple up here to put their garb on and take them down ready for the nuptials. Schnell, schnell.'

Valentine took Fanny's hand and led her out of the Chapel. 'Come with me, girl and I'll help you with your wings.'

Whilst Fanny was becoming ethereal, the wedding party dressed and were taken downstairs to the back parlour in readiness for the bridal procession up to the chapel, where the Bishop of Drury was waiting. Valentine grabbed Fanny's arm and pulled her down the stairs from the dormitory where Rosa and the female servants slept and pushed her into the ceremonial room. He told her to jump on the chair behind the toilette table, that was now the altar, which supported two tall church candlesticks with huge wax candles in the shape of phalluses.

'I won't light them until just before they enter, as

they like to see them in all their glory and not dripping,' said Valentine. The processional music started up, the air from Handel's 'Water Music'. Although played on a single fiddle, it didn't sound too awful. However, Fanny would have preferred to hear it with the other forty-nine musicians.

Valentine had lit the incense earlier, and he handed the chain to her. 'Get swinging, girl.' Fanny coughed as the trails of sweetened smoke caught her throat. After a couple of swings, she found the rhythm and was rather excited when she heard the cheers of good wishes as the bride and groom climbed the stairs, His Majesty leading the way. The rather drunk bishop greeted them at the door, curtsied and slurred, 'As I am a justice of the peace, I shall take the service of your marriage. Take your places before me.'

'God blind me, old codger Whinyates is playing the bishop. He's in his cups.' Valentine, who was standing next to her but out of sight, proposed, 'I bet you sixpence he'll fall over before they say, "I do".'

'I don't gamble,' lied Fanny in a presumptuous way. If she did accept a wager from Valentine, she would take him for every penny.

As Valentine handed out the glasses of Canary wine to the now crowded room full of guests and bridesmaids, the king sidled out by another door next to the serving table. However, the loss of his magnificence was not dimmed as the radiance of the betrothed couple eclipsed him. The groom's face was powdered and matched the pale cream silk of his highly bejewelled coat and he wore heavy make-up with patches and a high wig with various stuffed songbirds nesting in it. His bride was even more extravagant. Her wig, taller still, was dusted white and the long length of hair fell freely down to mid-calf, cascading with feathers tied with ribbons and braids, entwined with threads of fine pearls. From a high tortoiseshell comb, a veil reminiscent of the Vestal Virgins tried in vain to soften her visage. The harshness of the rouge and lead face powder shone through, relentlessly.

'A toast to the Molly marriage,' said Valentine.

All the men replied in unison, 'The bride and groom.' And they knocked back the wine in one gulp.

Valentine was now busy refilling their glasses, while the even more drunk bishop recited the ceremony, inserting lewd comments into the known service. 'Will you, Sir Lecher.' The room cheered. 'Take, at least ten times tonight.' Another cheer. 'Mistress Bendover, on and off the nuptial bed, in any way you so desire?' The speech was long, accompanied by loud whoops of congratulations. In-between the good humoured hollering, the vows continued. 'I now pronounce you man and wife.' Mr Whinyates concluded. He bowed deeply, then crumpled to the floor. The celebrations began, with much open mouthed kissing amongst the wedding party. This was swiftly followed by serious letching, beginning with the bridesmaids joining the newly marrieds in bed and in flagrante delicto. The wedding guests returned to the main parlour, to perform various sex acts, and they continued to enjoy the party by drinking, singing bawdy songs and dancing outrageously until the sun was high in the sky.

'Ready to go home, Fanny?' It was Tom, looking pristine and puffing up the cushions.

'Yes.'

'How was it?' asked Oliver, looking very dishevelled.

'Acceptance of desire and happiness,' said Fanny,

smiling at her friends.

CHAPTER TWENTY-ONE

The First Secret

IN MRS BIG'S attic space, the few windows were opened to the warm breeze of June. The Little Troupe busied themselves packing up props and costumes for their working holiday in Cambridge, and Fanny wished she could accompany them. With Theo away, she felt apprehensive knowing all her closest friends would be out of London. They wouldn't be gone for long, but for some reason, she felt anxious.

Reaching the low door, she knocked three times. 'It's Fanny.' She waited for the bolt to be drawn. Her heart warmed when Mrs Big's smiling face greeted her. Fanny embraced this special, tiny woman, who had such wisdom and love and said, 'How I shall miss you all.'

'My dear Fanny, we shall miss you too but we must entertain, that's our life. On our return, we shall have such tales to tell. If I know the boys, they will be up to all sorts. It will take most of my time to keep them in order and out of the taverns. Now, before I forget, Fanny. Here are the keys to the garret, should you need to visit. Please take great care of them as all our most precious possessions are here. I know you will keep them safe. As an extra precaution, I have threaded them on a ribbon to wear around your neck.'

'Don't worry, Mrs B, I won't lose them. They will be returned as soon as you are home again. How is Betsy?'

'Good news, my dove, her scars are healing, and she can be moved. Letty and Samuel will be showing at the Midsummer Fair, so we are taking Betsy with us. I shall travel with her on their wagon and help to care for her. She will feel part of the troupe, and laughter is a fine medicine.' Fanny wanted to beg Mrs Big to take her too, but work was busy at her aunt's, and the theatre had a new play coming in. Mrs Bovel was all over the place sorting the costumes, and she relied on Fanny to keep her calm. The month would pass quickly, she hoped.

'I can see how busy you are, I shall take my leave of you. I hope you have fun and carry my love with you.'

'You will always have ours, Fanny. Do not worry, we shall be back in a twinkling of Mr Big's eye.'

As Mrs Big unbolted the door, it opened to reveal Jack Mann. His first words were, 'The King is dead.'

'What's the difference? He was never here when he was alive. Good riddance, that's what I say,' Mrs Big proclaimed.

Humphrey Busby was in his counting house, balancing his accounts. On the table he'd emptied out the contents of the strongbox and put all the coins in piles, relating to their denominations. Something was wrong, and it disturbed him. He was always so precise, he couldn't have made a mistake. He opened the paper deeds of the leases, freeholds and other business contracts, including any debts due to him, hoping to find coins that had accidentally found their way into the folds but no. There was only one explanation, someone was stealing from him. He rose from the chair and searched the room for the coins he had hidden in various places, many were missing. He sat down again, and as he wondered who the thief could be, his anger swelled. The only person who had access to the key was his wife. He crept into the parlour where she was stitching.

'Husband, you startled me, I did not hear you enter. Come, let me take my sewing things off the table–'

'Have you taking other things, Marie?'

'What are you speaking of, Humphrey?'

'Have you been taking things that are not yours? It is a simple question, even for your little brain.'

Madame Marie started to rise. Humphrey pushed her back down into the chair. 'Have you been taking money out of my strong box?'

'No. Why would I do such a thing?'

'I don't know, why would you steal from me when I have been so good to you?'

'Husband, I have not stolen from you.'

'There are coins missing from the box and also from secret hiding places. Only you have could have taken the key. You are a thief. I shall call for the constable and have you thrown into gaol.'

'No, husband, I swear on the blessed bible, I have not done such a thing.'

'Do not blaspheme.' Anger flushed through him. He hit her hard across the face with his clubbed hand. 'Liar, you have taken my gold.'

'Husband, no, think about it. If I was to rob you I would take the necklace I bought to the marriage, it is far more valuable. It doesn't make any sense for me to steal coins from you.'

'Are you saying I am mistaken? I am never wrong,

Marie. Except when I married you. You bewitched me, you were the devil.'

'No, husband, no.'

'I knew you were nothing more than a whore and a gambler. What a fool I was to be seduced by you. Now, you are a stone around my neck, thieving from your own husband.' He hit her again. This time the chair toppled over, tipping Madame Marie onto the floor. She knew what was coming, covering her face with her hands, she cowered into the corner of the room.

Fanny gave a few pennies to the flower seller in Fleet Street. She carried home a small posy of white roses as a small gift for her aunt. Arriving at the milliners, all was quiet. There was no sign of Kitty, who was probably with Gideon, and she sensed her uncle was out. When she heard Sous-Sous whining, she called out, 'Aunt Marie, it is me, Frances.' She followed the sound to the parlour, where her aunt was sitting on a chair at the table. Her head was in her hands and she was sobbing. 'Dear Aunt, what is distressing you so?'

'Go away, Fanny. Please go to your room.'

'I can't leave you like this. Does this have anything to do with my uncle?' Fanny dropped the roses on the floor, where they started to die.

As Madame Marie lifted her head, Fanny saw the livid bruise purpling around her right eye and the red soreness on both sides of her face.

'My god, did he do this to you? I shall kill him.'

'No, Fanny, sit down. I need to speak to you.'

'Let me get a cold compress to put against your bruising.' Fanny went to the scullery to find cold water. In the corner, on her thin bed, was Martha. She was very still and shivering, her eyes meet Fanny's. 'Martha, did you witness this attack?'

'Oh no, miss, I wouldn't do anything like that, miss, I would be too frightened to do that, miss. Please, miss, it were nothing to do with me.'

'Of course, Martha, I'm not blaming you for anything, and I understand your blindness to this violence.' Martha started to weep. 'Do not cry Martha, it's over now and something will be done to stop this happening again. I don't know what exactly, but something will change. Take my shawl, it's cold in here. Try to sleep.'

Fanny returned to her aunt and sat next to her while she cleaned up Madame Marie's battered face. 'Aunt, you must leave this man, he is dangerous.'

'Dear Frances, that is impossible. I have no money, and he would not be able to face the humiliation of his wife deserting him. It cannot be done. He does not love me and therefore finds me annoying. But I know how to become invisible to him, most of the time. Fanny, I have to tell you something of great importance. I do fear for my safety and you must know these secrets, now.'

'What is it, Aunt?'

'Anise, who raised you, was not my sister. She was my greatest friend, a good woman and we loved each other very much. After my mother and grandmother both died in the same year, my fortune changed. Anise and I travelled to this country from France. My grandmother, Hortense, had a glittering life, but after she fell from favour, her gambling debts increased and she died penniless. When I arrived in England I was poor, but because my grandmother had been known to the English court, through her connections I became a courtesan. I was the mistress of an important man, who was a member of the English aristocracy and married. I found myself with child. I was very frightened. Pierre, who you know as your grandfather, knew my family well and after the birth, he took my beautiful baby girl back to Anise, in Wiltshire, who raised her as her own.'

'But I have no sister, Aunt.'

'No, indeed not. Anise had no children.'

Fanny's mind was swirling, trying to make sense out of these facts. As the truth settled, her mouth and throat lost all moisture and the beating of her heart started to pound. She managed to find her voice. 'You mean, do you mean you are my mother?'

'Do not be angry child. I had no choice. I had no money and no future so I could not look after you. I had hoped once I married Humphrey I would be able to tell him, and he would accept you. But when I realised how cruel he was, I couldn't take you away from your safe home. Forgive me, child.' Madame Marie held onto Fanny's hands and wept out her sorrow.

'Of course I forgive you, Aunt. No, I mean, Mother?'

'Yes, Frances, I am your mother.'

Nothing made sense, and yet it all made sense.

'My dear, there is something else. Please bring me that ginger jar, on the right side of the over-mantle.'

Fanny picked up the valuable porcelain and placed it on the table. Madame Marie removed the lid and lifted the jar over her other hand. Out fell a silver neck chain with something on the end of it. 'This is yours, Frances. I had it made for you, just after your birth. Now, is the right time to give it to you.'

Fanny, still trying to take in all that Madame Marie had said, looked closely at the necklace. The chain held a strange looking ring, a gold band with engravings of what looked like triangles and on the inside was an inscription that could not be read, a jumbled succession of swirls and loops. 'What is it?' she asked.

'I cannot tell you what it is exactly, you may never need to know. Please remember these words, Fanny. "You will know when you see it."

'What does it mean?'.

'Forgive me, I cannot say. Maybe, one day it will all become clear to you. It is in the hands of God. Please, always wear it, and think of the mother who loved you from afar and try to forgive her.'

'There is nothing to forgive. My mother was the kindest of all people and she bought me up as her own, and now I find I have another mother who loves me the same way. I am truly fortunate.' Fanny wrapped her arms around her true mother, and they smiled and laughed.

'There is one more thing to tell you. In Humphrey's strongbox there is a ruby and diamond demi-parure. It is mine, given to me by my mother. It is a family piece, and I pass it on to you. It is extremely valuable, so if you should need money, you have it to sell. Make sure you get it from Humphrey if I should die. It is all I can leave you.'

Fanny had an idea. 'My dearest Mother, let us take the necklace set and sell it. We can live somewhere else, maybe out of London, far away from Busby. We could set up as milliners together.' Fanny imagined the life of independence she longed for, now that love and security was within her reach. From a situation so damaging and malignant, could happiness and contentment blossom? A new beginning. 'We simply have to get the necklace and earrings, then escape.'

'It is impossible now, my dear, as Humphrey has accused me of stealing money from the strongbox. He will never let me handle the key, ever again.'

Fanny felt guilty. The coins she had taken to give Gideon, had been partly the cause of this fight. But the coins in the box? Who else knew about the coins? Kitty. It had to be Kitty. Gideon must have told her about them. Humphrey was too besotted by Kitty to accuse her of theft.

Fanny would get Kitty to steal the demi-parure for her so she and her mother could flee. If Kitty didn't agree, Fanny would put it into Humphrey's head that Kitty had used his key.

'I shall get the jewellery, Mother.'

CHAPTER TWENTY-TWO

Fury

GIDEON WAS AGITATED. 'I need more money, Kitty. You have to take all the coins and items from the strongbox. Clean it out.'

'And what? Me, hanged at Tyburn? Oh, no. We got to get away, Gideon.' Kitty was scared.

He sighed. 'All right. Get me the gold, and we'll go.' Gideon had no intention of fulfilling his promise. Kitty had served her purpose, and sexually he was beginning to tire of her. He had Fanny in his sights now and the value of her maidenhead. Kitty was extraneous to his needs. Fanny was in love with him and would do anything he asked of her.

'Gideon, if I do this for you, will you marry me?'

'What? Kitty, be reasonable, my family would never agree to it. My father is threatening to stop my allowance, this gold will stave off that action. I can't marry you, Kitty. What a preposterous idea.'

'You promise to be my protector? Live with me and keep me?'

'Just get the gold, Kitty'.

Kitty and Humphrey were reckless, and neither

worried about his wife being in the house. Kitty ignored Madame Marie, and Humphrey hit her. The two lovers lived as man and wife, as though it was the most normal thing in the world. Madame Marie slept with Fanny in the attic, and the illicit couple shared the marital bed. However, Kitty longed for the day when she could leave this household and the deformed Humphrey Busby. But while he was in lust with her, she would take great advantage of his generosity. Each day they went shopping, and he bought her extravagant gowns and many jewels. He might as well have left his strongbox open for her, as she was costing him far more. Kitty didn't keep the gifts. She passed them on to Gideon, who was delighted.

The next day, when Humphrey was out at his lawyers, Kitty planned to rob what remained in the strongbox. She would take the stash to Gideon and be free forever from the foolish old man.

Kitty met her love in the morning and told him, she would bring all the treasure to him that night and be ready to run away with him. She returned to the milliners later than she expected, delayed by Gideon's sadistic enjoyments. The house was empty, except for Madame Marie who was in the attic bedchamber. Kitty knew Humphrey would be returning soon. She quickly took the copied key and went to the strongbox. It opened the box easily, and Kitty robbed him of the coins and snuff boxes. The demi-parure, she would keep as her own surety.

She was moving through the parlour when she heard the shop bell, it must be either Fanny or Humphrey. Kitty looked around in panic to where she could hide the gold. She saw Fanny's sewing bag lying on one of the chairs of the card table. Sous-Sous sat on top of it. She shooed the monkey off, opened the bag, dropped everything in it and placed it by the side of the chair. She turned just in time to see Fanny coming into the parlour. 'Fanny, what are you doing here?'

'I live here if you had forgotten. What are you doing? You look guilty of something. Ah, let me think? Could it be you have been stealing from Humphrey's strongbox?'

Kitty was thrown by this. 'I don't know what you can mean.' She started to turn towards the stairs. Fanny caught her wrist and faced her.

'I won't say anything to Humphrey if you will steal the necklace for me. I want it to pay for my aunt and me to go away. Once we are gone, you can have Humphrey and all his wealth to yourself.'

Kitty wasn't expecting this, but always being someone, open to any suggestion, she weighed up what Fanny proposed. The shop door bell jingled again, and the young women looked at each other and said under their breaths, 'Humphrey.'

With his usual lack of grace, Humphrey Busby strode straight pass Fanny without acknowledgement and told Kitty to go upstairs with him. She looked back over her shoulder towards Fanny, as though considering which decision would be in her own interest.

Fanny climbed the stairs and passing the first-floor bedchamber, she heard the unrelenting noise of passion without love. When she reached the attic room, she could see Madame Marie also had been enduring this demeaning performance.

'Cards, Mother?

'What an excellent idea. It is clear we shall not be disturbed for a while.'

The two women tiptoed down to the parlour. Fanny sat down in her usual chair, next to her sewing bag, and placed her card box on the table. They started to gamble.

Madame Marie was playing well. Never losing the touch of an excellent card sharper, she explained to Fanny the finer points of how to improve her cheating.

Humphrey was dressed to dine out and as he descended the staircase, the voices of the two women playing cards carried to his ears. He paused at the foot of the stairs to listen to what they were saying. 'If you are going to cheat, Fanny, you must do it in such a way that your charm and refined tenderness, will blind the other players to your intention.'

Humphrey flared up. He was beside himself with anger, it rose in him like a hot eruption of lava. He believed Madame Marie had used this feminine manipulation to entrap him into marriage, and now he wanted rid of her so he could be with Kitty. That's all he craved for, all he cared about: Kitty. He was furious with hatred and rage.

As he roared into the parlour, Madame Marie and Fanny froze. They reeled from his seething madness. 'Gambling. Gambling in my house. You are a sinful, wicked whore.'

Fanny swept the cards off the table and into her sewing bag. She noticed it was heavy. Humphrey continued shrieking, this time at Fanny. 'Give me those cards. You will go to hell for what you have done to me: bringing sin into my God-fearing house.'

This was too much for Fanny. She pushed her chair back, put her sewing bag on the table and shouted back. 'Sin? You are the one who bought sin into this house. You beat your wife and debauch a girl, who is young enough to be your daughter. How dare you speak of God, when you are the devil who worships only himself and his money.'

Fanny stepped around to the front of the table to confront him. Humphrey grabbed at the bag. 'Let me have those evil cards.' Fanny clasped the bag to her chest and took a step forward in defiance. A mistake. She was too close to him. He was threatened. With all his weight, he trapped her between himself and the table. He opened the bag to take out the cards but withdrew the necklace. 'What's this?' Fanny's mouth dropped as he lay it on the table. He put his hand in again to find the snuff boxes, and while staring at Fanny with malevolence, he brought out a handful of sovereigns. His rage was incandescent.

'I didn't take those. I didn't steal anything,' Fanny cried.

Humphrey went berserk. 'Liar, thief. You will hang for this.' He put his strong, right hand around her neck and started to squeeze.

No-one noticed Kitty enter the room. It took her a moment to take in what was happening, as she stood behind Humphrey.

Fanny started to choke and was desperate for air as he tried to strangle her. Madame Marie screamed in a primaeval way and flew at him, causing him to release his hold on Fanny. She fought him to the ground. On his back, Humphrey was disadvantaged. He shuffled towards the fire grate, trying to fling off this irritating mouse who had now become a lioness. Madame Marie pummelled and scratched ferociously whilst Humphrey flayed about, trying to grasp anything he could to defend himself with. His right hand felt something cold and hard. It fitted well into his palm, as his fingers wrapped around it. He raised the iron poker, and brought it down onto Madame Marie's head numerous times, until she stopped struggling and fell back, lifeless.

Fanny screamed, 'Mother, no!' She stared at Humphrey with horror and intense loathing, then hurled herself at him. But he managed to seize her again around the throat, while he punched her head with his clubbed hand. He hit her twice before a fast-moving shadow jumped at him. Sous-Sous with claws bared, scratched him from forehead to jaw, nearly taking his eyes out. Whilst Humphrey screamed in agony, blinded by the flood of blood, Kitty ran to the wooden corner cupboard and took out the pistol, already primed. Humphrey felt his way back towards Fanny and took her by the neck again.

Kitty pointed the gun at him and said firmly and calmly, 'Let her go, Humphrey.'

He turned to Kitty and through the scarlet veil, he saw the gun trembling in her hands. The smile he adored became ugly and full of contempt. 'You little whore.'

'Yes, that's me. Let her go, Humpy.' Her disdain was naked. She smiled at him. 'Or, there will be a big bang.'

He knew that even if she aimed to maim she probably would kill him, the firing range being too close to survive. He could try to grab the pistol, but knew Kitty would fire before he reached her. He released Fanny, put his hands up and whispered, 'You are all bitches.'

Never once taking her eyes off Humphrey, Kitty said to Fanny, 'Put the things back in the bag and get out of here.' Fanny, although in shock, did what she was told. She looked around for Sous-Sous who was hiding behind one of the ginger jars on the over mantle. She called the little monkey. 'Sous-Sous, come.' Fanny could no longer see the necklace,but assumed she had already put it in the bag.

She took a last look at her uncle and at her dear mother, lying dead on the floor. As she ran to the shop door, Sous-Sous jumped onto her shoulder. Standing behind Kitty, the two of them moved backwards towards the door.

'I shall shoot you if I have to, be in no doubt. I hate you, Humphrey Busby. You are a cruel and lascivious old man and you disgust me. I just wanted your money. I'm going to back out of here and I shall keep the pistol on you, so stay where you are. Don't think you can stop me.'

Humphrey couldn't see anything through the red waterfall from his eyes, but he did hear the shop bell jingle.

Mario the printer listened to the violent argument and the screams coming from the milliners. He was worried and ran next door to Charles the bookseller.

'Charles, there is a dreadful fight going on at Mr and Mrs Busby's. I am concerned and think we should intervene.'

'That awful man is always fighting with his wife, it will pass.'

'No, Charles, this is serious–' Before he could say any more, they saw Fanny and Kitty run past their windows followed by a shout of, 'Murder. Thief. Murder.' Mario and Charles rushed outside and watched the women flee through the Inner Temple gate onto Fleet Street. The men rushed into the milliners whilst summoning the constable, who heard the cry and immediately hurried to join them.

They opened the shop door and were shocked by

what they saw. Busby was standing in the middle of the room covered with blood. His shirt and coat were saturated as it poured from his eyes. On the floor was Madame Marie, with her skull caved in. Busby held out his hands saying, 'My dear wife has been murdered by that evil girl, Frances, and her accomplice Katherine has robbed me of my gold and jewels. Dear God, catch them. Murder, murder…' He dropped to his knees, sobbing and muttering like a mad man.

In this confused murder scene, the constable appeared and formally asked Humphrey, 'Who has committed this heinous crime?'

Humphrey, seething with hate said, 'Frances Tomlinson murdered my wife by hitting her with a fire poker. She had tried to stop the accomplice, Katherine Woodford, from stealing my gold. When I intervened, the young bitch tried to scratch my eyes out.'

Quietly, from the dark shadows came a thin figure who is normally invisible to others: the maid of all work. Martha called out in a strong voice, 'It ain't her, it were him what done it, I was here. I heard it all. He knocks the nice French lady about, often like. I can hear him. Slapping and beating her until she falls, bang on the floor. I keeps me nose out of it, I don't want no trouble. But he did it all right. She's only little and he hit her hard with the poker. I saw it with me own eyes. Fanny wouldn't hurt a fly. She's lovely, she is.'

Humphrey's rage broke through again, and he reached for the poker to strike Martha, only to realise all eyes were upon him. He froze and spat out, 'Shut up you stupid girl, don't you know your place. It's all lies.'

'No, it ain't. I'd swear it on the bible. It was him

what did it. He killed her.'

CHAPTER TWENTY-THREE

The Escape

THE WOMEN RAN straight over Fleet Street and headed towards Lincoln's Inn. Fanny was leading Kitty, as she knew her way around the small squares and alleys, having discovered the layout of the Inn with Theo. Sous-sous chose his own path, either scampering beside Fanny or jumping high over buildings, whichever was the most direct route. They ran for their lives. Citizens on the streets heard the hue and cry and joined the posse who chased the female murderer and robber. Fanny now understood how a fox or deer must feel when the hounds picked up the scent: the intense fear caused by the increasing bay of the pursuing hunters. Both the girls were running out of breath and needed some respite, they had to find somewhere to hide. Fanny remembered the Inn's chapel. She caught Kitty's hand and swerved under the arches to drag her up the stairs into the place of worship. Halfway down the aisle, Fanny opened one of box doors and pulled Kitty in. Sous-Sous surfed over the tops of the pews and joined them. They all hid under the wooden bench and listened. If they were caught, there was no escape. Maybe, they could plead sanctuary but Fanny doubted it. Kitty held the gun close to her, knowing it was ready and primed. They kept still and silent, only the heaving of their lungs would give them away. Their senses were screamingly alert, and they listened to the men congregating under the arches beneath them. Their leader shouted above the rabble.

'They will either try to escape into the narrow courts around Holborn, where it's easier for them to disappear or run further into the villain's hide-out of Field Lane. Those areas give more cover than to go west onto the open Lincoln's Inn Fields. They will head towards Shoe Lane. Follow me, men.' The clamour started up again and the women heard the mob running towards the gate onto Chancery Lane.

'How could they not think we may be above them?' Fanny whispered.

'Pray for their stupidity,' answered Kitty.

'Let us stay here a while until all is completely quiet then we shall walk out slowly as if we have nothing to hide. You will have to leave the gun, Kitty, it will give us away.'

'No, we may need this where we're going. I'll find something to hide it in.' She slowly raised her head above the pew and when certain there was no-one around, she looked for something to use. 'There is an alms basket for food, I'll get it.'

'Be careful, Kitty. Be as quite as you can, just in case someone is listening for us.'

Kitty lifted the latch and tiptoed down the aisle to the altar steps, where the basket sat. Bending down, she carefully emptied it of the food whilst noticing it was lined with a cloth. On her way back, she took some flowers from the ewer at the foot of the lectern. Once safely returned to her position on the floor, she placed the weapon in the basket and covered it with the linen, placing the flowers on top. It was a perfect prop. Anyone would think they were returning from the market or about to visit friends.

'A bit different to the last time we were at church, eh, Fanny?'

Despite their dangerous circumstances or maybe through nerves, Fanny burst out laughing. Kitty joined in but put her finger to her lips to try to shush her.

They waited in the chapel for about half an hour, it seemed forever. Fanny took this opportunity to thank Kitty. 'You saved my life. I shall never forget that, despite our differences. You needn't have put yourself in such danger. You were brave and I thank you. If there comes a time for me to repay you, remember, I shall be by your side.' The women embraced.

In this intimate moment, Kitty asked, 'You called out "mother" when Madame Marie fell. Why was that?'

Fanny wondered how to answer her. She decided it would be too complicated to explain what had been confessed. Better to keep things as they were. 'I felt a void opening up within me, the same as when my mother died. I just called out, trying to heal the great loss I was suffering from the death of my dearest aunt.'

'I'm so sorry, Fanny. You find it so easy to love and be loved. I find it too difficult.'

A door opened and closed at the back of the chapel with a loud bang. Adrenaline shot through them both, and Fanny said to Kitty, 'On your knees and start praying.'

'That won't be too hard to do.'

It was another poor woman who came to the chapel

for prayer. She past them in the pew, knelt at the altar and prayed very quietly to the Virgin Mary.

'Let's go,' said Fanny.

They crept up the aisle with their heads bowed, opened the door with no sound and descended the stone staircase. At the bottom, Sous-Sous jumped into the basket and hid under the cloth. They took a quick look around and felt safe, seeing only men of the law speaking earnestly to each other and ordinary people going about their business. No one would notice two women ambling over Lincoln's Inn fields, busy gossiping to each other.

'Where are we going, Kitty?'

'The only place we can go, the tenements of St Giles. First, we have to visit Covent Garden market.'

As they crossed Drury Lane, a man shouted, 'Frances Tomlinson, stop.'

The women raced down Russell Street and Kitty yanked Fanny into the side alley of the Fleece Tavern. 'Stand against the wall, Fanny, and grab the first man that comes along and offer him sex.'

'What?'

'Do what I do,' Kitty instructed. Fanny's heart fell. She had no alternative. In the distance, were three men running towards them. They would catch them hiding in the alley.

'Sous-Sous, up.' At Fanny's command, the monkey jumped high, onto the tavern's sign. She knew he would fly at anyone who attacked her. The movement caught the attention of two other men who saw the attractive women lifting their petticoats. Kitty beckoned to them with her index finger. As they came across, Kitty wasted no time. 'Hello pretty man, it will only be a shilling for one such as yourself. Here let me ease your desire. My friend will give service to the other gentlemen.' She quickly undid his breeches and took hold of his penis. More importantly, she nuzzled her face into his chest so she would not be recognised. Fanny copied all her actions and was thankful for the experience of quick changes of breeches in the wings, but she was dreading the main act, what was she meant to do? She remembered the Molly house, and it all became crystal clear.

The noise of men running past the alley kept the both of them busy, but as soon as the danger had passed they removed their hands from the men's half erect phalluses and ran, much to the consternation of the unfulfilled gentlemen.

As they headed for the market in the Piazza, Fanny asked, 'You do have the gun, don't you, Kitty?'

'A man's weapon is never too far away from me, Fanny. Slow down, let us meander and compose ourselves under the colonnade.'

Fanny called Sous-Sous and tapped her shoulder, he jumped up and enjoyed the view of the busy square.

They made their way over to the stalls and trolleys of the costermongers and approached a man selling potatoes and vegetables. Kitty knew him, and she hoped the news of the murder at the milliners hadn't reached him yet.

'Kittycat, how are you? Don't see much of you around the market these days. Whatcha want? 'Cos it's always something you want when to talk to old Joe.'

'Joe, you are such a gentleman. I want to ask you, how you are?'

'Nah you don't, you want something. Spit it out, Kittycat.'

'I want two large potato sacks.'

'That'll cost ya.'

'No, I want two empty sacks.'

'Watcha got to give me, then?'

'I'll give you a quick squeeze, like those hoity-toity ladies do to your tomatoes.'

'How you know that?' They both laughed. Joe bent down and picked up two long hessian sacks from under his cart and gave them to Kitty. 'You owe me, Kittycat.'

'I won't forget.'

'How's that Da of yours? Still robbing with his cups? Serve them right if they fall for that old trick. Off you trot now, I've got toms to sell, and I see a St James's lady wanting a squeeze of them.'

The girls went on their way towards St Giles's tenements, carrying two empty sacks and a gun.

If Fanny thought Field Lane was a collection of filthy slums, St Giles was far worse. She had never seen such poverty. The people who lived in these vermin-ridden hovels were so dirty, they looked like chimney sweep boys. There was no colour, everything was brown, black or grey, even the people's eyes. It was squalor in it most raw form.

Kitty didn't seem to notice the deformed beggars or the children crying through hunger. She was blind to the mothers, catching the rags of others and pleading for victuals of any kind. The stench was overpowering from the waste tipped out of the windows of the toppling lodgings. Fanny couldn't stay here, she knew she wouldn't be able to bear it. She had the key to the garret, how clean Mrs Big kept it, like a palace compared to this hell. She would go there and hide. But she remembered the man in the posse saying, the fugitives would flee to Holborn area and particularly Field Lane. She couldn't put her friends in any danger. She would have to stay with Kitty, in this vile place.

They wound their way deeper and deeper into the labyrinth of atrocious deprivation and with every step, the daylight diminished and the pathways became narrower and darker. The lane was so confined by the lodgings either side that only one person could walk along it. If another approached from the opposite direction, the two foul-smelling bodies would have to ease past one another, contaminating each with new reeking odours, fleas and lice.

'Here we are,' Kitty said as she reached the doorless threshold of a crooked house. 'Hold on to your bag and don't put it down.' There were no locks on these doors, as none of the inhabitants had anything of value to steal. On the first floor hung a battered door with a pair of dead rats nailed to it. Kitty kicked it open with her boot. The room was dark, lit by one small window that was so filthy, the sun had given up trying to penetrate it.

'Hello, Da. It's Kittycat.'

In the corner, playing with orphaned baby rats, was a man in rags and a battered tricorn hat. He sat eating a chunk of dry, mouldy bread. He sucked it more than bit it, having only two black teeth left in his mouth. Fanny shuddered.

'Who's this?' he asked, pointing at Fanny.

'It's a friend of mine. Can we stay a while?'

'What you done?'

'Nuffink. Do I have to have done something wrong to see me own father?'

'Yes, you do.'

Fanny was confused and asked Kitty, 'Is this your father?'

Kitty replied, 'Unfortunately, yes.'

'You said your parents were dead? Killed by native Indians in the Americas?'

'Yes, that was good, wasn't it? Fanny, you got to stop believing any bleedin' fairy tale someone might tell you. Da, can we stay a while?'

'If you pay your way, girl.' He picked between his two teeth with a sharp knife.

Kitty held up one of the sacks and took her own knife, out from her stocking garter, and cut the hessian in three places. She threw it at Fanny and said, 'If you don't want your clothes eaten and pissed on by the rats, take them off and hang them over the pole, you can keep your shift on 'cos we wash them once a week.' She pointed up to the rafters where hooks and rails were suspended.

'Kitty, what shall I wear?'

'The sack.'

There was a partition in the room and Fanny took refuge behind it, out of sight of Da. She removed her mantua and put the sack over her head. She could no longer hold it in, she shivered violently and burst into tears.

'You all right?' asked Kitty as she came across the room and sat next to Fanny. 'It's the shock coming out, you'll be fine. Kitty's here.' She put her arms around Fanny. 'Don't you worry. Kitty won't leave you.'

Somehow, Fanny managed to sleep through the night, resting her head on her sewing bag, using it as a pillow and for safety. When she first awoke, because of the lack of light, she believed it was still night and she was alone. But out of the darkness, close to her face, a woman spoke in a strong Irish accent.

'Ah, there she be. We all been tiptoeing around, not to disturb you. Only this once mind, you have to work your shift and bring the pennies in. Kitty be back soon. She's a good girl that one, wish I were her real Ma. But

I'd be not married to any man, oh no. The gentlemen all love me, but I've promised myself to Thomas Jackson. I am his mistress and he keeps me in the best luxury and gives me fine clothes,' she said whilst twirling around showing off her cluster of dirty rags, as though it were the most expensive gown imaginable. Fanny wasn't sure if she was being ironic or deluded. 'My name is Kathleen. My friends call me Kathleen Garrett, so mind you do. Now, you'll be wanting a nice cup of tea, my brother brings it over from Dublin for me: the most delicious tea you'll ever drink, nectar of the gods. Sit up, me dear.' Kathleen Garrett helped Fanny rise and at the same time, without Fanny realising, she also helped herself to the sewing bag. Fanny shot up and grabbed it back.

'Give it back. It's mine. Don't touch it. Ever,' she warned.

'All right, all right, calm down. Just trying to help.' The grimy woman tilted her head and arched one eyebrow. Kathleen Garrett looked very untrustworthy. 'What you got in there? Let your friend take a look.' She tried to seize the bag again. Fanny held on to it tightly and for a moment they see-sawed back and fro, each wanting to possess it.

Fanny won the tussle and again warned this strange Irish woman, 'Don't you dare touch it again.' She looked around in panic realising Sous-sous was nowhere to be seen, 'Where's my monkey?'

'What?'

'My pet monkey, where is he?'

'Oh, him. Our Kitty has him, he followed her out.'

'Where is Kitty?'

'She'll be back soon. I'll get you that cup of tea.'

'Thank you,' said Fanny.

The tea, of course, never arrived. Fanny waited

nervously for Kitty's return. She wondered if she had stolen Sous-Sous and left her in this godforsaken place to rot with the vermin, the only company being a woman who could be mad. Fanny had to find a way to escape from this nightmare, but how could she when she was wanted for murder.

The door opened and Sous-Sous danced across the floor and onto Fanny's lap. He seemed quite happy and Fanny calmed down a bit.

Kitty came in carrying the basket from the chapel, it was full of food. 'Hello, Fanny. Here, Kathleen Garrett, take this, it's clean bread and some cold meat and beer.'

'Where you get the money for them, girl?' asked Kathleen.

'None of your business, keep your nose out and cut up the food, so we can eat. Where's Da?'

'At his work.'

Kitty sat next to Fanny who whispered to her, 'Where did you get the money, Kitty?'

'Where you think? A sovereign comes in handy to buy food.'

'From my bag? How did you do that? I was lying on it all night.'

'Fanny, you are going to have to learn fast. I come from a long family of divers, we pick pockets. Don't tell me no one's tried to thieve from you, this morning?' She looked quizzically at Fanny.

It took a moment. 'Yes, Kathleen tried to take my bag.'

'The whole bleedin' bag, we'd never see her again. With the money from them fenced goods, she'd really have the jewels and gowns that she thinks she has.'

'I'm sorry Kitty, she was clever and quick. But I held it fast, and she didn't look inside.'

'She's good that woman, that's what attracted Da to her, but he's better than she is. If you ask him nicely, he'll maybe teach you how to pick pockets and locks … if you give him a bit of advice on the cards?'

'I don't know, Kitty. My mind is a blur at the moment. Let me settle and get used to what is happening.'

'Food,' called Kathleen.

'A word of warning. Don't call her just Kathleen, always Kathleen Garrett. She takes awful bad against it. Dunno why. Best to play safe. She plays innocent, but she's got a temper on her, that one.'

'Is this yours, Fanny?' Kathleen asked and she handed over Mrs Big's garret keys. Instantly, Fanny put her hand to her neck, the keys had been taken but her ring was safe.

CHAPTER TWENTY-FOUR

New Skills

DA RETURNED HOME wearing a big, loose coat and like a magician, conjuring up everything one could imagine: silk handkerchiefs, watches, lace, wigs, stays, a small piece of pork and even a cooking pot. Fanny had to admit his skill was pretty impressive, and she was a little in awe. He dropped the pork into Kathleen Garrett's cradling hands and said, 'Get that knuckle in the pot and put it on the fire, my precious. After we've eaten, I'll take you to the tavern.'

'You treat me like a princess, Thomas.' Kathleen pressed her voluptuous breasts into his face and said intimately, 'And when I get you home, I'll take a close look at your crown jewels.' Da walloped her backside.

Once the lovers left their lodgings, Kitty poured Fanny a small beer, whilst she opened a bottle of gin. With no chance of being overheard by Kathleen Garrett, Kitty asked Fanny, 'Where did you hide the necklace.'

'Nowhere, it's in the bag,' Fanny replied.

'No it a'int, I'd of felt it. Where did you put it, Fanny? Don't mess with me.'

'Kitty, I swear it was in the bag. I could ask you the

same thing, as I know you had your hand in it this morning.'

Their eyes locked and each waited for the other to back down. As they were both telling the truth, neither did so.

After a minute or two, the anger subsided, and they had time to think about what could have happened to the ruby and diamond necklace. The dangerous moment passed and Fanny said, 'Kitty, I wouldn't take the necklace from you, and I don't believe you would do that to me, either. It must have slipped out of my bag when we were running away or when we were sheltering in the chapel. If it was left in the pew, hopefully, it will be sold, raising alms for the poor of the parish.'

'I can't believe what you are saying? Are you really that good?' Kitty threw her hands up in the air. 'You got to change the way you think, Fanny, if you are going to survive this kind of life.'

'I know, I know. What are we going to do with the gold?'

'I promised it to Gideon.'

'Why?' asked Fanny.

'I have to tell you the truth. He's not my uncle.'

'Who is he?'

'I'm a whore, a good one, but business can be up and down if you get my meaning. When I met Gideon, I was about to be thrown out of my lodgings, and I didn't want to come back here. Gideon helped me, by getting me into the Busby's home. We both had to lie. He was very good to me, Fanny, I'd do anything for him. He's a gambler, not a good one. He has great losses and he's about to be disowned by his family unless he can pay his debts. I had to help him. I stole from Humphrey. I have to give the gold to Gideon,

Fanny, I have to.' Fanny looked at Kitty and could see her devotion to Gideon, but she had no idea what the relationship was really about.

'Take the gold, as I too, want to help Gideon. What he did for you was the act of a true gentleman. We must both do what we can to help him. Go tonight and explain what happened. Tell him, I shall find money to send to him. What about the necklace? Surely, he was relying on its value.'

Kitty hesitated, but only for a moment. 'I only went to the box once, I didn't know it was in there, so neither did he.'

Kitty put her hand in her pocket and felt the earrings.

That night Kitty met Gideon. After she explained what had passed at the milliners, he held her firmly and said, 'Don't mention my name, Kitty, whatever happens.'

'I won't. I love you. Shall we go away together now?'

Gideon looked closely at the items and coins that Kitty has brought to him. 'No, Kitty, the value of this stuff is not enough, we need much more. Fanny is our only chance, her virginity can be worth a great deal of money. Go back and protect her. She must not find out that no prosecutions are being brought against her, or that Humphrey Busby has been charged with murder.'

'Gideon, she is a good person, I don't want to use her in such a way. She has nothing now and is living in poverty. I don't think she has the strength to survive such a hard life. The foolish girl says she will find you money to help you settle what you owe, and she wants to see you again.'

'Good, excellent. Now, go home and we shall meet

again next week. Bring me money, Kitty.' He held her by the shoulders and lied, 'Don't forget to stay hidden, you are still wanted for robbery and that's a hanging offence.'

Every day Fanny woke up a little more depressed. Her world was shrinking, and she was trapped in this hateful den of thieves and robbers. Having no control over her choices, she had no escape from her confined existence. Kitty roamed the streets of London in the evenings looking for trade, and Fanny spent most of her time in the slum with mad Kathleen Garrett and the unpredictable, but strangely fascinating, Da.

An unexpected relationship grew between Fanny and Da. It started when Kitty suggested they play cards together. Da was a good player, Fanny was impressed by the way he counted the cards and used sleight of hand. He was as proficient as Fanny. Like a sharp-eyed blue jay, she watched him to find his weaknesses. She let him win until she knew how he did it.

'You got to work harder than that, my girl. I'll take you for all you got,' said Da, showing his two black teeth.

'Give me a chance, Da.' She looked at Sous-Sous and nodded her head. Immediately, the monkey found a high perch directly behind Da. When play started, Sous-Sous read the cards and made noises or scratched his head and limbs, in the secret language Madame Marie and Fanny had taught him. She won every hand, but not too many for Da to work out what was happening.

'What you up to, you little devil. I knows you're cheating but, I can't work out how.'

'That's the point, isn't it, Da?'

'You're good. You could rake in a fair bit. I'll have to watch you or you'll be leaving me behind.'

Leaving Da behind. This was the answer. She realised this gambling system was the way out of this hideous life.

'Da, would you show me how to win at dice, and ball and cup?' It was worth asking, although Fanny knew cheats never gave away their secrets. She enticed him, 'We could work the streets together and double our takings.'

Da moistened his lips, she knew he wouldn't be able to resist this temptation. 'Alright. I go and get them.'

He taught Fanny both gambling tricks and showed her how to mislead and deceive. His precious Kathleen would file down the dice, to weight them, allowing them to settle on certain numbers. Fanny knew she had the ability to palm one loaded dice for a genuine one when required.

After a few sessions, Da granted Fanny his highest accolade. 'You, my dear are one of the best. I shall take you out tomorrow with my barrow, and you can be my lookout.' Fanny tilted her head, not willing to accept this position. Da gave in. 'Alright, you win. You can be my partner.' He rubbed his hands together, thinking of promised riches. 'What a team we shall be.' And they were. Fanny worked hard, copying Da's patter and method of working. He was generous with his guidance and when Fanny asked him why he was helping her, he answered, 'I had hoped Kittycat would follow in the tradition of the family profession but sadly, no. She likes a more relaxing position and can't get out of bed until eleven. She's back in one, by noon.'

Fanny divided her share of her income into quarters. One, to pay her master, Da. Another to pay for her keep and the third, to give to Kitty to take to Gideon. The final forth was for herself. It was a meagre sum, but it was a start.

When Da was sure Fanny was secure in her crimes, he let her go out alone, using his barrow. Danger was everywhere. Firstly, someone could recognise her as a wanted murderer and secondly, she could be arrested for gambling.

Da warned Fanny to be careful and not to take risks. To look more like a legitimate coster, she needed a full barrow. He suggested that Fanny persuade people to wager their fruit and vegetables first, before retiring to a discreet area to gamble money. Soon, she would be overflowing with produce, which she could sell throughout the day.

Fanny realised she would have to take breaks from this illegal work, or the chances of being caught would become too high. She could be followed and her pitches remembered. She needed a change of clothes and a disguise. She also wondered what else she could do to make money. The answer came to her as if Mrs Big were whispering in her ear, "You are a performing Indian princess, my dove."

Fanny kept to the shadows as she made her way to Field Lane. As she climbed the rickety staircase to Mr and Mrs Big's garret, she had a sense of coming home, and a feeling of wellbeing flooded over her.

She took the keys from around her neck and unlocked the chains and door bolts. The familiar smell of the room and the atmosphere of happiness nearly overwhelmed her, she wanted this life back.

She closed the door and looked around. The ropes the acrobats used for practise were hanging motionless from the rafters, and everything else was clean and tidy, in its place or packed away. Against the far wall was a mountain of boxes and bundles containing props and costumes, all with written lists of their contents. She dragged over the only table in the room and climbed up on it to reach the rafters, where she started to read where the items would be found. She remembered there was something unusual about the box that held the Indian gown, but she couldn't see the image in her mind's eye. Fanny moved the table back out of the way, to get to the bottom row of sturdy skips and chests. There it was, in the middle of the row, how had she forgotten? It was a paupers coffin and across the long side, were written the words: DEAD ANIMALS.

It took her a while to dismantle the wall of boxes and she was careful to note how to replace them in exactly the same order. When the coffin was accessible, she saw that a heavy chain had been wrapped around it, secured by a strong lock. She wondered why someone had gone to such trouble to protect dead animals and a dancing costume. Maybe the carcasses were new and rank, and therefore dangerous to touch until they desiccated. If that was the case, the costume would have been removed and Fanny would never find it.

She opened another small box in which Mrs Big had stored the hoop earrings. It was full of paste jewellery. What she was looking for, was two long hat pins.

'Exactly what I need,' exclaimed Fanny as she picked a pair up, bending one over at right angles to make a tension wrench. Da had taught her how to use these simple tools, to pick a lock.

The lock released with ease, and she removed the chain. Once the lid was off, she saw a pile of old sacking. All she could smell was dust and leather.

Fanny took out the hessian, reminding her of the sack she wore at Da's, to reveal the Indian dancer's gown. It was just as beautiful as she remembered. It was always a little big for her, but now it would fit her perfectly. She lifted the patchwork of velvet out of the box and smiled at the tinkling of the tiny brass bells. Fanny held the gown to her body and spun around. It made her happy. She wanted to find the bangles and belt, they must have slipped down under the other costumes. She rummaged through the layers of fabric and threw a brightly coloured scarf on the floor, next to the gown. She was relieved she didn't come across any dead animals. Halfway down was a carefully folded blanket, and as she lifted it out, she saw a collection of leather bags, and scattered amongst them were the bangles. She reached down to move a saddlebag out of the way, but it was too heavy to lift. Fanny could not deny her curiosity. She untied the thong and opened the flap to see what was inside. She was so shocked, she reeled back. It was full of gold. Never in her imagination had she seen this amount of gold: coins, watches, precious jewellery, even bars of gold. And this was only one of the bags. She blinked several times checking she was not dreaming and found she was riveted to the spot. What was this huge amount of treasure doing in the Big's garret?

Fanny felt her chest drumming and she became fearful, not because someone may catch her, but because she had found it. It was obviously well hidden, and now it looked as though someone had come to find it. She didn't know what to do and felt panic rising in her. Quickly retying the leather laces, she put the sacking back. She wrapped the chain around the coffin, snapped the padlock closed and replaced the boxes and bundles, as they were. She wanted to get out of the garret as fast as possible. She started to head towards the door, and stopped, remembering the Indian dancer's gown. It was still on the floor, she had forgotten to put it back. What should she do? It would take a long time to dismantle the wooden mountain again, and what if one of the troupe returned to London, early? No, she had to go, now. She swept the gown off the floor with the scarf and wrapped them in her shawl. Locking the door behind her, she ran as fast as she could, down the stairs and out into Field Lane. She may have taken the gown, but she had stolen something far more valuable: the secret of the gold.

CHAPTER TWENTY-FIVE

St Giles

FANNY RAN ALL the way along High Holborn back to St Giles. She hoped she would be alone, to think about what she'd found and what she should do. At some point, Mrs Big would discover the Indian gown was missing and would know Fanny was the only person who could have taken it. She feared Mrs Big would never trust her again and disown her. Fanny decided to avoid the troupe on their return to London.

As soon as Fanny opened the door, Kathleen Garrett was upon her. 'You'll be wanting a nice cup of tea, Fanny.' This woman seemed to materialise out of thin air.

'Thank you, Kathleen Garrett, that would be most welcome.'

'Sit yourself down. What you got wrapped in that shawl?' The woman in rags started to pick at the wool, like a bird. Fanny knew nothing would stop Kathleen Garrett eroding the lies that Fanny could offer in explanation, so she unfolded the shawl to reveal the gown. Screeching with delight and snuggling her face into the soft folds, this childlike being, who existed one degree beyond others reality, asked, 'For me? For

Kathleen Garrett?'

'Kathleen Garret, it cannot be yours as I need to wear it to beg and sing ballads, and it is too small for you. When I have enough money, I shall make you a gown just like it,' promised Fanny.

'No, it's mine.'

'The gown I make for you will be even more beautiful. I shall use emerald green and light blue velvet, the colours of the grass and sky of your home country. Would you like that, Kathleen Garrett?'

She considered this with one eye closed and her tongue in her cheek, wondering if she could believe Fanny. When?' she asked.

'I do not know, but you have my word I shall sew you a gown like this. You have to trust me.'

Kathleen had never trusted anyone in her life, and she wasn't even sure what the word meant. 'Let us spit in our palms and shake hands.' They sealed the deal.

In the afternoon, Fanny decided to go out and sing for money. The city would be full of people, a good time to perform on the street corners, or if lucky, on a table in a tavern. She dressed in the Indian princesses gown and tied the scarf at the back of her head like a gipsy.

'Good-bye, Kathleen Garrett. I shall return tonight.' The woman took no notice, she'd slipped through to another world, dancing around with her imagined lover in her arms.

Well disguised, Fanny felt confident she wouldn't be recognised, so ventured towards busy Covent Garden. This area was the most dangerous for her. The community knew her. She relied on her belief they would not give her up, as they themselves had crossed the law.

'Well, Sous-Sous, let's see what happens. I'm not

sure of my voice or my dancing, but I have no choice. I need money. I have to beg.'

She settled herself outside the coffee shop on the corner of Russell and Bow streets.

'Let us make our pitch here Sous-Sous. Ladies and gentlemen will pass on their way to the theatre, and I hope they will be in generous humour. This is my stage now. I shall make the best of it.'

She began dancing, making the bells tinkle. Once the movement caught the eye of passers-by, she started to sing a ballad about a fair maid of Islington. Soon, she had a small crowd around her, and they dropped money into the little purse the monkey held up. When heavy, Fanny emptied the coins into her pocket. As she started another song, she saw Tom Mercutio approach. She knew it was too late to run as it would attract attention, so she held her nerve and continued her act. Finishing to applause, she picked the coins up from the ground. As she kept her head down, Tom came up to her and said, 'You have a good voice, have you worked on the stage?' He hadn't recognised her. Fanny shook her head. 'Well, you should.' He turned away towards the theatre. She was safe but sad. She missed her friendship with Tom.

On her way back to St Giles, Fanny found a hidden archway where she counted her earnings. For an afternoon's work it was good, but not as much as gambling could make. Either way, her cut was always little. From the street winnings she had to deduct Da's portion and from the gilded salons of St James's, she paid Gideon a percentage. Fanny would never save enough to leave the tenement. She needed to learn more devious tricks.

Kitty was in high spirits when Fanny arrived back,

partly due to the amount of gin she had drunk.

'Fanny, I have been to see Mother Stroker, and she wants me to visit her bagnio every evening, as she believes me to be a great talent. Not only as a whore but as a singer. She will allow me to sing to the company throughout the night. Soon, my name shall be on theatre bills, all over London.'

Fanny had listened to Kitty's voice and it wasn't pleasing. Mother Stroker had used the promise of performing as bait to get Kitty into her clutches.

'Do you really want to work in a brothel, Kitty?'

'How dare you ask that, you are not so high and mighty yourself now, are you, Fanny? Begging on the streets? Whereas I shall wear new clothes of the latest fashion.'

'How shall you get these gowns?' asked Fanny.

'Mother Stroker has picked out the best for me, and I shall repay her back from my earnings.'

'And how much will you have to repay her?'

'I shall pay her back very quickly, using my great flair with gentlemen.'

Fanny was concerned. This was a notorious way of a bawd taking full control over her girls, tying them to the brothel. They agree to give most of their earnings to the Mother and pay over the odds for the other items her house provides. These girls were never able to pay back the money owed, and when they became troublesome, grew older or got caught the pox, the Mother would send them to the debtors prison, to rid herself of the unwanted whores.

'Take care, Kitty. Do not believe false promises'

'Oh, you always want to spoil my happiness.'

'No, Kitty, I want you to be happy. I only warn you because I am your friend.'

'Enough of this, I'm going to the tavern to celebrate

with my real friends.'

Kitty flounced out leaving Kathleen Garrett unimpressed. She's seen this behaviour many times before. For Fanny, this confrontation opened her mind to see further into Kitty's character. Only now, when the two women were living together on equal terms, had Kitty let her guard down. She'd stopped pretending who she wanted to be and showed the underbelly of who she really was. Living in the pitiful, rat infested hovel of a home and seeing the fractured relationship with Da, Fanny realised their experiences of childhood and family life could not be more different. Fanny had felt completely safe and loved by Anise and Pierre. The village people all knew her, and a caring eye watched over her wherever she went, making her feel secure. She had no doubt that her life would be simple but contented. The people around her treated others with respect. They had a kindness and an openness of understanding, which instilled in Fanny, a sense of fairness and acceptance of difference. Now, Fanny's life had capsized, and she feared the tumultuous storm waters of fate that drown the destitute of London. She clung to her childhood beliefs, certain she would not only endure but thrive on her experiences. Fanny had faith. Kitty never had a chance to believe in herself. From day one, the only thing she needed to do was to survive, without any help from others. She had no love, no support and no guidance. She did have aspirations, but they were based on pure imagination. Kitty lived by her wits, using her good looks and lack of empathy to endure a tortuous life. But for all her selfish actions, when faced with a life and death choice, she instinctively chose to save another. Fanny would always be her champion, whether Kitty wanted it or not.

CHAPTER TWENTY-SIX

London Bridge

KITTY SLEPT, WHILST Fanny awoke. She looked across at the young woman lying on the floor and supposed she would rest for most of the day, until the effects of the gin wore off. Fanny dressed in her Indian costume and without waking Da or Kathleen Garrett, she took the wheelbarrow with the loaded dice, three cups and ball and went outside. She felt in her pocket for the few coins she had, not many. If she couldn't make more money, she would have to sell her teeth.

Pushing her barrow along Great St Andrews Street, she approached a coster. Fanny needed to win some fruit or vegetables to put in her barrow. 'Fancy your chances on the roll of a dice, sir? I have coins to wager against your fruit.'

'I'd rather have a roll on you. How much?'

Fanny stepped back. Her instinct was to run. She knew that would bring attention. Since her arrival in London, she had avoided direct sexual advances. Now being so vulnerable, Fanny realised this would not be a lone proposition. She remembered how Briddy shook off an unwanted admirer in Vinegar Yard, behind the theatre. 'Got the pox, love. Don't get your sugar stick near me, dear. I'm here for another type of business. All I wants, is four of your oranges and apples. You win, I gives you pennies, you lose, I get the fruit.' Up to four throws Fanny could cheat on, any more and the chance of being discovered was high.

'All right. Don't wanna do it here though, too open.'

Fanny was happy to move somewhere quieter, she didn't want spectators examining her play. She took him to Neals Yard, where there were fewer people. All went well until after the third throw. The man was loosing, which he didn't appreciate. 'You napping me? I don't like that, girl. Cheats should be arrested.' He grabbed her arm, looked around for help and shouted, 'Stop thief! Call the constable, a gypsy is stealing my money.' Fanny struggled and slipped his clutches. She dashed out into Queen Street, with the barrow swerving before her and ran back to the tenements.

Kitty was up and wearing her sack when Fanny, out of breath, burst in with the barrow.

'What's up Fanny?'

'The constable was called, I was frightened they would take me.'

'What you nicked?' asked Kitty.

'I was throwing dice for some fruit to fill my barrow to start my day's gambling.' Fanny slumped on the floor, dejected.

'Blimey, not worth being locked up for that. You better come with me today, and we'll do some diving for valuable stuff.'

'Kitty, I'm not sure I'm clever enough to pick pockets,' said Fanny.

'You got good fingers, I seen your sleight of hand, you just need confidence through experience. Here, I'll put on Da's coat and you can have a go.' Kitty took one of the stolen handkerchiefs hanging on a line and stuffed it in her pocket, in the other one she put some coins. 'Now, don't tell me what you're going for. We shall circle around the room and I shall pretend to stop and look at some books or goods and you can pick a pocket. Off we go.'

Fanny had to laugh at the sight of Kitty haughtily moving around with her head held high, wearing old sacking and an oversized coat. 'What you sniggering at?'

'Nothing Kitty, I was just impressed by your acting.'

'Thank you. Well, better you keep watching as one day you'll see me stepping right up onto the Theatre Royal's stage.' Kitty dipped an outrageous curtsy.

Fanny moved around her, sometimes getting near and at other times, shying away. An idea came to her, she motioned to Sous-Sous to come over and sit on her shoulder. She pointed to the left of Kitty and the monkey hopped, skipped and jumped up to the rafters, this startled Kitty and distracted her, Fanny was able to dive both coat pockets and held the handkerchief high in victory, dropping a stream of coins to the floor. Kitty spun around at the noise, saw the beautifully stolen goods and gave Fanny a huge smile and said, 'I think it's time we all go to church.'

'Not dressed like that, you won't,' said Kathleen Garrett. 'Here, take the big hoop and the round-about pocket.' She picked up a boat hook and reached up to the rafters, lifting down the support garments worn by a thief. She handed them to Kitty to wear and raised the hook again. 'I'll get Da's Sunday best down, as well.' She lowered a man's silk coat and breeches.

'Go through everything once more for me, Kitty,' asked Fanny.

'They'll be three of us, Da the pusher, me the diver and you the receiver or if you want to patter flash,

"Miss slang all upon the safe". It means you stand a safe distance away from the thieving, ready to receive the stolen goods. Either Da or I will pass them to you. In that way, if I'm discovered or as we say, smoked out, I won't have the stuff on me. Make sure you get away and disappear into the crowd looking innocent, like.'

'What does Da do?'

'He sets it up. We may go to the bridge before the church, as it will be busy with carriages and carts, and what he does is helps a genteel lady cross the road. Watch him carefully, 'cos you and me are waiting for Da to distract the lady and hold her hands up, saving her from being run down by the horses. That's when I go in and either cut her pocket or dive for the stuff. Now, you have to get close to me, so I can pass the goods to you and we both scuttle off. Or, if you're real lucky, and Da is in total control of the lady, he may let you dive the other pocket. He's the boss.'

'And the church?'

'It'll be crowded as people crush in. We shall follow Da on that one, he'll push the crowd and disorientate them, and that's when you get a chance to dip. Both of us will empty their pockets. Be confident and it's easy.'

'I hope so,' said Fanny.

'Now, you'll be wanting a nice cup of tea before you set out,' offered Kathleen Garrett.

Both the women in unison said, 'Thank you, Kathleen Garrett, that would be most welcome.'

Surprising them both, one cup of tea mysteriously appeared for Da on his return. He nonchalantly took it as though it was the most normal thing in the world. 'Thank you my precious, I've been waiting a long time for this.'

'About ten years,' Kitty whispered to Fanny.

The trio dressed up smartly, and Fanny ripped the openings in her petticoats to make easier access to the pockets. Kitty's wide hoop acted like a large cage, hiding the oversized round pocket, where the stolen goods would be stashed. 'Are we ready, ladies? Yes? Right, to London Bridge it is,' said Da and led them out on a new adventure.

Kitty was correct, London Bridge was very busy, making it difficult to cross the road in between the carts, carriages and chairs. The three of them sauntered along one side of the bridge, looking for victims. Da told them, 'When we're done, meet up on the north side of St Magnus. Ah, I see a mature lady of high class, waiting on the other side, looking to cross. I can handle her, easy. You girls get to the right and the left of me, and I shall gentlemanly help her to avoid the carts. Fanny, I'm going to let you dive, as well as Kitty. Remember, once I got her hands up in the air, in you come. Ready?'

'Yes.' Fanny hoped her nerve would not fail her.

A carriage passed too close to the lady, which startled her. She put her foot out to cross, once again. This was Da's cue. He rushed towards her, blocked her way and grabbed her hands, lifting them high up in the air. 'Madam, have a care. Allow me to assist you. Hold onto me.'

'I thank you, sir. You are most kind.'

Still keeping her hands above her head, he manoeuvred her side to side, trying to avoid the carts, making her confused as he guided her to the centre of the walkway. Keeping her attention on him and in conversation, allowed Kitty to cut the string of her pocket whilst Fanny took a watch and six crowns from the other. In the hurry of the commotion, the lady knew nothing of being robbed. When Da released her hands, she dropped into a fine curtsey and thanked him for his consideration.

The three thieves, separately and with purpose, returned back to the north end of the bridge. Fanny was both exhilarated and hot with trepidation, expecting a shout of 'Stop thief.' But all was quiet. They met up as planned and Da decided they would head home to St Giles, to view their goods. Fanny was pleased with herself. Da congratulated them. 'Well done, my girls. Later, we'll go out to St Ann's in Soho, for Evensong.'

Back at Da's, Kathleen poured ale as they told her of their exploits. Excitement was running high amongst the thieves and Da yearned for more. 'Well done, girlies. What a team. What next?' An idea came to him. 'I ain't done the sham kinchin for a while. Let's have some fun.'

'What's that?'asked Fanny.

'A false belly, so you look with chid,' answered Kitty with a wink.

'Get the belly and arm down, my precious, I'm taking my young wife to church.' Once again, Kathleen Garrett hooked from the rafters a large pillow with what looked like a long arm attached to it. Da took it from her and said, 'Get a cloak down too. Do you remember how to do this, girl?'

'Yes, Da. It's one of me favourites.' They both laughed.

Kitty tied the pillow around her waist and passed the gloved end of the arm, through the right pocket slit of the cloak. She pinned the cape closed. The false arm, bent at a right angle looked as though she were caressing a very pregnant belly.

'Is the hand ready, for your dear husband to hold? '

'Yes, dearest,' answered Kitty with an artful smile, her head against Da's. 'We love to feel the movement of our baby. Our hands resting on its heart.'

'Come on, let's go. The service must start soon.'

Fanny stepped out in high spirits, this seemed an easy way to make money. They arrived at the steps of St Anne's, Soho, where a line of carriages discharged their occupants for the evening service.

Da whispered to Fanny, 'Follow us, but keep a few people in-between, so it looks like we don't know each other. I have taken a fancy to that elderly lady with the black lace fichu and the gold necklace. Fanny, once we've sat down, ask if you may sit at the aisle end of the pew.' He took Kitty's arm. 'She's coming closer. Come on, Kittycat, let's get in behind her.'

As instructed, Fanny followed them inside the church making sure she separated herself from them by a couple of parishioners. The lady went to open the open pew door and Da said, 'Please, let me be of service.' He helped the old lady to her place. 'May my wife and I join you?'

'I would be delighted. Is your baby due soon?'

'Indeed. It cannot be too soon for such excited and loving parents,' Da said. The lady settled herself at the far end of the pew and Kitty sat next to her with Da on her left. He cuddled up close to Kitty and looped her real arm through his. With his left hand, he reached across Kitty's belly to take the false hand. He left just a little room by the pew door. Fanny arrived and asked if she might join the worshippers. They all happily agreed and shuffled along a little, to allow her to sit comfortably. The lady took from her pocket a repeating watch, checked the time and replaced it.

Kitty looked at Da and smiled.

Towards the end of the service, Kitty slipped her left arm from Da's and pulled it inside her cloak. Now, she had both her hands concealed, waiting to work. While the lady slept through the sermon, Kitty used her right hand, hidden by the fabric, to empty her victim's pocket. Like a well-oiled chain, Kitty passed the stolen items across her lap, under the cloak, into her left hand, then pressed them into Da's hand. He passed them along to Fanny, who put them in her pocket. Kitty gracefully replaced her arm through Da's, as a loving wife. As the service ended, the lady woke up and looked at the charming couple next to her. She saw that they had held onto each other hands, all through the service and said, 'How charming to see such a devoted couple, I wish you every happiness with your new child.'

Fanny rose and stepped out of the pew, as Da thanked the lady and said, 'Please forgive us that we cannot stay to accompany you to your carriage. Joan's mother is sick and awaiting our return.'

'I quite understand, my dears.'

Kitty and Da joined the faithful in the aisle, pleased with their thieving. But something was wrong, very wrong. Fanny, thinking it had all been so easy, decided to pick a pocket of a gentleman, as he passed her whilst leaving the church. As she scooped up the watch and chain, his hand grabbed her wrist in his pocket, and he held it firm. 'Thief. I have her here. Call the constable.' From his coat, he pulled out her hand still clutching his gold watch.

Kitty and Da saw what was happening, and they moved away as fast as they could.

'My god, they have Fanny. What are we going to do?'

'Nothing. She has all the stolen goods on her. We are in the clear, Kittycat.'

'I must help her,' Kitty cried.

'Oh, no you don't. Get home, now.'

Kitty and Da arrived back at the tenement, feeling a mixture of shock and relief. Kitty was shocked and Da was relieved.

'Da, they will hang her.'

'I expect so. Rather her, than me.'

'There has to be something we can do.'

'Pray for a miracle?'

There were three deafening knocks on the door.

'Who's that?' said Da.

'The law?'ventured Kitty.

'Nah, we got away. Go and answer it, my precious.'

Kathleen Garrett was confused over the consternation, but did as asked and opened the door.

Jack Mann stood there with a large blackthorn cudgel. 'Who are you?'

'I am Kathleen Garrett and you are Jack Mann, you remember Kath don't you, Jack? I helped you get out of Newgate, I got my brother to bring you tools, remember? I'd never forget you Jack, handsome man that you are.' Jack did recollect a mad Irish woman in gaol with him, who did help him, in return for money to bribe her way out of Newgate. 'I heard you was inside. Short stay?'

Jack wiped the sweat off his brow. 'It was. For the last time. I'm looking for a girl named, Kitty.' He looked about the room, noticed Kitty making a move away from him and strode over to her. 'It's you, ain't it? I was told you were pretty.' Kitty smiled. 'Pretty untrustworthy.' Kitty dropped her smile. She looked at Da for protection. He backed away into the shadows.

'Where's Fanny?'

'I don't know who you mean.' Not believing her for a moment, he took hold of her arm and twisted it tight. 'I know all about you, Kitty Jackson. And, your Da.' Jack looked straight at the man hiding in the corner, who'd lost all bravado now that Jack Mann was angry and in the same room.

Jack twisted Kitty's arm further. 'Now Kitty, we can do this the nice way or I could beat you up. Pretty face like yours wouldn't take too long to become ugly.' He threatened her by raising his club as if to hit her.

'Stop. What you wanna know?'

'Simple, where's Fanny?'

'Well, she ain't here.' Jack waited with an inquiring look. 'She were had.'

'Where?'

'Soho church. She was diving when she shouldn't. She was our Adam Tiler, we'd made a good speak and we'd passed it on to her. All she had to do, was walk out with it. But no, she had to have a go herself and was caught with her hand around the watch in his pocket.'

'When was this?'

'I dunno. An hour ago, maybe.'

Jack mopped his brow again. 'You all right, Jack?' asked Kathleen Garrett. Jack nodded. 'You want a nice cup of tea?' Jack shook his head in refusal and also to help clear his head. He was hot with a fever. He paced up and down the dirty room, thinking what to do. The others remained standing, watching this famous criminal mind at work. Jack stopped and turned to Da.

'Winyates, the Justice?'

'Yea, that old goat.'

'That's good, he'll take a bribe, and I've got a lot on him. Kitty, you are to go to the Crown alehouse in

Compton Street to find out who the victim is, and where to find him. Tomorrow morning, go to the rotation office where Winyates will be presiding. Wait for Fanny to come out.'

Kitty interrupted Jack. 'She won't come out, she had the goods on her. They'll send her back to Newgate, to wait for sessions.'

'She'll come out. Wait for her and find your way to St Ethelreda's chapel, at the old Bishop's Palace in Holborn. There should be no one around as the place has returned to the wild. There is an unused small confessional, in the Crypt. Take her there and leave her. Wait at the Mitre Tavern, where Fanny will join you later.'

'No, I can't Jack, they're out to get me for Humphrey Busby's robbery, I'll be done for.'

'No, Kitty. Busby's been found guilty of murder. He lied about everything. You're not wanted for any crime.'

'What?'

'You are innocent. Of that crime, anyway.'

'How long have you known this, Jack?'

'A couple of weeks. Why?'

'Gideon told me I was still being hunted.'

'Who is Gideon?'

'The man I love.'

CHAPTER TWENTY-SEVEN

Newgate

FANNY, WITH FEAR running through her veins, was taken straight to Newgate. The gaol rose like a black monolith to despair, the stench of pestilence and filth permeating its stone walls. Conditions in Newgate were terrible: the foul smell of the unwashed prisoners, bodily waste and the prevailing reek of stale alcohol. The miasma wrapped itself around the dejected, ill or dying prisoners.

'Garnish. Give it me,' demanded the cellar-man, whose breath smelt rank and acrid from gin. Fanny had just enough money for the committal, which would save her from surrendering her clothes. But she had no more to pay for bedding or food. She was taken to Waterman's Hall, one of the women felon's wards, a dreadful dark and stinking place with a floor of soiled oak planks. Close to this ward was water to drink, from a cistern made of lead.

She was not manacled, yet. Fanny knew that could change. If she was charged for the murder of Madame Marie, combined with grand larceny of having been caught with her pocket full of stolen goods, the irons would be fitted. Her future was bleak. If she did not succumb to gaol fever, she would hang at Tyburn. As her friends were away from London, not knowing she was in Newgate, there was no one to pay for privileges. As for Da and Kitty, he was penniless and didn't care about her, and Kitty would be too frightened to visit, being sought for robbery. She was alone and would be left to rot with the dirty, half-naked women who picked lice from their hair, pinching them as they crawled over their bodies, in the vain hope that fewer parasite faeces would save them from typhus.

Fanny found somewhere to sit in the darkness. She leant against the wet wall, and in the raked light from the meagre window, carvings and candle smoke marks appeared. These recorded the types of crimes and the names of those who committed them. Dates were scratched in the stone and rows of single strokes denoted the days spent incarcerated: a mural of desperate hopelessness. As she ran her fingers over these markings, a shadow loomed above her, a little blacker than the wards dullness. It was the ward-woman,

'Here you, Miss Hoity-Toity, do ya want to earn enough for some food privilege tonight? I'll take you to the Stone Hold in the men's quarter, and you can have a blanket horn-pipe with one of the boys.' There was laughter and taunting by the other prisoners. They knew Fanny was an innocent in the ways of this hell on earth, and that the Stone Hold was the most dreaded of wards, underground with no daylight. Fanny shook her head as she realised the gruesome dilemma she was in, to prostitute herself or starve.

'No, not tonight, thank you.'

'Suit yourself.' The cellar-women receded into the blackness. Crushing the crawling creatures on the floor, Fanny groped her way to an empty space in a corner and curled up in the foetal position. She considered what made her skin creep more, the lice, fleas and rats or being raped. But to hang, made her blood run cold.

By seven the next morning, Fanny was exhausted. She'd spent all night listening to the inmates moaning and screaming. Through the long hours, she recalled the chain of events that led up to this final destiny. Once again, she was alone and powerless. Nothing had changed. She was still the penniless little orphan from Wiltshire. If a hand was offered to help her survive, to show her a way out of Newgate and to avoid the gallows, she would take it and be loyal to her rescuer, forever.

'This way.' A rough man heaved her up. 'Winyates' ready for ya.' She was manhandled and taken to the rotation office. Here, she would discover if the prosecution was strong enough, to send her to the next sessions. Fanny started to scratch her scalp and skin, it made her shudder.

The room was small with one window, close to the ceiling. Sitting in the middle of a row of large gentlemen, was the Justice of the Peace. Fanny kept her head down, not wanting to acknowledge the reality of the situation. She couldn't stop shaking.

'What is your name?' the Justice asked.

Because Fanny was using her ears and not her eyes, she was more sensitive to sound. She knew this voice.

Lifting her head, she looked straight at the speaker. With a small smile, she said, 'We have met before, Bishop Drury, at a wedding.'

She had Justice Winyates' full attention. Their eyes met, and she knew he recognised her from the Molly house. In irritation and anxiety, he shouted at her, 'You are mistaken. I repeat, what is your name, girl?'

'Frances Tomlinson, Bishop.'

The Justice took a long slow intake of breath, growled then pursed his plump lips and through squinted eyes said, 'The victim has decided to withdraw his evidence, so there is no case against you.' He lent over closer to Fanny. 'Now, listen to me, Frances Tomlinson, I shall remember you. Do not cross my path again, do you understand? Keep your mouth shut, and get out of here before I change my mind. Leave.'

Fanny couldn't believe her luck. Shocked, she didn't move, until he shouted, 'Get out.'

Still reeling from disbelief, she staggered outside into strong daylight, not knowing what she was doing. A shrill whistle caught her attention, and on the other side of the street was Kitty standing with a shawl covering most of her head and face. She beckoned Fanny towards her. 'Kitty, I'm so pleased to see you.'

'Quick, we have to go.' Kitty held her hand and they both hurried towards Holborn Bridge. As they reached St Andrew's, Kitty slowed down and asked, 'You all right?'

'Not really, I can't believe what just happened. They let me go, why?'

'You got Jack Mann to thank for that. He organised it with bribes and threats. Good friend of yours, Fanny? You never told me, I would have probably behaved meself better, if I'd known.'

'Why did he do it? How did he know I was there? None of this makes sense, Kitty.'

'Don't worry your head about that, he'll explain. I gotta take you somewhere. Come on.'

'Kitty, even if he got me off for stealing, what about Madame Marie's murder?'

'Ah, that. Well, Busby's gonna hang for that. There was a witness who saw and heard it all.'

'Who? We were the only ones at the scene.'

'Well, that's what we thought. The unseen and unheard was there all the time.'

'What do you mean?'

'Martha.'

'Martha? Oh, Martha.' Fanny started to laugh. 'Martha, Martha, Martha, I love you.'

This made Kitty laugh too. 'Yea, good old Martha.'

They were so happy, they ran and danced through the overgrown fields of the old Bishop's Palace, scattering rabbits to run for cover. On the far side was the chapel, overgrown with ivy. As they opened the heavy door to the undercroft, they smelt the dampness of the stones. Inside was silent and dark. They nearly tripped and fell down the steep, stone steps that led to the body of the crypt.

The sun from the east shone through a small pair of gothic stained glass windows and spread a shaft of light that illuminated the confessional and a small altar.

'In you go. I'm to leave you here and you must meet me at the Mitre Tavern, when you are ready. Make sure to tell Jack I did all right.' Fanny nodded and kissed Kitty on her cheek. 'I'm glad you're out, girl,' said Kitty and with that Fanny opened the confessional door and sat down on the small bench. It was very dark. A wicket was pulled across and a man's voice said, 'Put your shawl over your nose and mouth and keep well away from this opening, where any remaining lice could craw through.'

Fanny would know this voice anywhere. The relief of feeling safe in the presence of this man was palpable. 'Jack, how can I thank you. You saved my life. I shall always be indebted to you. May God love you and keep you.'

'He probably will soon, if the devil doesn't get me first. Fanny, I'm not well and I shall die soon. I escaped Newgate again, but this time I carried out something to remember it by.'

Fanny felt dread rise up in her. 'No, Jack, please, not that.' She knew he as talking about gaol fever. 'Does Betsy know?'

'No, I don't want her to know. Fanny, I need you to do something for me.'

'I shall do anything you ask of me, but may I ask you how you knew I was in Newgate?'

Kitty had not left the crypt, curiosity getting the better of her. She crouched down outside the confessional and was able to overhear the conversation.

Jack explained to Fanny. 'I live in Seven Dials, and I saw you running away with your barrow, wearing the Indian Princesses costume.'

'Oh, I see. I think.' Very carefully and purposefully she said, 'Mrs B gave it to me.'

'Fanny, Mrs Big is away from the city and it was still there after she left.' Jack waited for her to work it all out.

'Jack, you know.'

'You went to Mrs Big's garret to get the costume that was in the box with the words DEAD ANIMALS written on it. What else did you find there, Fanny?'

Her heart was in her mouth. She couldn't lie. 'The gold.'

Outside the confessional, Kitty's eyes nearly

popped out of their sockets. It took all of her concentration not to gasp. She now knew where Jack Mann's treasure was hidden. She put her hand over her mouth to silence her fast breathing, but the excitement was too much, her heartbeat wouldn't slow down. She needed air. Creeping up the steps, she opened the heavy crypt door and silently fled the church to the alehouse.

Jack's voice rose as though touched by another soul. 'Yes. My gold. If I wasn't going to die, I would probably kill you for finding it.' Fanny listened as Jack's mind slipped little, wrestling with his emotions.

'Is there anything I can do, to help you?' There was no reply. 'Jack, I have to ask you this. Have you watched me ever since I arrived at the Swan Inn?'

He focused. 'Yes.'

'Why?'

'All will become clear to you, soon.' He calmed himself. 'I have studied you and your actions. You are an extraordinary human being, naturally kind, talented, ingenious and intelligent. These attributes are polished through the adversities of this harsh city. As a master cuts a precious diamond, your potential is exposed. Though hardship, you learn to be fearless, inventive and quick thinking. You will become a fine commander of others and yourself. You are a true London apprentice.'

Fanny didn't realise she'd grown and changed so much. 'All I have done is to remember what others have taught me, through observance and consideration. It is the people I've met, who have given me these gifts.'

'And you will continue to use them, to survive.'

'I have nothing, Jack. No money, no work and no

home. I wouldn't call that surviving.'

'Things will change, the wheel always turns. Do you trust me, Fanny?'

'Implicitly, Jack. You saved my life.'

'I'm giving you half my gold when I die.' Fanny caught her breath. 'This is payment for what you agree to do. I need you to take care of Betsy and Mr and Mrs Big for me. You are to use the other half of the gold, to invest for their benefit.'

Fanny couldn't believe what he was saying. And there was another strange thing happening. His voice had changed, like an actor dropping his stage accent as he transforms back into his real self. Jack was speaking in a refined manner. Fanny was confused.

Jack continued. 'I have a house that will be yours. I know this must seem unreal, but one day soon you will understand everything.'

He handed Fanny a folded piece of parchment. 'This is to introduce you to my lawyer, Mr Beaudelaire. When I die, take this to him at the address written in this document and everything will be arranged. Do not worry, Fanny, all will be well.'

'No, it won't Jack. You won't be here.'

Before Gideon made his way to the bath house, he smoked opium in a Pall Mall den. He felt pleased with himself, as today he'd arranged a plan with Madame la Comtesse. She would invite chosen licentious, wealthy gentlemen to enjoy the auction of a virgin. One of these men would outbid the others to ravish and rape Fanny. She would be introduced to each man for valuation.

It was imperative Fanny believed this meeting to be an evening of gambling. She must not become suspicious when the bidders asked her questions, whilst taking in her physical beauty. The gambling house in King Street was opulent and discreet enough for Fanny to feel comfortable. Each bidder left a non-returnable holding fee, which the two conspirators shared. The final, winning payment would be paid at a later date. The night Fanny was raped.

As planned, Fanny met Kitty at the Mitre.

'Well? What happened?' Kitty was hoping Fanny would tell her about the gold, and they could go and get it. But she didn't.

'Jack's not well, so he wants me to do some things for him.'

'What things?' Kitty guessed Fanny meant moving the gold.

'Nothing much, but as he has been so good to me, I must do my best for him.'

'I'll help you, Fanny. You can tell me all about it. What do you have to do?'

Fanny passed over this request this and said, 'He gave me some money for us to go to the Kings Bagnio for a proper bath. He noticed I was scratching and said it was important I got rid of the lice.'

'That's a treat,' said Kitty.

'He gave me this too.' Fanny placed a leather pouch on the table. Kitty wondered if it contained the gold. Fanny opened the bag, and it was full of the items stolen from London Bridge and St Anne's. 'I have taken some money, as I need to live on something. But you and Da, can have the rest. They are your pickings. I don't want them. It's all yours.'

'Are you sure, Fanny?'

'Yes. Now, let's go.'

Kitty decided she wouldn't tell Da about Fanny's offering, but keep the gold and silver for herself. What had Da ever given her? A few beatings, nothing else.

Part of the gold, she would take to Gideon. He had some explaining to do.

There were many bagnios in Covent Garden, but this one stayed true to the Ottoman style. Upstairs, were rooms to rent by the hour, day or night, for a gentleman to entertain a lady or an assignation between a married woman and her lover. In the basement, were the baths.

Even before Fanny entered, she could smell the addictive aroma emanating from the ground floor. 'What is that delicious smell, Kitty?'

'It's coffee, Fanny. You've had coffee before. Haven't you?'

'No.'

'You are such a simple girl. What would you do without me? We'll get a gentleman to take us in, after the bath. Trust me.'

A strong man, whose skin was the colour of polished walnut, guarded the door to the baths. He wore a strange hat similar to a large pumpkin and pinned to it was a jewelled brooch, holding a plume of ostrich feather. He smelt clean. Fanny hadn't realised there was a specific smell for true cleanliness. It reminded her of boiling linen in the washer woman's copper: the scent of steam and soap.

'Stop sniffing him, Fanny, and pay the man,' Kitty advised.

Fanny handed over some coins, and the man clapped his hands to summon a young woman dressed in newly washed and pressed linen, who led them downstairs.

'Please undress, ladies, and cover yourselves with a towel. A girl will be with you soon.'

'What's going to happen next, Kitty?'

'The second thing best in the world. Being clean.'

'What's the first?'

'I'm told it's love.' She paused. 'I'm not sure, I don't know what that is anymore.'

'Oh, Kitty.'

The door opened, and in walked a rather fierce looking woman, with muscles to match Sam the Strongman.

'I am here to clean you,' she said and rolled up her sleeves. 'First, I do your hair. It's filthy.' Fanny wasn't going to contradict this indomitable female. 'My name is Burcu, it means a sweet smelling woman, in Turkish.'

Fanny took her opportunity. 'Hello, Burcu, my name is, Fanny. I have a friend called Fatima. She is a dancer, do you know her?'

'Ah, Fatima. Yes, our families know each other. She is a beautiful dancer. '

'Indeed, she is,' replied Fanny. 'Umm, you are very strong, Burcu, and I'm a little bit tiny. Please bear that in mind.'

'Don't worry, Fanny. I will not rub you until you disappear. Well, not completely. We start now. I do your friend next.'

Kitty muttered, 'I can't wait.'

There was something very pungent in the soap. It didn't smell nice, but after her hair was rinsed, it had never been cleaner and the itching had stopped. Burcu pushed, pulled and pummelled until all the muscles accepted defeat and relaxed. Still shaking slightly, Fanny and Kitty were escorted by Burcu to the sweat room. Here, they were gently switched with birch, as their pores opened and toxins sudated from their bodies. Once the heat became too much, Burcu led them into a vast room with a high ceiling. They immersed themselves into the cold plunge pool, covered by a pergola supported by pillars.

'It's what heaven must be like,' said Fanny as she dipped down again, submerging herself and came up laughing. 'I'm going to do this every day, when I make my fortune.'

'In that case, your be pretty dirty for a long time,' teased Kitty.

Too soon, the time came to leave the womb of steam and warmth. They dressed in their gowns, now clean and smelling sweet from the sponging and sprinkling of lavender water and they combed their hair, pinning it up. Almost floating on air, they made their way to the main floor, and as they walked to the coffee house to enjoy a fresh brew, a man said, 'Ladies, how fortunate for me to rest my eyes on such beauty.'

Kitty spun around. 'Gideon, what are you doing here?'

'The same as you, Kitty. Bathing. Would you care to join me for coffee?

'Yes. Thank you, Gideon,' Fanny replied, as she looked longingly into his eyes.

'It is my greatest pleasure.' He raised her hand and kissed it, with savour. Kitty noticed this and instantly interrupted this intimate moment, by linking arms with him and pushing in front of Fanny. When they were settled at a table, Gideon ignored Kitty and spoke directly to Fanny.

'Frances, my dear, I have good news. There is a group of card players who are interested in your ability and also, may I say, your considerable charms.' Gideon smiled. Kitty flinched. She was worried about this friendship that had risen up without her realising it. 'The game will take place next Sunday evening and

I shall meet you at the Temple church as usual. We shall take a carriage to Madame la Comtesse's elegant salon, in St James's. Do you have a suitable gown, Frances?'

'Do not worry, Gideon, I shall be appropriately dressed.' Fanny would have to spend the money she stole, to buy a secondhand mantua and add trimmings.

'Have you finished your coffee, Fanny?' asked Kitty.

'Yes.'

'Please leave us. I have to speak to Gideon, privately.'

'Of course, I shall see you Sunday, Gideon. Farewell for now.' He kissed her hand. Fanny knew Gideon watched her as she crossed the room. She needed him to desire her. Turning back her head, she looked over her shoulder and from the corner of her eye, Fanny held his stare.

It wasn't only Gideon that kept his eyes on Fanny. Kitty watched her every movement. She noticed a subtle sashay had crept into Fanny's gait, and she realised her friend had blossomed into an assured and attractive woman. Kitty would have to watch this girl from now on. She turned on Gideon.

'What do you think you're up to?'

'I don't know what you are referring to.'

'Oh, yes you do. I see the way you look at her. Don't you dare cross Kitty.'

'My dear girl, do behave. I have no idea what you are implying.'

'I know when a man is acting and when he ain't, and the way you look at Fanny is too truthful. It's me you love, don't forget it.'

'Kitty, we have an arrangement. Once I have the

money from Fanny's loss of maidenhead, we can change our relationship.'

'You mean you will marry me?'

'I have explained to you all the reasons why that is impossible. Kitty my sweet,' he stroked her cheek gently. 'Don't spoil what we have. We share the same feelings and desires. Now, would you like to spend the afternoon with me, upstairs?'

Kitty's anger dissipated. 'Yes, of course, I do, Gideon.' Kitty wouldn't chance breaking this close bond with her lover. Today, he was being nice to her and she refused to jeopardise this feeling of love, by confronting him with the question of why he'd told her she was a wanted woman.

CHAPTER TWENTY-EIGHT

Back at the Theatre

FANNY TOOK THE familiar route towards the Inner Temple. Knowing she was no longer hunted, she was free to pass through the double gates to the bow-fronted shops, without fear of meeting her friends.

Through the window she saw the bookseller, sitting in his usual chair, immersed in the book he was reading. She opened the door, and the bell announced her arrival. Mr Jordan looked up and hesitated. Removing his spectacles, he brushed the chequered blanket onto the floor and held his arms wide open. 'Fanny, my dear child, I am so relieved to see you again. Come here.'

Fanny ran into his welcoming arms, relieved to feel the warmth of an embrace. She began to weep, as he comforted her. 'That's right my dear, let the tears carry away the hurt and anxiety. You have nothing to fear now, you are with Mario and me. Come. Sit down.'

The shop bell rang again, and Mario burst in. 'Fanny, you are safe. We have been worried. What a dreadful day it was when poor Marie…' Mario broke down. Mr Jordan secured the latch on the shop door. He turned to Mario and held his hand. 'Now, now,

Fanny is well and we have her home. There is nothing to get upset about.' The bookseller kissed Mario with much tenderness, and he took the patchwork handkerchief from printer's pocket to dab the tears away.

Mario leant his head on Mr Jordan's and said, 'Si, scusami, mio caro.'

The three friends sat down and discussed the dreadful events that had led to this happy reunion.

'We were out searching for you, the day you ran away,' explained Mr Jordan. 'Tom saw you crossing Drury Lane and the three of us called your name, but you ran off. We tried to keep up, but you disappeared.'

Fanny remembered how she and Kitty had raced from the men, who they believed were another posse. She laughed at the idea of her friend's reaction, if they had found her in the alley with the men.

'I'm sorry to laugh, it wasn't funny. I wish I'd known it was you, dear friends, who were chasing us.'

'Fanny, we need to tell you what happened after you fled. We were certain it was impossible for you to harm to your aunt, and running by our shops, we saw no blood on either of you. The parlour was, dear God, horrible.' Fanny held onto Mr Jordan's hand. 'There was blood everywhere and Humphrey was drenched in it. When Martha appeared and told how she had witnessed the whole scene, he raised the poker to strike her, and it was at that moment the constable had no doubt of his guilt. He is certain to hang, Fanny.'

She replied, as cold as ice, 'I have no sympathy for him. He was a violent and cruel man, and it seems just that it was his servant, whom he treated with contempt, who was the one to condemn him. I wish to forget all about Humphrey Busby.'

There was a tapping on the window and a shout of,

'Mario, it's Tom, to pick up the playbills. Would you two gentlemen stop entertaining a very pretty young woman and let an old girl in?'

Charles unlocked the door. 'Forgive me, Tom, we have company.'

'I know. How could I forget such an innocent face with a quick, knowing mind. Hello, darling.' Tom opened his arms and Fanny almost jumped into them.

'I've missed you so much,' said Fanny.

'Well, of course. I am extraordinary, did you not know? Do you want your job back in wardrobe? Mrs Bovel is having a lot of bover.'

'Yes, yes, oh, please, yes.'

'Are you looking for lodgings'

'Yes, now that I am working. Do you know somewhere?'

'You need looking after. You can stay with me.'

'Thank you, Tom, thank you.' She gave his cheek a big kiss.

'Well, that seems to be settled. See you this evening. Au revoir, mes amis.' And in a tinkle of a bell, he was gone.

Fanny returned to the place she loved most: backstage at the Theatre Royal, Drury Lane. On her way to work, she repeated those four words to herself, almost as a chant, accompanying her wish to act upon that great stage.

'Theatre Royal, Drury Lane, Theatre Royal, Drury Lane. Oh, good evening, Fred.'

'Well, well, if it ain't that little Frances Tomlinson. We all been worried about you, disappearing as fast as a shilling off a tart's palm. Welcome back. I hope you got a hankie, Mrs Bovel will be all over ya.'

'Thank you, Fred. It's good to be back…home.'

As Fanny climbed the stairs up to the attic wardrobe, she listened to the conversation of two girls running down the stairs towards her. It was Briddy and Dolly, still arguing over borrowed stockings. All was normal.

'I've had enough this time, Dolly. You pinch my stockings one more time, and I'll stick me leg out in the last scene and trip you up.'

'You wouldn't dare do that.'

'Oh, wouldn't I? Then put me stockings back.' She pulled Dolly's hair as they rounded the corner of the second landing.

'Aaooou, let go, Briddy. Oh, Fanny, what you doing here?'

'I'm back to work with Mrs Bovel. I'll see if I can get you another pair of stockings, Briddy.'

'No. She'll have a new pair and I'll be stuck with the darned ones,' wailed Dolly.

'Next time, you will get the new pair. Does that make you happier?'

'You promise?' Dolly said as she looked Fanny up and down in approval. 'Well, well, Fanny, I see the competition's grown up. You're looking good. How's that nice young cousin of yours, you know the one with the lovely manners?'

'Theo? He's been in Scotland, and I don't know when he is due to return.'

'Scotland, eh?' Briddy cupped her breasts in her hands and said, 'When you see him, tell him he can explore my highlands any time he wants.'

Not to be outdone, Dolly retorted, 'And me lowlands could do with a gentleman wandering about in them, too.'

Nothing had changed.

Mr Big's Little Troupe were back in London. As the fire at the Swan had almost destroyed the building, her friends had made the Dolphin Inn at Pye Corner, their home from home. Mr Big decided there should be a celebration for their return and to discuss the upcoming performances at Bartholomew's Fair. Everyone who should be there, was there: the little people, Letty and Sam, William the knife thrower and butcher, who enjoyed a new contract of supplying this Tavern with meat, and Betsy, who had made a remarkable recovery thanks to Theo. Fanny took Tom Mercutio along as her guest. He loved it. When the entertainment started, he was up in a second and did a whole routine of a farce about the late King. It was hilarious, and he received a standing ovation. Mrs Big translated her husbands questions. She asked Tom if he had written the play himself. 'Yes, I do a bit of writing.' Mr Big signed something else.

'My husband asks if would you be interested in being paid, for his company to perform the farce at the Fair?'

Fanny had a broad smile across her face, Tom looked at her. She nodded repeatedly and he turned to Mr Big and said, 'I would be most honoured, sir.'

The two men shook hands, and a toast was taken to the great success of Mr Thomas Mercutio's masterpiece: *The King is Otherwise Engaged*.

Tom turned to Fanny and said in the most theatrical way, 'Do you know me? I am Thomas Mercutio, playwright.'

CHAPTER TWENTY-NINE

Elizabeth

MRS ELIZABETH ROCHESTER Mancini was a disarming, intelligent beauty whose wit was sharp and who had gained respect from the highest, most influential people of the land. She was of middle height with iridescent skin and shining, seductive hazel eyes, which drew the desired into her web. She was no longer young, but her beauty and charm remained mesmerising and ravishing, exhibiting all the qualities of a high courtesan. Her femininity belied her adroitness and fierce ambition. To betray her, may call down the revenge of Medea. Elizabeth was a woman to admire and fear. But here, in this exquisite drawing room, full of delightful, delicate collections of china, glass and timepieces, she was the only mother that Jack Mann had ever known. Sitting in a French bergère, was a sick man wearing an oiled coat.

'Let me help you out of that disgusting piece of clothing. We must be sure you are free of lice.'

'No, I do not have the strength and keep your distance, Elizabeth.'

'Fear not, Jack, I shall go to the baths tonight, and Juliette has given me one of her potions that will protect me from contagion.'

'Still the magician's daughter?' he said, laughing with affection.

'Do not question your great aunt's gifts. Her mother, Olympia, was an excellent potion maker. Anyway, I am strong and determined.'

'I have typhus, Elizabeth. Even you, cannot frighten it away.'

Elizabeth wanted to steer the conversation away from such distressing news. 'I see your collections have grown, Jack. The jewelled snuff boxes are particularly splendid. My great uncle, Cardinal Mazarin, would be envious of those diamonds. Tell me about Frances.'

'She is out of danger and out of St Giles. She shares lodgings with a friend from the theatre, so is no longer under the bad influence of Kitty Jackson. I have explained to her what she is to do upon my death, and how she will inherit this house and all that is in it. You will like her, she has the traits of her great aunts.'

'Unlike you, Jack, who chooses to follow in the rakes path of your grandfather, Rochester, and the violence of your father, Sackville, I was never fond of him. Thank goodness you have at least inherited the love of fine things from your grandmother's side of the family.'

Jack explained again to his aunt. 'You know I crave excitement and freedom from convention. I have to find a way to release the uncontrollable passion and confusion that rages within me. It is only here, alone in my home, I can give in to the allure and quietness of beauty. My spoils have made me a great deal of money, and profit from trading goods has allowed me to enjoy these trinkets'

'Does Frances know of her forbears?' Elizabeth

asked.

'Not as yet. I shall leave that to you.'

'I'm surprised dear Marie did not explain but, of course, she had no knowledge of what that brute, Busby, would do to her. I would have rid her of him, years ago.'

'You had no reason to look over Frances whilst she was in Wiltshire or with her mother, here in London,' Jack reassured her.

'Once I was informed she was a victim of that dreadful, Humphrey Busby, I had to intervene. She is of our blood: the direct line of the illegitimate children of Rochester and three sisters of the Mazarinetts.'

When Fanny left the stage door after the show, she saw Briddy draped over Theo. He looked very uncomfortable and she did not save him immediately. Theo was such a gentleman that he didn't know how to extradite himself from Briddy's clutches. Although Fanny didn't want to be cruel to him, it was rather amusing to watch. She decided that the dancer had embarrassed her cousin enough and said, 'Leave him alone, Briddy, he's mine.'

Theo looked at Fanny, wishing she meant the words. He was hers, heart and soul if only Fanny felt the same way.

Briddy didn't give up easily. 'Stopping my fun, Fanny, don't do that. I'm happy to share him, how about that, sir?'

Theo turned bright scarlet, and Fanny stopped this teasing by instructing Briddy to leave off, or she wouldn't get a new pair of stockings.

Fanny slipped her arm through Theo's, and they made their way towards Brydges Street. Her touch triggered Theo to speak, he couldn't help himself. 'I wish you did want me for yourself, Fanny. I have missed your company and the sight of your lovely face. Have you considered my proposal?'

'Dear, Theo, I cannot promise myself to you. You must find someone else.'

Fanny could see how much this hurt him, it was if a cold iron bar had been thrust through his chest. She felt terrible and wished she could love him as much as he loved her. But her heart was Gideon's.

To change the mood, she spoke of Jack and how ill he was.

'Is there anything that can be done, Theo?'

'No, the disease will take its course. Death will come relatively fast. Typhus is spread by lice and Jack has never been one to honour cleanliness. Keep away from him, Fanny. You have been through such a bad time, if only I had been here, maybe I could have helped you.'

Fanny realised that although she yearned for Theo's friendship when she was so in need, she would have hated for him to see her so vulnerable.

'Will you see Jack?'

'There is nothing I can do to help. He will have high fevers and headaches and become confused. All I can suggest is to balance the temperature to make him comfortable. I'm sorry, Fanny.'

'He needs someone who loves him to be by his side. I shall go. Theo, may I ask you something?'

'Anything, Fanny.'

'I think you may answer me, as Jack is so ill. What are the packages you bring to him?'

'I don't fully understand it myself. I shall tell you what I know. Jack makes money from criminal means. I do not approve, but more important to me is to help people needing medical treatment. You know I have a dream of my own hospital?'

'Yes, Theo, it is an honourable desire.'

'Jack pays me to deliver those packages. I save the money towards my ambition.' Fanny nodded her approval. 'Fanny, Jack has been ill all his life. He trusts me with this secret.'

'What do you mean? He has always been strong and healthy until now.'

'I speak not of his body, but of his mind. He fights demons still not understood by doctors. It is as though there are two characters fighting each other, within him. He tries to control the fury, but the urge of switching personalities is too strong. The one thing that keeps him relatively sane is his collection. The money he makes from villainy he uses to buy back pieces of his family inheritance. I do not know his history, I only accept payment for sourcing and negotiating the items he wants. Jack is very precise in his description and provenance. I travel easily to France and ingratiate myself with the people who own the precious articles. I know nothing more, except the families I speak to are rich and important. Once the brokering is agreed upon, the objects are given to me, wrapped and with a waxed seal of the letter M. Jack is obsessed with collecting these specific little treasures, and I imagine he lives in poverty to be able to afford them. It is a mystery to me.'

Jack Mann was also a great mystery to Fanny.

The next evening, Tom gave Fanny a piece of paper with an address written on it. 'A man, hunched, wearing a very dirty oiled coat, came to box office and asked me to give you this. He was good looking, but there was something unpredictable about him. He wants you to meet him at his lodgings tonight, in

Queen Street at the sign of the two fish and scallops. I think I should come with you.'

'No, Tom, I know who it is. I have trusted him with my life. I shall see you tomorrow.'

The lodgings were not only a part of a house, they were the whole house. Fanny lifted the heavy, iron door knocker and let it drop. She waited until the door was opened by a regal looking lady, with a high powdered wig, who asked her to come in.

From the doorstep, she could see the hall was lit by crystal and ormolu candelabras and chandeliers. It was an elegant home.

'Forgive me, madam, I seem to have the wrong house. I'm sorry to disturb you.' She turned to go.

'No, Frances, you are in the right place, at last.'

Fanny didn't understand.

'Come in, my dear. Let us join Jack.' She closed the door. 'Before we do, I must ask you to take this draft. Do not be afraid, it will not harm you. It is a potion that your great-aunt mixed, to keep the typhus away. Here, drink.'

Fanny did as she was asked, without any hesitation. For some reason, she trusted this sophisticated woman, implicitly. The fashionable lady led Fanny upstairs, to the drawing room on the first floor. Fanny had never seen such a beautifully appointed house, there were treasures all around.

The first thing she saw as she entered the room, was a blazing fire and in its glow was Jack, not in his oiled coat, but in an oriental silk banyan. He was sitting in a wing chair with his slippered feet supported on an ottoman.

'Ah, Fanny, my dear. Forgive me for not standing, but I am rather sick at the moment. I see you have met Elizabeth. My mother, Laura Mancini was Elizabeth's cousin. She died giving birth to me, and since then, Elizabeth has raised me as her own. A task that has not been easy for her, as I continuously rebelled against her admirable standards.'

'Why are you telling me all this? It has nothing to do with me. Why am I here? I'm confused.'

Jack smiled at Fanny. 'I'm not surprised in the least. There is a lifetime of unspoken truths to comprehend. We shall not try to unravel all tonight. In time, you will slowly become familiar with them and therefore understand everything. Sit down opposite me, Fanny. Elizabeth, would you be so kind as to bring us all some brandy?'

'Of course, my dear boy.'

'Jack, I asked Theo to help you, he wanted to —'

Jack held up his hand to stop her continuing. 'Theo is a good man, and I know he would help me if there was a way, but there isn't. I have seen many men die of gaol fever, so I have no surprises in store. Thank you for trying to help me.'

Elizabeth re-entered the room and handed the glasses of brandy to Fanny and her nephew.

As Fanny took the glass, she glanced at the floor and saw a carpet with exactly the same design as the one in the Madame Marie's parlour. Elizabeth spoke next.

'My dear, Frances, I shall try to explain some facts to you. To help you understand, I have some small portraits to show you.' She reached over to the open glass display table and took out a porcelain miniature of herself, as a young woman. She handed it to Fanny. 'This is not me. It is my twin sister, Celeste.' The image was familiar. 'We were twins and very close. As we were to our cousins: Juliette and Laura. The four of us were born of the same father.' Elizabeth replaced the miniature with another, a handsome young man with prominent eyes and a full, sensuous mouth. 'John Wilmot, 2rd Earl of Rochester. He seduced three of the Mancini sisters when visiting Paris: Hortense, Olympia and Marie Anne.' Elizabeth handed over a delightful image of the three sisters. 'Being the libertine he was, he planted his seed in each sister. His lovers were spectacular women, and they were our mothers. As premier courtesans, they were known for their beauty and promiscuity at the court of Louis XIV. They all became wives or mistresses, sometimes both, to the greatest men in Europe.' Fanny placed the two miniature portraits on her lap to make room for another. Through the oval glass peered a stern looking man with a high forehead and piercing dark eyes. Wearing his cardinal robes, he showed great intelligence. 'Their uncle was Cardinal Mazarin, who had been Louis's chief minister. The King had relied on him for all things, thus the Cardinal had great influence. This is my mother, Hortense Mancini.' She pointed to the beautiful dark-haired beauty who exuded sexuality. 'Hortense gave birth to twins: myself and Celeste. Celeste had a daughter by her lover, Louis, Le Grand Dauphin.' Another portrait, this time of a Prince of France, wearing the royal colour of blue. Once again, Fanny recognised this man's face. 'That child was Marie, your mother.'

'What?' interrupted Fanny. This was an absurd story. Why had this woman made it up?

Jack spoke. 'Please be patient, Fanny. I appreciate these facts come as a shock, but you must understand who you are.'

Elizabeth continued. 'Listen to me, my dear. When Marie's mother, Celeste, and her grandmother, Hortense, both died in the same year, she was no longer protected. So, Marie, my fourteen-year-old niece, joined me in London. I looked after her, as best I could. Your mother, Marie, before marrying that dreadful man, Humphrey Busby, was mistress to Henry St. John, 1st Viscount Bolingbroke, who is your father. You carry the bloodline of Rochester, Mancini and Les Rois de France.'

'No, that cannot be true. I am a poor girl from Chilton Foliat.' But something was nagging at Fanny's memory. She remembered the miniatures her mother had shown her, the first day they met. The captivating and seductive girl who Marie explained was her mother, Celeste. She would be Fanny's grandmother. And there was the elegant man, wearing a French blue silk sash. The royal colour. 'It cannot be possible.'

Jack spoke to her gently whilst Elizabeth sat opposite but close. 'Frances, you were a poor girl from Chilton Foliat, but now you know you are the last of this illegitimate, but noble line. And thus, you will inherit all that this family has. When I die, you will live in this house with all the treasures I have collected, and your great-aunt, Elizabeth, will train you to run her highly successful business, which you will eventually head.'

'What business? I don't know anything about business.'

'You have nothing to worry about, Fanny. Elizabeth will guide you, and you have the temperament, ability and may I say flair to enhance her business empire.'

'What such business is this?' asked Fanny.

Elizabeth rose to her full height, her face lit by the refection of golden flames and said, 'The business of vice.'

CHAPTER THIRTY

Awakening

SUNDAY ARRIVED AND Fanny dressed in her new gown, which she had embellished with lace and ribbons. Her mind was still racing with the extraordinary things she had been told, and they would not settle in her brain. She was to meet Elizabeth later this week and hear her plans. Things were moving so fast, she felt swept off her feet. Fanny recalled Shakespeare's words: "There is a tide in the affairs of men, which, taken at the flood, leads on to fortune." Was this her moment?

She longed to share her news with Gideon. But something told her to wait. Arriving at the porch of Temple Church, Gideon greeted her and moved close. 'You look enchanting tonight, Fanny. You remind me of my mother, she was as loving and alluring as you. Here, come into the shadows with me.' With her back to the cold stone, he held her arms tightly by her side and kissed her. This was a different kiss from the previous chaste brush of her lips, now he forced her mouth open and impaled his tongue into her. Fanny wasn't sure she liked this, it felt invasive and somehow remote. He released her right shoulder and lifted her petticoats out of the way, so his fingers could find the place that he believed they were made for. Fanny was pinned by his tongue and his body. She squirmed and wanted him to stop, but he pursued his desire. As she moved her hips from side to side, trying to free herself, she sensed a watery sensation between her legs. Her intimate area began to swell, becoming sensitive to every small movement of his fingers. She began to feel hot, and her nipples reacted to her linen shift brushing against them. A wave of desire and lust came over her as Gideon rubbed her more rapidly, bringing her to climax. She didn't expect him to pull away from her so suddenly. She felt completely exposed, as he held her at arm's length and studied every shudder of her body. She had no control over her reaction, and she liked it. And wanted more. As her breathing slowed, he said, 'Did you enjoy that, Fanny? Has that happened before? Do you love me, Fanny?'

'Yes, I love you, Gideon.'

'Would you like me to do that again?'

'Yes, Gideon.'

'That's what I like to hear.' He dropped his arms and patted down her petticoats. 'Well, not tonight. You have other more important things to do. Remember that feeling, Fanny, I want you to desire it all the time.'

She felt flushed and had never felt so desirable. She had a natural knowledge that men would find her irresistible in this state of arousal. Maybe Gideon would excite her again this evening before she sat at the tables.

Gideon kissed her hand. 'You are of great value, Fanny. Come, let us find our carriage.'

Gideon knew if the men could see Fanny in this state,

they would pay an enormous amount to be the one to take her virginity. Maybe, he could arouse her again this evening, just before meeting her buyers.

Sitting next to her in the carriage, Gideon made certain that his hand rested on Fanny's lap, teasing her of what he might do next. From his experience with women, he knew that Fanny was ready and willing. He found it almost impossible to deny himself the pleasure that could be his, but he knew the great value of this particular virgin.

The carriage stopped in King Street, outside a large stone house with steps rising up to the front door. On either side were liveried footmen. Once inside, they were directed to a small, intimate reception room with only one gaming table. A striking dark-haired lady extended her hand towards Gideon. 'Bonsoir, Monsieur.'

'Bonsoir, Madame la Comtesse.'

There was no further introduction and they took their seats at the table.

'I shall not be playing this evening, Monsieur. However, I shall sit in, for company.'

'As I have decided to do,' said Gideon.

Fanny looked at the other three men around the table, they were all old and corpulent and there was something about them that repulsed her. They asked her questions, and she answered them politely.

At the end of the evening she came away up with reasonable winnings. Gideon was content. In fact, he seemed exceedingly happy.

'Madame la Comtesse, thank you for a most delightful evening. We must take our leave of you, now.' Gideon helped Fanny on with her cloak. As they left the mansion, down the steps to the carriage, Fanny asked, 'Gideon, shall we lay together tonight?'

'No, my dear, let us keep that pleasure for a little while longer.' He smiled and patted her knee like a child. Fanny flinched. Couldn't he see? She was a woman now.

Once again Kitty felt her life shattering. Time and again she made the same mistake. All her life, she clung to anyone who gave the impression they would protect her, only to be disappointed when they used and discarded her. As Kitty grew up, her alliances became more fluid and one by one, they all let her down. Despite her bravado, Kitty depended emotionally on other people, whereas Fanny had taught herself never to rely on anyone but herself. Kitty was panicking at the thought of losing Gideon, and she started to drink heavily. When drunk, she caused a rumpus at Mother Stroker's, and that night she was dismissed from the bagnio with a warning to sober up. Defiantly, she went straight to the Fleece and ordered a pint of gin. With only her own fears of loss as company, she slid into a black mood and went to find Gideon. After checking his usual haunts, she discovered him with a wench on his lap, at the Plough and Harrow tavern in St Martin's Lane.

'Get off him, you whore,' screamed Kitty.

'Don't mind me, I'm sure,' said the red-headed girl.

Gideon slapped the girl on her rump. 'Be off, I have some business to do. Kitty, that wasn't nice.'

'I don't care, you're mine. I won't let no woman take you from me, do you understand? I know too much about your goings on, and I'll ruin you if I have to.'

Gideon held her arm firmly and whispered to her, 'Outside, Kitty. I'll not be made a spectacle in a common tavern.' He dragged her, kicking and screaming into Goodwin's Court.

'Ger off, you're hurting me.' She struggled to free her arm that was now turning blue with bruising. He pulled her across him with force, and her head hit the brick wall.

'Now listen to me, Kitty, I've had enough of your histrionics. A man of my breeding cannot be expected to put up with such gutter behaviour. I've had enough of you. I don't want to see your face again.' He threw her down into the wet mud and started to walk away.

'No, no, Gideon, don't leave me. I love you.'

'Stop it, Kitty, you're just a whore. Why would I want you? What do you have to give me that I need?' He began to laugh.

Kitty caught him by his ankle, looked up from the dirt and said, 'Gold.'

'Don't be ridiculous. What do you know of gold?'

'I know where it is.'

'Let go of me, woman. It's all lies.' He turned away again.

Kitty desperately pulled on his ankle once more. 'No it ain't. It's Jack Mann's gold, his treasure.' Gideon turned around. 'I overheard him tell Fanny where it was hidden.'

A pause and Gideon knelt down to her. 'Where is it?'

'You won't leave me, Gideon?'

'Tell me where the gold is, Kitty.'

'Promise you won't leave me, and I'll tell you.'

Gideon sighed and smiled at her with contempt. 'No, I won't leave you. Where is it?'

Kneeling together on the ground in the dark passage, Kitty looked into his eyes and told him. 'He said it was at Mrs Big's garret, in a box marked DEAD ANIMALS.'

'Who's Mrs Big?'

'I dunno.'

'Well, that's helpful.' He squeezed her cheeks and pushed her back. 'Find out, Kitty.'

'Fanny ain't staying with me no more, I don't know where she's gone.'

'I am finding this rather tedious, as you are very stupid. Go and find her. Then come and tell me who this Mrs Big is and where she lives.'

'Do you love me, Gideon?'

'Of course, I do,' he replied with a smirk.

The next evening, Tom and Fanny were enjoying a drink at the Rose and gossiping about the actors, when he stood up and said, 'Sorry, I forget to tell you something, which may be important to you.'

'What is it, Tom?'

'When we were at the tavern with the Troupe, Little John told me he was playing Nano the dwarf in Ben Johnson's, Volpone, at Lincoln's Inn Theatre, in November. Apparently, they are looking for a young actress to understudy and asked me to keep an eye out. Well, here I am with an eye on you.'

'Me, Tom?'

'Why not? You can do it easily. Would you like me to have a quiet word with those who matter? Get them to put you forward, for an audition?'

'Would I? Yes, Tom, that's wonderful, thank you.'

'Don't get too excited, they'll be lots of girls wanting the job. But I think you could do it, and you need experience before you play the great Drury Lane.'

'Tom, do you really think I could play the Lane?'

'Tread the boards a few times and find out where the notches are, and Mr Cibber may use you.'

Fanny jumped up and gave him a big kiss on the lips.

'Do not tell anyone you did that. And don't tell Cibber Dibber I'm fraternising with the enemy, Rich.'

The next time Fanny was to play cards for Gideon, they met at their usual place by the Temple Church. She reached up and kissed him. 'I have such exciting news. I am to audition for Mr John Rich, at Lincoln's Inn theatre.'

'Really? Is that exciting? I imagined the theatre was a failing place of entertainment.'

'Gideon, please be happy for me.'

'Does this mean you will be adored by the male playgoers? I don't think I would like that very much. In fact, I don't want you to do it. I'm asking you not to.'

'I must. This is what I want, to be a successful actress.'

'I refuse to allow it. That is my final word.'

'Gideon, I am going to do it. Nobody tells me what I can and can't do.' With that, he raised his hand to strike her. 'Gideon, no. What is the matter with you?'

He looked within himself and realised his true feelings. 'I must be jealous, an emotion I have never felt before. I believed it impossible for me to love anyone, again.' He drew her towards him, his face almost too close to hers. 'You have bewitched me. Nothing matters except being with you. I love you, Fanny.'

She took a small step back and put both his hands in hers. 'Gideon, I have waited to hear you speak such words. You must know, I love you too.'

But did she love him as much as his mother? The adoration: so possessive and satisfying. He'd returned her love completely, as a son and a man. He yearned for the pure physical love he'd shared with such a beautiful and caring woman, with whom he was obsessed. For the first time, he kissed Fanny gently and with affection. It was a remembered emotion. 'Fanny, will you marry me?'

Her reaction was not as he expected. She drew back from him. 'Gideon, I have no wish to marry any man. It is important to me to become independent. Only then, shall I have my complete self to give.'

Gideon didn't like this, he wasn't used to being refused anything. 'I shall leave you alone if you don't need me.'

'I don't need you, Gideon. I choose to spend time with you. Please understand.'

He didn't understand. She had to be his, all the time, she was never to leave him. He spoke with a vein of ice running through his words. 'Perhaps you do not think me suitable? Do I embarrass you? I have never been introduced to your friends. Do you have any friends, Fanny?'

'Of course, I do. It's just that I like to keep them private.'

'So, I am not important enough to meet them.'

'Would you like to meet them? They are not of your class, Gideon. They are performers, they show at the Fairs. The next one is Bartholomew's. Would you like to come with me, to see them?'

'Yes, Fanny, I would. What are their names?'

'Mr Big's Little Troupe.'

CHAPTER THIRTY-ONE

Bartholomew Fair

GIDEON AND FANNY walked through the Inns of Court to reach Holborn. 'I'm sorry to delay our journey, Gideon, but Mrs B asked me to pick up a basket of props from her garret. It's not far.'

'I am pleased to be of help. Which way are we headed?'

'To Field Lane, close to Smithfield.'

Gideon was unnerved and uncomfortable in the squalor of this street of slum tenements, and he found the stench revolting. He raised his handkerchief to cover his mouth and nose.

'I wouldn't do that if I were you, somebody will snatch it out of your hands and add it to a line above our head.'

Gideon looked up at the bunting of silk squares. He replaced the kerchief in his coat pocket, not so much out of fear from theft, but from the threat of bodily harm that may accompany it.

'Here we are.'

The door was nearly off its last hinge and had to be lifted up to clear the threshold. Gideon had never been so close to such poverty and was shocked that people lived in such wretched dwellings. He couldn't wait to leave this place. But first, he had to see where the gold was hidden.

'Follow me up the stairs, there are mantraps to catch robbers. Don't worry, I know the way. Watch where I put my feet and hold on to the handrail. We'll climb to the top floor.'

After careful navigation of the staircase, they arrived at the low door. Fanny opened it with the two keys, which hung around her neck. Gideon followed her in and looked around.

'What is this space? It looks more than just lodgings.'

'It's where the troupe practise, they are acrobats and tumblers. Now, where is the basket?'

Gideon saw the wall of boxes and a tarpaulin draped over them. He stepped up close and pulled the covering down. 'What's all this?' he asked and surreptitiously scanned the pile of boxes.

'Boxes full of things the troupe need when performing. Ah, here it is. We can go now.'

Gideon had to find the box containing the gold. 'Have you opened any of them?'

'Only a few. Not much to see. A lot of dust though. Come on, we should hurry.'

Gideon started to cough. 'Fanny, would you bring me some water please, I think dust has found its way down my throat.'

'Yes, of course. Just a minute.'

While Fanny's back was turned, Gideon kicked away the folded blankets that were laying at the base of the wall of boxes. He saw it. DEAD ANIMALS.

'Here you are Gideon, this will stop you coughing.' He took the pot and drank it, all the while looking over its rim at the long coffin-shaped box, dreaming of the gold within. He smiled. He was looking at his future.

They walked along Cock Lane. The street was aptly named, after the business conducted against the walls and in the lodging rooms. The noise from the fair and revellers combined with the smell of roasted pork, promised a good afternoon. At the end of the street was a narrow alley turning north, leading to the back door of the Dolphin Inn, where they would enjoy some wine before joining the milling crowd in West Smithfield.

In the spirit of the fair, the Innkeeper and his wife portrayed Harlequin and Colombina. They both wore bonnets and colourful clothes. The Innkeeper dressed in the classical diamond patterned costume and carried a slapstick, used probably not to magically change any scenery but to control the raucous drinkers throughout the day. His wife, as the coquettish Colombina, looked alluring in an off the shoulder, multi-coloured gown of rags and patches.

'Hello, Alice, I see you are in the spirit of the occasion,' said Fanny.

'Welcome, Fanny, to the exciting, bizarre and irreverent world of Bartholomew's Fair.'

Mr and Mrs Littlewit were ex-performers and having saved their earnings, found they could buy this hostelry and have a more settled life. They provided a warm reception, good ale and regaled many colourful stories to their customers.

'And who's this fine fellow?' asked Ned Littlewit.

'This is Gideon, a good friend of mine.'

'Looks as though he's a very good friend,' said Ned, eying Gideon's hand around Fanny's waist. 'A beer or wine, sir?'

'A fine Claret. Do you have such a wine?' asked Gideon, as he looked around the room with distaste.

'Indeed I do. However, fine wine deserves a high price. It that to your liking, sir?'

Fanny was embarrassed by Gideon's rudeness and said, 'Ned, I am sure your wine is the best and truly delicious. Please be so kind as to bring us a bottle.'

'My pleasure, Fanny.' Ned walked away towards the casks.

Alice followed him and when out of earshot said, 'If it weren't for Fanny, I'd spit in it.'

'Have no worries, I'll do better. I shall take a separate glass of true wine to Fanny as she is not a drinker, so will not partake in the adulterated flask. It will be him, who has the piquant taste of my piss in his wine.'

Alice laughed and nudged him in the ribs. 'Serve him right. There's something about him I don't trust. I think I shall warn Mrs B.'

Ned served the wine to Gideon. 'I hope it is to your liking sir. It is one of Ned's special wines.'

'Just pour it, and go.' The innkeeper smiled, nodded and returned to other, more joyful customers. As Ned predicted, Fanny drank just one glass of wine, whilst Gideon drained the bottle.

'Shall we go, Gideon? My friends will be looking forward to seeing us.'

Gideon reluctantly rose, and together they walked out to Pye Corner. Here, they were engulfed by the throng of fair-goers and the clamour of shouts, rattles and drums that called punters towards the myriad of sideshows, which showed at least six times a day. People crowded around them with enticing promises. A man in a leather jerkin, wearing a crown made from horseshoes, shouted, 'Here, see the Horse But Not a

Horse. His tail where his head should be and his head is where his tail should be. You could say, he talks out of his arse.' He neighed loudly and the crowd roared. A man on stilts cried, 'See a real man with no legs, walk on his five-foot arms, follow me to the corner of Hosier Lane.' Blocking Gideon's path, came a girl wearing a wig made of rather smelly seaweed and who held in her hand, a tall pole with a crossbar. Hanging from both ends were blue and silver paper fish. She hawked, 'Swim with the shoal to the Hand and Sheers in Cloth Fair, and for the price of a shilling you can stroke the scales of a real life merman.'

Gideon pushed all of them away, declaring, 'What nonsense is this?' He pulled Fanny towards a gin seller, sitting next to a dancing bear. Showering the drunk woman with a few low value coins, he took a large swig from her bottle. He looked at the chaos around him and shouted, 'This place is madness. What in God's name am I doing here?'

'You wanted to meet my friends. Please, Gideon, let us go to their pitch.' The couple weaved their way through the pressing rabble, towards a row of large booths by Hospital Gate. Here, the drolls were staged: condensed writings of popular plays. A large number of people had gathered outside the rope walkers booth, where Mr Big produced his show. Fanny waved her hand, catching the attention of Sam the Strongman who controlled the line of people, crushing towards the tent. 'Sam, Sam, it's me, Fanny.' He saw her and beckoned them forward. 'Hello, Fanny, how good to see you, do you want to see the show?'

'Yes, please, Sam. This is my friend, Gideon.' She turned, only to discover he'd disappeared.

'It that him?' asked Sam. Gideon stumbled up the stage stairs, the gin making him falter. Sam and Fanny elbowed their way to Gideon, and the strongman reached out to support him by the arm. 'Watch your step, son.'

Gideon had to stretch his neck up to take in Sam's height and weight. Not to show inferiority to Sam's obvious strength, Gideon commanded, 'Get off me, you are not my father. Please be so civil to call me, sir.'

'I'm begging your pardon, sir. I shall not aid you again.' Sam took an instant dislike to Gideon.

'Come on, Gideon, let us go and meet the troupe.' As Fanny passed Sam she whispered, 'I'm sorry, Gideon is not feeling well at the moment.'

'Yes, I can see that, Fanny. Go round backstage to see the boys before the show.'

'I will. However, I must leave for the theatre before the performance starts. Gideon will stay.'

'Well, before you disappear, run next door to see Letty. It's been too long. She's working with the conjurer Issac Fawkes. She and his son are the posture masters.'

'I shall certainly make sure I see her today, Sam.'

'And, Fanny. Tell her I love her.'

'Yes, I will.' Fanny wanted all the world to be in love.

Fanny drew the printed canvas aside and showed Gideon the way to behind the stage. 'Watch the steps,' she warned. He did not take well to her concern but took care before following her down. When the boys caught sight of her, they called out, 'Mrs B, it's our lovely girl.' The troupe crowded around her.

'Let me introduce you to my friend, Gideon,' Fanny said proudly. When Gideon lifted his head up from watching his step, Noble, Luke and John immediately recognised him from the Swan Inn, when he jeered at them and called them freaks. Luke advanced on Gideon and once again, Noble and John held him back, whispering, 'Fanny.' Although Matthew and Mark were not present at the earlier confrontation, they picked up that something was wrong. Shoulder to shoulder, in a defensive row, they all looked menacingly at Gideon.

'Mr and Mrs B, this is Gideon.' Mr Big wandered over to the receiving line of his Little Troupe and saw that the new visitor was not welcome here. Mrs Big watched from afar and when the silence became too much for her, she stepped forward, outstretched her hand and said, 'As a friend of Fanny's, you are most welcome.' She looked back at the little men. 'Isn't she boys?' Not a word was spoken. Fanny was bewildered. Gideon bowed to Mrs Big and kissed her hand gallantly.

'What a pleasure it is to meet such a…', here he paused, 'a unique lady.'

Mrs Big acknowledged this with a curt nod and turned to Fanny. 'Well, my dove, happy birthday. Sixteen today, it's such a joy to see my sweet girl grow into such a beautiful woman. We shall celebrate at the Dolphin on Sunday.'

Fanny, feeling a little guilty said, 'Forgive me, I have to see Gideon on Sunday evening.'

'I see,' said Mrs Big, disappointment and worry etched on her brow.

Mr Big signalled to the troupe. It was show time and with relief they filed pass Fanny to the wings. 'See you soon, Fanny. Take care of yourself,' said Luke and shot Gideon an icy look.

Mr Big signed to Sam to watch Gideon closely during the show. Sam nodded and waited to accompany him to his seat.

Fanny, leaning close to Gideon said, 'I must leave you now, I have to go to the theatre to work. I shall see you on Sunday.' She looked into his eyes with adoration, before turning away.

'This way, sir.' Sam took hold of Gideon's arm despite his objections and called after Fanny, 'I'll see you soon. Go and see Letty.'

Sam manhandled Gideon to his seat. 'Sit here and behave yourself.'

'Take your hands off me.' He tried to shake Sam off.

'I hope I have no cause to do otherwise. Sir.'

Gideon shook himself free and drank from the bottle of gin.

Towards the end of the performance, Gideon's drunkenness became verbal, and he started to heckle. 'Why don't you grow up? Look at you, you're not men, you're freaks.'

Mr Big knew what Gideon was screaming, he didn't need hearing to understand the word, freak. He nodded to Sam who stepped in front of the other spectators and seized Gideon by his collar, dragged him in front of the audience and threw him down the front steps into the mob of the fair. The boys didn't need a signed order from Mr Big, to make them run off the stage to find and follow Gideon. They fanned out around him, flanking him, ready to move in for the attack. Sam kept his distance, out of sight, ready if required. The liquor had made Gideon hungry and he followed the smell of roasting pig. He saw a banner, "William Bull's Famous Spiced Sausages and Spit Pig". Behind the trestle table was a large man in a butches apron and next to him, his petite wife, Lizzie.

'Two sausages.'

'Yes, sir. Please wrap them for the gentleman,

Lizzie,' said William. Gideon fumbled for the coins to pay, not noticing the little men were closing in on him. But William did. 'Thank ye, sir.' In readiness, the butcher wrapped one of his hands tightly around his carving knife, and in the other, he held one of his throwing knives.

With a large hot sausage in each hand, Gideon turned to face six very angry dwarves, two with stones and slings, and Sam the Strongman standing behind them with his arms folded, waiting for trouble.

Before Gideon could do anything, Luke ran into him and head butted him in his solar plexus. He doubled over in pain and John, with his fingers of both hands locked together, swung them up from his knees with great force, to hit Gideon under the chin. He reeled back as Matthew ran at him, backflipped and struck Gideon's groin with his heel. Gideon clutched at his crotch, his mouth open in agony as the stones from the slings hit his temples. At the same time, Mark rammed into the back of his knees, crumpling him down onto the ground. The men watched him crawl back to the table, where he pulled himself up. Gideon was not finished yet. As he turned to face his aggressors, he slid a meat knife into his hand and threatened the troupe. The line advanced on him and William the butcher came from behind his meat bench, brandishing his knives. Gideon knew he would have to find a way to flee. He glanced at Lizzie and dashed behind the counter to grab her whilst his knife cut the air in front of him. 'I have her,' he cried and he started to back away from his aggressors, using Lizzie as a shield. William halted, dropped one of his knives and held his hand up to stop his friends attacking further.

William shouted, 'Leave him, Lizzie is more important. Let him go. Please.'

The troupe were not happy, their blood was up and they wanted to maim Gideon in such a way that he would never again use the word, freak. But they let him go.

'Next time, Luke,' said John.

'Next time, I shall kill him.'

Kitty spent the afternoon cleaning Gideon's wounds, listening to his rantings about Mr Big's Little Troupe, and how he would take revenge. His anger slowly subsided and when exhausted, he fell asleep for a few hours. On awakening, he insisted on more wine. Soon, the two of them were fast in liquor and once again, screaming at each other.

As the boy carried the tray of wine and glasses across the landing to an upstair's room at the Rose tavern, he sighed with boredom at the sound of a violent argument coming from the Mermaid Room. He did not pause in his duties, as this was not an unusual occurrence. He knocked on the door and waited for the gentleman to open it. Gideon's timing of avoiding the missile Kitty threw at him was remarkable, he ducked just in time to see the carcass of the capon hit the serving boy in the face. Gideon's reaction was fast, and he caught the two bottles of wine before they toppled off the platter. He turned around, re-entered the room and slammed the door shut with his foot. The boy narrowly escaped a broken nose.

Gideon poured the wine, whilst Kitty complained. 'I said I wanted gin, not that stupid wine.'

'You will drink what you are given. Anyway, you've had too much gin tonight. You are getting very boring, Kitty.'

'You didn't say that when I was on my knees to you, with my hands tied behind my back.'

'That's all you're good for. You have no conversation. You're drunk most of the time, and I don't wish to be in your company any more. Leave me and send up another girl.'

'No. No, Gideon. Let me stay, I'll be good, I promise.'

'Leave me alone.'

'I have something you want to know. Give Kitty a kiss and she'll tell you.'

'Kitty, there is nothing you can tell me, or do for me that I require. Get out.'

'I know where Jack Mann's gold is.'

'So do I.'

'What?'

'You are too slow and of no use to me. I know where the gold is.'

'How do you know?' Kitty grabbed his elbow to make him look at her.

'Fanny very kindly took me to see it.'

'What are you talking about? She wouldn't do that, she's friends with Jack.'

'I have my ways of getting what I want. You should know that, Kitty.' He poured a glass of wine for himself.

'What do you mean? What have you been up to with Fanny?'

'It's none of your business.'

'It is. I love you. I've done everything you've asked of me. All you have to do, is to love me back.'

'Quiet, woman. Go home.'

'Home? Where's home? I don't have a home, Gideon. My home is with you. I need you.' Kitty flung her arms around his neck and tried to kiss him. 'Don't send me away, I'll be on the streets.'

'Where you belong.'

'Gideon, no, don't say that, you look after me, right? I ain't got no one else now. Mother Stroker has thrown me out.'

Gideon's laugh was cruel. 'Too much gin, eh, Kitty?'

'Yea, I'll stop though, I'll do that for you. I promise. I'll just sit here quiet like and be no nuisance. I'll be good. See, Kitty's quiet as a mouse. You have a drink and I'll wait for you, forever, Gideon.'

CHAPTER THIRTY-TWO

Trouble

THE COLD-BLOODED business of the auction served as a prelude to the hot-blooded climax of the victor. The bidding for Fanny was fierce, the gentlemen willing to pay above the normal rate, for such a fine specimen of a virgin. Although Gideon found it almost impossible not to ravish Fanny, he knew monetary gains were more satisfying than the swift, first bite of the apple. The three sexually deviant men were well known to Madame la Comtesse, Mrs Juliette Mancini. All had great wealth and expensive addictions to gambling. It was the infamous, Charles Chartris who outbid his debauched rivals.

Juliette ran the most elegant and renowned salon in London, known for the excessive wagers placed on all types of bets. This gaming house complemented the luxurious brothel, close by in Pall Mall that was the headquarters for her cousin's empire, of all things immoral and enjoyable.

In the carriage, Gideon was flirting and kissing Fanny to make her lips swell and redden in the most delightful way. As he moved his mouth towards her breasts, he murmured, 'You are perfect in every way and ready to enjoy the sensations of seduction. Would you like that, Fanny? Will it be tonight? I think it will.' Fanny's ardour left her breathless, as he slid his hands under her petticoats. She couldn't bare Gideon not to take her in the carriage, immediately.

'Have your desire, my love. I can no longer wait to have you inside me. I beg you, Gideon.'

'Later, Fanny. Keep yourself excited for me. Will you do that Fanny?'

'Yes. All evening I shall think of what we shall do.'

As he moved away from her, he hooked his fingers under the ribbon that held Mrs Big's keys. 'Fanny, please allow me to remove this just for tonight, the coarse ribbon is out of place with your soft skin.'

She lifted the keys over her head and put them in Gideon's hands. He placed them in his pocket, where a little box filled with warm wax was waiting to enfold the penetrating iron key.

The carriage pulled up in front of the mansion. 'We are here. Dearest Fanny, enjoy this evening and be lucky.'

Passing through the great hall of the mansion, they were ushered upstairs to an intimate room, furnished with comfortable chairs, a card table and a grand bed with dressings of white silk, falling from a gold coronet. Juliette Mancini, Madame la Comtesse was sitting next to a player who Fanny recognised from a previous game. She welcomed Fanny. 'Ah, the delicate and exquisite Frances, how beautiful and radiant you look this evening. You have met Mr Charles Chartris. He is very enamoured with you, my dear.'

'Indeed, I am. Thank you, Juliette, for inviting me to relish Frances's beauty.' Chartris raised Fanny's hand and kissed it with his plump lips, secretly licking it. Fanny flinched as he locked his eyes on her. 'Please, my dear do sit next to me.'

'Gideon, how handsome you are. Please join me.' Juliette Mancini patted the upholstered seat.

Fanny looked to Gideon for security. He gave her a seductive smile.

Wine was served, and Fanny was coaxed to drink it as fast as she could, not knowing a small amount of opiate had been added. This would relax her, stopping any resistance from Chartris's assault, which was fast approaching.

Once Juliette could see the draught working, she nodded to Gideon and excused herself from the room. 'I shall meet you in the public card room, later.'

'Indeed, Madame la Comtesse, I shall look forward to speaking to you.' He gave her a deep bow.

'Au revoire, gentlemen.'

Content with the amorous proceedings, Juliette retired from the virgin room into her adjoining business salon. Maidenhead contracts could be sensitive, so she took personal management of them. As a great deal of money was at stake, everything had to go smoothly. The two footmen opened the double doors, and she hurriedly crossed the floor to a small, devotional folding tryptic, hanging on the wall. She opened the wings and put her eye to the virgin's halo where there was a spy-hole. She saw Chartris begin to stroke Fanny's arms and whisper sweet things in her ear. It wouldn't be long. Gideon would stay until Chartris led the girl to the bed when it was obvious the pact would be concluded. He would then retire and wait for Juliette to join him, to share out the money.

A fog was descending over Fanny. She took deep breaths trying to clear the mist, as her focus pulled in and out. She felt the hands of the man next to her, slip over her body and pull out her nipples, over the top of her corset. Fanny started to panic. 'Get off me.' As she managed to push Chartris away, the chair toppled over and she crumpled to the floor. It was then that she saw Gideon. She recognised the beady look in his eyes, the one of desire and power. His smile was sly as he slipped his hand down his breeches to caress his penis. 'Gideon, help me.'

'I'm the one to help you, my pretty one. Let's get you up on the bed.' As Chartris bent over to lift her, he thrust his hand towards her sex.

'No!' Fanny flailed her arms around trying to free herself from her assailant, making it easy for Chartris to catch her wrists and pull her up, trapping her in his arms. She felt his warm and foul breath close to her face as he fumbled to kiss her. Fanny twisted her head away, only to be rewarded by a stinging slap.

'Behave yourself, and I won't hit you. You're a pretty one, and I want to keep you that way. I shall have you many times. I'll teach you a lot.' As Chartris dragged her towards the bed she saw Gideon walk to the door and leave her.

'No. I said, no!'

'Quiet.' Chartris slung her onto the bed, face down and Fanny crawled up the counterpane trying to break free. He caught her by the ankles and hauled her down the bed like a sack of grain. Fanny grasped at the linen trying to get some control, but the tugging continued until her feet touched the floor. 'Leave me alone, stop it. Let me go.'

'No, my dear, I shall never leave you alone. You are mine now, to do with whatever I please. And you will obey me.' He tossed her over onto her back. 'Now, show me your pretty bud.' With all her strength,

Fanny managed to sit up and with her fingers outstretched, she lunged them at Chartris' face, catching his eyes. White hot fury flushed across his face. 'How dare you. It's time you learnt who your master is.' He untied his stock and stuffed it in her mouth. 'Know your place, girl.' He climbed up on the bed and knelt astride her, trapping her hands above her head. Fanny struggled to free herself but Chartris was too heavy. There was no escape. In his fervour, he ripped her petticoat away and forced her legs apart, using his own to keep them prised open. 'Stay still, you little bitch. Let me take a close look at you.'

Elizabeth waited to be announced by Juliette's footman. 'Madame. Your cousin, Mrs Elizabeth Rochester Mancini.'

'Welcome Elizabeth. You have visited me on a quiet, but profitable evening.'

'Good. Do tell me all about it.'

'We have the libertine, Chartres, in the virgin room. He is about to deflower a young girl. He paid a fortune for the honour. The man has more money than sense. However, I must say, that this girl has something about her that is entrancing.'

'Pour me a glass and I shall see how the old dog mounts her.' Elizabeth sat down and made herself comfortable. In every room, there was an iced bucket holding a bottle of chilled, white wine within Juliette's reach. She poured two glasses, ignoring the conventional rule of being served. The women toasted each other. 'To the house of Rochester and Mancini'.

A scream came from the next door room. Juliette smiled and said, 'Ah, the mongrel is about to cover his bitch.'

Elizabeth stood up, put her glass down and went to

the spy hole. She saw the young girl lying face down. Chartris lifted the girl by the waist to position her over the edge of the bed. As he held her hips, he dropped his breeches. The girl twisted her anguished face around to him. 'Stop, please stop.'

'Oh, my god!' Elizabeth recognised who she was.

She swept out of the salon, like a galleon in full sail and burst into the virgin bedchamber. 'Get off her.' Chartris looked over his shoulder, in surprise. 'I said, get off her.'

'I've paid for her. Leave us, Madam.' Elizabeth rushed up to Chartris and prized him away from Fanny. 'How dare you, she is mine, I paid for her.'

'I shall repay you. Leave her be.' Elizabeth raised Fanny off the bed and said, 'Go outside, to Juliette.' Fanny stumbled towards the door where Madame la Countesse was standing, bemused.

'I refuse to be treated like this,' blustered Chartris with his breeches around his ankles.

'If you do not accept my repayment, you will be blacklisted from all my palaces of pleasure. Do you understand?'

Very reluctantly he agreed. Elizabeth started to withdraw. She stopped at the door, turned around and said, 'And Charles,' Chartris looked up at her. 'Put your prick back, dear.'

Back in Juliette's business salon, Fanny slumped in a chair whilst Juliette questioned her cousin. 'What's going on? He is a good customer.'

'Juliette, she is one of us. She is Frances, Marie's child.'

Juliette gasped, the blood draining from her face. 'What? No, that cannot be.'

'It is, I tell you. I spent an evening with her and Jack.'

'No, no,' Juliette muttered to herself as she fell back into the chaise.

Elizabeth poured a large glass of water and sat next to Fanny, urging her to drink all of it. She wanted to flush the drug out of Fanny's system. She wrapped a blanket around her to help ease the shock. 'Fanny, you're safe. No one will harm you here, I promise. Drink the water and the feeling of disorientation will fade.' Elizabeth turned to Juliette. 'Who sold her?'

Juliette had calmed herself, and she stared ahead with hatred. 'Gideon Woodford. He is waiting in the main salon for me to give him his share of the winning bid.'

Ready to surge into battle again, Elizabeth said, 'You stay here, I shall deal with him. We shall make sure that he is excluded from society. His life in London is finished.'

Fanny was woken by a beam of morning light, gilded by the autumn sun. As it stretched towards the bed and touched her face, she turned her head away from its brightness. She felt as warm and safe as a baby bird in its nest, cocooned in down. Her hands stroked the silver grey satin cover as she luxuriated in the softness of voluptuous pillows. As Fanny emerged out of the state of sleep, she looked around the room. Above her, the domed ceiling was of dark cobalt blue, studded with silver stars of the night sky, and the bed, made of gilded carved beech was in the shape of a curled scallop shell. It seemed to float on the clouds that were painted on the floor, allowing glimpses of the landscape beneath her. The effect was magical. When she stepped out of bed, it was as if she were walking between the heavens above and the earth below.

The door opened and the dream world was lost.

'Good Morning, Frances. I hope you slept well.' Fanny shrank back from the striking black haired, dark-eyed woman, whom she remembered from her waking life nightmare.

'Get away from me.'

'Frances, you have my sincere apologies. I didn't know who you were.'

'It doesn't matter who I am. It should never have happened.'

'Yes, my dear, but that is the way of the world. This city is based on vice. I mean you no harm, please believe me. Elizabeth has kept a caring eye on you, since the death of your poor dear mother. Marie chose to follow a different path to us and trusted the wrong man, but she loved you and did what she believed was right, in order to give you safety and happiness. But now, your life is in London, and you are of our blood, so we shall protect you as she did. Please, Frances, join me for some breakfast. Elizabeth will arrive soon. My dear, come with me.' Juliette held out her hand. Fanny took it but with reserve.

Juliette's living quarters were on the floor above the gambling rooms. Flowers and exotic perfume filled every opulent room. She led Fanny though to her private sitting room. On the floor, lay a large silk carpet, the same design as in Jack and Marie's houses. Because of its size, Fanny could read the intricate pattern. There were two coats of arms. One, a pair of silver fish on blue, and the other, three golden scallop shells on red with a triangle of black eagle's heads. Beneath each shield was a name: Mancini and Wilmot. On the carpet's dark blue background, a golden pentagram was woven over the zodiac belt of the heavens. She looked for her own sign, Virgo, and found there was a chair placed directly over it.

'Please sit, Frances,' Juliette gestured to the same seat.

By her side was a small marble and gilt rococo table, and upon it were bite-sized pastries and a chocolate pot and bowl.

'Please help yourself, whilst we wait for our guests.'

As if Juliette had conjured up her appearance, Elizabeth was announced at the door and by her side was Tom. Fanny ran to greet him.

'You've gone up in the world, Fanny,' he said, looking around with a big grin. 'Your friend has missed you and so have I.' Tom opened his coat to reveal Sous-sous, who jumped onto Fanny's shoulder and wrapped his arms around her neck.

'My dearest, Sous-Sous.' Fanny stroked the monkey to calm him. 'I'm so pleased to see you again, Tom. How is it you are here?'

'Apart from being scintillating company, desired in all the best salons in St James's, you mean?'

'Stop teasing me, Tom.'

'Mrs Mancini's footman asked me to step inside her divine coach, for a word.' Tom raised his eyebrows. 'It's not often I receive such a request, so how could I refuse?'

'Tom, get on with it, please.'

'Mrs Mancini is a good lady. Trust her, Fanny. She is your friend. She will look after you and show you a better life. I believe her and so must you.'

Elizabeth interrupted. 'Please, Thomas, do take a seat and have something to eat.'

Tom pinched himself and under his breath, asked Fanny, 'Am I dreaming?'

'No, Tom, it's really happening.'

Elizabeth eased herself into a splendid velvet settee. 'Now, Fanny, I thoroughly approve of Thomas, so you are to remain living with him until my son's time comes to leave us. Tomorrow, I wish you to start work at my establishment in Pall Mall. You have a great deal to learn, but I have every faith in your ability and loyalty. Thomas, you are welcome at any time.' Tom sat up straight and looked extremely excited.

Fanny spoke. 'Elizabeth, I am auditioning for the role of understudy at Lincoln's Inn Theatre and I hope to one day play Drury Lane. I need to follow my ambition as an actress.'

'Really, Frances,' Juliette interrupted, 'Elizabeth is offering you everything anyone could wish for, and you bring up the theatre.'

'Juliette, my dear, I shall decide what is right for Frances, and for us. I see no reason for you to give up your dreams, Fanny. In fact, a celebrated and respected actress would be an asset to our establishments. Many a well placed wife has begun her career as a whore or an actress. Or, indeed both. There is no reason for you not to succeed as an actress and a businesswoman. You have my blessing, and I shall help you in any way I can.'

Fanny knelt before Elizabeth and kissed her hand. 'Thank you, dear Elizabeth. You will be proud of me.'

'I know I shall. I only wager on winners.' As Fanny rose, the ring attached to the silver chain fell forward and Elizabeth held it. 'I see you have the ring.'

'My mother, Marie, gave it to me. Can you tell me its story?'

Elizabeth released the ring. 'No. It will be your story to tell.'

CHAPTER THIRTY-THREE

The Beginning...

FANNY AND TOM travelled in Elizabeth's coach to their lodgings in Maiden Lane. For once in his life, Tom had no words, so overwhelmed was he by the day's events.

Fanny stared at him, waiting for some sort of reaction. 'Speak to me.'

'I know I'm going to wake up in a minute, and I don't want to.'

'Oh, Tom,' said Fanny, shaking his arm gently, 'this is going to be fun.'

'Fun, Fanny? This is going to be amazing. I'm not letting you out of my sight. Without you, all this will dissolve like a stage transformation scene.'

'I'm not going anywhere. I know now, who my true friends are, and I will keep them close.' She hesitated and asked, 'Tom, did Elizabeth tell you about last night?'

'Yes, Fanny, she did.'

'And about what Gideon did to me?'

'Yes, she did.'

'I was in love with him, Tom.'

He put his arm around her and offered some wise

words. 'You won't be the first or last girl to fall for a bad man, the best of us seem to be attracted to the worst. Friends can see the danger, but when the heart beats with the blindness of passion, we are deaf to such truths. Forget him, Fanny.' Tom kissed her on the forehead and gave her a squeeze. 'What about that nice cousin of yours, Theo? He likes you.'

As if clear blue sky broke through the dark storm clouds, Fanny imagined Theo's kind face, and she felt terrible about the way she had dismissed him so easily when he felt so strongly about her. 'I must see him. What a fool I have been. He has been my kindest friend and always looked after me. I must thank him and ask his forgiveness for my foolishness.'

'Do you love him, Fanny?'

Without warning, the carriage pulled up sharply and veered to the left. Fanny and Tom were thrown forwards, out of their seats.

'Why have we stopped, Tom? Is it highwaymen?'

Tom lifted up the leather blind of the window and looked around. There was a girl lying in the road. Tom called to the coachman, 'What's happened?

'That woman, she threw herself in front of us. I did what I could. Honest, sir. Gawd, is she dead?'

'I don't know. I'll get out and see.'

'I'll come,' said Fanny.

'No, wait. Let me go first.' Tom stepped down as the coachman joined him. They both went over to the ragged body. Miraculously, she had missed both the hoofs of the horses and the wheels of the coach. Tom turned her over. She was alive but nearly starved. He ran back to the coach where Fanny was leaning out to see if she could help. Tom came up close to her and said, 'She's alive. It's Martha.'

Two weeks later Martha was looking better, Theo had attended her and Fanny and Tom fussed over her. She had become part of the family that lodged in Maiden Lane, and it took all of Tom and Fanny's attention to prevent Martha from rising from her bed, to cook and clean for them.

'Martha, don't work now, you have to gain your strength and rest.'

'No, miss, you have been so good to me, I have to pay you back somehow.'

'Please, Martha, you saved me and Kitty from Tyburn, I am happy to help you, in your time of need.'

'You know he hung, don't ya?'

'Yes, in August.'

'I were there. I weren't gonna miss that old bugger swing. There was thousands of people turned out for the day. Old man Busby, well, you'd have thought he was off for a day at the races, all gentility itself in his mourning coach and best coat. But when it came close to him being turned off, and he had his chance to speak to the crowd, he were a proper coward. Oh, yes. No airs and graces then. Just crying and swearing, pleading for mercy, saying he didn't mean to do it, then saying he didn't do it and in the end he said, he did do it. Shouting out that his wife was a hell cat and he, but a poor, put upon faithful husband.' Here, Martha spat to punctuate her feelings. 'I knew he was no good the moment I set me eyes on him. If I ain't been so young and a foundling, I'd of chosen the rope meself, rather than work me fingers red and sore for such a beast. Kitty were there.'

'What?'

'Yea, I saw her, up close she was. Must've waited all night to get the best place. Screaming and shouting she were, throwing everything at him, including a dead cat. At one point I were sure he seen her. He shut up and just stared forward. It were the most scary part. Him like a demon from hell caught looking into the eyes of the devil himself. It weren't an easy drop, he writhed and twitched like a twisted paper ribbon, hung over a flame. I had nice piece of ginger-bread and come home.'

'Well, a good day out, Martha.'

Jack's house in Queen Street was dark with the shutters closed, except for the window of his bedroom on the second floor, where a single candle was lit. A weak flame reached out to illuminate the last vestige of night, as the life of Jonathan Sackville slipped away behind the dawn.

Elizabeth's footman, dressed in mourning, opened the door to Fanny. 'Hello, James.'

'Please follow me, Mistress Mancini.'

'I'm not called…' Fanny stopped herself, it was not the time for such matters. 'Thank you, James.'

The room was dim and the figures floated about as murmuring shadows. Kneeling by the bed was Elizabeth in devout prayer, her hands clasped together reciting the holy rosary. Opposite her stood a priest, making the sign of the cross and waiting to give extreme unction to the dying man. In juxtaposition, Juliette Mancini walked about the room in tight, anxious patterns and repeated magical incantations. Only a powerful, respected family could practise two opposing beliefs at the same time. Fanny was astounded and a little afraid. Elizabeth looked up at her. 'My dear, come here. Jonathan was asking for you. I hope it is not too late, he has slipped into sleep.'

'I came as fast as I could, Elizabeth.' She approached the bed and sat down on Elizabeth's chair. The strong smell of incense made her eyes water, adding more tears to the ones that flowed from her heart. 'Jack, I'm here. It's Fanny, can you hear me?' She took his hand and lifted it to her lips. 'Jack, you are so special to me, I look upon you as an older brother. Stay with me.'

Jack opened his eyes and spoke in a whisper, using the small amount of life remaining in his body. 'Fanny, do not grieve for me, you have much to do. Everything our family has worked for, will come to you in time. Use your gifts and intelligence to make the house of Rochester and Mancini, greater than ever.' Fanny nodded and wept as he added, 'You will carry my love with you until we meet again in heaven.' He turned his head towards Elizabeth and called out, 'Mother.' She rushed towards him as the priest administered the final anointing.

The interment was at St James's Church, Piccadilly. Jack was laid to rest with Laura Mancini. The mother and son parted at birth, were now reunited in death. Fanny insisted that Betsy attend. This caused no indignation. The Mancini women understood the young girl's life, having been in the same situation themselves at some time. They treated her with kindness and respect. Fanny promised to explain everything to Betsy, as soon as Jack's estate was distributed. In the meantime, Fanny would look after Betsy. She would have everything she wanted.

The family being rather eccentric and not conforming to the usual expected customs, decided once the funeral was over, mourning would no longer be worn. They believed the precious fine chain of life between family members, should be celebrated and not mourn the loss of one link.

It was with mixed emotions that Fanny moved into

Queen Street. She opened the shutters, allowing the sun to fill the rooms, which Jack had left his indelible mark upon. Looking around, she noticed Jack's oiled coat, wrapped up in a corner, its disposal overlooked. Fanny touched it and ruminated on what a tortured man he must have been. It seemed there were two people in one body. Jonathan Sackville, who was refined and kind, and the other, Jack Mann who was passionate and violent. Fanny experienced both identities, and the one thing that stayed stable between the double personality was a sharp intellect. She was aware of the strong connection with him in this house, she looked around the drawing room and called, 'Jack, I'm here.' A feeling of warmth settled over her, as she swept off the silk coverings that protected the precious items on every surface. She turned to Tom, who was helping her open up the house. 'I can feel Jack's presence in every object and think I see him appear when I turn my head. Everything I look at makes me miss him, so much.'

'Jack wanted you to care for his home and collections. You must be happy that you are carrying out his wishes.' He opened the lid of a glass display table. 'Look at these beautiful portrait miniatures. Who do you think they all are?' He picked up a small piece of paper, which rested on top of an image of a man with a narrow moustache and sensuous lips, dressed extravagantly. 'This one has a note. It says it's for you.' Fanny picked up the pendant and examined the delicate enamel on metal. In Jack's hand, was written: 'For Dearest Fanny. This is Louis XIV of France.'

'My goodness, why would he give that to you?'

'He is my great-grandfather.'

'What? Stop fooling me, Fanny.'

She put her head to one side and looked at him. 'It's

a long story, Tom. One day I will tell you all about it.'

'You certainly will.'

Another covering was being ripped off a table, not half a mile away. This was not of soft silk but rough hemp. Kitty, heavy with liquor, decided she didn't like the second pint of gin she was served. 'This is piss, give me something drinkable, nice and strong.'

The woman who ran the gin shop, lifted Kitty up by the elbow. 'Get out, we don't want your sort drinking here.'

'What you mean, my sort?'

'Get back on the streets, you hedge whore.'

Kitty slapped the woman around the face, screaming, 'I'm not a common whore, I'm one of Mother Stroker's girls, and I have a rich protector.'

The woman didn't slap her back, but hit her in the eye, with her fist. 'I heard Stroker threw you out, as you weren't no good, no more. So you won't have a protector much longer. Look at you, dirty poxy whore. Get out.' She held Kitty by the back of her stays and kneed her out of the door, onto the street.

'How dare you. I am going to be Mrs Gideon Woodford, you hear me? Someone important, you'll see.' The door slammed in Kitty's face.

Fanny lit the candles, casting a spell of splendour over the drawing-room.

'This is a wondrous house,' said Tom. 'We should celebrate your good fortune. Shall we go to the theatre and see a play?'

'In the audience, Tom?'

'Where else?'

'I've never been in the audience.'

'It's about time you did. You can study how the

acting appears from the front and the way actors work the house.'

'Do let's go. Maybe Theo would like to join us? He is working at the apothecary. I can run over to him later and bring him back to the theatre.' The door opened, it was the new housekeeper. 'Hello, Martha, do you need some help?' asked Fanny.

Martha giggled. 'No, miss, that's what I says to you, not you to me. Thank you for me frock, I've never had such a beautiful gown before.' Martha caressed the bodice and petticoat with pride. 'And me shoes. I ain't had no proper pair of shoes, neither.'

'Martha, there is something else I am going to give you, now you are living in a fine house.'

'What's that?'

'Aiches.'

'Aiches, that's what I say, aiches, I know it ain't hayches,' said Martha, stressing the first syllable with a strong exhalation of air.

Tom looked at Fanny, hiding his mouth under his hand to conceal his laughter.

'Very well thought out, Martha. We shall speak about this later. Tom and I are going out so you may go shopping to buy yourself something nice. Please take this money.'

Martha looked at the coins, transfixed. 'For me? All for me? To get what I want?' Fanny nodded. 'Oh miss, I shall buy a bonnet and I shall be,' Martha took a breath, 'hall hairs and graces.'

'Enjoy yourself, Martha and when you come back you can relax, as I shall be attending the theatre. After the performance, I shall return home to rest in my bedchamber, before I meet my dear friend.'

Kitty staggered her way to the Plough and Harrow

where she had found Gideon before. It was the same scene, Gideon drinking wine with the redhead sitting on his lap.

'Get off him, whore.'

'Not again,' said the Titian beauty. 'Is this your wife, Gideon?'

'Soon will be,' Kitty said, as she pushed the girl off her lover.

'My best wishes and good luck to you, sir. I'm off. I can't deal with all this trouble.'

'Sissy, don't go. We'll retire upstairs, in a minute.'

Kitty caught the girl and roughly pulled her close, warning her, 'Upstairs? You ain't going nowhere, except out in the street. Go on, get out.' The girl left, tossing her flowing mane of red curls, whilst Kitty took her place on Gideon's knees. She wrapped her arms around his neck and kissed him violently. 'You're mine. Don't forget it.'

He threw her off and wiped his mouth with his sleeve. 'Stop clinging to me. Go away, Kitty.'

'No, I ain't going, nowhere. You promised yourself to me. You begged me to be only yours. You have to love and keep me, now that I need you so much.'

Gideon disentangled himself from her clasp, took her by the arm and led her outside.

'Kitty, how many times do I have to tell you, I don't want to be with you. It's over. You bore me, and you are of no further use to me.'

'What do you mean, Gideon?' Tears started to pour down her face, washing narrow channels through the layer of soot.

'Kitty, I have no money, no status, no life. My father has disowned me for my drinking and debts, and I am refused entrance to any of the gambling houses. The higher society has turned its face away from me. I am penniless.'

'No Gideon, I will help you get money, I'd do anything for you. I love you.' Once again she clung to him, tighter this time. Gideon caught her wrists, pinned down her arms and spat out, 'I do not love you, Kitty. Look at yourself, you are ugly now. You can no longer hide the pustules and chancres, with patches. You have the pox, Kitty. You are no use to anyone.'

'No, Gideon, please do not be so cruel. You are a good man.' She stroked his face.

'No, I'm not. I don't love you, Kitty. I love someone else.'

Kitty wasn't expecting those words. 'Who? Who do you love? You can't love anyone but Kitty. No one else is so good to you, like Kitty is. Who is it?'

'Fanny.'

Kitty was silenced, her mind racing. 'Fanny? It can't be. Fanny?'

'Yes, I love her. I have made terrible mistakes and used her for my own advantage. But I intend to make up for my bad behaviour. I know where Jack Mann's treasure is, and when I have it, I shall shower her with diamonds and love. Fanny will be mine and we shall live together in great wealth.'

In disbelief, Kitty said, 'No. No. This can't be. Fanny? But she is my friend.'

'She has loved me for a long time now.'

'No.'

'She kept it a secret.'

'No, she wouldn't do that to me. I have been so close to her. She couldn't have lied so well.'

'She did, Kitty. It was our secret. Never have I felt so much love and desire for any woman, and one so beautiful and entrancing as her.'

Kitty looked into the distance and quietly vowed, 'I shall kill her.'

CHAPTER THIRTY-FOUR

...of the End

KITTY LEFT GIDEON in the tavern and ran up New Street. She ignored the calls thrown at her as she crossed the Piazza and made her way to Little Brydges Street. She opened the stage door and out of breath, asked Fred, 'I want to see Fanny. Is she here?'

'The lovely Mistress Frances Tomlinson may now be found at Lincoln's Inn Theatre. She is rehearsing with the company for the upcoming production of Volpone.' Kitty stared vacantly at Fred. 'In other words, she ain't here. Be off with ya.'

What was this? Fanny working as a legitimate actress? Kitty was shocked and stunned by Fred's revelation. But more than that, she was furious. It was she, who was going to be the famous actress, not Fanny. How could this be happening? Fanny was stealing her life.

Fanny whispered in Tom's ear. 'I'm going to get Theo. I won't be long.'

'Good timing, Fanny. Cibber's monologue is due to start, and he's not a good tragedian. It promises to be awful. Let's go. I've agreed to meet Oliver at the

Fleece, not my favourite tavern but my favourite man. We'll leave through the pass door.'

Reaching the keepers cubby hole, they called out, 'Goodnight Fred.'

'Didn't know you were in. Sign out, please.' Tom made an indecipherable spider mark and Fanny wrote her name legibly.

'Going somewhere nice, you two?'

'Off to the tavern. Must keep it in business. See you tomorrow, Fred,' said Tom.

Outside, the temperature had dropped and the autumn air brought the oncoming winter dampness with it. 'Watch how you go, Fanny. Keep to the main streets.'

'When did you become my father?' She kissed him farewell.

Tom turned right towards Brydges Street and Fanny in the opposite direction along Vinegar Yard, towards the apothecary in Chancery Lane. Tonight, her heart beat a little faster with the desire of meeting Theo. Did that mean she was in love with him? Or, was it because she had so much exciting news to tell. He still understood her to be living at Tom's lodgings and would be astounded when he saw Jack's House. There, she could spend time alone with him, not interrupted by either of them running off to do different tasks. She imagined them sitting in front of the fire, drinking hot negus wine during Advent, and at Christmas, they would celebrate Letty and Samuel's wedding. She decided she would hold his hand all the way back to the theatre.

Kitty sat alone in the shadows of the Rose tavern, as her miserable jealousy turned to thoughts of vengeance. She needed fuel to fire up the smouldering hatred glowing inside of her. She ordered another pint of gin. The more she drank, the more depressed she became. She watched the tavern door open and recognised Fanny's friend, Theo. Under her breath, she said, 'Another fool who has fallen under that witches spell. I'll take him from her.' She shouted over the hubbub of the tavern. 'Here dear, over this way. That's right. It's Kitty, remember me?'

Theo approached her and because of the low light and her dishevelled appearance, he scarcely recognised her. 'Are you Fanny's friend?'

'Yes, dear. Kitty. Sit yourself down next to me and buy a girl a dram.'

'You have some gin, Kitty.'

'You being rude? Who do you think you are?'

'I'm looking for Fanny. I'm early. She was to meet me at my shop, later. Have you seen her?'

'Fanny. What's so special about Fanny?' She took a long draft of the burning liquor.

'I'll go and see if she is at Tom's.' Theo felt uneasy about this girl.

'Don't go, dear. Fill up my pot.'

'No, you have had enough. It will cause you harm.' Theo tried to take her gin away.

Kitty trapped his wrist on the table. 'Don't you tell me what to do. I'm going to be famous, one of the best actresses in London and people will love me, hundreds of them. Just you see.'

'Fanny has the same ambition.' He'd lit the fuse.

She slammed her fists down and cut in, 'Don't talk to me about Fanny. She's a liar and a false friend. That one is a bitch.'

Theo jumped up, knocking the chair over behind him. 'How dare you. Fanny is a kind and innocent young woman.'

She pressed her face close to his and hissed, 'She ain't, she's the devil itself and I'm gonna find her and shoot her.' She spun around and made to leave the tavern. Theo stopped her, grabbing her by the arm. 'What are you saying? Don't threaten such things.'

'I'm not threatening, I'm going to do it.' She threw him off and ran from the tavern.

Theo left the tavern, at exactly the same time as Fanny was imagining spending Christmas with him. As she walked east, towards Chancery Lane, he made his way, west, to Tom's lodgings in Maiden Lane. His progress was hindered by prostitutes of every type. He tried to be polite but became brusque as his frustration grew. He must warn Fanny of Kitty's threat to harm her. He knocked on the front door of a dwelling, ironically named, 'Peace House'. The din from within nearly drowned out his hammering. Nobody opened the door to him. He knocked even louder and hollered up to the first floor. 'Fanny, Fanny, it's Theo. I must speak to you.'

A window was pushed up and a middle-aged woman's head poked out. 'What's all this shouting about?' She couldn't see his face under his hat, but when he looked up at her, she smiled and leaned out further, causing her breasts to tip out of her stays. 'Well, what a good looking boy you are, my dear. What do you need young Fanny for? What you need, is an experienced woman in the art of loving.'

'No, I don't.' Theo was getting annoyed at being accosted during a time so worrying. 'Is Fanny there? It is of the utmost importance that I speak to her.'

'Well, my dear, I think you've woken the dead, let alone Fanny. No, she ain't here.'

'Do you know where she is?'

'Nah, she went off with that Molly from the theatre.'

'When was that?'

'I dunno. This morning? She's probably in one of the taverns, or you could try the theatre. Look, do you want to ride with me or not?'

'No, thank you.'

'Please yourself.' She shut the window with such force, a pane of glass cracked, fell and shattered next to his feet. 'Oh, bugger it,' she said.

Fanny cut through Lincoln's Inn. She passed under the arches of the chapel, where she had hidden the day Marie was murdered. If it were not for Kitty, she would never have escaped. Fanny felt bad she hadn't seen her for a while. Her busy life was no excuse for not seeing her friend. She would make the effort, although she wouldn't look forward to revisiting St Giles' squalor.

Opposite the Gate House, stood the apothecary with its window full of blue and white Delft jars. Fanny loved to study the different cartouches, with their peacocks and angels with outspread wings. Theo would describe what each jar contained and for what illness the medicine was prescribed. To her surprise, the shop was closed and dark. She called, 'Theo. It's me, Fanny. Are you there?' No answer came. Being so punctilious in his arrangements, it was strange he wasn't home. Something must have happened. She wasn't worried though, she would see him tomorrow. Fanny decided to return to Jack's House to take a rest before she visited Pall Mall, later that night.

As dusk fell, Gideon waited outside the Big's tenement to see who came and went. From his hiding place, he could see the top window. It remained dark.

Nobody was in. For the tenth time, he checked his pocket for the attic keys. He had to make his move, now. He looked around, checking all was clear and pushed away the tenement's door, which was off its hinges and resting across the threshold. Guided by the light from the full moon, he climbed the dangerous staircase, being careful to remember Fanny's warning of the open traps. Reaching the top, he crouched down and listened at the little door. Silence. Lifting the two keys, still tied to Fanny's ribbon, he turned the locks and the door opened. He stepped in. The wall of boxes faced him, covered by the painted tarpaulin. He ripped it down. There, on the bottom row, was the box he was looking for. To access it, he had to remove those above it. Dragging the table over, he climbed up to reach the top tier. Carefully and quietly, not to attract attention, he began to demolish the mountain of wooden, metal and wicker trunks. At last, the man-sized box with the writing DEAD ANIMALS on its side, was exposed. He tried to move it forward, but he'd not considered the weight of the gold. He panicked. How was he going to carry it all? It would be impossible. He hadn't planned properly, his greed and impatience for riches overpowering his reason. In the little time available, he would only take the most valuable pieces. At a later date, he'd return to rob Mrs Big of the rest of the hoard. What could a little freak woman do to stop him? With Jack Mann dead there was no rush. The violent criminal was no longer skulking in the shadows, ready to slit Gideon's throat.

The dead weight of the gold held the box firm. Gideon struggled with the chain and padlock. His fear together with his obsession focused his strength, and he managed to slip the chain off the narrow end of the coffin. He prised open the lid. What was this? All he could see were dusty costumes. In anger, he threw them on the floor around him. He thrust his hands in again, to empty out the last garments. Panic rose in him. Where was his gold? As he flung a serge coat behind him, it uncovered the leather bags. He could hardly breathe. Here was his salvation. Untying the strappings, he upturned the pouch and the contents spilled onto the floor. He gasped. The amount was staggering: rings, earrings, brooches, necklaces of coloured stones and even a coronet encrusted with diamonds that caught the light of the moon. Gideon swept up the jewellery with both hands, lifted it above his head and showered himself with starlight.

Kitty paced her way home to the slum in St Giles, and with every step, her imagination painted more and more vivid scenes of situations that never happened. In one, she saw Gideon and Fanny in bed together, drinking the finest champagne and laughing at their clandestine love affair. In another, Gideon bought Fanny jewels and gowns, with the gold that Kitty had stolen for him. She put her hands over her ears, as she heard them joking about the falsehood of Fanny's friendship. Bile rose up into her throat. How she hated her. Fanny was to act upon the stage and be adored by high society, whilst she, wretched with syphilis, would die on filthy streets of London. Unloved. They had made a fool out of her.

Her rage grew. When she arrived at Da's hovel, neither he nor Kathleen Garrett was there. She ran over to the spot where the pistol was hidden under the floorboards. As she held the weapon, it calmed her. All emotion drained, and a coldness descended over her. 'I shall have my revenge on Fanny Tomlinson.' She picked up the basket taken from the altar of the chapel of Lincoln's Inn. Once more, Kitty concealed the gun under the cloths. Now armed, she would find Fanny.

Sitting on the floor of the Big's garret, Gideon stuffed his pockets full of jewels and gold. So engrossed in his avarice, he didn't hear the light footsteps on the stairs, until a voice said, 'Stop, the door is open. Someone has broken into the garret.'

Gideon recognised the Irish accent. He ran across the room and flattened himself against the wall, behind the door. His heart thudded in his ears, but his mind was sharp and clear. When the dwarves came in, they would see the gold and boxes strewn over the garret. Gideon gambled on the fact they would instinctively move straight towards them. Once they'd passed him and were at the far end of the attic, he would slip out and down the stairs. Gideon held his breath.

'Ready boys? In we go.'

The troupe burst through the door. As Gideon predicted, they ran to the far end of the room. 'What's all this?' said one of them.

'What does it look like, stupid.' Luke bent down to pick up some of the jewels. As he did, he saw movement and spun around. 'You. You scabby thief. You're mine now.'

The others turned and looked at Gideon with pure hatred. For a moment no one moved, then all together they surged forward. Gideon moved towards the door as the dwarves ran at him. At that moment, Mrs Big appeared in the doorway and took in the whole situation. 'Stop.' She held one hand up towards the men and the other, close to Gideon's face. 'I know what you want to do with him, boys, but I ain't letting you.' She turned to Gideon. 'Now, you have the jewels on you and we are all witnesses to this theft. I suggest you empty your pockets of everything, and we shall let you go.'

'What?' said Luke.

'As long as you swear, never to show your face around here or see Fanny again. Do you understand?'

'No,' shouted Luke. 'That's too good for him, let me at him.' Mark held him back.

There was a standoff. Gideon had no intention of leaving his treasure. He lied, 'All right.' He reached into his pocket and pulled out a small handful of jewels. 'Here.' He threw them into the men's faces whilst he grabbed Mrs Big around the waist, tucked her under his arm and raced down the stairs.

'Get him,' cried Luke. Gideon couldn't have had any idea of what came next. The boys went into performance mode and repeated movements they had always done for fun. Now, there was much more at stake, they had to save Mrs Big.

Matthew and Mark jumped on to the hanging ropes and like monkeys, swung from one to another, quickly descending down the centre void of the stairs. At the same time, Luke and John ran to the window on the top landing, opened it and pulled one of the ropes towards them, which was attached to a pulley higher up. They looked down into the small, contained courtyard below and saw that the large water bucket was full. They nodded to each other.

As Gideon reached the bottom of the staircase and was about to run out of the building, he came up against Noble and Livewell coming through the doorway. 'Stop him. He has Mrs B,' shouted Matthew to them from above. They knew they were barring the only escape route, as the courtyard was enclosed by high walls. They stood firm. 'Put her down.' Gideon paused only for a moment, challenging them with a fierce look. Then, he made his first mistake. He turned around and headed into the courtyard, only to find there was no other exit. Matthew and Mark slid down the stair ropes, and somersaulted down the last eight foot, to the floor. Gideon watched as they guarded the only way out of the courtyard. He heard the whistle of the pulley high above him, and he watched the two dwarves drop down while the heavy bucket flew up. John jumped off the rope and secured it to a cleat on the wall.

Gideon was surrounded. Luke stood opposite him on the other side of the well and commanded, 'Let go of her. You cannot escape, you are trapped like a rat. Call us vermin? You are the vermin, and you will die in a trap and be left to starve.'

Gideon increased his grip on Mrs Big. 'Leave me alone or I shall kill her.'

'No, you won't. You are surrounded by those who want to harm you and there is no escape. Now, put her down.'

Gideon was trapped, and he knew it. There was no way out. He panicked. That was when he saw the well.

'You win, I shall put her down.' Gideon took two steps forward to the edge of the well. 'I shall put her down, there.' He thrust out his arms straight until Mrs Big hung over the centre of the round abyss of the well.

The men started for him, but he made a sharp movement as if to let her fall. 'Opps, nearly dropped her. Sorry about that.' The men froze. 'Now, do as I say and you can have your little freak back. You behind me, move away from the doorway and get to the other side of the courtyard, you can join your very rude friend. Oh, I'm forgetting my manners. Please.'

Mrs Big, speaking for the first time said, 'Do as he says, he will drop me, I know he will.'

Matthew and Mark joined Luke and John on the far side of the well, opposite Gideon. 'And you two,' he said to Noble and Livewell, 'Off you trot, you little cockroaches.' The men shook with loathing and anger but kept their ground. 'Are you deaf? Move!'

Mrs Big had comforting words for her friends. 'Move over dears, and I shall be cooking your supper as soon as we all return upstairs. Do it now, my dears. Off you go.'

Very reluctantly they joined the others, spitting at Gideon as they passed. Now his exit was clear, he lowered Mrs Big a couple of inches. Addressing the six men standing on the other side of the well, he said, 'You know, you should all be cleared off this earth. I can only play my small part.' He released his grip and dropped Mrs Big down the well.

CHAPTER THIRTY-FIVE

Fearlessness

THE SOUND OF Mrs Big screaming as she plummeted down the narrow well, would stay with the little men all their lives. Rushing to the edge, they looked down through tears of grief.

'I caught a rat.' All heads turned towards the courtyard opening. There, stood Sam the Strongman carrying Gideon, unconscious in his arms.

'He threw Mrs B down the well, Sam,' said Mark, weeping.

Gideon stirred. Sam hit him again, and he passed out with a few more bruises this time.

'Do you want me to strangle him?'

Luke, although in fury and distress, took a moment to think. 'No, he deserves a worse death than that. Take him upstairs, and if he comes round hit him again. Harder.'

Four of the men followed Sam upstairs, baying for revenge. They wanted to see Gideon's blood flow. Livewell and Mark stayed in the courtyard, with the vain hope of saving Mrs Big. Mark released the bucket rope from the cleat and shouted to Livewell, 'Mind your head.' They both watched the bucket hurtle to the ground, with the last of the water spilling out of it. A massive knot at the other end of the rope prevented it from flying up and through the pulley. 'Quick, send the bucket down the well.'

'Wait,' said Livewell. 'Maybe we can hear her. Now it's quiet.' They both leaned over the edge of the stone. 'Mrs B, can you hear me?' Nothing. 'Mrs B, it's Mark. Make a noise, please.'

Livewell said, 'Her voice is so small, we shall not be able to hear her, she is too far down' He shouted down into the blackness. 'We're sending the bucket down as fast as we can Mrs B. Try and get in it, and we shall pull you up.' They knew there was little chance. The fall would break her body and the water drown her. But still, they lowered the bucket. They felt it hit the water. There was no noise or movement. 'Oh, Mrs B.' Mark let out his emotions and Livewell tried to comfort him, taking the rope from Mark's hands and embracing him. At that moment of lost hope, Livewell felt a slight movement of the rope.

'Mark, she's moving the bucket. The vibration is tiny. If she is alive, I don't think she has the strength to get in it. What are we going to do?'

Mark dashed to the wall where a large butchers hook hung. 'Pull the bucket up, and tell her we're going to send the hook down and all she has to do is hook it through her clothing and we shall lift her up.'

Livewell shouted the instructions down the well and told Mrs Big not to worry, they would get her out. Mark untied the bucket, replacing it with the hook. Down it went. It seemed an eternity until it reached the water.

'Hook it on to you Mrs B.' Mark lent over so far he nearly lost his balance.

'Be careful, Mark, I'd never get you both back up. Have you got it, Mrs B?'

'I can't hear her, Livewell. It's wishful thinking. She's dead, I know it. Dear God, please help us.'

His prayer was answered. Livewell felt a shaking of the rope, as it moved on its own accord. He tugged it and felt weight. 'She's on it. Mark, she's done it. She's secured the hook. Get her up.'

They both pulled with all their strength, and slowly the rope brought up the hook.

'Thank God,' Mark said, as they saw the shadow of a tiny figure nearing the top. But their happiness returned to sadness, when they saw what was on the end of the hook. A dying and broken doll, The Tiny Pearl.

Fanny arrived home at Jack's House and Martha opened the door in her new bonnet, which was rather overloaded with feathers. 'Do you like it, miss? I feel like a great lady in this here hat.'

'It looks lovely on you, Martha. Would you like me to come with you next time?'

'Oh yes, miss, I would be honoured,' Martha said with strong emphases on the first syllable. 'I saw that Kitty when I was out. Cor, she were worse for drink, that girl. She said she hadn't seen you for a while and where was you living. I told her you had a bit of luck and were living in a grand house, here in Queen Street. She said she'd visit you.'

'I will see her, Martha. I'm going to rest now and come down later, to meet my friend.'

'Yes, miss.' Martha curtsied and retired to the basement.

Fanny was feeling rather alone as she had much to tell people, but they all seemed to be busy, doing things without her. As she climbed the stairs, she changed her mind about resting. She would visit the Big's, instead. They were always excited to hear her news, and she loved their company. Also, she had to explain how she lost the garret keys. She wouldn't get them back now, as she certainly wasn't going to see Gideon again. The temperature had dropped outside, so she went to her room and opened the trunk of new clothes, which Elizabeth's seamstress had made for her. She unfolded a long, velvet cape with a hood. Although a little creased, it wouldn't be noticed as it was dark outside, and the damp air would smooth out the fabric.

With much happiness, Fanny closed the door to her house. Her mind full of stories to tell Mr and Mrs Big.

Theo, was at Drury Lane stage door. 'Good evening, sir. My name is Theo. I am Fanny's cousin. I was to meet her this evening. Is she in the theatre, by any chance?'

Fred sucked on his clay pipe. 'I know who you are. She's a popular girl tonight. Another friend of her's, come by earlier.' This made Theo nervous. 'Fanny went with Tom to the tavern.'

'Which one?'

'It's usually the Rose with that lot, or the Fleece.' Theo rushed off. Fred shouted after him, 'If you see her, tell her Cibber wants a word.'

Fanny hurried through Holborn to reach Field Lane. She gathered up her cloak as she climbed the familiar staircase. Once at the top, she saw the garret door ajar. She thought it strange, as it was always locked. Entering the room, she took in the chaos inside. 'Oh, no,' she thought. 'Someone has stolen the gold.' The room was lit by moonlight, showing the mountain of boxes, broken down. In the middle of the room was something covered with a black cloth. She nearly fell over it, as it didn't belong there. She heard a groan. Lifting the covering, she found Gideon tied up on a wooden board, with a gag in his mouth. The ropes held him secure, crisscrossing his body, anchored by nails catching the turning of the ties. He was badly beaten. She knelt down and removed the rags from his mouth.

'What happened?'

'Fanny, forgive me. I love you.'

'Don't start that, Gideon. I don't believe you, and I should just leave you here.'

'No, Fanny. Don't desert me. They will murder me. They kept saying they wanted to.'

'Why would they say that? They are good people.'

Gideon paused a second. 'I tried to steal the gold. I did it because I wanted to give you the life of wealth, you so deserve, Fanny.'

'Stop it, Gideon. You are deluded if you think I have any feelings for you. I despise you and want you out of my life. I don't need you or anybody.' She looked at his bindings. 'Why did they only tie you up? Any one of them could kill you. They are small but very strong. They could strangle you, using one arm around your neck.'

'They said, I would die of a hundred cuts. They're coming back. What does it mean, Fanny? Untie me, and stay with me. Please.'

Fanny sat back on her heels, covered her face with her hands and wondered what she should do. She knew the boys would murder him and when the crime was discovered, they would be imprisoned in Tyburn, to await hanging. She must protect her friends. But this situation had put herself in danger. By now, the troupe would have worked out that it was she, who had told Gideon where the garret and gold was. Fanny's betrayal would incite them to demand revenge on her. Once they found out she'd rescued Gideon, they would come to kill her. Neither leaving Gideon to his fate nor freeing him, could save her. She felt sweat rising in her palms. Her mind spun with contradictory scenarios.

There was one way she could protect herself. To kill Gideon, here in the attic, and wait for the return of the troupe. She would be united with them in justice. Looking at the board again, things fell into place. She realised the meaning of death by a hundred cuts. This was William Bull's target board, she had positioned herself against it at the May Fair, whilst Chief Lightning Thundercloud threw knives at her.

'So, that is their plan.'

'What? What are they going to do?'

'They have gone to fetch the knife thrower. He will bring his sharp weapons, to torture you. You won't die of one well-placed stab, but by a hundred cuts, severing nerves and blood vessels. It will be a slow and painful death.'

'No. They can't do such a dreadful thing. You must save me, Fanny.' Gideon struggled to free himself, but with no avail.

Looking coldly at this pathetic man, Fanny decided on the only alternative to such a slow and terrible death. She would cut his throat.

Fanny loathed Gideon. She wanted him gone, to be free of this man who'd manipulated her into surrender and crime. Fanny walked to the small table by the stove and picked up a knife. She touched the edge. It was razor sharp.

'Hurry, Fanny. Get me out of here, before they return.'

Fanny was calm. She knew what she had to do. She bought the knife to the side of his throat. Only a little movement was required. Sliding the blade to the right, his neck would unfurl, spilling rich velvet blood to bloom, as red roses over white Carrara marble. Her pupils turned black, as strength and revenge pulsed down her arm. She jerked the knife. But she pulled it to the left, away from his throat, cutting through the ropes.

'I'm not doing this for you, I hate you. I am saving my friends. Tonight I shall hide you, and tomorrow you will leave London. You are never to return.'

Theo was very concerned now. He had to find Fanny to tell her to take care and not to see Kitty, under any circumstances. He hadn't found her at the Rose. Maybe she was in the Fleece tavern. He entered the drinking parlour, which was thick with smoke from the fire. He moved around the drinkers, asking if anyone knew Fanny. A large guffaw drew his attention to a table close to the window. Theo saw a pretty young man flirting with another fellow, whom he recognised. Theo approached the young men. 'Excuse me, I am looking for Fanny. Have you seen her?'

'You're a nice looking gentleman, come and sit beside me,' said Oliver.

'Quiet, Oliver. Who wants to know?' asked Tom, turning towards the voice.

'Theo, her cousin.'

'Oh, hello, Theo, I thought you were with her. She left the theatre to find you. I would have accompanied her, but I became a little distracted.' Tom patted Oliver on the thigh.

'Well, we must have missed each other. If you see her, tell her not to see her friend, Kitty. Make sure you warn her of that.'

'Is there trouble?'

'I hope not,' said Theo. 'Do you have any idea where she may have gone?'

'Not really. Oh, what about Mrs B's?'

'Yes, that's a good idea, I shall go there. Thank you.'

CHAPTER THIRTY-SIX

No Turning Back

FANNY SUPPORTED GIDEON as they slowly progressed towards Jack's House. He was badly beaten and in pain. As he limped along, Fanny spoke to him as if he were drunk. A whore and her customer would raise no interest from passers-by if it looked as if she were taking him to a room to do business.

'Now, sir. You hold on to Meg, and she'll take you for a nice lie-down.'

As Fanny walked, she plotted a plan to get Gideon out of London, quickly. She had friends at the stable in Great Queen Street. They would help her.

It was late when they arrived home. Not to disturb Martha, she let herself into the house and helped Gideon up the stairs to her bedchamber. The fire was lit and the bed turned down.

'Get on the bed and try to sleep. I am to find a wagon that will take you to the north of this country, and you will never return. Do we have an agreement?'

Gideon could hardly speak, the exertion of the evening had exhausted him. 'Yes, Fanny, I agree.'

'Good. I'll take back my keys.' Gideon was cold and in shock. 'You're shivering. Let me pull the covers up high, to keep you warm, and I will wake you when the wagon arrives in a few hours.'

Gideon pulled the counterpane over his head and instantly fell into a deep sleep, as Fanny closed the heavy bed curtains around him. She then left the house.

Theo arrived at the Big's garret, to find the door wide open and the room in total disarray. Whatever had happened here, was violent. Fanny was nowhere to be seen: his distress mounted. He rushed down the staircase and was greeted by a gathering of neighbours, gossiping and looking up to the top floor of the building. He asked a washerwoman what had happened. 'A young man by the name of Gideon Woodford threw Mrs Big down the well. He escaped and Mr Big's Little troupe are out hunting him down.'

'No, it can't be. That is terrible. What can I do? Where's Mr Big?'

'I don't know, dear, I told you all I know.'

'Have you seen a young woman by the name of, Fanny?'

'Fanny? No, dear. I ain't seen her around, for a while.'

'Thank you. I must hurry back to Covent Garden, I want to be the one who breaks this awful news to her. I must find her.'

Kitty found Jack's House by the sign of fish and shells, hanging above the front door. She didn't think it grand, it was similar to the other new houses being built in the area. She knocked on the door. It took a while for Martha to answer.

'Hello, Martha, it's Kitty, Fanny's friend. I've come to see her.'

Martha rubbed her eyes to clear her head. She hadn't expected to be awoken before morning, and she was still befuddled from sleep. She remembered, Fanny told her she would be meeting her friend tonight.

'Can I come in?'

'Yes. Fanny said she would come down after she rested. Follow me and you can wait in the drawing room, upstairs.' Martha saw the basket and asked, 'What you got in there, Kitty?'

'A surprise for Fanny. She's not expecting it. I've been waiting to give it to her.'

'That's nice.' They had reached the first floor. 'Sit down in here. She told me not to disturb her and that she'll come down on her own accord.' Martha lit the candles of a candelabra on the side table, next to where Kitty was sitting. 'I'll leave you, now.'

'Thank you, Martha.' Kitty sat and waited until Martha went downstairs and all was silent in the house. She looked around and her jaw fell open as she took in the wondrous things in the room. It could have been the King's palace with such treasures on display. How could Fanny be living here, she wondered. Her jealousy began to flare again, her imagination flourishing. Fanny must have ensnared a rich protector. Or Gideon had lied to her with his stories of being rejected and having no money. Both of them must have accumulated this wealth behind her back, getting her to steal for their benefit, adding to the spoils of their pot of gold. Now she was no longer of use, they rejected her.

She felt her heart racing and blood rushing to her head. Enough, she decided. It was time to be rid of her enemy. She almost spat the words out, her hatred raw. 'I was kind to you, Fanny, and you've repaid me by treachery. You will get what you deserve.' She lifted the basket and took the gun from under the cloth. As she made her way to the staircase, she picked up one of the diamond encrusted, gold snuff boxes and put it in her pocket.

The stairway was dark, lit only by a few night candles, causing her tall shadow to drape itself down the complete flight of stairs. Reaching the second-floor landing, she listened for any sounds. The main bedchamber was usually at the front of a house, so Kitty put her ear to that door. She could hear shallow breathing, from one in a deep sleep. That was good. Fanny would not stir, and Kitty's nerve would not fail from fear of Fanny waking. She opened the door. The room was in total darkness except for a chink in the heavy curtains, which sent a shard of silver light towards the four-poster bed. The velvet drapes were pulled around, to keep out the cold. Kitty raised the gun in front of her. She was not hesitant, as she believed her justification sound to be rid of Fanny. She tiptoed to the side of the sleeping figure and softly eased back one of the drapes. There, wrapped up and hidden from any intruder, was the body of the sleeping occupant. Kitty brought the barrel close to the concealed head, which rested on the pillows. As the pistol touched the fabric, the figure roused a little and began to turn towards Kitty. That small signal of movement was enough for Kitty to pull back the trigger. The gun fired. Kitty watched the head explode, just after recognising the steely blue eyes of Gideon Woodford.

Fanny was nearly at the stable yard, at the end of Great Queen Street, when she saw a man rushing towards her. 'Fanny, thank the good Lord I've found you, I have been searching for you.' He held her very close.

'Theo, something terrible has happened.'

'You've heard? Fanny, I'm sorry. I wanted to be the one to tell you.'

Fanny stepped back, confused. 'What do you mean, Theo?'

He looked at her, realising they were talking at cross purposes. 'What is the terrible thing that has happened, Fanny?'

She looked at him unsure. 'The troupe tied up Gideon when they found he had been trying to steal Jack's gold from the garret, and they were going to torture him to death. What is it you need to tell me, Theo?'

'Fanny, prepare yourself for bad news.'

'Theo, just tell me what it is, please.'

He held her close to him. 'Gideon threw Mrs B down the well. She is dead, Fanny.' There was absolute stillness, followed by such an outpouring of grief that Theo thought her crying would never stop. 'Fanny, I'm so sorry.'

'What a fool I have been. What an evil man he is and I never saw it. Even tonight, I believed he had good inside of him.'

'The troupe is out looking for him. I fear what they will do to him when they catch him.'

Fanny looked up at Theo and held his eyes. 'They won't catch him, Theo. He is at my lodgings.'

'What? I don't understand.'

'I'm on my way to order a wagon to take him to the north and out of all our lives. I feared the boys would kill him, and they would be caught and brought to trial. I couldn't let that happen, so I helped him escape. I didn't know what he had done to Mrs B. If I had, I would have killed him myself.' Fanny hung her head and let the tears fall to the ground.

Theo embraced her again. 'We shall get the night watchmen and go to your lodgings. I will not leave you for a second.'

'Dear Theo.'

'Fanny, there is something else.'

'No, not more.'

'I met Kitty tonight. She was in a bad way and she threatened to shoot you. You must keep away from her, do you hear me.'

'She said she'd shoot me?'

'Yes, Fanny, but I am sure she hasn't a gun.'

'Kitty does have a gun, but she would do me no harm, Theo. We are friends.'

The screams were so loud, they woke the whole area of Seven Dials. The night watchmen had to clear a way to the house and hold back the onlookers, as Fanny opened the front door. Martha sat on the stairs shaking uncontrollably, rocking back and forth. She held Sous-Sous in her arms, each taking comfort from the another. Fanny bent low and asked in a soft voice, 'What's happened, Martha? Tell me.' The housekeeper couldn't speak. All she could do was to point upstairs to where the wailing was coming from. The night watchmen ran up the stairs, and Fanny and Theo followed. The four of them entered the bedchamber where Kitty was bending over the bed, embracing a bloody body.

'Kitty…' Fanny started but was interrupted by one of the night watchmen.

'There's the pistol, at the woman's feet.' His counterpart seized the weapon and sharply retracted from the killer.

Fanny made a move towards Kitty, but the murderess turned on her with wild fury. 'Don't touch him, he's mine, I love him and he loves me. He's with me now, and you can't have him, ever. Stay away.' Fanny put her hand over her mouth in horror, when she saw Kitty was covered in Gideon's blood, her face smeared with it from cradling the head, no longer with a brain inside.

'I am taking you in, for the murder of this gentleman.' The night watchman clasped Kitty's arm.

She shook him off and flew at him. 'I'm not leaving him. He needs me. I've always looked after him, until that evil woman turned his head. I hate you Frances Tomlinson. You took him away from me. You took everything away from me. You stole my dreams.' Kitty wept and wept.

'Kitty, I didn't. I was your friend.'

CHAPTER THIRTY-SEVEN

Return to Newgate

FANNY HAD TO turn her mind away from Kitty's distress and breathe some fresh air, away from Newgate gaol. She walked around all the streets that had become her world, and she thought about the characters who had moulded her into the woman she now was.

After resting at home, at Jack's House, she prepared for the visit of her dearest friend, Theo. Fanny relaxed in her drawing room, listening for the door knock that announced his arrival.

'Good evening, Martha,' Theo said.

'Good evening sir, may I take your coat and hat?' offered Martha, beautifully spoken.

'Thank you. May I say you are looking well this evening, Martha?'

'Oh, yes, sir. I'm much better thank you, sir. Miss has taken great care of me, sir, after that dreadful night of the killing of Gid–'

'Yes, Martha. Best to leave that in the past, though?'

'Indeed, sir.' She gave him a small curtsy. 'Follow me, please sir.'

Fanny heard Theo's footsteps on the stairs. She

didn't wait for him to come into the room. Instead, she ran to him. Whilst embracing him, she said, 'Theo, I have longed to spend an evening with you before the fire, drinking Negus and talking to each other. Please take a seat. Martha, would you bring up the wine, please?'

'Certainly, miss.' Martha looked at both of them holding hands and put her head to one side, smiling. 'Opps, nearly forgot…' she curtsied and retired, closing the double doors behind her.

'Fanny, are you going to explain how you are living here, in this splendid house? You said Jack Mann left it to you, but Jack was a villain, and I imagined he lived in simple lodgings. Not a house filled with such exquisite things.'

'Some of which you recognise?'

'Yes, but I had no idea of his wealth. I don't understand.'

'When your wine comes and we get settled, I shall tell you the whole story, Theo.'

'I have something to tell you too, Fanny.'

'I hope it is good news.'

'Indeed it is. Actually, I have two things to tell you.'

'Tell me.'

'Mrs B is recovering well.'

'How happy I am. Dear Theo, you have worked miracles on her tiny body. I was certain she would die of her dreadful injuries. Will she be as able as she once was?'

'I'm not sure. But she is the queen of determination, and if she says she will recover fully, who am I to say she will not?'

Martha came in with the hot wine, not just a glass but a silver jug full. 'I thought you would sit long into the night and would need sustenance.' She poured the sweet cinnamon wine and rested the jug on a trivet by the fire.

'Martha, Mrs B is recovering.'

'That is good news. I have never met the lady, but please pass on my sincere, good wishes.'

'Well, Martha, you shall see her at Christmas. There is to be a great celebration here at Jack's House, and you will be part of it.'

'Thank you, miss.' Martha sniffed tears of happiness away. 'I'll leave you now. Please ring if you need me. I don't think you will…' Martha backed out of the room as though she had met the King.

'You talked of other good news, Theo.'

'Yes, it's about Humphrey.' Fanny froze for the moment. She had managed to forget him. At the mention of his name, the past jerked back into her mind, just for a second. 'It seems that I am the full beneficiary of his estate. He disregarded his brother, probably because they hated one another, I think my father knew exactly what Humphrey was really like. For all his hideous faults, he was clever with money and had protected his wealth against any eventually. Even if found guilty of murder. He used Gideon's family to draw up various legal trusts and investments, and his entire estate has come to me. I am rather overwhelmed with the fact. He had a very large property portfolio, including many acres in Kensington, sharing part of the park with the King. I am a wealthy man, Fanny. I shall now able to open a hospital with good research facilities and continue my ambition to further the understanding of medicine.' Theo fell back in his seat as the revelation had exhausted him. Fanny laughed.

'That is what you deserve, Theo. You are the best of men.'

'Thank you, Fanny. I have something to give you.' Out of his pocket, he drew her mother's ruby and diamond necklace. 'I was surprised to find it a ginger jar, on Aunt Marie's overmantel.' He handed it to Fanny. 'It's for you.'

'It is the necklace that Marie asked me to take, should anything bad happen to her. How did it get into the jar?'

Sous-Sous was alerted when the sparkle of the gems flickered over him, as he rested on his luxurious bed at the top of a climbing pole. He scampered down and jumped into Fanny's lap, took the necklace and placed it around his neck. 'Sous-Sous, you clever monkey, you hid it when I wasn't looking. Thank you, Theo, I shall treasure it. Now it is my turn to ask you something. I believe I may have hurt you in the past, will you please forgive me?'

'Of course, I will. You have nothing to feel guilty about, Fanny. You know how I feel about you, I want you for my wife.'

'Theo, I am going to tell you about me now, and what I am about to do. You may not want a wife who is an apprentice to vice.'

Theo took some wine, touched the tips of his fingers together and prepared himself to learn more about this extraordinary woman.

Working for Elizabeth was not at all as Fanny had imagined. The vice empire was successful and well respected. The splendid seraglios and gambling houses of Mrs Elizabeth Mancini, were far removed from the dingy bagnio where Kitty took Fanny. But even after several months, she had not visited the magnificent entertaining rooms. They were spoken about in hushed tones, amongst the employees she worked with. On her first day, she entered by a rear door and was taken straight up to the top storey, where she was introduced and tutored by Mr Nicholas Foxwit, the book-keeper. He was a studious gentleman, neat and tidy who rubbed his hands together as though washing them, whenever he had important thinking to do. The room was in the attic. It seemed to Fanny, she had spent all her time in various rooms, under the tiled roofs of London. She would quite enjoy coming down in the world, if just for a different view. However, this was her classroom for the time being. The room was sparse, with only the necessities required for book-keeping and the running of Elizabeth's business. Adjacent was another room, with a large table and chairs around it. Here, future projects and finance were discussed, with outside accountants and lawyers. Mr Foxwit oversaw his two scribes, Peter Moody and Phineas Pott. In these offices, there were no crystal chandeliers or champagne, no silk and satin, only the invaluable knowledge of how a successful enterprise should be run. It fascinated Fanny, and she was eager to learn.

After one long day with dry ledgers, learning and writing, she yearned for the oasis of the theatre. As soon as she was released from her days work, she hurried across town to the stage door.

'Hello, Fred, have you seen Tom?'

'Yes, he's up with Cibber. By the way, did that cousin of yours tell you, "Himself" wanted a word?'

'Do you mean Theo? No, he must have forgotten.'

'Cibber won't like that. You'd better run up there now. They're having a meeting about casting. I heard you was up for something.'

'Really? Goodness, I hope I'm not too late.' She started to run passed Fred.

'Hold on, young lady. Sign in.'

Fanny took the stairs two at a time. When outside number one tiring-room, she smoothed her gown and knocked on the door. Colley Cibber inquired, 'Who is requesting entrance, I pray?'

Fanny crossed her fingers for luck. 'It's Frances Tomlinson sir.'

'I don't think I know you. I once did, but you disappeared. No longer interested in the art of the muses, Melpomene and Thalia.'

'Yes, I am. Please, Mr Cibber, I do want to be an actress. May I come in. I'm sorry I did not receive your message, requesting to see me.'

'You were summoned by the great Colley Cibber, and you refused the call.'

'Please sir, forgive me.'

Another voice spoke through the door, one she knew well. 'He's only jesting, Fanny. He's laughing his cap off.' Tom opened the door to a worried Fanny. 'Come in.'

'Enter,' sang Colley Cibber.

Fanny stood just inside the door, too frightened to say anything. 'Frances, my dear,' started Mr Cibber. 'You will have to grow a thicker skin and judge when people are being amusing.' Fanny nodded enthusiastically. 'Tom was explaining the difficulties you have experienced recently. Remember my dear, everything may be used in the art of acting and brought to one's performance. Remember the emotions, and present them to your audience.'

'Yes, sir.'

Tom leaned back on his chair and smirked, he was enjoying this. Fanny shot him a withering look.

'Frances, this fine Theatre Royal is putting on one of

Shakespeare's lost plays, Double Falsehood. Although, I am not convinced of that claim. However, it will be played on this hallowed stage. I am offering you the part of Violante.'

'I beg your pardon?'

'Tom, bring her to life, please.'

'Do you want to play the part of Violante, here at Drury Lane, in December?' Tom asked.

'Yes, yes. Oh yes, thank you. I don't know what to say, I'm delighted.'

'Good, I like enthusiasm from my actors. Tom, give her the lines to learn, and we start rehearsals a week before we open. Off you go.'

'Thank you, Mr Cibber. Thank you.'

'Yes, yes, enough. Go and learn your lines.'

Kitty was imprisoned in Newgate for nearly two months. She was held until the next sessions took place in October, and Fanny was in the courtroom when Kitty was condemned to be hung in November. The judge put on the black cap and gloves to pass sentence. 'The law is that thou shalt return to the place whence thou camest and from thence to a place of execution, where thou shalt hang by the neck 'til the body be dead. Dead. Dead. And the Lord have mercy upon thy soul'.

Fanny entered Newgate with Kitty and paid the garnish for committal. She arranged for her to stay in the masters side, which was not the hell of the commons where Fanny had been held. She paid all the money needed to make sure Kitty had good food and clean bedding. It also enabled her to buy liquor in the tap room. Fanny visited regularly, taking in pretty things that she knew the prisoner would like. Kitty was not the vivacious, attractive girl Fanny had first met. She was only eighteen years old, but she was decrepit. Her body was slowly and painfully decaying, her nose being eaten away and her face unrecognisable.

Kitty's mind was failing due to the anxiety and syphilis that was ravaging her body and brain. She insisted that Theo give her a mercury cure. He didn't want to prescribe it, but Fanny argued that it would make no difference, as the disease had gone too far. It would calm Kitty to believe her beauty would return. Medicine mattered little as Kitty would die soon, her execution day being the twentieth of November. The day drew nearer, and Fanny would travel with her to Tyburn in a mourning coach, with the blinds pulled down. No one would see her disfigured face and taunt her.

Fanny was on her way to a sparkling future. She had everything she had ever dreamt of: good friends, a family, a fine man who loved her, a fortune and a beautiful home. She was now heiress to a great business empire and was starting out on the path of a successful career, as an actress.

Kitty had no future. Her dreams were gone and her life would end in anguish. It didn't matter to Fanny what circumstances had led Kitty to such an end, Kitty had been her friend and she would continue to love her until the final moment. She would accompany Kitty, in the execution procession, to Tyburn.

The night before hanging day, Fanny sat in the prison chapel together with the voyeurs of the macabre, watching the condemned sit around a coffin during their funeral service. Afterwards, she paid gold to the keeper, allowing her to see Kitty, who was fettered in the condemned cell.

'Fanny, stop them, I can't hang. I'm so scared. Do anything, to stop tomorrow morning coming.'

Fanny was lost for any comforting words, so she spoke the truth.

'My dear friend, there is nothing I can do to change the path of justice. I give you my word I have done all that is possible. I shall be with you all the time and I shall hold your hand to give you strength to prevail over your fear.'

'You promise not to leave me? You will stay with me on the cart until they turn me off?'

This request pierced Fanny's heart. Kitty was asking her to sit by her side, as she stood on the flat wagon with the halter around her neck and her eyes covered with a nightcap. Fanny would hold her hand, as the horses were whipped away and the wagon slid from under Kitty's feet, leaving her suspended under the gibbet. Fanny wasn't sure she had the strength of will to do this for her friend.

'You promised once, never to leave me, Fanny. Make it true, I beg of you.'

Fanny closed her eyes for a moment, opened them and assured Kitty, 'I shan't leave you. I shall hold on to you until the very end.'

The morning was foggy and damp, the perfect cold setting for such a gruesome day. Fanny paid the turnkey for admittance into Kitty's cell. St Sepulchre's bell tolled. As Fanny knelt on the floor, wrapping her arms around Kitty, she smelt fear.

'I'm here. I won't leave you.'

Four men and two women waited for death at Tyburn that day. During the night, they'd picked straws from the floor to decide in which order they would go to their hanging. Kitty picked the longest, she would be last.

They waited in the condemned hold, where Fanny changed Kitty into the finest gown she had ever worn. Although the mantua hung from Kitty's emaciated frame, she smiled and spun around. For one more time, Fanny saw her as she once was.

At around seven o'clock, the prisoners shuffled through Jack Ketch's kitchen and out into the Press Yard. Kitty shivered as her leg irons were removed and the halter of the rope, tied with a slip knot, was dropped over her head. The remaining long tail wrapped around her body, in readiness of being slung over Tyburn Triple Tree's hanging beam.

'What's that noise, Fanny?'

It was the sound of the mob. Thousands had gathered along the two and a half mile route to jeer at the execution cortège.

Fanny stepped up to the keeper and chaplain. 'Please, take us to our mourning coach.'

The young women sat in silence as the procession rumbled out of the courtyard of Newgate, towards Tyburn.

Throughout the journey, liquor was offered to the condemned. No-one went to the gallows sober. At St Giles, the carriage pulled up and the door was opened by a man in a tie wig and full coat and breeches. It was Richard Arnet, the hangman. 'It's time to take a toast with your executioner. Please join me in lifting a glass to no hard feelings. Forgive me, as it is my job.' Brandy was brought out from the Bowl Inn and Kitty drank it thirstily, whilst Fanny gave three guineas to Arnet to ensure a clean hanging. He would pull on the legs of the convulsing body, to hurry death. Fanny looked outside the carriage. She saw the four men taken off the wagons to imbibe. Those who refused a second drink, got back on the wagon.

As they arrived at Tyburn, the noise of the crowd reached a crescendo.

Fanny turned to Kitty, who was reeling and disorientated with terror. 'Kitty, listen to me. This is the most important performance of your life. You must play the part of a great lady, with decorum and benevolence.' Kitty couldn't stop trembling. 'Kitty, look at me.' Fanny lovingly turned her head towards her. 'I will be with you. We shall play this scene together, and the crowd will roar at your acting talent.'

The door of the coach was opened and one of the armed guards, chewing tobacco said, 'It's time now, get out.' He spat in Kitty's face. Fanny started to react to this insult but stopped herself. Kitty was a murderer who had killed her lover. But by doing so, she had destroyed her own spirit.

'Are you ready, Kitty? It's time to take the stage.' This once beautiful and smart woman, looked at Fanny, her eyes not quite focusing. She opened her left fist. There, sat the lost pair of diamond and ruby earrings. Kitty calmly put them on. Fanny was aghast. 'Where have you been hiding those?'

'Up my ladies money pocket. I was keeping them for a special day.' Kitty smiled at Fanny and regally alighted the carriage, accompanied by loud cheers from the crowd. In her altered mind, she believed that she was stepping onto the stage of the Theatre Royal, Drury Lane.

'I am the resurrection and the life.'

Kitty's time had come.

'He that believeth in me.'

In the last minutes of her life, Kitty's mind cleared. She needed forgiveness. She looked into her eyes of her dearest friend, whom she had tried to murder. Fanny comforted her with a smile so full of love, it eased Kitty's terror. It wouldn't be long now.

'Though he were dead.'

It had been a crime of passion, ending a life of passion. Now, with peace, Kitty accepted her fate with repentance.

'Yet he shall live.'

Kitty prayed. 'Lord, forgive me.'

This was the end.

'And whosoever liveth and believeth in me.'

Kitty closed her eyes as the chaplain gave the final signal. The cap was pulled down, the rope secured around her neck and the horses jerked forward. She hung from the gallows.

'Shall never die.'

Fanny bowed her head and prayed. 'And the Lord have mercy upon your soul.'

THE END

Covent garden 1720

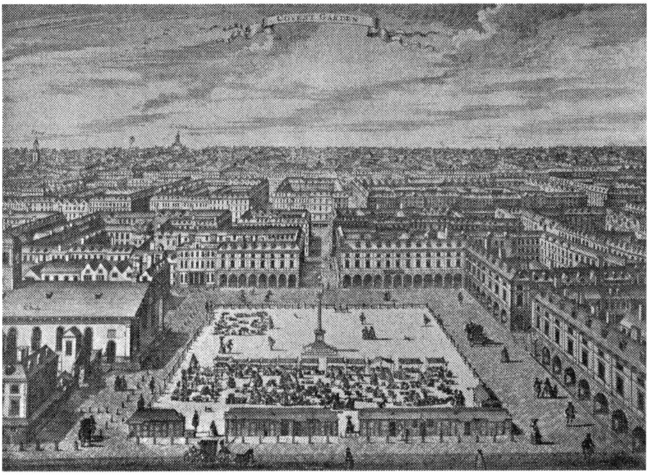

Acknowledgments

Thank you to all the characters who fill my life and dreams. Particularly those in the theatre, with whom I have laughed and cried. If you didn't think I'd listened, now you know I did.

Special thanks to

GHP, Suzanne, Pattie and Dame B.

Follow me on Facebook

About the Author

JUDY'S FAMILY CAN be traced back five hundred years, to living and working on the wharves below St Paul's, before the great fire of 1666. London is in her bones. As a child, she met colourful and eccentric people amongst the blackened terraces of the East End: factory girls bantering with the costers of Chrisp St market, dockers who carried anonymous brown paper packages under their arms and soft shoe buskers ready to sand the pavements of the West End.

Her father was a tallyman in Poplar, who taught her to treat everybody the same, always with respect, until they no longer deserved it. Her family settled east along the river Thames, but Judy still worked in the city. From modelling in Mayfair salons, to taking pattens to the schmutter houses in Bow, from dressing photographer's sets in Battersea to interior design in Kensington, she's met the gamut of London citizens. She's drunk pints in pubs with theatre crews and sipped champagne in palaces, with Royalty. All these wonderful people, sparked the creation of fictional characters on the page.

Her genre is fast moving historical fiction, which she hopes is easy to read, about accessible characters who face predicaments that remain relevant today. Nothing really changes, only the time and setting.

The stories are wrapped up in technicolour locations and the dramatis personae are dynamic and memorable, in homage to the time she was an actress in the West End.

When not writing, she paints and prints whilst still living in the greatest city in the world. London.

About this Book

A LONDON APPRENTICE is a fast moving, sometimes bawdy story set in 1726.
The underbelly of London is dramatic, with eccentric and theatrical characters creating situations of mystery and adventure.

Innocent Fanny Tomlinson, becomes destitute and homeless when her mother dies. Her only relative is Aunt Marie in London, to whom she will apprentice. Leaving all that is familiar, she is abducted into the dangerous underworld of eighteenth-century London but befriended by sideshow performers.
Fanny is intelligent, but to survive she must absorb the energy of London. With every step towards her desire, events happen that challenge her principles. Will her association with villains and outcasts destroy her or make her stronger?
Unknown to Fanny, she carries a secret, which will only be revealed if she is worthy.
From slum garrets, gaudy brothels and molly houses to the bewitching Theatre Royal, Fanny collects colourful characters whose actions could teach her independence. Will she be brave enough to become a true citizen of London?

This book contains mature situations and adult themes.

Links

IF YOU HAVE enjoyed **'A London Apprentice'** please leave a review on Amazon. Thank you.

Having worked as an actress, you may enjoy my reading of the Audiobook of this story. It will be found on Amazon / Kindle, Audible and iTunes.

Social media links for **'A London Apprentice'**:

Wesite: alondonapprentice.com
Authors Facebook page: Judy Graham
Facebook: A London Apprentice
Twitter: @londonapprentic
Instagram: alondonapprentice

Printed by Amazon Italia Logistica S.r.l.
Torrazza Piemonte (TO), Italy

10955464R00237

A LONDON APPRENTICE

Innocent Fanny Tomlinson, becomes destitute and homeless when her mother dies.
Her only relative is Aunt Marie in London, to whom she will apprentice.
Leaving all that is familiar, she is abducted into the dangerous underworld of eighteenth-century London.

Fanny is intelligent, but to survive she must absorb the energy of London.
With every step towards her desire, events happen that challenge her principles.

Unknown to Fanny, she carries a secret, which will only be revealed if she is worthy.

From slum garrets, gaudy brothels and molly houses to the bewitching Theatre Royal, Fanny collects eccentric characters whose actions could teach her independence.

Will she be brave enough to become a true citizen of London?

ISBN 9781916086500

90000

9 781916 086500

alondonapprentice.com

Cover design by
Judy Graham

£9.99